"Rollicking fun and sharp as a brass tack, this book is everything steampunk should be."
— Cat Rambo, Nebula Award winner

"An intriguing alternate world, filled with sharply amusing dialog and lively characters. VERDICT: A delightful gaslamp fantasy that will please readers of Gail Carriger and Kate Locke."
— Library Journal

"I loved *The Brass Queen*: hilarious, with a very tongue-in-cheek dry wit and delightful imagery. One of those books that you don't want to put down because they're just so much fun."
— Genevieve Cogman, author of the Invisible Library series

"Razor-sharp wit and immaculate worldbuilding make this debut one to savor . . . a genre blockbuster."
— Leanna Renee Hieber, award-winning and bestselling author of **The Spectral City**

"With a satisfying bite, this steampunk venture includes an insightful twist on the British Empire . . . Best of all, Constance stays center stage: a feisty, lovable heroine who is capable of rescuing herself, thank you very much."
— Foreword Reviews

"At times wondrous, at times romantic, and very often gut-bustingly funny. Elizabeth Chatsworth . . . will be one of your new favorites!"
— David Farland, New York Times bestselling author of The Runelords series

"Elizabeth Chatsworth infuses her writing with humor, charm, and adventure . . . I can't wait to read more."
—Rebecca Moesta, New York Times bestselling author and award-winning coauthor of the Star Wars: Young Jedi Knights series

"A fun, frothy blend of fantasy and romance . . . Fans of humorous fantasy and headstrong heroines will be delighted."
—Publishers Weekly

"Simply a joy to read!"
—James A. Owen, bestselling author of **Here, There Be Dragons**

"Lush, exciting, and endlessly inventive, *The Brass Queen* is a grand adventure of manners and espionage—perfect for readers who like a little magic in their retro science escapades."
— Cherie Priest, award-winning author of **Boneshaker**

"You'll find yourself cheering for this heroic cowboy and his unexpected love for a jinxed red-head who is dead set on saving the world (as well as finding her place in it) all before teatime, of course . . . Stocked with whimsical gadgets, sky pirates, weird science, and mustachioed villains this race-against-the-clock adventure scratches the steampunk itch and leaves you wondering what will emerge from the aether next."
—A. L. Davroe, author of The Tricksters series

The Brass Queen

Elizabeth Chatsworth

CamCat Publishing, LLC
Brentwood, Tennessee 37027
camcatpublishing.com

Hardcover ISBN 9780744300093
Paperback ISBN 9780744300109
Large-Print Paperback ISBN 9780744300369
eBook ISBN 9780744300123
Audiobook ISBN 9780744300130

Library of Congress Control Number: 2020937704

Cover design by Lena Yang
Cover art and chapter illustrations by James A. Owen
Book design by Olivia Croom Hammerman

1 2 3 4 5 6 7 8 9 10

Dedication

Dedicated to Doris Ann, always in our hearts.
"Sharp as a tack and kinder than the world deserves."

And to my very own Trusdale, my husband.

Epigraph

"Oh, when she's angry, she is keen and shrewd.
She was a vixen when she went to school. And though
she be but little, she is fierce."
—William Shakespeare

"Why can't everyone be reasonable, like me?"
—Miss Constance Haltwhistle

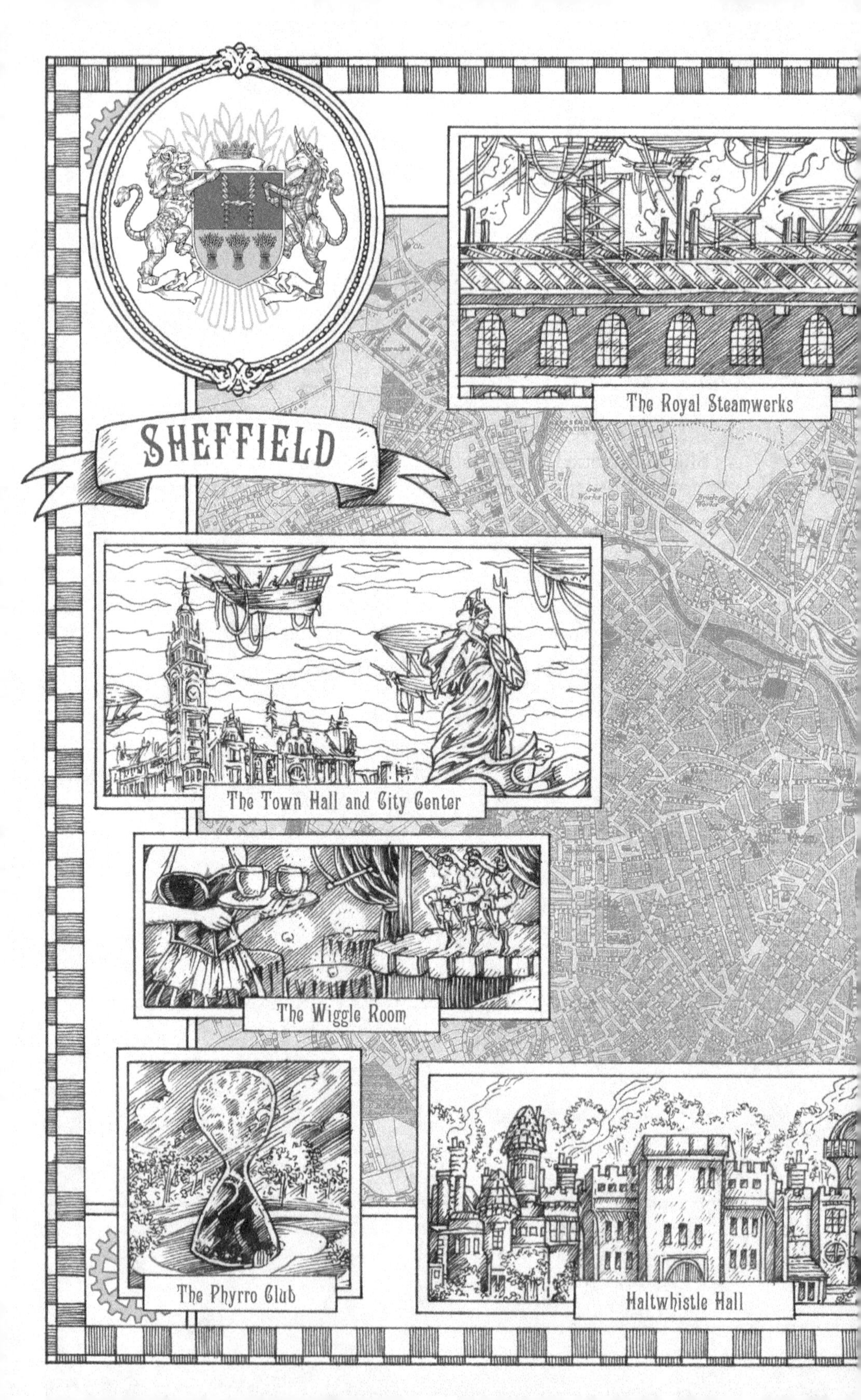
SHEFFIELD
The Royal Steamwerks
The Town Hall and City Center
The Wiggle Room
The Phyrro Club
Haltwhistle Hall

Le Paon Pompeux
The Royal Steamwerks
Exhibition Dome
and the Royal Steamwerks
Wedgeworth Warbling
Vulcan's Folly
PINDER'S
PRINT EMPORIUM
PINSTONE STREET
SHEFFIELD
ENGLAND
The Manor

Chapter 1: A Night to Remember

Tuesday, May 18, 1897:
The Royal Steamwerks Exhibition Dome, Sheffield, England

THE GRASS WAS ALWAYS GREENER in another dimension. Miss Constance Haltwhistle imagined that in a parallel world, she was actually enjoying her coming-out ball. A taller, less red-haired version of herself was waltzing in the arms of a dashing beau. Young noblemen, resplendent in white tie, were lining up for the opportunity to propose holy matrimony.

And no one had tried to kill her in weeks.

Her score for the evening stood at marriage proposals, none; embarrassing incidents, two dozen and counting. Dropping an ivory fan into the punch bowl had raised eyebrows. Wearing steel-toed ankle boots instead of dance slippers had drawn more gasps than she'd anticipated. And mistaking a cigar in an earl's pocket for a concealed weapon, then demanding he disarm himself before she damned well did it for him . . .

Alas, sometimes a cigar was just a cigar.

She strode through the crowd, recalled her need for an instant husband, and added a coquettish swing to her bustled behind. She glanced over her shoulder as laughter erupted from her aristocratic guests. Her unmarked dance card lay upon the parquet floor.

She'd missed her bustle pocket. Again.

Cheeks aflame, she scooped up the errant card and scurried into a forest of willowy debutantes. Each swan-necked beauty held the attention of at least three bachelors, none of whom spared Constance a second look as she made her way toward the center stage.

Mentally rehearsing her—hopefully crowd-pleasing—speech, she skirted the edge of the dance floor. Shoulders hunched, she snuck glances at her guests as they clustered in their favorite cliques. They posed and preened, blissfully unaware of the multiverse, ever secure in the knowledge there was safety in numbers.

Thanks to her portal-tripping mad scientist of a father, she, alone, knew better.

Perhaps in one of those alternate worlds, she was already dead? A pale corpse, slumped beside the dance floor, crimson life staining the parquetry as the orchestra played on. Or she was dying, cradled in the arms of a love-struck Adonis who dabbed her brow as she murmured, "No, really I'm fine. Do try the vol-au-vents."

Oh, how he'll miss me.

The dance floor teemed with euphoric couples gazing into one another's eyes. Drunk on champagne and true love, they eddied like rose petals in a whirlpool. Constance stomped by, thoroughly regretting her choice of footwear. The floor trembled beneath her boots as three dozen formally attired couples waltzed to "The Blue Danube" with the precision of an infantry brigade. Heirloom tiaras glittered in the gaslight under the vaulted glass dome—a crystal bauble beneath infinite darkness, built by humans who reached for the heavens but fell short. Without the dazzling lure of the exhibition hall, she'd have been a party of one, but the gallery's artistic display of military hardware had proven to be an irresistible draw for her two hundred guests.

Constance held her breath as she passed through clouds of cigar smoke tinged with lavender perfume. Her guests' fine silk gowns and waistcoats blurred into a pastiche of jewel tones and monochrome blandness as she weaved between the nobles. Her reclusive life on the family estate had not prepared her to sail through the starched sea of British gentry with the poise displayed by every other attendee. It was all down to her speech to prove herself worthy of their respect. *This is it, my one moment to shine. I'll make them all love me or die trying. Nothing and nobody will stop me from—*

Her face slammed into a muscular chest. She staggered back, clutching at her nose as tears welled, and blinked up between her fingers. A tall, dark, almost-handsome stranger gazed down at her. His eyebrows were raised over ridiculously blue eyes, bright as sapphires against shockingly tanned skin. Neatly trimmed sideburns and a square, clean-shaven jaw framed a nose that appeared to have involved itself in numerous brawls. Such a nose must assuredly belong to a ruffian.

Heart pounding, she brought up her fists, ready to punch the potential assassin.

The ruffian grinned.

Strike or smile? A decade of Mistress Ying's kung fu instruction kicked in. She swayed her weight onto her rear boot, leaving her front ready to smash his kneecap with as much violence as the situation required.

The trespasser raised his hands in surrender.

If he was an assassin, he was certainly taking his sweet time about it. And there didn't seem to be any telltale lines of hidden weapons beneath his clothing. But what odd clothing it was. The lone stranger was apparently unaware that a gentleman never wore a hat indoors.

Particularly not a black Stetson that seemed to have survived one too many cattle drives. His all-black ensemble would have suited a gunfighter on the cover of one of Papa's dime novels, save for his leather gloves and lack of a revolver. Did he think this was a costume party?

"Are you all right, miss?" His voice resonated with a suspiciously American accent, deep and slow, conjuring images of deserts, mountains, and rolling plains bestrewn with bison. "It's a crowded spot for that level of speed. You got somewhere better to be?"

She narrowed her eyes at the inadequately armed gunslinger. "From your dialect, I'd venture you're from Texas, or Nevada, or Colorado, or Nebraska, or—"

"Do I get a say in this?"

"Wyoming?"

He shook his head. "That's five states down, forty to go. You some kinda language expert?"

"I read." Papa's thirty-two volume *Legends of the West* contained many thrilling tales, but none depicted uninvited cowboys invading white tie events in Yorkshire.

"If you must know, I was raised in Kansas. My mother was an army nurse, my father is a retired US Cavalry officer, and my siblings—"

"I don't need your life story, thank you very much." For heaven's sake, Kansas would have been her very next guess. Why couldn't he have waited for her to get there?

She scanned the crowd for quirked brows and dropped jaws at the cowboy's presence. Fortunately, the tiara-and-white-tie set was pointedly ignoring the stranger, as the British do when foreignness exceeds their comfort level to an unspeakable degree.

Or perhaps, they were pointedly ignoring *her*?

Constance dropped her fists and adopted a nonchalant pose. He didn't appear dangerous. For now, it was best not to make a fuss and further disrupt the party.

The American warily lowered his hands and bowed. "Justice Franklin Trusdale, at your service. You can call me J. F."

Her hasty reading of *Babett's Modern Manners* on her way to the party suggested otherwise. "I'll do no such thing until we are introduced by a mutual acquaintance, or by letter. Have I ever written you a letter?"

"I don't think so, Miss . . . ?"

"If I tell you who I am, that would be an introduction, which I cannot do without—"

"A letter. Got it." A generous grin spread across his rugged face.

Her heart drummed a little faster than was seemly for a well-bred lady. But she didn't have time to consort with cowboys. She leaned toward Trusdale. "Look, do you mind moving out of my way? I'm heading to the stage."

"Aha! That explains it. You're the entertainment."

"I beg your pardon?"

"Your crazy getup, the chain mail corset." He nodded toward her neckline.

Sure enough, the velvet ribbon she had stitched along the top of her gown had slipped to reveal her chain mail undergarment, her last defense against the knives of her family's enemies. She groaned. "Oh, for goodness' sake."

Constance grabbed the metal links and tried to wriggle them back down inside her gown, keeping her eyes on Trusdale. The cowboy's grin widened, but he raised his gaze to the ceiling. He studied the stars twinkling through the glass dome as Constance swore softly at the unruly links. "This place must be somethin' to see from up there."

"The locals call it the crystal octopus, presumably because of the display halls that splay out from the dome. The glow of the lamps can be seen from over a mile away." A violent shimmy sent the offending links below the velvet ribbon.

Trusdale glanced down at her with a smile. "Consider me impressed."

She tugged the ribbon high, wincing as stitches snapped.

He chuckled. "Interesting armor. Boy, I sure do love carnival acts. So, tell me, are you a fire-eater, or do you have a partner who flings knives at you? Is there a rotating wheel involved?"

She gasped at the very thought of such theatrics. Admittedly, the chain mail had stretched her green silk ball gown to the bursting point over her prominent bosom and cruelly cinched waist. The tautness added a burlesque flair to what should have been the most stylish ensemble of her life. But a fire-eater? *Heavens, no.*

"Sir, I'm no entertainer. As you're clearly not an invited guest, I suggest that you leave before the authorities are called."

"No need for that, now. I'm here with—"

"You'll find the exit to your left, sir." She fixed him with her sternest stare. The one that made her stable boys stop playing cards and saddle her horse in record time.

He blinked and stepped out of her way.

She swept by the interloper. She'd have words with the security staff about letting in undesirables. It would be unusual for a professional assassin to don a Stetson. In her experience, hired killers tended to be rather dull in their choices of hat, seeking to blend in rather than stand out.

She's certainly had her fill of assassins over the last few weeks. It was such bad timing that one of her oldest arms clients had decided to terminate her contract, and her with it. As if planning a ball wasn't demanding enough, she'd had to deal with inept thugs at every turn. All this, for nothing but a simple shipping mix-up? Admittedly, King Oscar II of Sweden had lost a war when his globally prohibited armaments had been accidentally sent to Scunthorpe instead of Stockholm, but still. Such administrative misunderstandings could surely be resolved without bloodshed. *Why can't everyone be reasonable, like me?*

Beside the raised stage, Dr. Maya Chauhan—who happened to be her *favorite* arms client—winked mischievously. Maya was happily plump and perfectly comfortable in a voluminous gold sari that could double as a sail in the event of high winds. The gray-haired, Delhi-born genius was the Empire's most celebrated military scientist and head of the Royal Steamwerks, Britain's war laboratory. Maya was a prominent example of Queen Victoria's realization that intelligence and innovation were not solely limited to those born within a day's ride of London. Victoria might be a despotic, parliament-disbanding, mass-hanging-of-opponents type of queen; but she knew talent when she saw it.

Maya's grin stirred memories of childhood science classes filled with laughter and learning. Papa had signed young Constance up for the Steamwerks' classes, ignoring her cries that she'd learn more by his side in his lab than from any dull tutorial. But she'd soon grown to love Maya's warmth, her intelligence, her decision to allow eight-year-old Constance to roam unsupervised through the Exhibition Hall to play with automatons and tie together visitors' shoelaces.

But Maya didn't know, *couldn't* know, that Papa had absconded to another dimension to live with an alternate version of Constance's late mother. Maya would no doubt find the technology used intriguing, but she was duty-bound to share such secrets with her Royal employer, and that would never do.

Constance winked back. Maya beamed and downed a glass of champagne with impressive gusto. Beside her stood her two long-time colleagues, bespectacled Dr. Zhi Huang and lanky Dr. James McKinley. Both men gazed at Maya with undisguised admiration. Constance suspected the duo had been locked in a silent battle to win their supervisor's heart for decades. At their current rate of progress, all three scientists would reach their seventies without a word spoken on the topic of love. Constance resolved to kickstart the potential love triangle at her earliest opportunity. It was the least she could do to thank Maya for her use of the Exhibition Hall.

Maya swiped a fresh glass of champagne from a passing waiter's tray and raised it to Constance. "How is the belle of the ball? Has a handsome prince plighted his troth amid all this finery?"

"No troths yet, and I've spent half my dowry on this wretched event. The bachelors here are so flighty. I discuss the weather, then casually mention that I need to wed by Friday noon. Wouldn't you think that at least one man would find my candor refreshing?"

"Your candor, dear girl, could kill an elephant at ten paces," said Maya. "Have you considered subtlety and guile?"

"I just don't have the time. Uncle Bertie's lawyers are determined to declare Papa deceased *in absentia*."

McKinley snorted. "I'm surprised it took this long. With all due respect, Miss Haltwhistle, four years is quite a long time to be missing, even for a gentleman scientist. Most botanists only get lost for a year or two at the most."

Constance glowered. "Papa's far more than an amateur botanist. He's an inventor, a relic collector, an explorer of unseen worlds. And he's not missing; he's merely misplaced."

"You're quite right, Miss Haltwhistle," said Huang. "Misplaced is a perfectly normal state for a man of science. I'm confident your father does what he can to keep in touch. Sadly, continental postal services aren't as efficient as the Queen's Royal Mail. Apparently, they don't hang their mail carriers for a late delivery. But perhaps you've received at least one or two letters that prove the Baron is alive and well—?"

"Of course I have. My hope chest is stuffed with missives overflowing with praise for the marvelous way I'm handling the estate. Do you know, I thrust a handful of them at the lawyers, and they had the cheek to suggest they might be forgeries! And I know Papa's handwriting better than anyone. I've been signing his name on documents for years."

Maya squinted at her. "People are so untrusting these days."

"And I'm sure you've responded to the Baron's letters and informed him of your plight," said Huang. "No doubt, His Lordship is racing back to England as we speak."

Constance's stomach clenched. Fat chance. Why risk the dangers of portal travel back here when his other England was so perfect? He'd found his parallel paradise. He was selfish, pompous—but Lord, how she missed him. "If, by some mischance, Papa fails to appear at the court hearing, how am I going to tell the staff that I've lost the estate? Two hundred farmers, shepherds, milkmaids, and servants look to me for a roof over their head and shillings in their pocket. It's their home, too. Where will they all go?"

Maya blinked at her. "Well, I—"

"For that matter," Constance said, placing her hands on her hips, "why do I have to be married to remain in my own home? What in my biological form declares me to be less deserving of respect than a male heir? Who decided that a single woman can't inherit property? Oh, I'd like to give *him* a piece of my mind, make no mistake."

Huang and McKinley stepped back, mouths agape.

Constance stomped her boot. "For heaven's sake, we have a woman on the throne. Why on earth doesn't Victoria make the laws more female-friendly?"

Maya paled as the surrounding crowd went silent. The scientist gave a nervous laugh. "Oh, Miss Haltwhistle, you and your jokes. Why, you'll be the death of me."

The partygoers, apparently satisfied that high treason had not been committed, returned to their chitchat.

Constance bit her lip. "Dr. Chauhan—Maya—I'm so sorry. This has been a very trying evening. I do realize the Royal Steamwerks is hardly the place to comment upon the Queen's—"

Maya held up her hand. "Please, let's change the topic, I beg you." She leaned in and murmured, "The redcoats can be . . . *overzealous* in their search for royal detractors. You don't wish to be branded a rebel, do you?"

Constance gasped. "Heavens, no, I . . . speaking of redcoats, don't you usually travel with a platoon of guards? I don't see a single scarlet uniform in here." She added loudly, "Incidentally, I adore the troops' stylish new double-breasted overcoats. Those brass buttons are so debonair. The effect is intimidating, yes, but delightfully so. Why . . ."

Maya tapped her arm. "Don't overdo it, my dear. Now, if you must know, the platoon was forming up when I suggested to the sergeant that we could safely walk here alone. After all, it's barely a quarter mile down here from the lab. We brought along a new engineering consultant who I wanted to have a chat with away from the guard's ears."

"A new—?" Constance surveyed the elegant crowd for a stranger in a lab coat, or even worse, oil-spattered coveralls.

"Yes, I hope you don't mind. Anyway, to cut a long story short, whilst the sergeant was filling out forms in triplicate asking his superiors for permission to consider the matter of whether we could leave, we slipped away. We'll be back before he completes the paperwork. Until then, we're sipping the sweet succor of freedom, aren't we, boys?"

The boys were staring at Constance's neckline.

Her hand flew to her chest. Sure enough, the chain mail had made another appearance. She shoved down the offending rings, wriggling and puffing. Huang and McKinley turned their backs as she struggled with her gown.

Maya scratched her ear. "Dear girl, if you're in need of protective underwear, I could run you up an armored corset back at my lab. Bulletproof, knife proof—"

"Invisible? That's what I need."

McKinley spun on his heel and stared at her. "What did you say?"

"I said—"

Clucking her tongue, Maya said, "That's enough discussion of lingerie. My poor boys are getting all overheated." She beckoned Constance closer and whispered, "Should I worry that I'm about to lose my favorite secret weapons designer?"

Constance pursed her lips. "Do you have more than one?"

Maya laughed. "No, one's more than enough. You're an inspiration, a true genius. You'll be pleased to learn that your latest flamethrowers are going directly to the Queen's personal guard. Some women collect hats. She prefers a nice incendiary weapon."

"Don't we all?"

"Naturally, I've kept your name out of the official reports." Maya gestured at the chain mail. "Dare I ask again about your armor?"

"It's a temporary precaution against a disgruntled client. I have everything under control. Mostly."

"It's the 'mostly' that concerns me. I'm not one to interfere, but this rush to marry is unlikely to end well. My dear, as grand as it is, Haltwhistle Hall is only a house."

"As Buckingham Palace is only a house, or the Vatican is only a church. The Hall is history, it's heritage, it's all I have left of Mama, of—" Her lip trembled. Constance bit it firmly into submission and tilted up her chin. "If you'll excuse me, Doctors. I'm afraid it's time for my speech. Duty calls, and all that." She turned away from the scientists and walked up the steps to the oak stage as if it bore her gallows. Solitude broken by the odd knife-wielding assassin she could handle, but public speaking? She shuddered.

From her elevated position, the view was outstanding. Within forty yards of the stage, scattered like battlefield wreckage amidst a sea of guests, loomed the dome's prized exhibits: an airship turret gun, five mechanical warhorses, and three towering infantry exo-suits. To soften the exhibits' threatening appearance, Constance had draped pastel streamers around the turret gun, festooned the steam-powered horses' articulated necks with pink rose wreaths, and topped the twelve-foot-high bronze-and-brass exo-suits with polka-dot party hats.

Even the jauntiest hat wouldn't disguise the exo-suits' deadly design. With a bulbous similarity to undersea diving suits, their chest cockpits were protected with a bubble of bulletproof glass. A burgundy velvet pilot's seat and a mahogany control panel added a genteel touch to the giant suits of armor. Each held a brass Phoenix F-451 flamethrower in its massive hands. The weapons had been repurposed as beverage dispensers for the ball. Any guest who dared to pull a flamethrower's trigger was rewarded by a squirt of champagne from its polished barrel.

Constance's pulse quickened at the sight of the weapons' deadly beauty. Hidden on the barrel of each Phoenix was her maker's mark, a crown on a cogwheel. The stamp was an assurance that you were holding an armament of superlative quality. Constance's secret life as an elite arms smith swelled her chest and shamed her soul. For a typical noblewoman, *any* career was unladylike.

And she'd at least appear to be a true lady tonight, even if it killed her.

Alone at center stage, she signaled the orchestra to cease.

All eyes turned to her. Hopefully, this was due to her regal bearing, not her provocatively tight gown or, heaven forfend, the chain mail.

She smiled. "My lords, ladies, and scientists. I am come amongst you at this time, not for my recreation and disport, but being resolved, in the midst of these battle machines, to present you with an evening of fine wine, delicious hors d'oeuvres, and the good company of your peers."

She paused to allow her audience to applaud her humorous purloining of Elizabeth I's famous battle speech to her troops, so fitting for the martial setting.

Silence reigned.

The orchestra conductor coughed and rustled through his musical score.

A waiter dropped a silver platter with a decidedly unmusical clang.

Is it hot in here?

Constance fanned her glowing cheeks with both hands. Trapped in the amber of the moment, she stuttered, "Um—well—that is to say, it's a truth universally acknowledged, that a single woman in possession of a good fortune, must be in want of a husband. Could all interested parties please line up—"

The ceiling exploded with a thunderous crash.

Shrieks pierced the air as shards of glass showered nobles and servers alike, sending them scrambling for cover. Constance snapped back her head as a huge iron cage plummeted straight toward her on a winch chain. Far above, a black airship was silhouetted against the stars. She froze, staring up with the dispassionate clarity that comes when a large metal cage is about to crush your skull, and your body refuses to move, convinced the entire incident is a figment of an overactive imagination.

What the dickens—

A heavy body slammed into her chest, propelled her backward off the stage and shielded her as the cage smashed it into splinters. Her spine thumped against the floor and she lay, breathless, sprawled upon the parquetry.

A warm weight lifted from her as J. F. Trusdale pushed himself up to stand. He offered her his hand. "My apologies, miss."

Winded but unhurt, she allowed him to pull her to her feet. She scanned the cowering crowd, fearing the worst. By some miracle, the debris seemed to have caused no more than minor lacerations and a need for stiff drinks all round. Peers and servants helped one another to stand, momentarily equals in shared adversity.

Thank heavens no one was seriously—

A clanking hiss from the champagne dispensing exo-suits drew shrieks from her guests. Despite the vacant pilot seats, the three exo-suits shuddered into life. Black smoke belched from their exhaust pipes as supra-coal ignited in their backside furnaces. Their brass control sticks moved as if possessed by ghosts.

The suits of armor turned to face the ruined stage and took their first steps as the nobles scattered, screaming.

It must be a trick. Someone was using strangely faceted mirrors, or piano wires, or—

The giants holstered their flamethrowers in the gun clamps attached to their backs. As one unit, the polka dot–hatted mechanicals strode toward the iron cage.

Constance turned to her inappropriately-dressed savior. "The suits are being stolen!"

The cowboy nodded. "I reckon so. Best stay out of their way."

Such common sense beneath her, she reached under her tiara and drew out her six-inch stiletto hairpins. She flicked off the tiny cork protectors that stopped the sharpened steel pins from damaging her scalp. But how could she use them to stop the suits?

The bronze behemoths took a sudden left and advanced toward Maya, Huang, and McKinley. The three scientists gawked up at their monstrous creations. With surprising speed, the suits grabbed their elderly prey, tossed them over their metal shoulders, and made a beeline for the cage.

Constance raised her hairpins. *What if I stab one of them in the . . .*

Trusdale yelled, "Hey, leave the lady alone!" and sprinted behind the suit that held Maya captive. Constance's jaw dropped as the cowboy flung himself onto the back of the exo-suit. He hooked his left arm around the suit's gun clamp, dipped his right hand into his coat pocket and drew out a knuckle-duster. He punched at the suit's shoulder seam, splitting it open to reveal a tangle of lubrication tubes. Trusdale yanked the tubes loose, spraying oil over the parquetry. The exo-suit stuttered and slowed.

Ah, the joints are the weak spots. Constance darted between the two functional suits as they clomped up to the cage. One pulled open the door and tossed Dr. Huang unceremoniously inside before entering. The second suit followed the first, holding McKinley on its shoulder.

Maya drummed her fists uselessly against her captor's armor plating. As Constance raced to help her, the scientist grabbed Trusdale's hand and held it. She muttered something incoherent as the exo-suit shook like a wet dog to throw off Trusdale. He fell from its back as Constance rammed her hairpins deep into the suit's knee seam. Hot steam blasted into her chain mail corset from a punctured cable and she yelped more from shock than pain.

The exo-suit dropped to its knees but still managed to lean forward enough to clamp a bronze hand onto the cage door. Chains clanked, and the makeshift prison rose into the air with the exo-suit dangling.

"No!" Constance leaped for the bars. A strong arm grabbed her around the waist. Trusdale dragged her back to earth as the cage shot up through the gaping hole in the great glass dome.

She wrestled herself from Trusdale's grip as the airship sped away with the cage swinging beneath it. The damaged suit hung by one arm from the open door as Maya flailed upon its shoulder. The black airship soared silently toward the stars, almost invisible against the night sky.

Constance barely restrained herself from running right out the door after the airship. The debutante Miss Haltwhistle would *not* bolt from her own coming out ball, scrambling over hedges and ditches to follow a ship in the night.

No. Miss Constance Haltwhistle would tend to the wounded, would wait for the constabulary to arrive, and would give a detailed report of the theft of her dearest friend.

Her alter-ego however . . .

Constance placed her hands on her hips, jaw set.

Fly while you can, villains.

I'm coming for you.

No one crosses the Brass Queen.

Chapter 2: One Lump or Two?

RAIN TAINTED WITH SOOT BLEW in through the broken glass of an iron-barred window at the Sheffield Police Station. The grimy water trickled down brick walls painted an uninspiring institutional green to pool on the flagstone floor. Trusdale's teeth chattered as cold, damp morning air seeped through his black shirt and waistcoat to settle on his skin. Rumbles of thunder outside were echoed by the protests of his empty stomach. He sat on a three-legged stool as Detectives Barnard and Chester applied their phrenology expertise to his aching skull.

For seven hours, the detectives had taken great care to ensure his skull matched one of five phrenology profiles. It was a matter of departmental pride that any suspect brought in for questioning could be scientifically assigned to the correct criminal category. This was achieved primarily through the application of heavy objects to the suspect's head until its bumps matched the charts. After a night of applied phrenology, Trusdale had been officially profiled as a cat burglar.

He was no longer a fan of the scientific method.

Shoulders slumped, he studied the cracks in the stone floor, sneaking the occasional glance up at his two captors. The brown bowler hat of authority sat heavily upon the detectives, as did the white shirt of self-righteousness, and the pinstriped pants of due process. Barnard's ginger horseshoe mustache was beaded with sweat on a face red with exertion. The portly detective held a white phrenology bust over Trusdale's throbbing head. At three pounds, the life-size bust was the department's heaviest interrogation aid.

Detective Chester frowned at a stack of profile charts clutched in his meaty hand. Pulled down tight, his hat pushed his ears out at ungainly angles. An earthy odor of last night's beer was his chosen cologne. "You know, we could move him up from 'cat burglar' to 'anarchist agitator' if his benevolence lump wasn't quite so large."

Barnard tapped Trusdale's skull with the bust to see if a new lump would help.

It didn't. Trusdale winced and swayed back on the stool, so the next tap wouldn't hit in the exact same spot.

Barnard snapped, "Stop fidgeting, or you'll be back on your knees on the floor."

"I told you a stool was too good for the likes of him. We should save stools for the locals, not some heathen cowboy from the back-end of beyond," snarled Chester.

"I'm an Episcopalian." Trusdale pulled aside his shirt to show his bone crucifix, hanging on a leather thong.

Chester's nostrils flared. "Episca-whatever isn't the Church of England, now is it?"

"Actually—"

"As I said, you're a heathen, with a penchant for jewelry. Now pipe down, or else." Chester flipped open a notebook as black as his bushy beard. "Right, let's review the notes." The officer cleared his throat. "Point number one. Prisoner is suspiciously large and refuses to fit stature to size required by profile charts. Prisoner is two inches taller than chart limit of six foot."

"I can't help—ow." Trusdale flinched as the bust thudded into his temple.

"Shush," said Barnard. "We are being procedural."

"Point number two," continued Chester. "Prisoner has been suspiciously pleasant throughout the interview. Prisoner has stated that he understands that we are 'just following protocol' and that he knows we 'have to be thorough.' Said reasonableness was delivered in a resonant baritone malignantly designed to inspire trust and confidence in the attending officers. Prisoner has stated that he served as an army engineer in his own country of Kansas."

"That's true. Well, Kansas isn't a country, but I did serve as a captain in the US armored cavalry. If you send a telegram to my former commander, Lieutenant Godfrey Gillingham, he can verify—ow." Stars lit Trusdale's eyes as the bust tapped him again.

Chester said, "Being a former member of a foreign army isn't exactly an endorsement in these parts. Now, shut your trap."

Trusdale bit his tongue. All he had to do was stay polite and reasonable, and at some point, they'd have to let him go. *No one in their right mind would believe I masterminded a kidnapping the same day I rode into town.*

Chester continued, "Point number three. The prisoner trespassed onto Steamwerks property and invited himself into a hoity-toity party at which the top scientists in England got yanked up into the night sky. This led to the arrest of said prisoner upon the request of the party hostess, a woman named Constance Haltwhistle." Chester frowned. "Now, she wouldn't be any relation to that Baron Haltwhistle, would she? Rumor has it that he got captured by headhunters in the jungles of Peru."

Barnard scratched his chin. "I heard it was pirates off the coast of Burma." He glared at Trusdale. "Do you possess any pertinent information on His Lordship's whereabouts?"

"I can honestly say I don't have a clue where he is, and I sure don't know any of his relatives. The only person I met at the party last night was a sharp-tongued fire-eater who wouldn't tell me her name."

"I'm adding 'fire-eater, suspected collusion with,' to the notes," said Chester. "Point number four. Prisoner offered eyewitness testimony to the kidnapping of the esteemed scientists and several armored suits of death. Prisoner stated that he believed the airship used in the attack was a short-range transport ship, possibly an R78 model, and that the cage was of a type used to contain livestock. As the cage was approximately twenty feet high, prisoner suggests that we look into exotic animal air transport for zoos and circuses." He glowered at Trusdale. "Zoos and circuses? In Sheffield? You must think we're idiots."

Trusdale studied the floor and said nothing.

Chester leered. "Cat got your tongue, has it? I'll tell you right now, Johnny Foreigner, you've managed to be in the wrong place at the wrong time. The crown judge has a fondness for handing down fast sentences to out-of-towners. Mark my words, you'll be dangling from a noose by noon. We like a good hanging around here, don't we, Barnard?"

"Grand day out for the whole family."

"Even better than a circus, wouldn't you say, Barnard?"

"That I would, Chester. So much better. Almost as good as a zoo."

Cold sweat trickled down Trusdale's spine. Whatever the scriptures said, there was no such thing as justice here on earth, only good luck or bad. He should've known he was due for a dive, after convincing Dr. Maya Chauhan that he was—

He shifted uncomfortably on the stool.

The role of his own late brother, the esteemed electrical engineer J. F. Trusdale, was not one he had ever wanted to play. Every agent needs a cover story, but this one hit too close to home. He was getting hanged for all the wrong reasons. Hang him because he was a US spy. Hang him for believing that the British Empire wasn't doing the world a whole lot of good. Hang him for impersonating his late brother in what would have been the highlight of J. F.'s career. But to be hanged for going to the wrong party?

He whispered, "It just ain't right."

Barnard leaned close. "What's that now? Did I hear a confession?"

Chester closed his notebook with a snap. "That's grand news, Detective. I reckon we might make it to the pub by lunchtime after all." He leaned down close to Trusdale's face. "You ever seen a hanging, son? Nasty business. Very, very, nasty."

Chester wasn't wrong. Trusdale could almost feel rope fibers tightening around his throat. An angry mob of locals surrounded him, jeering up at him on a makeshift wooden stage. He balanced on the same stool he now sat on, waiting for the moment when the executioner kicked it from beneath him and he fell, jerking his neck, but not quite breaking it. A short drop to eternity, punctuated by a lingering death. The crowd hooted and hollered, taking bets on how long his legs would kick, how long 'til his eyes bulged and his lungs gave out.

He could barely remember the idealist he'd once been, before the Military Intelligence Corps turned him into a man who watched, listened, and betrayed; a man forever caught in twilight. The MIC brass told him it was his duty to serve, but he had little to show for his sacrifice. No shiny medals, no wife to hold him, no children to carry on his name.

Damn, I'm almost ready to tie the noose myself, just to get it over with.

Chester snickered. Clearly, extinguishing all hope in the condemned was a favorite amusement. He said to Barnard, "We might get this cowboy sentenced by eleven if we get a move on."

The iron door to the interrogation room flew open with a force that made all three men jump. A blue slab of sergeant stomped in. Behind him trailed an elderly male servant with the air of a depressed stork. The silver-haired retainer wore an emerald tailcoat cut in a style that had been popular in the 1830s. Gold buttons, an ivory ruffled shirt, mint-green silk pantaloons, pristine white stockings, and black buckle shoes completed his archaic ensemble. The servant carried a silver tray that bore Trusdale's black frock coat, leather wallet, silver fob watch, and beloved Stetson.

A lump formed in Trusdale's throat at the sight of his hat. He could almost feel the sun beating down as he rode alongside his brothers on the summer cattle drives. Forty ornery steers, dust in your eyes, and wolves on your heels. Papa yelling that the herd was heading too far south, J. F. grinning like a cat, saying he knew a faster route to the next watering hole. He always was the brains of the family, caught up in his imaginings, a practical dreamer.

Maybe, somewhere, there was a world where J. F. spotted the runaway carriage bearing down on him and didn't freeze. Maybe he jumped out of the way, dirt flying up in his face, half-crying, half-laughing for the close call on his life. Maybe he'd traveled here, to England, instead of dying a senseless death in a New York gutter.

What Trusdale wouldn't give to live in such a world.

The sergeant and the servant stepped aside as the curvaceous fire-eater from last night's party swept into the room in a fountain of white lace cinched with a scarlet corset. A glint of metal through the delicate lace covering her décolletage suggested that she still wore armor next to her pale skin. Her waist-length red hair flowed over her shoulders like molten lava. Atop her tresses perched a ruby bowler hat set at a jaunty angle. Trusdale swallowed hard and smiled at his green-eyed visitor.

She surveyed the room with undisguised distaste.

"Her Ladyship here," said the sergeant gruffly, "is considering dropping the charges against—"

"I would only be 'Her Ladyship' if I were a married woman and my father had died in the night. Unless you can produce for me both a husband and a corpse, the correct form of address is 'Miss Haltwhistle.'"

The sergeant threw Trusdale a sympathetic glance and backed out of the room.

Detectives Barnard and Chester snickered, but stopped when Miss Haltwhistle fixed them with a glare. Both men became momentarily fascinated by their shoes.

Trusdale frowned. *Charges? She's the one aiming to get me hung? But, why?*

Miss Haltwhistle stalked up to Chester and held out her palm. The detective reddened and handed her the black notebook. She flicked through the pages, brow furrowed.

Trusdale drew in his breath deep and slow, just as he'd been trained to do. It was nine years now since he'd passed out of West Point, seven since he'd graduated the MIC. Keeping relaxed under pressure was the most useful skill he'd picked up along the way.

He exhaled and flashed his warmest smile at the redhead. "Pardon me for asking, miss, but am I to understand that you asked these fine gentlemen to arrest me?"

"It was a private party. You were trespassing."

So much for the calm and charm approach.

Miss Haltwhistle turned to Chester. "A cat burglar? Really? Look at the size of him. He's as big as a steam engine. What makes you think a man of his bulk could climb drainpipes and slide through skylights?"

The detective stammered, "W-well, he has been talking a lot about circuses, and there was a mention of a fire-eater, so maybe he's in league with a gang of acrobats—"

She clucked her tongue. "Ridiculous. Did his paperwork check out?"

"Ah, well, he didn't have any documentation on him, save for a return steamship ticket to New York with a sail date of Saturday. Or is it steam date? Anyway, in four days' time this blighter was set to abscond from the scene of the crime. Slowly, like, on a ship. But it's still absconding. He said any other paperwork that could prove his identity were stowed in his suitcase at his place of lodging."

"So, you sent someone to retrieve these documents?"

Chester shook his head. "No need to, miss. We're relying upon the scientific principles of phrenology. You don't need paperwork when you've got science on your side."

Trusdale kept his voice steady. "Not to belabor the point, Miss, but didn't I save your life last night?"

"I believe the technical term for pushing a person off a stage is 'assault.' I have no doubt I could have sidestepped the falling cage without your interference."

"You know that ain't true."

Her glare burned with such ferocity, his toes curled. "What I know, Mr. Trusdale, is that you were not on my invitation list and you stopped me from pursuing the kidnappers."

"With all due respect, Miss, I stopped you from dangling off the leg of an exo-suit as it flew away to Lord-knows-where on the orders of heaven-knows-who. Did you think you could defeat all three suits with a couple of hairpins?"

Miss Haltwhistle sniffed. "I'm sure I would have thought of something."

The silver-haired servant quirked an eyebrow at her.

She balled her hands on her hips. "I would, and that's that. Now, Mr. Trusdale, what prompted you to attend my coming-out ball?"

Chester coughed. "Actually, Miss Haltwhistle, we—"

"Are interrupting my investigation. Kindly desist, or I shall report you to the Lord Mayor for wasting my valuable time."

The detective blanched. Miss Haltwhistle turned her attention back to Trusdale. "This is the last time I shall ask. Why did you invite yourself to my—?"

"I didn't. Dr. Maya Chauhan invited me to tag along with her. Seems she, McKinley, and Huang thought I would enjoy this shindig of yours. It was my first day working as an engineering consultant to the Steamwerks, and they thought I'd like to meet the locals. Let me assure you, I haven't. Not one damn bit."

Her eyes widened. "Oh. That's . . . gosh."

The servant sighed.

Constance tapped her chin. "But if you've started a new job, why do you have a steamship ticket?"

"In case the job didn't work out."

"Hmm, very well. In light of this new information, I will drop the trespass charge, for now." She turned to her footman. "Cawley, please return to Mr. Trusdale his valuables."

The retainer approached him with a low bow and proffered the silver tray as Miss Haltwhistle retired to the doorway.

A fresh start. Hope on a silver platter.

After a long night of police procedure, Trusdale was stiffer than a winter oak. He stood slowly, stretching out his big frame with a crack of his neck joints. He kicked the stool behind him, smashing it against the wall.

Chester and Barnard took a wary step back.

Trusdale ignored them. He reached down for his Stetson, casually running his fingers inside the silk lining. His fingertips brushed the secret pocket he used to smuggle items through customs checkpoints. The pocket had carried codes, maps, and skeleton keys, but until last night had never held a mysterious artifact.

Through the silk, a tingle of electricity nipped at his hand. The source was the one-inch metal triangle Maya had pressed into his palm as she was dragged away by the exo-suit. She'd whispered simply, "Hide it." From who or what, he had no idea.

Her trust gnawed on a conscience he didn't need. He'd bluffed his way into the Steamwerks to reconnoiter her work, not to feel dread at what might be happening to the gray-haired genius with the impish grin. As for Huang and McKinley, they weren't exactly the evil scientists he'd anticipated. More like classics professors with a taste for weekend alchemy.

Why did they have to go and get themselves kidnapped, anyhow?

There was nothing he could do to help them. He had his own problems to solve. With a sigh, he pushed his hat firmly onto his bruised head, swung on his frock coat, and headed for the open door.

Miss Haltwhistle stepped in front of him, but he pushed by her with a terse, "Miss," and the barest tip of his hat. He ignored the sweet scent of orange blossom and roses emanating from the devil in a bustle. He wasn't a man given to rage, but the threat of hanging did not dispose him kindly toward her.

She said, "I think I may owe you an—"

He strode out of the cell without a backward glance.

Chapter 3: The Lone Stranger

TORRENTIAL RAIN DROVE A PUNGENT stream of horse manure down the cobblestones of Waingate. Trusdale trudged uphill against the deluge with his sodden frock coat wrapped tight around him and his hat pulled low. From the shelter of store doorways, stout women in bustled skirts and long work aprons gawked at his outlandish appearance. Stetsons in Sheffield were as rare as suntans. A man with both a Stetson and a tan was evidently a most unusual sight, on par with spotting the Loch Ness Monster swimming up the High Street.

Fifty yards ahead, an ornate iron monorail spanned the rooftops. A steam locomotive styled as a bronze snail puffed slowly along the track, drawing five cylindrical glass carriages in a glistening trail. Gas chandeliers illuminated smartly-dressed passengers seated on plush sofas and winged armchairs. Some enjoyed their aerial view of the city center, others read books or newspapers. A few brave souls tried to drink tea from the restaurant car without spilling it over themselves or their fellow travelers.

The snail slithered along its rail, meandering between the airship freight cranes and landing platforms that bristled atop the city's slate-tile roofs. A handful of cargo airships bobbed like children's balloons against their cable tethers, seemingly anxious to soar up and greet the lightning that would surely spell their doom. No doubt most dirigibles had been safely stowed in the industrial hangars that ringed the city like a black eye.

Trusdale plodded on. His narrow-toed Western boots were designed for horseback riding, not pounding the pavement in a downpour. Water seeped into his woolen socks, adding a squelch to every step. He avoided eye contact with approaching locals, turning to gaze into storefronts that boasted displays of bone-handled cutlery and desolate watercolors of windswept moorland sheep. Legions of clockwork garden gnomes rode saddled hedgehogs, fished from toadstools, and played the drums with abandon. Such a racket would surely drive hungry birds far from ripening raspberries and strawberries.

He paused outside a curiosity shop. A steam-powered diorama of Sheffield provided an avian's eye of the Armory of the Empire. A dark forest of Steamwerks smokestacks enclosed a medieval maze of timber-framed Tudor pubs, marble-columned Regency villas, and red-brick eighteenth-century emporiums.

The miniature city teemed with life. Pedestrians slid on tracks along the cobbled roads, dodging brewer's drays and fancy carriages pulled by trotting ponies. A bandstand with an automaton orchestra held the captive attention of two dozen spectators. Emerald parks dotted with gardens of red and white roses provided a haven from the busy thoroughfares. Water glistened in a silver pond speckled with ducks. They pecked at breadcrumbs thrown by toddlers under a uniformed nanny's watchful eye. The detail was so precise, Trusdale scanned the model's High Street, curious if his Stetson-wearing self was staring into a storefront.

He rubbed his eyes. *I'm getting delusional. Gotta get me some food and hit the hay.* But he still had five miles to go before he reached the comfort of his room at the Pyrrho Club, and there wasn't a single for-hire Hansom cab in sight.

He squelched on, imagining a warm welcome and a hot toddy upon his arrival at the club. The exclusive enclave for Steamwerks scientists and their international guests boasted state-of-the-art laboratories and an excellent wine cellar. Unfortunately for him, it had been built well outside the city center so any accidental explosions wouldn't inconvenience the local townsfolk.

Almost every shop window he passed displayed a bright yellow poster that read, "Reward offered for tips regarding the kidnapping of scientists from the Steamwerks Exhibition Dome on Tuesday, May 18th. Contact Haltwhistle Hall via Pinder's Print Emporium for more information."

Huh. Miss Haltwhistle had sure worked fast to insert herself into the situation, he'd give her that. Why wasn't she content to let the police do their job? Or the redcoats, for that matter? Weren't upper-class ladies supposed to pass out on the fainting couch at a mere sight of a spider, never mind a violent kidnapping? Why wasn't the belle of the ball having her fevered brow mopped by maids and the like?

Why does she care so damn much?

Nope, this wasn't his mystery to solve. A change of clothes and he was out of this miserable town for good. Maybe he could catch an earlier steamship home? The mission had been a failure, but at least he wasn't swinging at the end of a rope, and that was a mighty fine thing.

He strode on, splashing through the puddles. If he'd died here today, would the MIS have informed his family of his demise? Or would they have kept it a secret, just as they had J. F.'s accidental death? Would his mother lose two sons in two weeks, and never know the truth behind her loss?

Thunder rolled across the heavens, deep and low as a mourning bell.

Or even worse, would they tell her everything? Would she know that instead of coming to tell her of J. F.'s death, he'd agreed to step into his dead brother's shoes and head to the Steamwerks for an undercover mission? Would she cry, knowing that he'd put his country's needs before those of his family?

It was a crazy plan to start with. Convincing Maya and her team that he was J. F., the brilliant electrical engineer they'd hired to work on a secret project, had taken every ounce of his acting skill. Fortunately, they'd never met the real J. F. in person. They'd bought his story of travel weariness and hadn't yet put him to work. Within a day or two, he could have snooped around the labs to see what the Empire was building next. He'd have left the country before anyone got any the wiser.

But now the kidnapping posters taunted him. The unsolved mystery—who, what, why. He wasn't going to stick around for the answers, but maybe Miss Haltwhistle would get lucky in her investigation? Perhaps the lure of lucre would loosen a few tongues around town. Not that any of this was his problem. After all, it wasn't his job to be a hero.

A wave of exhaustion swept over him. Iron-gray clouds thundered like cannons, shooting down a fresh barrage of rain. He hunched his shoulders and trudged on.

The only poster more prevalent than Miss Haltwhistle's was a red-white-and-blue affair. It appeared he was going to miss an opportunity to see Queen Victoria in the flesh. This Friday, "In celebration of her diamond Jubilee, Her Majesty, the Royal Family, and European Heads of State will parade through the city to Endcliffe Park. Witness a flying salute by military airships and a thrilling battle in the clouds between the *HMS Subjugator* and a sky-pirate fleet."

Sounds like one hell of a show. Trusdale studied the streets that would soon welcome the self-styled Empress of India. A royal visit explained the abundance of sodden flags and garlands that hung limply from every building and iron gas lamp, two days too early. Someone was just a little too efficient around here for their own good. Hopefully, Her Royal Highness wouldn't mind damp decorations.

The despotic queen's temper was legendary. There were rumors of courtiers losing their heads over the slightest infractions of dress or manners. Becoming a member of Victoria's inner circle was both a blessing and a curse. As was becoming an imperial colony, vassal, or protectorate. Yes, you could rely on the redcoats to defend your land against invaders, but who defended you from the redcoats? The armed tourism of the British military had stationed troops in over sixty countries. Nowhere were the soldiers more prevalent than right here at home.

Trusdale turned up his collar as he passed a squad of the scarlet-clad troops. White ammunition bandoliers crisscrossed their double-breasted coats with brass buttons above bleached calfskin jodhpurs and polished black boots. Brass pith helmets kept the rain from dripping onto their callow faces. *Every year they seem to get younger.*

He kept his eyes cast down and his hands clearly visible as he walked by. It was one thing to deal with the local police, but it would be quite another to grapple with redcoats. The soldiers held the royal authority to be judge, jury, and executioner to anyone deemed disloyal to the crown. One false step and his dress, speech, or foreign birth could easily earn him an introduction to the wrong end of a bayonet.

For once, good fortune was with him. The soldiers were too preoccupied sharing the contents of a snuff tin to notice him. He walked by, taking care not to splash mud toward their boots.

The town hall's clock tower bell tolled nine o'clock over the slate roofs of Sheffield. Atop the Gothic monolith stood a strapping bronze statue of the city's patron saint, Vulcan. The burly Roman god of the forge thrust his golden hammer in defiance toward the stormy skies.

Horses clip-clopped along the street behind him. Ever wary in a foreign land, he glanced over his shoulder. Two bay mares drew an elegant green carriage. A driver's box sheltered two men in matching emerald coats. The bald driver's brawny build suggested that he could have been the sculptor's model for the statue of Vulcan, save for his impressive walrus mustache. Beside the driver sat the silver-haired retainer, Cawley. From the domed carriage roof behind the men protruded a stovepipe that puffed out a trail of black smoke. Baronial shields on the front of the carriage displayed an armored knight kicking a red dragon up the derrière.

Trusdale increased his speed to a fast walk.

The horses broke into a trot and drew alongside him, then slowed. He gave them a sideways once-over. The mares were fine examples of the Yorkshire Coach breed. For a saddle horse, he was a Morgan man, but for a carriage horse, the Yorkshire Coach was king. His antagonist possessed excellent equine taste.

A powerful female voice rang out, "Mr. Trusdale, may I offer you a ride?"

He gritted his teeth and marched on through the mud.

"I doubt they were actually going to hang you," said Miss Haltwhistle in a tone of voice that suggested only an unreasonable man would object to being hung in the first place.

His temple pulsed as he burst into a jog.

The carriage kept pace, rolling beside him.

"By the way, did you by any chance drop this?" A lace-draped arm lolled out of the carriage window and waved a black leather wallet.

His wallet.

The red-haired vixen had pickpocketed his wallet.

He stopped dead.

The carriage drew to a halt in a large puddle, casting a wave of mud over him. He marched to the carriage door, yanked it open, and bounded up the steps to give Miss Haltwhistle a piece of his mind.

The brass barrel of a blunderbuss greeted him, pointed squarely at his chest.

Miss Constance Haltwhistle held the gun steady, her fingers resting lightly on the trigger. It was a custom multishot Orphanator Mark VII, with a blast range of fifteen feet. Fine engraving on the flared barrel's polished copper showed a woodland scene of bunnies frolicking amongst daffodils.

"Please, do sit down." She gestured with the gun's long barrel toward the green velvet bench opposite her.

He groaned and sank onto the bench. The carriage rumbled along the cobblestones, gently shaking the end of the gun. His mouth went dry. If the blunderbuss went off now, it would probably kill them both.

"Sorry," she said, "I do hope you will forgive the Orphanator. I'm not accustomed to picking up strange men fresh from jail in the street. It's all a bit new."

He took several deep breaths and counted to ten. "It's your fault," he said, "that I was in jail in the first place. You had me arrested."

"True, but with good reasons. You invaded my event, assaulted me on a stage, and stopped me from pursuing the kidnappers. How do I know you're not dangerous?"

He raised his hands slowly. "How about, just for a start, the fact that I'm not the one holding someone hostage with a gun?"

She frowned. "That's a fair point, although I do think an abundance of caution is warranted when meeting new people, don't you agree?"

A slow chuckle rose from his empty stomach up through his chest until he shook with laughter. He was tired, wet, hungry, and in imminent danger of being shot by a woman in the most absurd hat he'd ever seen.

"What's so funny?" she asked.

"I can't believe I came all the way to England to get held up on a stagecoach."

"I'm not—oh, right, here." She rested the gun stock on her thigh as she tossed him the wallet. He caught it, flipped it open, and quickly checked the contents. Nestled against his US dollars lay one UK sovereign, three farthings, and a shilling, representing a currency system that made no sense to anyone but the British.

"It's all there," she said with a sniff. "I'm certainly not a thief."

"Nothing about you would surprise me right now."

"I doubt that's true. You'll be delighted to know that I've decided to offer you transport to your place of lodging."

"I'd rather walk." This statement was eighty percent true.

"Nonsense. Where are you staying?"

"The Pyrrho Club."

"Oh," she blinked. "The science enclave? My Papa visited there regularly. I understand their laboratory facilities are second to none."

"I only got to see the bar."

"I've heard that's even better." She sounded wistful.

A lady with a taste for science and a stiff drink? Trusdale couldn't help but dig deeper. "You never went there with your Papa?"

She shook her head. "Frankly, I've barely left the estate until the last few months. Papa always felt the world was too dangerous for me to face alone. If circumstances hadn't changed, he might have locked me up in a tower for my own protection. He seems to think of me as a permanent six-year-old, defenseless against all who would do me harm."

"Your gun suggests otherwise."

She glanced at the blunderbuss almost lovingly. "I see no reason that a lady shouldn't be well-armed if she so desires. I trust the fact that I keep such a weapon in my carriage shall remain our secret?"

Hmm. This was a classic way to build trust with a mark. Offer a 'secret' to bond the two of you. What game was Miss Haltwhistle really playing? Or was he reading too much into it? "My lips are sealed."

"They'd better be." She stomped her boot on the floor and called out, "Head to the Pyrrho Club." The carriage lurched as the ponies picked up the pace.

Miss Haltwhistle gave him a smile that didn't reach her eyes. "It will take us quite a while to reach the Club. In the meantime, may I interest you in breakfast?" She pulled a lever set into the carriage wall. An ominous hiss sounded to his right. He turned to see a copper Octistove with eight brass tentacles wrapped neatly around its potbelly. Water started to bubble within the glass water cistern beside the stove. A labyrinth of pipes channeled steam from the tank to a turbine. As pressure built, the tentacles unwrapped from around the stove and waved lazily.

His lace-bedecked companion must have deep pockets to own such a device. He'd have to think of a good nickname for her. Haughty Haltwhistle? Miss High-and-Mighty?

Ah, no, he had it. The British obsession with formal address begged for US informality on his part. It would surely irritate her if he called her Constance.

Or Connie.

Could he get away with a Connie?

Keeping a wary eye on him, Miss Haltwhistle leaned toward the stove and flicked a switch. She pulled back as a tentacle twirled to grasp the stove's door. The door opened, revealing hot coals and an iron frying pan. The tentacle drew out the pan and dropped it on the stovetop with a clang.

Mind you, she was holding a firearm. Perhaps he shouldn't call her either Constance or Connie to her face just yet.

Constance studied him and seemed to come to a decision. She laid the blunderbuss down carefully on the velvet bench, pointing away from her. Keeping one hand on the stock, she snapped a pair of pince-nez brass goggles onto her nose. She reached out to the padded carriage wall and pulled down a second lever.

A mechanism hidden in the roof whirred, and a panel slid open directly over the stove. The tentacles whipped into position just in time to catch four fresh eggs as they tumbled from the ceiling. The tentacles expertly cracked the eggs into the hot frying pan and tossed the shells inside the oven. More whirring overhead, and bacon, sausages, black pudding, and tomatoes dropped into the pan with a precision airship bombers would have envied.

"There's an icebox up there," said Constance, with a hint of pride.

The scent of sizzling bacon filled the cabin, and Trusdale's mouth watered.

His host pulled a third lever, and a four-foot panel in the floor slid back to reveal a compartment beneath the carriage. A drop-leaf table adorned with a white tablecloth arose from a bed of spinning cogwheels and insanely complicated steam pipes. As the table reached waist height, it flipped out its leaves with a triumphant bang. More compartments in the ceiling opened, and cutlery on delicate chains lowered to six inches above the table. The silverware was released from tiny claws at exactly the right moment to drop into a perfect formal placement on the linen.

"As an American, I assume you prefer coffee over tea?" Another lever, and a new ceiling panel opened. A silver tray on chains lowered to the table. The tray held a rose-painted tea and coffee set, with sugar and milk. A bottle of Scottish whisky also sat on the tray, beside a cut-crystal tumbler.

"I believe this is another US favorite." She gestured toward the whisky. "As you might refer to it, 'rotgut.' I've heard that whisky doesn't solve every problem, but it's sure worth a shot." She grinned. "That's an American joke I picked up from one of my father's periodicals."

Apparently, despite the pun and the gun, she was trying to be charming.

It was almost working.

The stove hissed to a steamy climax. The brass tentacles produced two pink porcelain plates, deftly filled them, and placed them on the table.

Miss Haltwhistle breathed a sigh of relief. "Good, it worked. This contraption can be a little temperamental. I can't tell you how many times I've ended up with egg on my face, but that's the price of progress. So much better than the olden days when one had to take one's cook everywhere, don't you think?"

"So much better." He'd never employed a cook but had no wish to antagonize an armed woman on an empty stomach. The bacon looked spectacular. It was a lean back cut, pink and crispy with just the right amount of fat tracing through the meat. He licked his lips. First, coffee.

He cautiously reached his hand out for the coffeepot. Constance made no move to bring up the gun. He relaxed, breathing easier. *Maybe she isn't as dangerous as she looks?*

"So, is that thing loaded?" He poured a steaming cup of coffee. He swallowed it fast in hot gulps, the full-bodied warmth chasing the chill from his bones.

She sliced into her bacon. "Of course it isn't loaded. Do you have any idea how dangerous it would be to use an Orphanator blunderbuss in an enclosed space? Particularly one with a large-bore barrel? I take it you don't know anything about weapons."

He knew more than he wanted to. Weapons were part of the spy trade, though he'd be the last to use one, given any kind of a choice. There were better ways to resolve most situations than waving around a blunderbuss, large bore, small bore, or any bore in between.

It seemed no one had ever mentioned that to Miss Haltwhistle. He sure wasn't going to start the trend.

Trusdale picked up a fork and set to work on the bacon. The sweet and salty flavor exploded in his mouth. He was in smoked-meat paradise. Nothing on earth had any right to taste so good. He closed his eyes as he chewed.

"I take it you like the bacon. You'll be happy to know that those pigs lived a wonderful life roaming the apple orchards at Haltwhistle Hall. Our pork has won first prize at all the major fairs. My family developed our own breed, the Haltwhistle Pink. It's quite famous in epicurean circles."

He snapped open his eyes. "You're a pig farmer? You don't exactly strike me as the shoveling kind."

Two rosy circles appeared on her alabaster cheeks. "I should hope not. I oversee the management of the estate livestock during my father's absence. I'm developing various lines of farm-produced goods—pork pies, woolen cloaks, and a wide range of ales and cider. I've also refined our equine breeding program, from fiery hunters down to shires and coach horses."

"Those two mares pulling the carriage?"

"Yes."

"Huh." Impressed, he kept on shoveling in the bacon, savory tomatoes, and smoky pork sausages with a hint of sage. He finally pushed back the plate, satisfied.

The redhead had watched him bolt through his breakfast, apparently fascinated by his speed and appetite. He said, a little shamefaced, "I haven't eaten in quite a while."

"I'd never have known." She laughed, and her eyes sparkled in a way he could almost find beguiling, particularly now that his stomach was full, and her gun was no longer aimed at his face.

He gazed a heartbeat too long. She raised one perfect eyebrow and cleared her throat.

Trusdale turned to wipe condensation off the window with his sleeve. Rain cascaded down the glass, smudging the industrial town with sooty tears.

"Right," she said, her tone taking on the sharpness it had held at the police station. "So, now you're fed and watered, let's get to business, shall we?"

He sat up straight like a naughty schoolboy before a no-nonsense nun. She seemed to expect nothing less.

"You understand, of course, that your incarceration is entirely your own fault. Nevertheless, I shall elucidate my decision to turn you over to the local constabulary."

So that was how matters stood. On purpose, he slouched again. "Is that your idea of an apology?"

"I never apologize when an explanation will suffice. Whilst you were sitting comfortably in your jail cell, I've been trying to mitigate the devastating consequences of the airship attack. Apparently, high society is abuzz with gossip about the theft of my drink dispensers, and my name is fast becoming a byword for poor party planning."

"I'll bet the kidnapped scientists aren't too thrilled either."

"Well, exactly. No one is happy. In addition, Maya is, well, she's more than a mere acquaintance. She was one of my childhood teachers. Over the years, she's become my confidant, my friend, my . . ." Her voice cracked and she blinked back tears.

He felt a gentle shift inside him, a ray of light through a dirty carriage window. He fumbled in his pocket for a handkerchief, clean or otherwise.

She pressed her fingertips to her eyes. "Please don't. It's just dust, that's all."

The carriage was spotless.

"Are you sure? I know I have a hanky in here somewhere."

She sniffed. "I'm fine. Suffice to say, Dr. Chauhan—Maya —is special to me and I want her back. I'd hate for her to . . . I mean, I'm sure the kidnappers wouldn't hurt her, would they?"

He shrugged. "Depends if they're after information, expertise, or are merely throwing a spanner in the Imperial war machine. I doubt they're after a reward so . . ."

She stared at him, all trace of tears vanquished.

"Ah, that is, I'm sure she's worth far more alive than dead."

"Isn't everyone?"

"I mean, you had no reason to think she'd be kidnapped from your party. You shouldn't feel guilty."

"I don't, really," she said, picking at the tablecloth. "But even if I did, there are other matters driving my concern. I have to set things right as quickly as possible if I'm to gain the public prestige required to elicit a marriage proposal by Friday noon."

His jaw dropped. "A marriage proposal from who, exactly?"

"Whom. And how should I know?"

He snorted. "Exactly how hard did you hit your skull when you went flying off that stage?"

She patted her head. "Fortunately, my pompadour was lacquered to such a degree that my cranium fairly bounced off the floor, but thank you for your concern."

"What I mean is—"

"I know exactly what you mean. Not that it's any of your business, but my father is misplaced in a foreign clime, and lawyers are plotting with my uncle to declare him deceased. Hence, I need an immediate husband to keep my home my own. The accursed inheritance laws are the bane of feminine existence, don't you agree?"

"I guess I've never really—"

"Of course you haven't. Few men do. I've noticed the American constitution maintains that all men are created equal, but what about the women?"

"Well, now you mention it, that doesn't seem—"

"Indeed. And don't get me started on the archaic laws I suffer under here. If I were in charge . . . but I digress. Sadly, it appears that the police have failed to ascertain the identity or location of the kidnappers and are at a loss as to how to proceed. I fear the assigned detectives lack the intellect to solve this case quickly."

A migraine jabbed at his temples. "Huh. If you're talking about those two with the phrenology bust, I agree. They're idiots."

"Therefore, I've decided to conduct my own investigation."

"You what, now? You can't possibly—"

"I noticed that in a room of your betters, you were the only man with the presence of mind to attempt to stop the kidnapping. Hence, you may prove to be of some use to me as I pursue the villains responsible. You may consider yourself enlisted as my aide-de-camp. That means—"

"I know what it means, and my answer is—"

"Splendid. I've used my contacts to scour the train stations, docks, and airfields. There's been no trace of the kidnappers so far, so I believe there's a good chance they're still in the area, lying low."

She lifted her chin, as if daring him to refuse her.

"I'm not saying no, but—"

She wiped her opera glove across the window, tingeing the white kidskin gray. "I would hope not. Then I would have to say things like, 'I'll reinstate my charges of trespass against you until I find someone else to blame for the kidnapping.' And I really don't want to be the sort of person who says things like that. Although, one does so need a scapegoat in these matters, don't you agree? Nothing personal, you understand." She nodded at the window. "I'm sure those redcoats over there would be kind enough to escort you back to your cell, should the need arise."

Through the rivulets of rain running down the windowpane a scarlet smudge of troops marched by. He grunted. "Back where I come from, they'd call that blackmail."

"Around here, it's known as leverage. Now, will you help me or not?"

He faked a smile. "I can't resist a damsel in distress."

"I can assure you, Mr. Trusdale, if there is any distress around here, I will be the one dispensing it."

His smile stretched into a genuine grin. "All right, Miss Haltwhistle, I'm in." It's not like he had any other plans for the next three days, besides coming up with an explanation for the United States government as to how he'd failed his mission. And if this was how she treated her friends, it made no sense to make her his enemy.

As smug as a canary-filled cat, she said, "I thought you'd come around to my point of view. I possess the most wonderful instincts about people. It's one of my many gifts." She wiped her dirty glove on her lace skirt, to the detriment of both. "Now that's settled, I have a few ground rules I'd like to set in place."

He tensed. "Oh?"

"First of all, let it be clear to you that I have a Plan. A Plan with a capital P. I have developed this Plan to find Maya and the others without alerting anyone that I am investigating the matter."

"Except for the posters offering a reward in every shop window."

She stared at him. "Well, yes, apart from that. Other than—"

"Bright yellow posters."

"*Other than* the posters, I intend to carry out my investigation as discreetly as possible. I don't want to be known as the 'debutante detective' or the 'socialite sleuth' or—"

"Ain't nobody ever gonna call you those things. You read a lot of dime novels?"

She pursed her lips. "The point is that I intend to carry on doing the things a lady does, including luncheons, parties, games of whist, et cetera, whilst simultaneously bringing the kidnappers to justice. I must appear at all costs to be marriageable material."

"I'm sure you could find a—"

"A *noble*man fit to marry the daughter of a baron. The next Baron Haltwhistle will be a highly respected gentleman. Which means I must remain—"

"Respectable. Got it."

"Which means you do too, if you are to be seen in my company. A cowboy engineer isn't exactly the type of company I should be keeping. I assume you have a change of clothes at the Pyrrho Club?"

He glanced down at his damp vest and pants. "Well, yes, I do, but—"

"Excellent. I'm sure it can only be an improvement."

"About this Plan—"

"It's on a need-to-know basis. I shall inform you at the correct juncture of your role, or not, as it pertains to the matter at hand."

"This Plan isn't merely waiting to see if someone responds to your posters, is it?"

She glowered. "Certainly not. Although that does play a part in the grand scheme of things."

He sighed. Lord, help him. This was going to be the longest three days of his life.

She sat back against the cushions. "I will now allow you to contribute your theorems and observations to my investigation."

"You want my opinion?"

"On certain matters. There are several aspects of the kidnapping that I don't understand. First, let's discuss your incursion into my party."

"Do we have to?"

"My cousin Wellington had reviewed my invitation list and specifically removed all known rakes, gamblers, and scoundrels—or as he prefers to call them, his closest friends. Everyone in attendance was therefore an upstanding aristocrat with impeccable social credentials. In short, you should never have gained admittance to the Exhibition Dome. Even by Maya's side, my servants would not have let in anyone without an engraved invitation and formal attire."

"It was quite the coronation—definitely fit for a queen."

"It was my coming-out ball, and white tie was mandatory. Don't sidestep my question—how exactly did you get in?"

He tugged at his earlobe. "Well, I didn't walk in through the front door."

"I know that."

"All right then. You've got to keep this information strictly confidential, understand?"

She laid her ruined glove across her heart. "I'm the soul of discretion."

"I'll bet. So . . . it seems the Steamwerks troops keep the scientists on a pretty tight leash. They're not allowed to leave the main facility without an armed escort. They sleep in their laboratories, work seven days a week, and rarely see the sunshine."

"And?"

"And over the years, Maya got a little tired of this setup. She pulled resources to build a secret passage between her lab and the Exhibition Dome. She heads there late at night to tinker with the exhibits or to steal out into town. As I didn't have a formal invitation to your ball, Maya thought it would be fun to give her guards the slip and sneak me in through the passage. Boy, you should see all the crazy traps, false walls, and dead ends she's built into her little escape route."

Constance arched one eyebrow. "I didn't know about the secret passage."

He shrugged. "Wouldn't be too secret if you did, now, would it?"

She sipped her tea. "So, could the exo-suit pilots have entered the same way?"

"I doubt it. It's more likely they came in through the service entrance before the party even began."

"But this doesn't explain why we couldn't see them. We had a clear view into the suits' cockpits. They appeared empty."

"That's true. So, tell me, Miss Haltwhistle, if the suits appeared empty but actually held pilots, what's the next logical step?"

"Wires? Mirrors?"

"Nope. Try again."

She rubbed her forehead. "Surely, Mr. Trusdale, you can't be suggesting that I'm looking for an invisible man?"

"No, miss, I'm not."

"Well, thank goodness for that."

"I'm suggesting you're looking for three invisible men. And lucky for you, I'll bet I'm one of the few people in this country who knows exactly where to start."

Chapter 4: A Man with a Plan

ONE SHOULD NEVER SCHEDULE THE assassination of one's queen and host a major garden party in the same week. Prince Lucien Albert Dunstan, third Duke of Hallamshire, thirteenth in line to the British throne, and Queen Victoria's favorite grandson, was having a devil of a time keeping the details straight.

He leaned over his Chippendale writing desk and smoothed out the map of Her Majesty's parade route through Sheffield with a manicured hand. Stacks of leather-bound biographies of his favorite tyrants, conquerors, and kings held down the edges of the printed sheet. The thirty-year-old nobleman traced the Queen's route from the rail station to the town hall and on to the green expanse of Endcliffe Park. From a purpose-built grandstand at the park, his grandmother, her closest relatives, and her extensive retinue would have a splendid view of the military airship maneuvers.

He sincerely hoped dear Gram-gram would enjoy the show, however briefly. What a shame he wouldn't be present to see the expression on her face when an imperial dreadnought opened fire upon the royal stand. A living funeral pyre with the aged widow on top. It was a fitting end for an obsolete warrior queen.

With a smirk, he picked up a golden fountain pen and drew the letter *X* three times in a row directly behind the grandstand. Effigies of British armaments covered with flowers would line the parade route through the city. His insertion of three real exo-suits disguised by roses behind the VIP seats should go unnoticed. The armored suits' flamethrowers would bring a fiery end to Victoria's cronies if any escaped the aerial bombardment.

He stood back to enjoy his handiwork. His bold X's stood in stark contrast to his military advisor's pencil scribbles, showing the exact locations of redcoat battalions and airships. Erhard might have his uses as an unofficial counselor, but he failed to grasp the most fundamental lesson of strategic planning.

True leaders aren't afraid to use ink.

Lucien poured a generous snifter of brandy and breathed in the heady scent of warmed plum and burnt gingerbread. Careful not to dampen his handlebar mustache, he took the daintiest of sips. It had taken three buxom French maids one hour to tease the ends of the hirsute adornment into perfect spirals. His barber could have styled it in just ten minutes, but the corseted maids added a certain *je ne sais quois* to the experience. Not to mention, their combined ability to polish his riding boots to a mirrored sheen was second to none.

Perhaps he should summon them? Mud from his morning fox hunt had sullied his boots and speckled his blood-red tailcoat, snowy silk cravat, and white calfskin jodhpurs. He could use a good polish.

A knock rapped upon the study door. He tossed a pile of receipts for party victuals across the map and bellowed, "Enter."

The tall walnut door opened, and Gunter Erhard bowed his way into the study. The stout Austrian bulged from the confines of a dark blue tailcoat. In a gray shirt, patched breeches, and scuffed brown riding boots, he looked more like a down-and-out coach driver than the right-hand man to one of the country's greatest aristocrats. A curved officer's saber in a brass and leather scabbard hung on his hip.

Lucien frowned. "Tell me, Erhard, which part of 'Never enter my home' is unclear to you?"

The Austrian paled beneath the dueling scars that marred his cheeks and straightened. His eyes widened as he took in the baroque splendor of the study. He gaped up at a ceiling painting of his master rendered as a Roman god, gazing down his aquiline nose at the world. God-Lucien drove a golden chariot pulled by white-winged horses across clouds lit crimson by a dying sun. His long corkscrew curls blew behind him in the heavenly wind. The tiniest wisp of a toga was wrapped around his Herculean torso as he brandished a sword at all who dared to cast their eyes upon his magnificence.

"An exact duplication of your illustriousness, Your Royal Highness," said Erhard

Lucien's chest puffed. "Yes, it does rather do me justice."

Below the painted hooves of the flying beasts stood Lucien's prize automaton, a twelve-foot-wide bronze globe dotted with tiny flags. Dr. McKinley's World-Domination Territorium rotated on a serpentine trunk of copper pipes. A haze of steam wrapped around the pipes as they snaked down through the oak floor. The boards vibrated gently from the steam engine below that drove the globe's rotation.

The seven continents were cast in relief across the Territorium's ribbed bronze sphere, and the outline of every country was rendered in silver ink. A cartographer redrew the borders of the more politically excitable countries almost daily. Holes peppered each nation to allow for the raising of a two-inch flag from within the device's innards. Two-thirds of the world flew a pink flag that marked the territories of the British Empire. Other nations flew the black flag of war with the empire, the blue flag of neutrality, or the green flag of alliance. The largest neutral country by far was the United States of America.

The Prince curled his lip at the US. Any country that started a revolution by tossing perfectly good tea into a harbor was clearly deranged. Why Victoria hadn't marched her redcoats back into Washington, DC, strung up a few thousand of the feistiest locals, and reclaimed the colonies was beyond him. Her error would be corrected once he'd ripped the crown from dear Granny's head.

A warning bell pinged within the metal entrails of the globe. The device was updated hourly by a telegraph operator with a direct line to the War Office in London. With a puff of steam and a grinding of gears, Ceylon's black war flag was drawn inside the globe. He held his breath. The bell pinged again and up popped the pink flag of colonial triumph.

Lucien breathed a sigh of relief. Finally, the embargo on serving Ceylonese junglefowl would end, and his dinner guests could delight once more in tasting the empire's finest wild bird. It was a victory for every epicurean host. *Well done, Britain!*

Erhard said in his precise, clipped accent, "Another glorious win for the empire. Congratulations, Your Royal Highness."

"Indeed. And you're here because . . . ?"

Erhard cleared his throat. "Please accept my profuse apologies for darkening your day with my ignoble presence. I trust that your fox hunt went well?"

"Better than it did for the fox." He gestured at the parade map sprawled across the desk. "I've made a few additions. Feel free to inspect."

Erhard scurried to the desk to view his handiwork. The Austrian studied the new X's on the map and broke into a wide smile. "An excellent embellishment. Three crosses, three exo-suits. Why, Alexander the Great could not have made a more fitting addition."

"I suspected as much. I can add a few more details—"

"Oh no, Your Royal Highness, surely Hannibal did not ask for one more elephant? Your plan is perfect as it stands. Additions would serve only to dilute such well-considered precision."

"I suppose that's true. We didn't have any problems acquiring the exo-suits, did we?" Lucien took a sip of brandy.

"Not at all; both the suits and the scientists are secured safely at your father's old folly in the forest."

The brandy turned bitter in his mouth. Lucien banged the glass down on his desk so hard fractures splayed through the delicate crystal. It held together, barely. He pushed the glass away. "I'm glad I've finally found a use for that damned folly. My father wasted ten years and half his fortune building that monstrous eyesore."

"The edifice provides a sufficiently remote location from your garden party tomorrow. For added security, our Swedish allies have sent armed commandoes to guard the place day and night. Your father would be horrified at his monumental work becoming a base camp for a foreign power. I'm sure he's turning in his grave as we speak."

"You never did tell me where you put the body."

"Which part? I recall you fed his heart to his favorite hound, and his spleen ended up . . ."

". . . served in the alms soup for the village poor. He always said he never wanted them to go hungry." Lucien snickered. "The blind old fool. However," he fixed his servant with a steely eye. "Unluckily for you, Erhard, I'm not cursed with Father's naïveté. You're clearly bringing up past triumphs to diminish current failures. What catastrophe are you so ably not sharing with me?"

Erhard stiffened. "I see that Your Royal Highness' keen intellect has once again hit upon the heart of the matter. Although we did procure both the scientists and the exo-suits, there were two small hiccups, for want of a better word."

"I loathe hiccups. Exactly how small?"

"Tiny, in the grand scheme of things. It appears that Dr. Chauhan was not carrying the artifact on her person when she was kidnapped."

Lucien twirled the end of his mustache. "Hmm. So, our informant is a liar?"

"We believe that she did have the Enigma Key with her at the party, but she managed to pass it to a male companion during the attack. We haven't been able to confirm his location yet, but we believe he's an American engineer called 'J. F.' Trusdale."

"Find him, kill him, take the artifact. And what, pray tell, is the other issue?"

Erhard sighed. "Haltwhistle's daughter survived, again."

"What? But—how is that even possible? I thought this time you were dropping two tons of metal cage on her head? For goodness' sake, how hard can it be to murder a debutante? Shoot her, stab her, boil her in oil. Strip away her flesh and leave her carcass for the crows. Toss her from a turret, smash her skull with a mallet, poison her claret. Drown her, hang her, burn her alive. My god man, these are merely the deaths I've administered to the worst of my servants over the past year. Surely you can apply a little creativity to the task at hand?"

The Austrian squirmed. "We've tried, my Prince. She rarely leaves her estate, and when she does, her servants keep as close an eye on her as the Queen's own guards. Even when our men do manage to sneak within striking distance of her person, she seems to have an uncanny ability to stay alive. Last week, two crossbow bolts fired into her midriff merely bounced off her. She shot a hard glare at the bowman and stomped off without so much as a word. She's an unnatural beast, Your Highness."

"Then send her screaming back to hell, or so help me . . ." Lucien viciously kicked the leg of the Chippendale desk. The desk withstood his attack. Pain shot through his foot as he howled and hopped across the study spitting a string of curses that would have made a sky pirate blush. "Dammit, Erhard, we need this wretched woman dead. Now. No more delays."

"The deed will be done, my Prince."

Lucien took a deep breath. "It better be, for your sake. The King of Sweden is adamant that *every* member of the Haltwhistle line must be eliminated. I can only assume that our good friend Oscar is related to the Borgias with his obsession with bloody revenge. Have you found out why he wants this family dead?"

"Not yet, my lord."

"The father is still missing?"

"No one has seen him for years. They say he might be lost in the Andes. Or Antarctica. Or—"

"Then the daughter's demise will have to do. I thought Oscar had sent his personal assassins to help you with this task. Are they incompetent?"

Erhard made a nodding motion to his right.

Lucien scowled. "Damn it, man. What's that supposed to mean?"

A male voice with a Swedish lilt spoke out of the emptiness to Erhard's right. "What he means, Your Royal Highness, is that we have placed an operative directly amongst the Haltwhistle servants. I can assure you that our team is working with you to the best of our abilities. Our new, *enhanced* abilities."

Lucien started like a spooked Thoroughbred. "My God, the invisibility serum actually worked?"

A disembodied voice affirmed, "It most definitely did. We can now roam unheeded through the halls of power. No secret shall be safe; no life shall be secure. Our supernatural stealth will allow us to eliminate all those who stand against us."

"May I introduce the newly invisible Captain Alvar?" Erhard waved his hand toward the last place inhabited by the invisible man.

The Prince addressed thin air. "Alvar, I applaud your courage in choosing to take part in this grand experiment. Progress would grind to a halt without men like you willing to take a giant leap into the unknown. Please continue to work with my servants to secure the artifact and terminate the elusive Miss Haltwhistle."

"As you wish, Your Royal Highness," whispered Alvar into Lucien's left ear.

Lucien bolted across the study to stand with his back pressed against the wall.

Alvar laughed, a high, musical laugh with a just a hint of yodel. It was the laugh of a man stretched too thin across eternity. *Perhaps the invisibility serum has a side effect of driving one's henchmen stark raving mad?*

Erhard cleared his throat. "Enough, Alvar. It's only funny the first ten times. We have much to do. An artifact to find, a Haltwhistle to kill. Perhaps we should begin?"

"Indeed," said Lucien, smoothing down the lapels of his tailcoat. "It's a fine day to hunt our prey."

Erhard bowed. "We'll soon run them to ground, my lord, I promise you."

"I shall hold you to that. Both of you. Do not fail me, for my wrath shall be as a dragon's, full of fire and fury. Now, begone. I have a garden party to oversee. Great hosts rely upon preparation above all things, and I've yet to choose the perfect canapé."

Lucien limped to his desk. He pushed the map of Victoria's route aside to study the menu choices supplied by his chef on twelve handwritten pages.

This would take truly exceptional planning.

The future emperor settled down to weigh his culinary options.

Chapter 5:
Mermaid Ahoy

STANDING AS A TESTAMENT TO the triumph of science over nature, the hourglass-shaped tower of the Pyrrho Club loomed two hundred feet above the treetops of Ecclesall Woods. Rain slid over the curves of the figure-eight edifice, slick against the black granite lower-half, glistening over the transparent top. Inside the tower's bulbous head, flashes of purple lightning crackled against the tempered glass. Outside, a violet vortex of unnatural storm clouds raged around scientific enclave.

Electrical energy tinged the forest air with the metallic taste of ozone so sharp Trusdale figured it could almost cut his tongue. The lavender lightshow transformed the ancient woods into a lurid alien landscape. For the first time in years, he felt homesick for the prairies of his native state. Folks could say what they liked about Kansas, but at least it wasn't a glowing purple nightmare. The Club's gravel driveway wound in a lazy spiral around the hourglass tower.

The weather seemed to be worsening the further they got from the city center. Silver sheets of rain blustered between the twisted trees. Trusdale was starting to appreciate the comfort of traveling in a warm, dry, carriage. Even if his companion was herself as odd as a seven-dollar bill, Miss Haltwhistle's seat was by far the plushest he'd ever sat upon.

Heedless of the storm, the Baron's daughter was trying to pull down the carriage window to get a better view of the tower. Swollen tight from the rain, the wooden frame wouldn't budge. Aha—here was his chance to curry favor with the woman who could send him back to jail.

Trusdale stood and pushed on the top of the frame with one hand, dropping the window instantly with a tinkle of broken glass.

"Most helpful, thank you." Her tone was colder than a brass toilet seat in the Yukon.

He sank back onto the velvet bench. "I can pay—"

"Not at all. Do excuse me."

She stood and leaned out of the window into the tempest. The wind whipped her waist-length hair into a frenzy around her tiny hat. There was something about her copper hair that reminded him of first true love, Milli. They'd spend every hour they could together, strolling through the meadows, tracking deer through the woods, sharing a bite by a roaring fire as snow drifted over the plains.

His dear, sweet, Milli.

The queen of Irish Setters.

Constance's auburn tresses darkened to a tawny red in the rain. When she got a clear view of the giant hourglass between the trees, she clapped her hands in delight.

He smiled, fascinated by the wild dance of her luscious locks. She'd have made a terrific mermaid. For all he knew, she could have been one. Who knew what she hid beneath that lace-covered bustle?

Constance murmured, "From the sky, it must look like a lighthouse for the gods."

Time to show off a little. As part of his cover, he'd memorized several science-related speeches. His brother had loved to explain complex power systems to all within earshot, whether they desired to learn or not.

He cleared his throat. "The purple lightning you see in the top half of the tower is the output of a high-frequency air-core transformer. It creates a powerful electrical field which burns at an extremely high voltage. The lightning arcs from the Tesla coil run to one hundred million volts or more. That energy provides wireless lighting and the raw power to drive the hundred bright inventions currently being developed within the club's state-of-the-art facilities."

"You seem rather well informed. Did you read the brochure?" She pulled back into the carriage. Seemingly unconcerned about her rain-soaked lace dress, she drew her two stiletto hairpins from beneath her scarlet hat. She deftly whirled her wet hair into a tight bun and pinned it with precision above the nape of her neck. She used both hands to smooth stray strands into straitlaced submission. The woman had transformed from potential mermaid to stern librarian in one swift move.

A vague sense of disappointment came over him.

She continued, "As you are clearly an expert, perhaps you can answer this question. Does it come in any other colors?"

He frowned. "What, the Tesla coil?"

"The lightning; it would be fabulous in green."

He couldn't read a single nuance from her expression. *Is this an example of dry British humor? It's so hard to tell.* Time to name-drop. "I'll ask Nikola for you when I get home."

Her eyes widened. "You know Nikola Tesla?"

J. F. sure did. "I sure do. When I was a student at West Point, he came to give a series of lectures. He asked me to serve as his assistant while he was there. The work was fascinating, to say the least."

"Really? Gosh. Tesla and West Point, what an interesting combination. Did Mr. Tesla demonstrate electrical weaponry? I've heard rumors that—"

He held up his hand. "I'm sorry, but I'm not at liberty to discuss the content of his lectures with nonmilitary personnel. State secrets, you know."

She sighed. "Just when you were starting to get interesting. In what year did you graduate?"

"Eighteen eighty-eight." He frowned. No, that was his own graduation date. When did J. F. pass out of the academy? "I mean, eighteen eighty-five."

Her lips narrowed. "I see." She sat back and folded her arms. Had she noticed his slip-up? Her face was unreadable. She said, "Moving on. Once you have changed into more suitable attire at the Pyrrho Club, we shall progress to the Steamwerks to investigate Maya's laboratory. Perhaps we'll find a clue the redcoats missed as to why she and the others were kidnapped."

"Other than being a weaponry genius? Such knowledge makes her valuable to the right parties."

Constance's brow furrowed. "True. I'd never really thought of it that way. I—that is, she, should have been more careful."

"I'll bet Maya's thinking the same thing. Listen, about trotting over to the Steamwerks and asking to poke around her laboratory—"

"Yes?"

"I doubt my temporary consultant credentials will gain me access without Maya there to oversee me, especially now that somebody has threatened the security of the place. You won't be able to get in at all. The Crown doesn't allow any Tom, Dick, or Haltwhistle to just wander in and snoop around, you know."

"Ugh, how tedious. Nevertheless, we shall try."

"I'm telling you that part of 'the Plan' isn't gonna work. I'd recommend—"

"Not with that attitude it won't. Your utter lack of usefulness to getting us into the Steamwerks aside, you have yet to share your knowledge of the invisible men who carried out this dreadful attack."

He glanced again out the window to reassure himself that the Club wasn't too far a walk. He'd been holding back his invisible man story on the impression that Miss Haltwhistle was the type of lady who might well throw a gentleman out of her carriage if she had no further use for him, and this was not an easy tale to swallow. He'd have to watch his words around her; she was sharper than a Bowie knife. "I must warn you, Miss Haltwhistle. You may find this tale hard to believe."

"Oh, I love a good story well told. Do continue."

"This is the true account of a man who was in the wrong place at the wrong time."

"Was it you?"

Yes. A younger, dumber version. "No, not me. It was a man with a close-cut black beard. Don't ask me his name, as they didn't mention it in the newspaper article that stirred my interest in this case. About two years back, a macabre series of murders occurred right here in England. The perpetrator was killed by an angry mob in a village called—well, that's not important. What *is* important is an incident that took place right before the villain met his grisly fate."

She leaned forward on the seat, her green eyes alight. "Go on."

"Our hero was an American tourist, just minding his own business, downing a few pints with the locals in a pub called the Jolly Cricketers."

She groaned. "I should have known any tale about invisible men was going to involve alcohol. Just how plastered was this tourist?"

He scowled. "He'd barely had a drop. Two pints, maybe three, of Burton ale. Anyway, as he shared tales of adventure with his newfound friends, someone burst into the pub screaming like a madman."

She gasped. "The killer."

"No, I'm getting to him. The fellow who ran into the pub was frantic with fear. He said that an invisible man was trying to murder him. To humor him we—that is, the locals—locked the doors tight. You can imagine the shock on every man's face as bricks came crashing through the windows, thrown by an unseen hand."

"Was it dark out?"

"That's not the point. The assailant was bent on killing us all if he got the chance. It seems he'd been a man of science who'd stumbled upon the secret to invisibility through a series of mad experiments. He used himself as a test subject, which rarely ends well. His newly discovered serum drove him into a ghostly world of madness and depravity. The things a man can do when he no longer has to look himself in the eye . . . but I digress. It was up to our American hero to save the day. He drew out his trusty service revolver—"

"So, he was a military man?"

"Once upon a time, I guess. Anyway, he pointed his gun out through the window at the transparent fiend. A policeman in the bar said, 'That won't do, that's murder.' Our hero replied, 'I know what country I'm in, I'm going to let off at his legs.' He fanned his shots, firing five rounds at knee height toward the invisible foe. One bullet hit, driving the madman away with a trail of blood seeping from his wound. The wet trail allowed others to track the enemy to his ultimate demise. The monster's murder spree ended that very night at the hands of the villagers he'd terrorized."

"Gosh. And what became of the invisibility serum?"

He shrugged. "That's what everyone wanted to know. There were rumors of a journal that contained the formula. Some say a local landowner got his hands on it, a certain Lord Burdock."

She blinked. "Are you sure? That name seems awfully familiar. I believe I may have invited a Lord Burdock to attend my coming-out ball."

"Well, isn't that a coincidence?"

Raised voices floated in through the broken window.

Constance stared into the rain. "Speaking of angry mobs, we appear to have run into one ourselves." She pointed to the entrance of the Pyrrho Club, under siege by twenty or so men and women clad in Steamwerks uniforms. The throng shouted insults at a couple of policemen guarding the club's black doors.

The carriage rumbled to a halt behind the proletarian protest.

As mobs go, they were quite smartly dressed. Chestnut-brown vests, bowler hats, white shirts, and suspenders were *de rigueur*. The ladies had put aside long skirts in favor of factory-friendly bloomers and high-laced boots. The men had tucked their moleskin pants into wool socks above hobnailed work clogs. Both sexes wore tool belts stuffed with the wrenches, spanners, and calipers required for successful tinkering, and stood in the deluge without coats or umbrellas. It seemed they had left the floor of the armaments factory in a hurry.

Two policemen clad in blue stood in the shelter of the arched doorway. Both had their arms folded. In England, two constables with folded arms were more than enough to keep a mob of twenty at bay.

The officers glared at the carriage, clearly expecting more problems to emerge from its elegant frame.

Trusdale grimaced. "You'd better stay in here." He reached for the door handle.

Constance leaned forward and whispered, "Please don't."

He stopped. She held up one finger, and waited.

Her elderly servant appeared by the door. With a flourish, the footman opened a large black umbrella and shielded the carriage steps as his own coat darkened from the rain.

"Would you mind awfully letting Cawley open the door?" She nodded toward the beak-nosed servant. "He gets quite miffed if you do it yourself."

"I can manage."

"I'm sure you can, but he'll sulk for days if you do. It's best to let him do things the way he thinks they should be done. He has a set procedure for almost everything."

"I suppose so."

The Baron's daughter appeared relieved. "He'll wait fifteen seconds to give us time to gather our belongings." She turned to press a brass button in the wood paneling behind her head. A panel slid open to reveal a rack of ten umbrellas and parasols in a rainbow of colors. She selected a scarlet umbrella with a handle whimsically styled as a fox. "Would you care for an umbrella?"

"No thanks. We're pretty close to the entrance."

"It's not for the rain." She nodded toward the Steamwerkers. "It's in case we need to defend ourselves. They might be anarchists."

"Anarchists don't tend to wear uniforms."

"They could be part-time anarchists. Stirring up trouble on their tea breaks. Brolly or no?"

"No thanks, and I think you should stay inside the—"

She was already halfway out of the carriage, holding the gloved hand of the servant for steadiness as she stepped down. She kept the umbrella furled and advanced on the group, ready for trouble.

He did so love a woman of action. Trusdale suppressed a grin and followed.

Cawley held his umbrella over his mistress, stalking behind her on impossibly skinny legs. The crowd parted before the woman's diminutive frame, her authority to interfere apparently confirmed by her upright bearing and confident stride.

She marched up to the policemen. They unfolded their arms and stood up straight.

"Right," she said. "What's going on here then?"

The two constables exchanged worried glances.

"They won't let us in," shouted one of the Steamwerkers.

"Yes, thank you, I can see that," called Constance over her shoulder.

The senior officer, a hatchet-faced giant with unruly sideburns, growled, "The Club is full. They can't stay here. There's no room."

His colleague, who was young and slender with a trainee mustache, said, "They're here because of the evacuation, miss. The whole Steamwerks has gone on lockdown for the next few days. There was a major security breach last night. The word is that three top scientists were kidnapped by an airship at a fancy party. Some debutante turned down the offer of redcoat guards in favor of her own servants, if you can believe that. Can you imagine the audacity—?"

"Let me stop you right there," said Constance.

The policemen studied her expectantly.

Constance raised her eyebrows. "Yes?"

The officers exchanged glances. "Aren't you going to say something?"

"Such as?"

The constables gaped at Constance while Trusdale smothered a smirk. "Ahem, officers, am I to understand that the Steamwerks is completely closed?"

Constable Hatchet Face said, "Not just closed, sir, locked down. No one is going in or out. National security, and all that."

The junior policeman added, "And the no one going in and out includes this lot." He waved an arm at the Steamwerkers. "Most of them live in the Werks' dormitories. Now they've got nowhere to stay, and every hotel in town is sold out 'cause of the Queen's visit. So, they're stuck out in the cold with no roof over their head."

"And they can't stay here," said Constable Hatchet Face firmly. "Can't have the hoi-poloi staying with the muckety-mucks, now can we?" This stirred angry muttering from the crowd.

Constance blew out her breath. "So, they're definitely not anarchists then?"

The junior policeman's expression softened. "No. They're just wet sods looking for a dry bed, Miss—?"

"Haltwhistle," she said, wincing.

This revelation drew a "well, I never!" several "oooh's," and a shocked "gettawaywiya" from the crowd.

Constance turned to face the Steamwerkers with the air of a captain going down with her airship. "Yes, all right. It was my coming out ball. I'm sorry you have all been inconvenienced by the nefarious villains that perpetrated this kidnapping. Nevertheless, I shall set things as right as I can." To the policemen, she said, "Is there a telegraph desk in the club?"

"Indeed there is, miss," said the senior officer. "In fact"—he raised his voice so the crowd could hear—"we've just used it to call for backup."

This raised a fresh grumble from the damp throng.

"Cawley," said Constance, "Do we still have all those camp cots available? The ones we used for the wounded soldiers last year?"

"Yes, miss," said the servant in a voice reminiscent of dried leaves crunching underfoot.

"Excellent. We'll telegraph Whirlow Junction rail station and ask them to run a message up to the Hall. The staff can set up the cots to accommodate our overnight guests."

Constance spun back to the waiting crowd and threw her arms wide. "Ladies and gentlemen, I'm delighted to invite you all to stay at Haltwhistle Hall. We have hot food, warm beds, and plenty of ale. Please *discreetly* spread the word to your colleagues, should they require lodging."

The Steamwerkers seemed torn between gratitude and gripes at the aristocrat who was both the cause of—and solution to—their current misery.

One stately woman with a supervisor's medal pinned upon her blouse looked around at the mixed feelings and took it upon herself to step forward. "Bless your heart, miss. We're most thankful for your kindness."

Strawberries of color lit up Constance's cheeks. "Yes, well, don't mention it. I do hope none of you catch pneumonia from this dreadful downpour." She turned her attention back to the senior policeman. "I assume you have no qualms about these . . . my new friends . . . waiting inside until I send for my carriages to pick them up?"

The unholy union of miss muckety-muck with the hoi-poloi was clearly above Constable Hatchet Face's pay grade. "I suppose that's all right, miss, as long as they stand right inside the doors and don't touch anything."

"Splendid," beamed Constance. She nodded at Cawley.

The aged retainer stepped between the policemen and grasped the hourglass-shaped handles on the two great doors. With a firm shove, he pushed the doors open to reveal a black marble foyer lit by glowing filament bulbs. The foyer was empty save for a coat-check counter and a tuxedoed, slick-haired club manager with a pencil mustache and the air of a *maître d'*. Two steel-and-brass doors strong enough to guard the Royal Mint stood closed at the rear of the foyer.

The manager stared aghast as the Steamwerkers stomped into his domain. He couldn't have looked more shocked had Attila the Hun and his rampaging hordes burst into the foyer demanding lemonade. He lit upon a known face. "Ah, Mr. Trusdale. You've returned. How was your first evening in the city?"

Absolute hell, thanks for asking. "Truly unforgettable. I think Miss Haltwhistle here," he gestured toward Constance, "would like to send a telegram, if you don't mind."

Constance appeared faintly bemused at this introduction. Trusdale added, "You can put it on my tab." As the Steamwerks were paying for his stay, he could afford to be generous.

"Absolutely, sir. The transmitter is in my office. And your other . . . associates?" The manager cast a disdainful eye on the disheveled Steamwerkers, who were dripping all over the pristine marble floor.

Constance said, "They will wait here for transport to my home, which is less than half an hour's drive. They will not be an inconvenience, I assure you."

The manager wisely chose not to argue with her. The Steamwerkers sat on the floor, a brown-and-white puddle of humanity brought low by fate and circumstance.

Trusdale leaned close to Constance and murmured, "That was mighty neighborly of you, offering shelter to the huddled masses and all."

She smoothed back her hair. "I just thought they looked untidy out there."

"If you say so. Well, I'm gonna head to my room for a half hour or so to clean myself up. It'll be good to get outta of these damp clothes."

She stared at his shirt as if she'd never seen it before, and her cheeks tinged pink.

Damn. Had he been indecorous? He cleared his throat. "I mean, I'm gonna strip off and scrub myself . . . I . . . you know what, never mind. While I'm gone, stay alert."

Constance cocked her head, one eyebrow raised. "Why do you say that?"

"I just have a feeling . . ." That he was being watched? Given that the entire Steamwerks crew openly gawked at his appearance with expressions ranging from amusement to mild alarm, it seemed like a foolish thing to say. Back home, his boots tooled with shooting stars wouldn't have drawn a second glance. To these folks, he was clearly something of an oddity. Yes, he was definitely being watched.

He shrugged. "I don't know. Just send your telegram and keep your guard up. That's all."

Constance rolled her eyes and sashayed after the manager through the vaultlike doors. Cawley trotted after her like a lapdog.

Trusdale took a final glance around the lobby. With a tip of his hat to the Steamwerkers, he strode into the heart of the Pyrrho Club.

Chapter 6:
Drunk Science

CONSTANCE HAD NEVER VISITED THE Pyrrho Club, despite the fact her papa was an honorary member. The Baron's groundbreaking thesis on the perceived sentience of certain archaeological relics had caused a sensation in the late 1880s. He'd head out to the club every Tuesday afternoon, returning hours later, blind drunk, and bursting to share news of the latest scientific advancements.

His tipsy state had been a vital part of the research process. The Pyrrho Club had been founded on the principle that exponential growth in human knowledge could be achieved through the liberal consumption of alcohol. Cocktail napkins around the world bore written testimony of the brilliant ideas that flowed through inebriated minds. Unleashing that creativity was the primary goal of the club's specially trained waitstaff. The correct application of an absinthe cocktail here, or a brandy there, might inspire the creation of a world-changing discovery.

It was ten o'clock in the morning, and the science was in full swing.

A-list scientists from the empire and beyond toasted their colleagues across tables piled high with research notes. Shoulder-buttoned lab coats adorned men and women of every creed and color. Tuxedoed waiters swung between the crowded tables carrying glasses of inspiration on silver trays. They padded silently across the black marble floor beneath the frosted glass ceiling. Beyond the glass, the purple lightning of the Tesla coil snarled and writhed like a hellish sea beast. Sedate by comparison, yellow filament lights glowed softly from the dark walls surrounding the circular room.

Constance turned to Cawley, who seemed to have walked three steps behind her since the day her one-year-old self first tottered out of the nursery in search of a snack. "Look, Cawley, electrical lights. Maybe we should install a few at home?"

The old man pulled a face that could have soured milk at ten paces.

She grinned. Cawley viewed anything more technologically advanced than a candle as bad news. In fact, he probably thought candles were a little on the flash side. Not that he'd ever openly proclaimed his disdain for technological progress. Like children, servants were expected to be seen and not heard. As such, their inner thoughts remained a mystery that revealed itself only through facial tics. This chasm between classes held benefits for both sides. As a benevolent dictator, she could assume her orders would be followed to the best of her servants' abilities. In return, they could bring to fruition her wilder ideas, safe in the knowledge that the results were clearly not their fault.

What would the servants do if she failed to marry and Uncle Bertie seized the estate? He'd never forgiven Papa for eloping with his only sister. But since Mama's death, his hatred of Papa bordered on insanity. Rumors flew that once Bertie gained legal possession, he intended to raze the estate, willfully destroying the livelihood of all who worked there.

Constance studied her retainer's crumpled-paper face. Not on her watch. The Brass Queen protected her own. She'd raise hell and bring down heaven before she let Bertie so much as throw a dark glance toward Cawley's silver-haired pate.

The object of her protection glowered at a Belgian scientist performing hiccup-laced equations for his cheering colleagues. Constance sighed. If only the scientists' great minds could discover her a noble husband in double-quick time. She would have paid a king's ransom for the device, serum, or lens that could reveal such a man, but the geniuses were focused on lesser mysteries of the universe than her love life, or lack thereof. Perhaps in another dimension, an alternate version of her could stand on a table and speak with such passion about the impending loss of the estate that they would flock to help her.

Alas, she could not be so bold in this one. Inquiries into Papa's current location could potentially be linked by the brilliant minds present to his obsession with arcane artifacts and his theories concerning parallel worlds. The thought of scientists learning Papa's secrets made her shudder. Scientists were the last people on Earth she'd want to know of his experiments. Not that they themselves were evil. But it seemed inevitable that at some juncture, their good work would be turned by others to nefarious ends.

Curiosity had wiped out many a world in the multiverse. Split this, shoot that. It was a slippery slope from the amusing images of a camera obscura to charred cities and ruined lives. This was why Papa had never let her travel to other worlds. Apart from the inherent physical danger of a portal transfer, he'd assured her that the sights she might see could ruin her outlook on humanity for good.

But shouldn't that be her choice to make?

Or did Papa truly know best?

And if ignorance was bliss, shouldn't she be much happier than she currently was?

She shook her head. She must stay focused. As both Miss Haltwhistle and the Brass Queen, saving the estate was job one. But perhaps it wouldn't hurt to learn a few new scientific secrets whilst she was here? Not full-blown curiosity, of course, but maybe just a smidge of natural inquisitiveness?

Constance followed the club manager on a weaving path between the crowded tables. At every opportunity, she peered over shoulders at complicated formulas written on napkins, tablecloths, and lab coat sleeves. The room hummed with conversation in a host of exotic languages. She cursed her lack of fluency. She was only proficient in nineteen languages, including French, Latin, Russian, Welsh, Portuguese, and nine dialects of Ancient Sumerian. Papa had always insisted that the key to understanding other cultures was to learn their language. A population with thirty-two words for love and only one for war experienced a kinder world than linguistically combative neighbors.

She strolled by the scientists, leaning in to catch snippets of their conversation. An experiment to galvanize corpses was a popular topic. This was matched only by the unearthing of bones from the giant lizard *Eotyrannus*. Inevitably, work was now underway to create a vast undead army of dinosaurs.

That could only end well.

She paused by a table of particularly inebriated geniuses. A petite Australian woman hiccupped, "*Äther* is the—*hic*—answer to all our—*hic*—energy problems, you mark my words."

Her Prussian companion nodded, downing a mug of hard cider in one long gulp. "*Äther macht's möglich.*"

Scientific discourse in action. Trusdale was so lucky to get to stay here and experience the intellectual milieu.

She glanced back. The American trailed slowly behind her, his blue eyes scanning the room. Stubble shadowed his square jaw, and his neckerchief was tied in a disheveled knot above his unbuttoned waistcoat. Apparently, he was still unaware that his hat should be in his hand, not on his head.

He noticed her stare and flushed beneath his tan.

Hmm, is that his guilty conscience showing? Perhaps he's realized that his hat is an affront to civilized society? Or is he hiding a sinister secret? In the carriage, he'd stumbled on his graduation date from West Point. And his story about the invisible man contained details he could never have gained from a newspaper article.

Trusdale glanced down at his waistcoat and fumbled to button it as he walked. Of all the men in the room, it was Trusdale who seemed least likely to have assisted Nikola Tesla. In fact, he seemed to be exactly the sort of man who might spend his evenings drinking in a pub before shooting a man in the knee. The invisibility serum might be real, but Trusdale's story rang hollow. Was it possible that he had been the gun-toting American tourist? And if he was, why lie?

The club manager stopped at a waist-height gate set into a brass railing that protected a twenty-foot-wide circular teak platform. Two overstuffed Chesterfield sofas faced each other in the center of the platform. A tasseled lamp illuminated a library table stacked with newspapers in a multitude of languages. A freckle-faced youth in an exuberantly gold-braided uniform stood beside a polished brass console with forty numbered buttons. At home, a press of a button usually led to the appearance of beverages, scones, books, or more logs for the fire. What wonders might this gleaming console produce?

The manager opened the gate and indicated that she should sit. The leather sofa creaked as she settled her bustle into place. Cawley sat beside her, his bones creaking far more loudly than the cushions ever could. The manager sat opposite, fiddling with his bow tie, and brushing his lapels beneath her gaze.

Trusdale strode over to the library table, grabbed a handful of newspapers, and collapsed heavily onto the sofa next to the manager. He stretched out his long legs, narrowly missing Cawley's shins with his enormous boots. The cowboy shook open the broadsheet newspaper with a loud rustle and began to read, flicking through the pages with what she deemed to be unnecessary enthusiasm.

She mentally added public reading to her list of things about Trusdale that irritated her. Perhaps she should start writing these down? Papa always kept a list of his friends' and enemies' strengths and flaws, to be used as ammunition in case of an all-out war. Trusdale wasn't exactly a friend, or an enemy, yet.

She'd have to create a column for "Potential Asset, and/or Annoyance."

The manager said to the freckled boy, "Floors one and four."

"Yes, sir," said the boy. He pushed several buttons and waited.

Nothing resembling tea, scones, or any other delights appeared. She folded her hands neatly in her lap and tried not to fidget. The English were known for their ability to wait, and she certainly wasn't going to let down her countrymen by making a fuss in front of Trusdale.

Two minutes later, the seat beneath her bustle vibrated. Almost imperceptibly, the teak platform began to sink. She gasped and grabbed the cushions for support.

"Don't worry, miss," said the manager. "It's designed to do that. You are riding upon a levitating reading room. They're all the rage in America."

"Are they indeed?" She glared at Trusdale behind his newspaper, but he failed to apologize for his country's lack of taste.

"It's fairly safe, Miss Haltwhistle," said the manager. "There's very little chance of asphyxiation. We take things slowly, as a precaution."

"I see." She sat for a while, watching the walls inch by. "And how long will this journey take?"

"Fourth floor, about twenty minutes."

"Right." She rubbed her temples. "So, would stairs be an option for this trip?"

"Stairs are considered to be old technology. This building is an avant-garde design, at the very forefront of innovation."

"Plus," muttered Trusdale from behind his paper, "stairs and drunks, not a good combination."

The manager gaped at him, apparently stunned by the American's lack of understanding regarding the intricacies of modern science.

Constance wouldn't make the same mistake. "I see. Most ingenious. And who designed this masterpiece of engineering?"

The manager puffed out his chest. "None other than Professor Pabodie. He also designed the Steamwerks Exhibition Dome. Are you familiar with it?"

"Indeed, I am. It is stunning. Although I do have to say I found some of the features over there a bit odd."

Trusdale dropped down one corner of his newspaper with a snap. "Odd how?"

"Well, for a start, the gift shop relocates itself every night."

Trusdale groaned. "Miskatonic architecture. Great. Just great. That's all we need. Rooms that move, floors that vanish. Creatures from beyond in the gents." He flicked up his newspaper with a particularly aggressive rustle and continued to read.

The manager looked as if he might well faint at such rampant philistinism. Constance studied the wall with new interest. From behind the newspaper, the American said, "Do you happen to have handy the guest list for your shindig last night?"

Shindig? She considered whether it was worth the effort to ask Trusdale to make a formal request using the proper vocabulary. But if she started down that conversational road now, the entire day could disappear into a tautological nightmare of explaining what words he could officially use according to Babett's definition of decorum. Even the very thought of trying to educate him to all the nuances of the English language tired her.

Perhaps in this particular circumstance, a simple response was best?

"I do indeed." She stood and reached backward into the hidden bag she had sewn into her bustle.

Trusdale dropped the newspaper and stared at her.

She rummaged around and pulled out a rolled parchment. She held it out to him.

He took it uncertainly. "Did you just pull this out of your—"

"Bustle. Yes. I do so hate to carry a reticule."

He lifted one unruly eyebrow at her.

"A reticule is a drawstring bag. I seem to lose them all the time, so instead, I have one sewn directly into my—"

"Bustle, right." He burst out laughing.

She flushed, sat, and folded her arms. The nerve of him. After she'd had the uncommon decency to refrain from mocking his horrendous hat. *If I wasn't such a lady, I'd kick him right in the—*

The teak platform shuddered to a halt.

"Here's your floor, sir," said the manager to Trusdale.

Eight black corridors led off from the platform shaft. Glowing filament lights ran the length of each corridor, casting shadows into dark doorways. A handful of guests walked the corridors, pausing here and there for clandestine chats with their colleagues.

The bellboy opened the gate for Trusdale. The cowboy strode down one of the corridors, drawing curious glances from the other residents.

"Next stop, fourth floor."

She might well die of old age before she got there. She tapped her boot on the platform, amusing herself by spelling out the word "bored" in Morse code.

After tapping her way through two Wordsworth sonnets, she reached into her bustle bag and pulled out her travel edition of *Babett's Modern Manners*. The bookplate declared in florid script that this edition belonged to Lady Annabella Pendelroy. She traced Mama's maiden name, the ink rendered almost invisible by her fingertips through the years. Mama would have been proud she was trying to follow the rules. Papa couldn't give two hoots for etiquette, but Mama . . .

Heavens, what would Mama have thought of Trusdale?

Constance flicked through the book, turning down page corners for those manners of which the American was devoid. It was so odd he didn't carry any identification in his wallet—not even a calling card. Uninvited party guest, cat burglar, liar. How could she find out who he really was?

He'd mentioned both West Point and Nikola Tesla. That was a starting point. Now, which of her American arms customers would be morally flexible enough to forge the paperwork to run a background check on Trusdale?

She slapped her thigh and grinned, raising the eyebrows of both Cawley and the manager. *Of course, Mr. Bobby "Two Fists" Malone of Chicago. He seems like a fellow unencumbered by rules and regulations.*

Delighted to have formulated a new aspect of the Plan with a capital 'P,' she sprang out of her seat as the levitating reading room approached her floor. The manager only just managed to open the brass safety gate before Constance strode through it down the steel corridor, a woman on a mission. She barely glanced into the windowed laboratories lining the corridor. Four gorillas sat at a table playing whist, as a white-coated scientist wrote notes on a clipboard. In the next lab, a white-coated gorilla with a clipboard wrote notes on four human scientists playing poker. Fascinating, but not enough to slow her progress.

A chill seized her as heavy snow fell unexpectedly from the ceiling. She blinked up at an oily green haze drifting below the steel plates.

"Malfunctioning weather machine," said the manager, hurrying to keep pace with her. "It has a tendency to puff out the odd micro-storm. That's probably yesterday's blizzard. Nothing to worry about."

She marched on.

The manager's office was notable for a fifteen-foot wide hole in the floor that plunged through four layers of lower laboratories to a granite bedrock.

"Small mishap in one of the labs," said the manager, switching on the telegraph transmitter on a battered mahogany desk.

"Raw aether?" she asked.

His eyes widened. "Why, yes, I believe so. Are you of a scientific bent, Miss Haltwhistle?"

"I am indeed. I'd love to chat all day about the do's and don'ts of safely utilizing aether without fracturing dimensional integrity, but time is of the essence. Are you ready to transmit?"

He nodded dumbly, hand poised to tap out her message.

"Address this to Mr. Robert Malone, a resident of Oily Annie's hostelry in Chicago, USA. Dear Bobby, I do hope my . . ." What would be a good substitute for the word flamethrowers? She couldn't recall this week's code word for incendiary armaments. Was it something to do with flowers? ". . . rose-scented candles . . . generated the pyrotechnic excitement you desired atop the cake at your niece's birthday party, stop."

She ignored Cawley's melodramatic sigh. He'd clearly missed his calling on the vaudeville stage. "I have a small favor to ask, stop. I've met one of your countrymen, a most curious Kansas cowboy. . ."

Chapter 7: A Close Shave

IT TOOK TRUSDALE TEN MINUTES and a smattering of his more colorful language to wrench off his wet boots. Water had swollen up his woolen socks to the point where sock and boot had become one entity. He peeled off his shirt and dropped it beside the free-standing copper bathtub. A nest of pipes encircled the base of the tub and ran through holes cut into the black marble floor. The same dark stone covered the walls and ceiling, where tiny filament lights twinkled like stars on a desert night. The subterranean bathroom's air, pumped down from the forest surface by softly whirring fans, was thick with the scent of wet leaves and ozone.

Three gold dolphin faucets arched over the side of the tub, surrounded by colored buttons. With no letters written upon them, he chanced pressing the red, blue, and green buttons. The copper pipes rattled, and warm water, green foam, and a cedar-scented oil cascaded from the dolphins into the tub. He screwed up his nose at the perfumed decadence. He'd have preferred a cold dunk in a horse trough to this European self-indulgence, but when in Rome . . .

He dragged off his damp pants and red woolen long johns. Stark naked except for his Stetson, he strode over to a gilded standing mirror around which flounced dolphins, seashells, and a winsome mermaid. Replace her golden hair with copper and she could almost pass for an aquatic Miss Haltwhistle. Not that he was thinking of her.

Turning his back, he glanced at his reflection over his shoulder. Dried puncture wounds peppered his skin. Splinters from the oak stage had drilled through his coat when he pushed Constance to safety. It sure said something about her character that she didn't seem to know the words, "thank you for saving my life," or even, "I'm sorry I had you arrested."

She probably thought *he* should thanking *her* for not letting him swing. Who knew, maybe he should be? A few hours in the company of Miss Haltwhistle, and the whole world felt topsy-turvy.

He flipped off his Stetson, hung it on the top corner of the mirror, and headed back to the tub. A shaving shelf behind the dolphins held an extendable mirror, a straight razor, a mug, soap, a badger-hair brush, grooming scissors, and a tin of mustache wax. Everything the modern gent needed to look presentable to the fairer sex. He ran his hand over his chin. He could sand tables with this stubble. No wonder the Baron's daughter kept looking at him like he'd just crawled out from under a rock.

The names on her party invitation list were well above his usual social circle. Lord this, Lady that, Dr. Maya Chauhan . . .

Stay strong Maya, if you're still . . .

Breathing.

The odds against rescuing the scientist from her captors were astronomical. But how could he share that with Constance? She clearly loved the Steamwerks matriarch. Admittedly, the women made a peculiar pairing.

One designed cutting-edge weapons.

And the other was a pig farmer.

Still, the thought of telling Constance that her friend was most likely . . .

Nope, I won't do that to her. It's always better to live in hope than despair. Besides, maybe his information about the original invisible man might tip fate's hand their way. On the party list, far below the names of Doctors McKinley and Huang, was the name Lord Peregrine Albertus Burdock. Constance appeared to have arranged the names not alphabetically, but by the order in which the attendee accepted her invitation. Was it significant that Burdock had accepted his invite after the scientists? He must have known they would be in attendance. Why would a man in possession of a working invisibility serum need a scientist, or three?

Beside Burdock's name, neat copperplate handwriting stated, "Lord B. left the party just before the speeches—claimed to feel unwell."

Miss Haltwhistle had clearly been making her own deductions from the list.

He scratched his stubble. Why in Heaven's name would Burdock steal the suits? If he already had the invisibility serum, he held more power at his command than most regents. Whether he used the invisibility serum for theft, murder, or mayhem, its very existence threatened the safety of all. No one on Earth could escape the clutches of an invisible lunatic—not queen, pauper, nor pope. If word got out that invisible predators were stalking the shadows, would any soul ever sleep peacefully again?

He sighed heavily. Sometimes, he wished he knew less than he did. Ignorance was a luxury he hadn't enjoyed in quite a while. It would be nice to take some time off now and again from the worries of the world.

The bath faucets clicked off automatically. No overflowing tubs here. He stepped in and sank into the cedar froth. Warmth enveloped his aching body.

Maybe the Europeans are onto something with their fancy bubbles after all.

Grasping the badger-hair shaving brush in his hand, he tilted the mirror to see his red-rimmed eyes. He swirled soap and water in the mug, creating white lather to slather over his jaw. As the foam softened his bristles, he checked the straight razor's blade with his thumbnail. It rang as sharp as truth. Holding the smooth bone handle in his right hand, he shaved his cheeks, flicking stray lather into the bathtub as he went. He tilted his head back, exposing his throat. Running the blade down over his skin, he paused as the hair on the back of his neck prickled.

The room was empty, with only the whirring fans for company.

Always paranoid. Why can't I relax and enjoy the moment?

He slowly ran the razor blade over his Adam's apple. He heard the slightest intake of breath. He tensed as an unseen entity shoved his own razor blade hard into his flesh, stinging, biting, slicing. The iron tang of blood filled his nose; a warm gush of life slicked his throat and panic churned his stomach.

Push back, push back, push back . . . against what?

He thrust his forearm out, twisting the razor away from his jugular, grunting as the invisible assailant thudded onto his chest and slammed what felt like a bony knee into his throat.

His skull cracked back into the copper tub as water filled his mouth, his nose, his ears, his eyes. Senses muffled, he blinked up through the water. Patches of green foam clung to parts of a body as naked as his own but on top, pressing down, still trying to twist the razor from his hands even as he drowned. He convulsed, tried to buck off the creature, tried to twist and turn, tried to turn the razor to his advantage. The assailant rode him like a prize bull, keeping his face submerged

One minute.

Two.

Lungs bursting, throat closing, sight dimming, he forced himself to relax. Crimson water cradled him to his grave. It was almost peaceful, letting go of the razor, surrendering.

Impatient, the assailant chased the blade as it slipped from his limp fingers.

A tilt of the creature's body weight, a slight lean to the left . . .

NOW!

Trusdale punched out with his left fist, connecting with what he hoped was an invisible jaw. It wasn't a full-strength punch, but the creature's weight rocked back. Trusdale surfaced, gasping for air, eyes and lungs burning with his assailant still astride him. Something bony slammed into his right eye. He grabbed for a wrestling hold. His fingers lit on . . . a wrist? He tightened his grip, and slid down into the foam, dragging his foe with him. He wrapped his arm around a surprisingly slender neck, keeping them both submerged. The attacker writhed, slick, and—

Wait. What?

Either his enemy had unnaturally well-developed pectorals, or it was—

A she.

In his bath.

This jarred his mind almost as much as the invisibility.

Sensing his distraction, she dragged herself from his grip. They broke water together, gasping.

"*Helvete!*" the woman swore as her elbow smashed into his nose, cracking it for the fifth time in his life.

Swedish? She's a long way from home.

Nose throbbing and eyes stinging, he shoved her out of the tub. She flopped onto the floor, winded. The green foam from the bath-water sketched the outline of her curves in empty space.

I've seen some macabre sights in my time, but this . . .

His flesh crawled.

She lunged toward his discarded clothes. Finding nothing of interest in his pants, she stood and reached for his hat hanging on the mirror.

The artifact.

"No!" He slopped out of the tub with the grace of a wet hound. His feet slid, and he fell back into the tub as the woman ran for the door with his hat. He lurched out of the bath again and shot after the invisible woman. His bare feet pounded on the marble floor as he chased the foamy female through the attached bedroom out into the hall.

She raced down the stone corridor dropping suds from her body, literally disappearing before his eyes. He bounded after her, eyes fixed on his floating hat. She sprinted for the levitating reading room, but the shaft stood empty, devoid of its teak platform.

Hah—gotcha!

She was trapped on his level with no stairs up or down.

The Stetson levitated to hover about six feet above the railing. Had she put the hat on and climbed up onto the rail? Surely, she wasn't going to jump?

He slowed, spreading his hands wide to show he was unarmed. "Ma'am, I swear I'm not gonna hurt you. Just toss me the Stetson, and you can be on your way."

A door to his left opened, and a woman screamed. He jumped as a female scientist thwacked him across his naked ribs with a furled umbrella.

The hat bobbed along the railing and swayed on the far side of the shaft.

The scientist's umbrella thwacked him again. He lurched toward the shaft. The hat leaped out into nothingness and dropped from his sight.

Fixed on his prey, he hurdled the brass railing. Time slowed to the pace of molasses.

Falling.

Like Lewis Carroll's Alice.

Through the air.

Nausea heaved up from his belly.

What if she hadn't jumped? What if she'd merely tossed his hat into the shaft?

He was falling to his death when he could have just waited for the Stetson to come up on the next platform rise.

He was gonna die looking like a damned fool unless . . .

The sound of a naked body slapping onto a leather sofa came from below.

He slammed onto the opposite sofa. A thousand angry hornets stung his spine. Stars flashed before his eyes as air burst from his lungs.

He groaned, his misery matched by a disembodied moan from the now-foam-free woman on the opposite couch. The Stetson levitated off the sofa as she rose. He tried to sit, rolling like an ungainly foal on the leather cushions, as his hat stumbled toward the gate. Its wearer flicked the latch open and trotted down the gray steel corridor leading from the platform.

She was a professional. No doubt about it.

He struggled up off the couch. The gaping, freckle-faced bellboy still stood by the library table. In his trembling hand, the boy held the broadsheet newspaper he'd been folding into a neat square.

Read all about it—foreign spies and assassins rain down in the heart of England.

He grabbed the boy's newspaper, slapping the *Yorkshire Herald* over his family jewels. No need to scare the ladies. He sure didn't want to get hit by any more umbrellas.

He followed his foe down the corridor. Blue bulbs lit up the steel walls every ten yards. He guessed they were on one of the laboratory floors.

The temperature was even lower than on the lodging level, and the air held a metallic tang. Beneath his bare feet, the steel floor was hard and cold.

From the sound of her footsteps, he guessed the invisible woman was at a full gallop and heading for the people at the far end of the hall.

Trusdale groaned as he recognized the trio. Why did it have to be them? "Stop that hat!"

Miss Haltwhistle spoke urgently to Cawley and the tuxedoed club manager. They stepped out of the way of the bouncing Stetson.

As the hat shot by her, Constance whipped out her umbrella's handle and hooked an invisible ankle. The hat shot toward the floor. A second swing of the red umbrella knocked the hat off an unseen head and propelled it toward the ceiling.

"*Va fan?*" screamed the assassin. Cawley, with impeccable timing, plucked the hat from midair. He turned and trotted toward Trusdale.

The club manager seized his chance to be heroic. He flapped his arms at nothingness. "Away with you, spirit. Return to the phantasmagoria from whence you came."

The spirit declined the invitation with a blow that bent the manager double. Trusdale winced for him. He knew that look—the assassin fought dirty.

A patter of running feet chased Cawley, and his head jerked backward as an invisible arm locked around his neck.

Constance ran to his aid. "Unhand my servant!" She swung her umbrella with venom. The assassin released Cawley and must have dodged out of the way, as Constance's brolly thwacked across the old man's spine. He yelped and dropped the hat.

Trusdale launched himself into a flat-out dive for the falling Stetson. The fingertips of his right hand closed around its broad felt brim. He slapped face-first onto the steel floor.

The assassin tried to wrench the hat from Trusdale's hand. They yanked the Stetson back and forth. The woman grunted as she pulled with all her weight against her prone enemy. He held on grimly, slowly drawing the brim closer.

A lesser hat would have split at the seams, but not a Stetson.

Miss Haltwhistle swung her umbrella ferociously and the carved fox handle clunked off bone—perhaps an invisible skull? He jerked the hat out of the assassin's grasp as Constance raised her umbrella to strike again.

Apparently, this was the straw that broke the invisible woman's back. Trusdale heard her bare feet slap past him as she raced down the hall with a whiff of cedar-scented bath oil. Miss Haltwhistle chased after the attacker, giving him a glimpse of her white boots as she ran. He gawped as her shapely ankles flashed by.

Focus.

He examined his hat. The ice-cold metal artifact was still hidden in the lining. Thank God the assassin hadn't found the triangle and done something extreme, like swallow it. He had no idea whether the contents of an invisible stomach could be seen, but he sure didn't want to find out. He crammed the Stetson onto his head and started to push himself up.

Cawley coughed. "Please, sir, don't stand. I beg you." The servant removed his emerald tailcoat, folded it, and presented it with a bow. There was a slight scent of mothballs, although whether that was from Cawley or the garment was difficult to discern.

Trusdale raised himself just far enough that he could attempt to put on the silk livery. The long-tailed coat was made to fit a slender man's frame. Rather than risk ripping the seams with his broad shoulders, he wrapped the garment around his waist like a Scottish kilt. The silk slithered over his bare skin as he tied the arms into a makeshift belt.

The color drained from Cawley's face at the use of his coat as a codpiece.

With a moan, the club manager uncurled from his bent position. Tears streamed down his flushed cheeks. His pencil mustache quivered on his not-so-stiff upper lip, and his bow tie was askew.

Cawley heaved a sigh and drew a leather clasp purse out of his silk pantaloons. He pulled out a thick wad of black-inked pound notes and handed the entire roll to the manager. "Please accept a token of Miss Haltwhistle's gratitude for your discretion regarding this unfortunate incident. She prefers that no arrests, gossip, or newspaper reports arise from this event." His world-weary tone suggested Cawley repeated this speech frequently.

The manager gestured at Trusdale. "He's broken the dress code. Still breaking it, for that matter. He'll have to go."

"Naturally," said Cawley.

Down the corridor, the levitating reading room was gone, and the uniformed boy was doubled over in pain next to the shaft's brass railing. It appeared Freckles had suffered the same indignity as the manager.

Constance stood next to the boy. Displaying the ultimate British bedside manner, she offered a firm, "There, there," with a gentle pat to his shoulder.

Maybe she was a little softer than she seemed? Her white dress fairly glowed in the electric light. Ethereal. Other-worldly. His eyes must be playing tricks, for he'd swear that snowflakes drifted around her, frosting her red hair as she comforted the boy.

Almost angelic.

He glanced down at his attire. How would the heavenly Miss Haltwhistle react if he approached her wearing only a tailcoat kilt?

And what if the invisible woman lurked behind her, ready to strike?

Cawley murmured, "I wouldn't go up there just yet, sir, if I were you. It's always best to keep an extra safe distance from such a dangerous woman."

Whether he meant the assassin or Constance, Trusdale couldn't say.

Chapter 8: The Cavalcade

IN LIGHT OF THE ATTACK by the invisible person, Constance's Plan with a capital 'P' was in dire need of revision. She stood on the driver's box of her green carriage with her furled umbrella in hand, peering down the Pyrrho Club's gravel driveway. Trusdale was still inside the Club, presumably finding something more appropriate to wear than the *Yorkshire Herald* newspaper. While she waited for him, she watched for the Haltwhistle Hall carriages, which would hopefully arrive before anything more bizarre occurred than a snowstorm in a corridor, gorillas playing whist, and a hat-stealing aberration of nature.

The rain had finally stopped, and the air was thick with the scent of wet foliage and earth. Drips of water beat a gentle tattoo through the ancient forest. The gusting breeze rustled leaves as thrushes trilled over a chorus of tree pipits, warblers, and redstarts. As the woods sang, the Tesla coil hummed a single note of power. Violet lightning crackled and danced within the transparent top of the hourglass tower. Beneath the trees, a hazy carpet of bluebells glowed in the unnatural light.

Science had transformed the idyllic landscape into an outlandish spectacle, potentially peopled by unseen predators. This raised many questions. First and foremost, why had the creature attacked Trusdale and not her? Based on King Oscar's obsession with destroying all Haltwhistles, it was only logical that she should be the focus of any and all violence, not some itinerant engineer.

Constance took as deep a breath of the metallic-tinged air as her corset allowed. *Surely I'm a more important target than Trusdale? Perhaps someone has mistaken him to be my bodyguard?*

Yes, that must be it. A simple error on the part of a villain.

Secondly, it seemed that Trusdale's outlandish tale of the original invisible man must be at least partly true. Once a lady had clunked her umbrella against an unseen body, there was no further room to doubt that a person can be both present and ethereal at the same time. Papa had speculated that the flickers of light some perceived to be ghosts were actually reflections of beings in other dimensions. An upstanding lady in this world might glimpse the shadow of her alternate self on a wall, leading to all kinds of fantastical conclusions. No wonder women were often called hysterical, when in fact, they were innately more predisposed to notice other people more than the typical man. Men tended to focus on what was right in front of them, while women observed the wider universe.

That was her theory, at least. She'd yet to meet a man who agreed with her.

But that didn't mean she wasn't right.

She exhaled the corrupted air. As dangerous to the natural world as science could be, it could also create effects that were almost magical. For instance, the purple light from the Club's electrical generator could be viewed as adding a bewitching majesty to Ecclesall Woods. If her unusual upbringing meant that she couldn't see the world through rose-colored glasses, perhaps a positive purple perspective could be the next best thing?

She resolved to purchase amethyst-tinted lenses for her brass goggle collection at the earliest juncture. The ocular accessory was ubiquitous in noble wardrobes due to the high status of science in the royal court. The more elaborate the goggles, the greater the implication that the owner was a science aficionado.

Constance gazed down at the assembled Steamwerkers, lined up in formation along the gravel driveway. The twenty or so engineers seemed unaware that they were missing a chance to impress with their ocular devices. From each of their tool belts hung mundane brass goggles. Why didn't they upgrade to the latest triple-lensed designs that included a magnifying loupe, barometer, and compass? Surely even Steamwerkers required more than basic utilitarian protection from their eyewear? After all, they were an integral cog in the Queen's magnificent war machine—didn't they deserve a splash of courtly style?

It was an oversight she should point out to Maya—

Miss Haltwhistle, the former student, swallowed back a lump in her throat. Her inner Brass Queen chided, *Stop that. There's no time for sentimentality today. Action, not tears, is the only way to make progress.*

Heavens, she wouldn't get anywhere if she allowed her two roles in life to bicker. Was it possible the stress of the last few weeks was beginning to take its toll?

She tilted up her chin. She must hold herself together. Too many people were relying on her to save the day in *both* capacities, and there was no reason to think she couldn't handle her dual responsibilities flawlessly.

Case in point, her driver, Hearn, glanced up at her, awaiting her next order while holding the carriage ponies' bridles. A black top hat crowned the brawny forty-year-old's bald head atop a well-fed face endowed with a magnificent walrus mustache. He had virtually no visible neck; his over-developed muscles were impressive evidence of his one true love after horses—bare-knuckle boxing. He was known throughout Sheffield as the only man to win the Norton Agricultural Show free fight three years in a row. Armed only with his mustache, he had head-butted, groin-kicked, and throttled at least ten other men before each victory. He was the pride of the Haltwhistle staff, many of whom bet heavily on him whenever he fought. Constance herself had won ten shillings on his last bout.

She'd heard whispers amongst the stable staff that Hearn's martial success was partly due to the intricate tattoos that covered his chest, back, and bulging biceps. No saucy mermaids or scarlet heart dedicated to his latest conquest marred his skin. Inspired by his Māori grandmother, Hearn boasted a jet-black spiral filigree carved into his flesh with bone chisels by Yorkshire's only genuine *Tā moko* artist. Hearn's numerous wins had inspired dozens of fighters to sit for similar tattoos, but most staggered out of the tattoo parlor sobbing long before the bone chisels finished their design. A barely-started Māori tattoo was the trademark of an amateur pugilist. Hearn relished taking on three or four of such wastrels at a time, much to the delight of his raucous fans.

Constance was glad he was there. It seemed her traditional way of dealing with problems was in need of an update. Usually, between Cawley's trunk of bribe money and Hearn's martial prowess, things had a habit of going her way. She'd always assumed there were few issues in life that couldn't be solved with the application of a hefty bribe or a hearty slap. But between the hunt for a spouse and the quest to find the missing scientists, she needed to approach matters with a little more finesse. It was time for her to become the heroine the situation deserved. She stood a little taller in her ankle boots, and jabbed her umbrella at the sky, challenging the heavens to trifle with the Brass Queen.

Muttering arose from the Steamwerkers. She'd forgotten they were watching her. With a polite cough, Constance lowered her umbrella and turned to face them, mere Miss Haltwhistle once more. The engineers displayed the ghostly pallor of those who spent their lives in gaslit factories. If not for a shared layer of grime, they would almost have been pale enough to pass for aristocrats.

Lord, she hadn't been talking to herself while she was mused, had she? She had a habit of doing that, but the Haltwhistle servants took such idiosyncrasies in their stride. Thank goodness Trusdale wasn't here to witness one of her more whimsical habits.

A brunette Steamwerker with gray streaks frosting her upswept hair stepped forward. It was the woman with the medal pinned to her chest who spoken up to thank Constance earlier. Now, her eyes were dark with concern. "Are you well, miss?"

Constance tilted her head. "Perfectly. Why do you ask?"

"You seemed to be having quite the conversation there with yourself."

Oh no. "Ah, well, my mumbles merely indicate that I'm composing an artistic oral interpretation of the day's events. I'm a part-time poetess."

Hearn's eyebrows lifted.

Constance shot him a warning glance, then returned her attention to the woman before her. In her most regal tone, she asked, "And with whom am I conversing?"

"Chief Welder Emily Lambert, at your service, miss." The welder curtsied with surprising grace.

Hearn pulled himself a little taller in his black riding boots as he gazed at the Steamwerker. He puffed out his barrel chest and tensed his burly physique so hard that he almost burst the seams of his emerald tailcoat.

Ah, true love strikes again. How freeing it must be to be free to pursue romance at every turn.

"Chief Welder Lambert, it's a pleasure. The carriages shouldn't be much longer. My cook will have a hot lunch ready for you and your colleagues upon your arrival."

"We're grateful, miss, aren't we, lads and lasses?" This drew a wave of nods from the crowd.

Constance beamed. "Splendid. It does appear that the . . . incident . . . at my party resulted in this unfortunate lockdown at the Steamwerks. It's yet another thing that the miscreants responsible should be held accountable for. By the police, of course. Not me."

A smattering of applause emboldened her to continue. "Besides, *noblesse oblige* and all that. It is my privilege to help the less fortunate. I always like to think that I do the right thing for those around me. Even if, at times, they do not understand what I'm doing, or why, or when, or even how. I'm always helping as best I can." Constance cast a meaningful glance at Cawley, who stood in the shadow of Hearn minus his green livery coat. She had never seen her loyal retainer in just his shirtsleeves before. Cawley straightened his posture, which she assumed meant he forgave her for slapping him with her umbrella.

Good. Another problem sorted. Perhaps things were starting to look up?

The club doors opened with a bang, and out strode Trusdale in his Stetson crown, carrying a travel-worn suitcase. He was every inch the unarmed gunslinger in his all-black ensemble. A leather duster coat swung like a cloak from his muscular frame. A frock coat, silk shirt, knotted neckerchief, svelte waistcoat and pin-striped pants complemented his cowboy boots embroidered with shooting stars.

Constance gaped. His outfit was a tad more decorous than the *Yorkshire Herald* newspaper, but not by much. The memory of his newsprint underwear caused a curious tingle beneath her corset. She'd never seen a strapping young man wearing only newsprint before. His strong, wide chest . . . it was a sight she wouldn't mind seeing again, should the opportunity present itself. She was curious about those well-toned muscles. How did a cowboy keep in shape? Was it all hard riding and lassoing things with rope and . . . ?

She fanned herself vigorously. The object of her newfound desire stared into the woods, searching for invisible foes. Her cheeks glowed at her own impropriety. Trusdale glanced at her and looked away, flushed. *Hah!* She wasn't the only one embarrassed about his nudity. *Good.*

She turned to check the driveway. Rumbling toward her was a veritable cavalcade of Haltwhistle carriages. The first was an open six-passenger landau driven by a green-liveried coachman. The formal black-and-gold carriage bore her family crest on the doors and was drawn by four jet-black Friesians, the offspring of Papa's infamously foul-tempered stallion, Beelzebub. The uncut manes and tails of the horses rippled in the breeze like the battle pennants once carried by their warhorse ancestors.

The next vehicle wasn't quite so illustrious. Two gray shires from the estate farms pulled an empty hay wagon. A rosy-cheeked milkmaid in a blue apron dress and two farm laborers in flat caps, white shirts, and Sunday-best pants rode on the front box of the wagon. The trio looked much cleaner than one would expect at noon on a Monday. Constance suspected they had taken a dip in the river and put on their church clothes to impress the Steamwerkers. Her instructions to the estate staff to host the townies at a servant's ball should allow everyone to blow off steam while they waited for Constance to announce either a betrothal or the end of the Hall as they knew it. With the Steamwerkers homeless, and her staff potentially about to be, they had more in common than they knew.

The last vehicle to arrive was one Papa had acquired in Japan. It was styled as a dragon whose snakelike body wrapped three times around the sides of the carriage. The red-and-gold monster held the driver's bench inside its gaping jaws, and its front claws stretched out menacingly toward the rumps of the chestnut Arabians drawing the carriage. The four ponies seemed remarkably unconcerned about the mythical creature roaring silently behind them.

Constance asked Hearn, "Which carriage is the fastest? We've wasted quite enough time here. I have a Plan to put into action."

Hearn thoughtfully sucked the air through the gap where his front teeth should've been. "I reckon that red-and-gold creature can hit a pretty pace. Regarding this Plan, miss, are we off to the Steamwerks, then?"

"Sadly, the security lockdown precludes my investigation there. We'll ride the dragon back into town. We're going to find Lord Burdock."

"Very good, miss."

The new arrivals pulled into a line behind her breakfast carriage. Cawley held up a gloved hand to help her climb down from the box.

Trusdale stood beside the Steamwerkers and fumbled with the combination lock on his suitcase. With its owner's attention distracted, his Stetson chose this moment to levitate off his head. Trusdale dropped the suitcase and grabbed his hat, yelling, "Oh no you don't! Hands off, you monster!"

Ignoring the gaping Steamwerkers, Trusdale tugged the Stetson free from a phantasmagoric foe and pulled it firmly down onto his head. Presumably chasing an invisible assassin, he sprinted into the woods and ran back and forth, waving his arms like a lunatic.

Welder Lambert asked, "Is he quite sane?"

The cowboy threw himself onto the ground to wrestle with a hawthorn bush. Constance declared, "Sunstroke." Several Steamwerkers glanced up at the overcast sky but made no comment.

Trusdale clawed at his throat and emitted rather vulgar choking noises.

Constance heaved a sigh. "Hearn, please go and assist Mr. Trusdale. It appears the woods do not agree with him."

"I don't see anything to slap, miss."

"You'll find something, I'm sure of it."

Hearn went to help Trusdale as the cowboy punched thin air. The approach of the burly coachman did the trick, as it usually did with malefactors, invisible or otherwise. Trusdale staggered to his feet unmolested. It seemed his attacker had given up, for now.

Constance rubbed her forehead. Why was the invisible fiend so intent on snatching Trusdale's Stetson? Also, had the world always been this perplexing, and she'd been too busy running the estate to notice?

Trusdale swatted at empty air as he returned to his dropped suitcase. He scooped it up and backed toward the carriages, keeping a wary eye on the woods. He tipped his hat to Hearn. "Most grateful for your help there."

"I didn't do much, but you're welcome," said Hearn.

Constance strolled toward the dragon carriage, taking her time so the servants could reach their positions before she got there. Hearn noticed her promenade and sprinted by her. He shooed away the junior driver and climbed up to sit in the gaping jaws of the red-and-gold reptile. Cawley hastened to check the open carriage seats for transparent enemies. Finding none, he stood by the steps and held Constance's hand as she climbed into the belly of the beast.

Painted murals decorated the interior walls and floor of the Japanese carriage. Two vast armies of red and blue armored samurai were locked in eternal combat upon a field of shimmering gold leaf. The battlefield was complemented by sumptuously cushioned seats upholstered in the finest spun-gold cloth. The seventeenth-century vehicle had been built to transport a warlord empress on a tour of newly-conquered lands. Somehow, Papa had acquired the carriage and shipped it to Constance from Kyoto as a gift for her fourteenth birthday. She'd have preferred that he stopped by in person on the day, but beggars couldn't be choosers.

She settled her bustle upon the cloth of gold. Outside, Trusdale had dropped to a squat upon the gravel to fumble inside his suitcase. He drew out Cawley's emerald tailcoat, locked the case, and stood. With the coat draped over his arm, he strode to the silver-haired servant and bowed. "Thank you for the loan of your coat, Mr. Cawley. Returning to my room would have been even more embarrassing without it."

Cawley took the coat gingerly, as if the very fabric might explode at his touch. He glanced up at Constance, heaved a dramatic sigh, and put on the coat.

Trusdale lurched up the carriage steps and tossed his suitcase onto the bench opposite. Her heart thudded as he plunked his huge frame right next to her on the golden seat. She slid away from him, cramming herself against the carriage wall. Did Americans have no concept of the British need for three feet of personal space?

Cawley raised both eyebrows at the implied intimacy of their seating arrangement. Lips puckered, he slammed the carriage door and stomped over to the dragon's head to sit beside Hearn. Technically, both retainers served the role of chaperone, but still, this situation was beyond awkward. She turned to Trusdale, prepared to deliver a rebuke for his forward behavior.

He scanned the forest, his brow furrowed over bruised blue eyes and a swollen nose. Almost hidden by his neckerchief, a nasty cut, congealed with blood and white styptic powder, scored his throat. Despite his injuries, his square jaw was clean-shaven, and his long, dark sideburns were neatly trimmed. Overall, there was a marked improvement over his earlier disheveled appearance. If it weren't for his complete lack of fashion sense and manners, in the right light, he could almost pass for handsome.

Quelle surprise. What a shame he wasn't an eligible nobleman.

Trusdale glanced at her. "What?"

"Oh, um . . . you're hurt."

"Could have been much worse." His eyes held a flicker of darkness, the look of a man who had faced death and won. Barely.

Her stomach dropped. "Oh dear. I'm so sorry."

"Not your fault."

Wasn't it? If the assassin was one of King Oscar's thugs, then Trusdale had simply got in the way of their true aim, eliminating her. Perhaps by saving her at the party, Trusdale had forced himself into the line of fire? On the other hand, his knowledge of the invisibility serum was in itself an odd coincidence. Was fate throwing her a winning hand, or were darker forces afoot?

The worst possible scenario rose in her mind. Invisibility was a dirty trick, even for Oscar. Perhaps a serum was to blame, but even that had to draw its power from somewhere. A ghost assassin suggested a body that had taken a slight step left into an alternate dimension, while still leaving enough of a physical form to interact and do harm. Trusdale seemed to have no inkling of this, but for her, it seemed a logical extrapolation. Was it possible that Oscar had started fooling around with interdimensional transference? Heaven forfend he'd finally got his hands on an Enigma Key.

If he had, then this world, and all others, were surely doomed.

And only the Brass Queen could save them.

Chapter 9: Secrets and Shenanigans

WITH THE WEIGHT OF ALL worlds now firmly on her shoulders, Constance sat back into the plush gold cushions of the dragon carriage. She called out to Hearn, "Head for Le Paon Pompeux restaurant." The carriage ponies broke into a brisk trot.

Trusdale gawped at her. "We're stopping for lunch? We were only just attacked by—"

"I see no reason to adventure on an empty stomach. It's been ages since breakfast. Personally, I like to eat at least once every three hours. It keeps one's energy topped up. But apart from that, this is the next stage of the Plan—"

"With a capital 'P'. Lord help me." Trusdale folded his arms, apparently unable to resist watching the passing forest for foes.

"If you must know, this part of the Plan is rather clever. We're going to find Lord Burdock. He's staying with Lady Pemmington, and she always takes her luncheon at the finest restaurant in town. Naturally, she'll bring her houseguests with her. Lady Pemmington has an innate ability to always appear in the right place at the right time for maximum social exposure. She's somewhat my idol in this matter."

"So, the Plan now relies on a society maven taking lunch? Ugh." Trusdale's head was still turned to the woods.

Constance huffed. She wasn't yet desperate enough to ask his opinion on what they should do. More importantly, surely, she was the better view? "Even if there was an entire army camped out there, you'd never see them."

"True, but it makes me feel better to keep a lookout. It's only a matter of time before that invisible woman figures out a better plan of attack."

She stared at the back of his head. "Not to nitpick, but how could you possibly know your assailant was female? The disembodied voice I heard during our encounter in the club could have been a soprano male."

"I know for certain, because, well—" He cleared his throat. "The thing is, she ended up in the bathtub with me. Briefly."

"I beg your pardon?"

He turned to face her, a flush creeping across his tanned cheeks. "It's not how it sounds. I didn't know she was a woman at the time. I thought she was a man."

"Well! Perhaps I should introduce you to my cousin Wellington. I understand he's quite free about his bathtub companions, both male and female."

"I also saw her legs and her backsi—um, so forth, covered in bubbles. I reckon we need to figure out a way to splatter some kind of dye or paint on our invisible friends to make them partially visible."

"Her 'so forth'?"

"What liquid doesn't wash off easily? India ink? That's soot and shellac, highly water resistant. And we'll need a close-range delivery system—"

"Baubles."

Confusion fell upon his face like rain on an English picnic.

"Baubles. Christmas baubles. The hand-blown-glass type, extremely delicate, easy to break, easy to throw. We could close them up with sealing wax."

"Huh. That's not bad for a short-term solution. I can see I'll have to watch myself around you, Miss Haltwhistle. You're not just a pretty face."

"I should hope not."

He chuckled. "No offense meant. So, you seem pretty unshaken considering you just met your first invisible assassin."

She stiffened. "I—well, what do you want me to do? Faint?"

He shrugged. "An assassin alone would scare most folks, never mind the otherworldly element. Is there something about you I should know, Miss Haltwhistle?"

She folded her arms. "Certainly not."

He studied her. "You don't trust me?"

"Of course I don't."

A tic in his cheek pulsed.

"Well, there's no need to take it personally, Mr. Trusdale. I don't fully trust anyone."

He stared. "Not even your servants?"

"That's different. They're like family to me."

"That's a pretty high endorsement."

"You don't know my family."

He leaned close, gazing deep into her eyes. "About that, where exactly is your father right now?"

She unfolded her arms and clasped her hands in her lap. She studied the stitching on her somewhat grimy opera gloves. *Don't mention he's in a parallel universe, or aether, or portals, or . . .* "Ah, well, Papa's traveling. In—Africa. Yes, that's it, Central Africa. He's steaming up the Congo River on a boat. I expect I'll be receiving a letter or three from him any day now. He writes to me all the time, you know."

Her mouth grew oddly parched beneath his stare. She licked her lips. "No matter what people say, he's alive and well. Enjoying the African sun and taking the most scenic route, as true explorers always do. Through the Congo. Which is where he is. On a boat, writing me a letter. I'm sure of it."

"Uh-huh. I think I'm getting the picture."

He grinned and sat back. She breathed a little easier. *Thank heavens I'm such an effective liar.* She bellowed to Hearn over the ponies' hoofbeats, "On second thought, take us by the glassworks and Pinder's Print Emporium *en route* to Le Paon Pompeux."

"Yes, Miss."

She said to Trusdale, "We had better get started on our anti-invisibility baubles as soon as possible, and we have just enough time to bring that about. Lady Pemmington takes her luncheon at two o'clock daily." She waved at the forest. "Judging by the height of the sun and the shadow from the trees I'd say it's about—"

Out of his vest pocket, Trusdale pulled a silver fob watch engraved with the heavenly constellation of Leo. He flicked the case open. "It's noon now."

"Oh, good." There was a miniature painted inside the top of the case. She craned her neck to view it. "Your relatives?"

He hesitated, then turned the watch so she could see. It was a family portrait, exquisitely painted with fine detail. An older version of Trusdale in a blue cavalry uniform stood with his arm around a kind-faced woman with blond hair and a baby in her arms. Two blond little girls and three gangly youths stood beside their parents. All three youths wore smart cavalry uniforms, just like their father. "That's me and my parents and siblings, back home in Kansas. The baby is Hope; the girls are Verity and Charity; the boys, me, Liberty, and Freedom.

"It's a beautiful miniature. Does your family still reside in Kansas?"

"Some do. Some don't." Trusdale contemplated the watch, his face crumpled into misery.

Kansas must have been an absolute idyll to elicit such visceral nostalgia. To lighten his mood, she smiled. "Heavens, Mr. Trusdale, you're so lucky to be part of a large family. I used to wish for siblings myself, but alas, I am an only child. Just between us, I think I would have made an excellent twin. Think of the trouble we would have caused. Constance and Ethel, out on the town, breaking hearts and windows like the wicked gals in the penny dreadfuls."

He didn't appear to hear her. She subtly coughed, increasing the volume and intensity until he stared at her in alarm.

"I see from your portrait that, like me, you were expected to follow your father into the family business?"

He furrowed his brow. "You mean, enter the military? I never really thought of it that way, but you're right. I guess it was always assumed that my brothers and I would join up as soon as we turned sixteen. We climbed our way through the ranks, never quite able to fill some pretty big shoes. My father was a hero in the Civil War. General Justice Franklin Trusdale, same name and rank as my grandpa, and his grandpa before. We have a long tradition of service to our country."

"And that's why you go by J. F., not your full name, to avoid comparison?"

"Huh—I guess so. It's funny, I never talked about this with—" He stopped and turned away, studying the woods with his jaw set tight.

His anguish was palpable. She reached out her hand to touch his arm, stopping short as her reading of *Babett's Modern Manners* came to mind. *One doesn't touch a gentleman in one's carriage. Mama would turn in her grave if she—*

Her heart wrenched as she almost felt the last hug her mother ever gave her. She was once more a ten-year-old girl, standing on the great drive outside Haltwhistle Hall. Lady Pendelroy, now Baroness Haltwhistle, was setting out on an adventure. Mama's dark hair was pinned up beneath her new pink pith helmet, bought as a joke by Papa but worn with pride by his fashion-forward wife. Four wagons packed with hatboxes, trunks, and supplies stood in line behind the black-and-gold landau on the driveway of Haltwhistle Hall. The horses stomped their hooves impatiently as Mama kissed her on the forehead and whispered, "We'll be home before you know it, my dear. Look after the estate; you're in charge now." She climbed up into the carriage. Papa took her hand as she settled down next to him. Two lovebirds heading to Egypt to search for hidden treasures.

Constance murmured, "Malaria."

Trusdale turned to her.

She swallowed hard. "My mother died in Egypt from malaria. Her brother, my uncle Bertie, never forgave Papa for taking her out there. Papa blamed himself, of course. He's never been the same since her death."

He rubbed his hands over his eyes. "I'm sorry for your loss. Was it recent?"

She dropped her head. "Seems like yesterday, but no, eleven years have passed. Papa stayed home for a while after the funeral, but he was restless. At fourteen, I took over running the estate as he roamed the world. I can't believe I'm on the verge of losing everything I've built since he left." Her hands clenched into fists. "But I digress. You were telling me about your mother."

"No, I wasn't."

"Tell me anyway."

He sighed. "Well, she was an army nurse when Papa met her. He and his unit had barely survived an ambush by a gang of outlaws they were tracking. He says he fell in love with her over a broken leg, two busted ribs, and a gunshot wound to the shoulder. She's a wonderful woman; no-nonsense, sharp as a tack, and kinder than the world deserves."

She sighed. "So, your parents married for love. How delightful. They must be so proud of you. The Steamwerks only hire the best."

He shrugged. "I don't know. Maybe. Not so sure what they'd make of me at the moment."

"Why is that?"

"I haven't told them . . . that is, no reason." His eyes hardened, and for a moment he looked almost sinister in his all-black attire.

Trust no one, as Papa used to say. Madmen, villains, and thieves—and she'd find even worse outside their immediate family. "Well, the watch is lovely, and I am sure it made your eighteenth birthday memorable. Tell me, when exactly is your birthday, Mr. Trusdale?"

He took just a moment too long to answer. "April twenty-first."

Bull, thought Constance. If his birthday were April twenty-first, Taurus the Bull would have been his star sign. But his watch was clearly engraved with the constellation of Leo, the Lion. If his parents had given him the timepiece as a birthday gift, then surely the engraving would have reflected his true zodiac sign. Her suspicions were confirmed; the cowboy couldn't be trusted.

Her heart sank to her ankle boots and stayed there for the rest of the journey.

Chapter 10: Pinder's Print Emporium

TRUSDALE TRIED TO KEEP AS low a profile as a Stetson-wearing giant could in Sheffield's bustling city center. Painfully aware that the jail he'd left mere hours before was within shouting distance of Miss Haltwhistle's ample lungs, he kept his eyes trained on the York flagstone path. The promenade was flooded with lunchtime shoppers and the child pickpockets who preyed upon them. Trusdale had to swerve to avoid running into surly Steamwerkers, fur-bedecked society ladies, tired nannies pushing baby carriages, and bowler-hatted businessmen.

Five feet ahead, Miss Haltwhistle maintained a straight course, expecting all to give way before her. To his surprise, they did, sweeping around the Baron's daughter like a stream around a statue of an ancient goddess—Artemis, maybe, or Athena. Certainly, the aristocrat's attitude toward him had been as cold as marble since the carriage ride. Lord knows what he'd done to offend her now. How her servants put up with her unpredictable moods was a mystery. No wonder Hearn had been eager to drive the carriage over to the nearest pub to "water the horses" while Constance shopped. He'd said he would bring back the refreshed ponies to La Paon Pompeux later.

As always, Cawley padded serenely at Constance's heels. The old man seemed to be an expert at riding in his mistress's wake. His arms were wrapped around four stacked boxes of hand-blown Christmas baubles, purchased within the hour at the local glassworks. Constance had spent a considerable amount of time ordering dozens of pairs of goggle lenses in varying shades of purple. She'd refused to share with Trusdale why she'd bought them. Perhaps one of her hobbies involved welding?

Now, they were on the way to a print shop to fill the baubles with ink. And also, for Constance to pick up her telegrams, and something about reviewing the VIP programs for the Queen's parade?

He sighed. Why was nothing ever simple when Miss Haltwhistle was involved? Never a straight line between A and B in her world. Anything and everything seemed to revolve around her need to show people that she was out and about doing "normal" fancy lady activities, not investigating a kidnapping.

Personally, he'd have rather marched around to Lady Pemmington's place and faced Burdock man-to-man, but apparently strong-arming a lord was a good way to get himself hung in these parts. Constance had sure been quick to point that out. Who knows, maybe approaching him in a softly-softly way at La Paon Pompeux was better?

Not that he'd tell Constance that. Her head looked big enough as it was underneath that tiny hat. No need to swell it any further.

Despite the constant flow of humanity on the promenade, Trusdale couldn't escape Miss Haltwhistle's ringing voice. She shouted over her shoulder like a tour guide, pointing out every point of interest whether he cared to hear about it or not. She clearly loved her soot-stained hometown, and despite her coolness toward him, she seemed determined that he would love it too. Another point of pride for her, he guessed. Still, this urge of hers to show her town in the best light was at least understandable to him. No matter where a person was from, most everybody saved a warm spot in their heart for the place of their birth.

He tuned back into Constance's narrative on Sheffield's premier landmarks. "And here we have Pinstone Street. This will be part of the Queen's parade route on Friday. She's coming to Sheffield to celebrate her sixty years on the throne and also to open our fabulous new Town Hall. It's taken seven years to build this stunning example of new Gothic architecture."

She waved her hand at the yellow-stoned municipal masterpiece ahead. "In the entrance vestibule, there's a bas-relief frieze of a knight killing a dragon. But not just any dragon. It's the same dragon that is being kicked up the derriere on my family shield. You wouldn't believe how much I had to pay the sculptor, Pomeroy, to add it into the frieze last month. But it's worth every penny to make my permanent mark upon this town."

"Maybe you could get them to name a street after you?"

"Pah. Don't think I didn't try. Perhaps after the Queen's Jubilee parade, the lord mayor will gain a new appreciation for my contributions in that matter. It's going to be an extravaganza of British military might, and flowers."

"I hope I'll still be here to see it."

Her stride faltered. "Oh, that's right, your steamship leaves on Saturday. I assumed you would . . . I mean . . ." she glanced back at him. "Well, you'd be an absolute fool to miss this parade. There'll be a mile-long procession of troops and brass bands, with magnificent airship maneuvers from the Royal Air Corps. The imperial dreadnought HMS *Subjugator* will battle an entire fleet of sky pirates over Endcliffe Park. It's only a mock battle, of course, but it should be quite spectacular, outdone only by the decorations along the parade route."

Trusdale squinted up. "I hope the town's got more going on than these soggy silk garlands draped between the lamp posts."

She bristled. "I'll have you know that those garlands are only the first stage of the floral extravaganza. There will also be legions of redcoats wearing rose boutonnieres, decorated arches honoring our colonial territories with their native flora, and two hundred flower-festooned effigies of the Steamwerks' greatest accomplishments—mechanical cavalry, armored exo-suits, warships, airships, et cetera. The list goes on and on. I know; I wrote the list."

"Let me guess, you're on the decorating committee?"

"I *am* the decorating committee. Everyone else quit. Artistic differences."

He laughed. "Really? Just like that, huh?"

"Not everyone is cut out for charity work, Mr. Trusdale. Someone has to make the big decisions, and it may as well be me. Oh, and the lord mayor and his council help with the remaining details, like arranging the sky pirate battle to entertain the Queen."

"Details indeed. They're lucky to have you on board."

She nodded. "That's what I keep telling them. I mean, any fool can order airships about, but fastening ten miles of garland to gas lamps to create a pleasing aesthetic, well, that takes real organizational skill."

"I assume you didn't personally hitch up these garlands?"

"Good heavens, of course not. I've employed over a thousand people, all working on various aspects of the parade. They've earned a substantial wage and performed work that doesn't involve being down a mine or in front of a furnace. It's been a real boost for the local economy, not to mention my social visibility. It's so hard to make a stunning debut into high society when hardly anyone knows who you are."

"I guess that makes you the second invisible woman I've met recently."

She scowled back at him. "My lack of visibility is not a matter for mockery."

"Just tryin' to lighten the mood. You seem to be wound a little tight right now."

"Oh, I do apologize." Her tone dripped honey. "Here am I, attempting to help a foreigner to understand his environment, whilst trying to save my friends and servants from ruin, and yet somehow, I'm not relaxed enough for your liking? Why sir, do forgive me."

He winced. She had a point. "I'm sorry, I meant . . ." The town hall clock tower bell tolled once. He glanced up at the Vulcan-topped clocktower on the new Gothic edifice. "I'm mighty impressed by the, er, stonework here. The Queen must be looking forward to the grand opening."

"I'm sure she is. Not many people know this, but a brand-new invention will be demonstrated to Her Majesty at the opening ceremony. The Queen will turn a key in a remote-control box in her carriage, and the gates will swing open as if by magic."

"Huh. Nikola Tesla's been working on remote control too."

Constance stopped and turned to face him. "Really? Does it work?"

"I honestly don't know."

"Oh. Interesting. Between us," she lowered her voice and beckoned him closer, "ours doesn't work at all. Three concealed men are going to pull open the gates with ropes, but from the outside, it will appear to be automatic. Tell no one. It's going to be a splendid surprise for the general public."

He put his hand on his heart. "Your secrets are safe with me."

"I'll hold you to that." She walked on. This time, he kept pace with her, shoulder to shoulder. It seemed his interest in her hometown and mention of Tesla had somewhat thawed her highness. For how long, he'd have to wait and see.

Constance pointed to a red brick Georgian building. "Ah, here's our destination, Pinder's Print Emporium. Nothing but the finest ink to weaponize our glass baubles."

"It doesn't have to be the finest—"

"Of course it does. I have no intention of creating a sub-par weapon. Even an ink-filled bauble must be the very best it can be. Without lofty standards, we are but beasts in the wilderness. And speaking of beasts, do behave yourself in the store."

"I wasn't planning on running amuck."

"This Emporium is the communication hub of Sheffield high society. Pinder produces the embossed invitations, letterhead, calling cards, books, posters, pamphlets, and other paper ephemera vital for the flow of information across the city. Between you and me, Mr. Trusdale, he's also the purveyor of ribald gossip he gleans not only from his customers, but also from the messages sent and received via his private telegraph service."

No surprise there. Public telegraph operators were guaranteed to share the contents of any remotely interesting telegram received. Private operators were a safer bet for spies and others with secrets to hide in their communiqués. But no telegram was truly secure, even if you used a frequently changed set of codes.

Trusdale held open the glass door for Constance and Cawley to enter the Emporium. The store boasted twelve-foot-high ceilings, ample floor space, and a long front window that provided a stellar view of the freshly planted Victory Gardens. The panorama of the park's manicured lawns, flower beds, and strolling citizens was blighted by a myriad of posters pasted unevenly across the glass. More posters covered the far wall in a kaleidoscope of color. Intrigued by the promise of breaking news, Trusdale passed behind Constance and Cawley as they stopped at the unattended oak counter. He scanned the end wall posters, keeping one wary eye on the deserted store.

The counter was littered with bottles of ink, stacks of books, an archaic cash register, and a polished brass bell. Behind the counter, a telegraph receiver and transmitter sat on a large desk in front of a sorting rack stuffed with yellow cards awaiting pickup. A collection of drying tables stretched to the rear of the store, where a steam-powered printing press the size of a Hansom cab hissed quietly. Four engraved plates on iron arms were poised to print upon a giant roll of green poster paper. The door on the machine's stove stood open, and the embers inside glowed a freshly stoked orange.

Trusdale glanced at Constance as she tut-tutted. "As usual, it seems our bird has flown the coop." She patted her bun, smoothing stray strands with her opera glove.

Trusdale gazed at the nape of her neck, pale as the moon beneath auburn tresses lit with copper highlights.

Nope. He wasn't going to be beguiled by the bold British beauty.

She stroked her neck, tilting her head . . .

Is it hot in here?

He filled his lungs and savored the woody scent of newly printed books. Tomes on the counter offered maritime adventures and gardening advice. On his travels across the globe, he'd always tried to visit esoteric bookstores and libraries. He especially relished fantasy novels that transported him to exotic worlds where love conquered all, and villains invariably received their just deserts.

Constance took in as deep a breath as her rather fetching scarlet corset allowed. A dreamy look settled over her porcelain features. Clearly, he wasn't the only one who enjoyed the aroma of ink and paper.

Cawley seemed unaffected by the scent. He placed the four boxes of Christmas baubles on the counter, then went to stand exactly three paces behind his mistress. Constance gave the brass bell a demure tinkle.

Trusdale studied the wall posters. One stood out with an image of a shepherd sleeping amidst a flock of sheep. The caption read: "Mr. Orwell's Security Sheep. Let your ewe protect you! Deter foxes, badgers, and poachers with Orwell's woolly guardians. The sheep that never sleeps blends in with your regular flock. Inquiries to Orwell's Fantastical Farm on Abbeydale Road. Head north to the Red Lion pub and turn left at the duck pond. If you reach the post office, you've gone too far."

Trusdale shook his head. You had to love English street directions. If there wasn't a pub or a post office near where you wanted to go, you weren't getting there.

Miss Haltwhistle rang the brass bell again, a little louder this time.

There was a movement to the rear of the printing press. A skinny dark-haired man crouched behind the device, identified by a brass nameplate as the "Wharncliffe Wonderpress."

Constance walloped the bell with her red umbrella. The bell rolled off the counter and hit the wood floor with a musical jingle.

The man in hiding heaved a dramatic sigh. He stood up and dusted himself off. His black hair was greased back over ears that looked as if they had been borrowed from a much larger man. His sparse eyebrows were knitted over eyes as sad as a scolded puppy. A wispy mustache straddled his lip with an air of defeat, as if it had once wanted to be a walrus mustache but had run out of ambition. A blue waistcoat and white shirt hung off the printer's thin shoulders, and his unfashionably slim green pants ran three inches too short of his ink-stained boots.

Constance said, "There you are, Mr. Pinder. I was concerned that I may have missed you. It is a bizarre coincidence that every time I enter this store, you disappear."

Pinder tugged the bottom of his waistcoat in an effort to smooth its well-set wrinkles. "The misfortune must surely be mine, Miss Haltwhistle. What an absolute delight that you have chosen to grace my humble establishment with your presence. Once more, I would like to stress that I would be honored to deal directly with your servants, not wanting to waste your valuable time with lowly printing matters."

"It's no trouble. I've several new matters to discuss with you."

Pinder groaned and shuffled over to the counter. The printer reached down behind the oak barrier and drew out a thick green ledger printed with the title *Royal Visit Paraphernalia*. He dropped the weighty tome with a bang onto the counter in front of Constance and opened it up. "Miss Haltwhistle, as thrilled as I am with your willingness to review the Jubilee programs and such for the lord mayor, I'm quickly running out of time for any more changes. Her Royal Highness will be here in two days."

"Not changes, corrections. And I am sure had I not been brought into this aspect of the planning at the very last minute, you and I would have fewer issues to fix."

"Let me guess, another person has quit the planning committee?"

Constance flushed. "That's hardly the point."

"Look, miss, with all due respect, I've already reprinted the Queen's parade maps, twice. I've upgraded the paper stock for the VIP tickets for the royal stand. I've corrected the grammar throughout the Jubilee souvenir brochure. What else could there possibly be?"

Constance stood a little straighter and narrowed her eyes. "I certainly don't mean to trouble you, Mr. Pinder, but I do believe that the impending visit of Her Majesty Queen Victoria, Defender of the Faith, Empress of India, might require that certain words, in particular, should be correctly spelled in the VIP commemorative program."

"Such as?"

"Her name is Victoria with a C, not Viktoria with a K."

Pinder frowned. "What? That's not possible. I've read that thing ten times."

"Page three, line seven."

He reached under the counter and pulled out a stack of printed booklets to review. His gaunt cheeks blushed a rosy red. "Ah, yes, a minor error, on the third page of the program, no less. I'm sure no one will notice. As the quote goes, 'The man who makes no mistakes does not usually make anything.' William Magee."

"I've got a quote for you too, Eli: 'The man who makes mistakes does not get paid until he gets it right.' Constance Haltwhistle."

Trusdale clamped down on a laugh.

Pinder grimaced. "Your delightful humor illuminates my world once again, Miss Haltwhistle."

"I should start charging you for the amount of illumination I've been able to cast. Don't you proofread?"

The printer sighed. "It's truly a miracle that I've been able to run this business for twenty years without your keen eye looking over my shoulder. Nonetheless, as this concerns the name of Our Gracious Majesty, I'll set up a new print run today."

"Excellent. Now to the second matter. Has anyone responded to my reward poster?"

"Not yet. Mind you, it was only posted a few hours ago. It takes time for word to get around to the types of people who might be willing to make a few quid informing on a crime."

Trusdale nodded, not that anyone was looking his way.

"I see. Most disappointing. Moving on, I have a rather unusual request for you." Constance indicated the neatly stacked boxes of glass Christmas baubles on the counter. "Would you mind injecting each of these baubles with your very finest waterproof ink before sealing them with wax? One wishes to be able to throw the ornaments at moving targets without getting one's dress covered in ink."

Pinder studied the redhead, perhaps looking for a hint as to whether this was a joke. "You really are one sandwich short of a picnic, Miss Haltwhistle, if you don't mind me saying."

"I do mind. Nevertheless, will you do it or not?"

"Yes, but it will cost you dearly. Ten shillings per bauble."

Cawley gasped at the exorbitant fee.

His mistress said, "Very well."

Pinder grinned at Cawley and took the lid off the top box. He plucked out a three-inch glass bauble decorated with glittering snowflakes. He peered at the ornament through his pince-nez spectacles. "Small, but strong enough to hold a fair amount of ink. You should be able to carry a couple in hand if needed. I'll assume, for sanity's sake, that you're planning on using these for tracking deer through the woods when hunting. May I make a suggestion?"

Constance nodded.

"Waterproof ink is hard to wash off, but if you fill the baubles with a gentian violet and ink solution, you'll be able to track your prey. For instance, if it splashes onto deer hooves, you'll get a purple trail to follow through the undergrowth. And your deer will have to scrub pretty hard with rubbing alcohol or vodka to get it off. Assuming your deer have access to vodka, that is."

"Yes, that sounds practical. I'll have Cawley pick up the filled ornaments in an hour. Now, on to the next matter. Is there any gossip I should know about?"

"Some maniac went running through the Pyrrho Club stark naked yelling at thin air."

Trusdale's heart dropped into his boots.

Constance shifted uncomfortably. "I've heard that rumor was made up by some drunk scientists. You know what they're like. They're a very unstable bunch."

Trusdale exhaled.

Pinder ran his hand through his greasy hair. "Really? Good to know. Other gossip—well, nothing you'd want to hear about."

"Like what?"

"Oh, just the small matter of some fancy party where the guests got showered with glass during an airship attack. Do stop me if you've heard this one—"

"Funny. Are people blaming me?"

Pinder smirked. "Let's just say your social calendar is about to open up to an unprecedented degree, and I wouldn't anticipate any new invitations for the next year or so. I'll get your telegrams for you."

Constance nibbled her lip.

It was the first sign of trepidation Trusdale had seen in the redhead. No invitations meant no chance to win herself a fancy husband.

Would someone like her ever marry for love?

He knew he wouldn't marry for anything less.

Pinder walked over to the telegram-sorting rack and ran his hand across the wooden slots. He pulled out an inch-thick pile of yellow cards and handed the stack to Constance. She flicked through them.

"I'll leave you to it." Pinder retreated to the printing press. He picked up an iron poker and stoked the machine's coal. Closing the stove door, he tapped on a pressure gauge and slid a brass lever to full ahead. The press rumbled into a deafening industrial din that shook the building to its foundations. The wooden floor juddered beneath Trusdale's boots as the engraving plates rotated through the printing cycle and posters rolled off the machine.

Pinder noticed Trusdale for the first time and sauntered up to the counter with a welcoming smile. "I'm sorry, sir, didn't see you there blending with the shadows. I was distracted by herself over there." He rolled his eyes at Constance, who stood reading her telegrams with a furrowed brow.

Despite the din of the printing press, Trusdale kept his voice low. "Tough customer?"

"The toughest. Put it this way, if she found a suicide note, the first thing she'd do is check the grammar."

Trusdale snorted.

Pinder grinned. "So, how can I assist you, sir?"

"I don't need anything. Just admiring your posters. Most interesting." He gestured at the wall.

Pinder glanced furtively toward Constance and leaned on the counter. He beckoned Trusdale nearer. Trusdale leaned in close enough to catch the anise whiff of absinthe on the printer's breath. "Perhaps sir is interested in the special collection of engravings we keep for our more selective male clients?"

Trusdale frowned. "I don't know what you mean."

Pinder reached down under the counter and pulled out a privacy screen. He stood the foot-high red silk screen upon the counter, blocking the views of Constance and Cawley. The printer leaned down and brought up a folio display album, opening it to the first page, where tissue paper protected a color chromolithograph. He gently pulled aside the tissue to reveal a woman in a yellow dress and an Easter bonnet sitting on a swing decorated with flower garlands. Both ankles peeked out provocatively from beneath the woman's long dress as she swung.

Trusdale gaped at the saucy picture and glanced over at Constance, who was still reading her telegrams. "Ah, no, I don't want this."

"I see sir has more specialized tastes. I do possess a titillating set of Parisian prints. Some go all the way up to the knee."

"I'm not looking for any . . . art."

Constance finished reading her telegrams, her face drawn. Without a word, she strode out of the print shop.

Cawley pulled out his coin purse and shuffled toward Trusdale and the printer. The silver-haired retainer caught sight of the woman on the swing, right before Pinder closed the book with a snap.

The servant gave Trusdale a very hard stare and pursed his lips in silent condemnation.

He stuttered, "Ah, no, Mr. Cawley, I can explain, I wasn't actually—"

Cawley held up a gloved hand to stop his excuses. "Eli, I believe this should take care of the poster printing and the bauble filling." The servant slapped a pile of pound notes down on the counter next to the naughty book.

Pinder nodded and took the money as Trusdale backed away and headed for the door.

The printer called out to him, "Feel free to stop by anytime, sir. We'll definitely find something for your particular taste."

Cawley tut-tutted.

"Oh, come on, Mr. Cawley," Pinder said. "Can't a man have a hobby?"

Trusdale cringed and shot out of the shop as fast as his boots could carry him.

Chapter 11: Le Paon Pompeux

IT MADE SENSE TO CONSTANCE that she would enter the Le Paon Pompeux restaurant alone. Servants and cowboys would surely not be welcome at the grandest restaurant in town.

Even she felt a little underdressed as she stood in the green marble vestibule outside the dining room. The scent of roast beef floated through the air, and her mouth watered. A tuxedoed *maître d'* stood at a podium carved into the shape of a fantailed peacock, checking his list for a lunch reservation she knew didn't exist. Le Paon Pompeux required that all reservations be made six months in advance.

Potential diners agreed to undergo a thorough review of their pedigrees, including the submission of written references from at least three peers.

The *maître d'* frowned at his reservation list. "I'm sorry, Miss Haltwhistle, I do not seem to see—"

"Perhaps it's under my father's name, Baron Henry Haltwhistle? Or my cousin, Lord Wellington Pendelroy? Of course, Lady Pemmington might know, if I could just pop in to see her—"

"Her Ladyship has not yet arrived."

"Ah, fashionably late as usual. Well, do let me know when she gets here. I'll show myself in." She strode toward the gold-tasseled curtains, halting as two brawny waiters in black tie and tails appeared from within. They stood with their arms folded, blocking her way.

Was it time to draw out her stiletto hairpins? What would be the social consequences of a minor skirmish?

Behind the waiters' dapper bulk, a gold-and-turquoise mural of dancing peacocks swept around the airy dining room. Light poured in through the vaulted glass ceiling, illuminating a golden stage where a string quartet played. The performers were surrounded by tables of patrician gourmets clad in formal luncheon attire. Plush aqua carpeting deadened the footsteps of tuxedoed waiters bringing an array of tasting plates to the epicurean clientele.

A silver-haired savior sat at the furthest table. Constance smiled. "Ah, I see that my godmother is waiting for me. Can you please inform the Dowager Countess of Benchley that her favorite goddaughter, Constance, is here, and wishes to join her for lunch?"

The *maître d'* blinked. "I apologize for the delay, Miss Haltwhistle. I had no idea you were connected to . . ." He nodded at the senior of the two waiters. "Inform the countess at once."

The waiter scurried into the dining room and obsequiously approached a stately aristocrat in her early seventies. Lady Margaret, the Dowager Countess of Benchley, raised her opera glasses to peer in Constance's direction as the waiter whispered in her ear.

Her goddaughter almost waved, thought better of the move, and curtseyed in her daintiest manner. She'd been allowed to call Lady Margaret "Auntie Madge" since childhood. It was the countess's only concession to whimsy in a life lived strictly by the book. The book in question was the expanded, annotated edition of *Babett's Modern Manners*, all seventeen volumes.

Madge nodded her approval at the curtsey and beckoned with a white-gloved hand.

The countess had deigned to see her. So far, so good.

Behind her, the *maître d'* coughed. "Sir, I'm sorry, but I'm afraid you must remove your hat. There are ladies present."

Oh no. She spun on her heel. Trusdale's leather duster coat hung open over his gunfighter ensemble.

She sputtered, "I ordered you to wait outside with Cawley."

He took off his hat. "So you did. Seems you didn't want to wait around to hear my opinion on that."

"Opinion? Why on earth do you think you are entitled to an opinion?"

"Why on earth do you think I'm not?"

"Oh, for heaven's sake. You're ruining everything. I demand that you—"

"Demand?"

She scowled at him. The *maître d'* glanced back and forth between them. "Are sir and madam dining together?"

She folded her arms. "Absolutely not."

"Yes, sir and madam are," said Trusdale. "I'm sure Miss Haltwhistle is far too lofty a lady to air a personal disagreement in public."

She couldn't disagree with that.

The cowboy smirked and fiddled with the lining of the hat. He palmed an object she couldn't quite see and slipped it into his right vest pocket. What was it he needed to move around his person so surreptitiously?

Most intriguing. Could it be that the invisible person's obsession with stealing his hat had little to do with a desire for Western headgear?

He shrugged off the leather duster and laid it over his arm. His black cotton frock coat was barely more suitable for the setting than the duster's weather-beaten cowhide.

The *maître d'* grimaced at Trusdale's accessories. "Does sir wish to check his hat and coat?"

"No, sir does not."

She glowered at the insufferable American and turned to pass through the gold curtains. This must have been how poor King George felt when the colonies rebelled.

Trusdale stepped up beside her. "Hey, don't take your bad news out on me. I didn't send you nasty telegrams uninviting you from every social event in town. I'm just here to help."

"It would help if you did as you were told. I'm more than capable of interrogating Lord Burdock, when he arrives, without your assistance. I'll soon find out if he has any connection to the invisibility serum."

He shook his head. "I admire your enthusiasm, but it's far too risky. Trust me, a fancy lady like you doesn't have the experience to deal with such a dangerous individual."

Little do you know. "Speaking of dangerous individuals, you're about to meet my godmother. I strongly recommend absolute silence on your part."

The string quartet mercifully drowned out his response with a stirring rendition of Schubert's *Death and the Maiden.* If the maiden ate at this restaurant, the cause of death was probably starvation. At every table, over-corseted women stared longingly at their male companions' tasting plates as they pecked at their own single servings. *Haute couture* was a harsh mistress, and the spring fashion for a corset worn over a lace dress allowed no fashion-forward lady a second helping of treacle pudding.

The buzz of conversation died as every eye in the room turned to judge her attire, plus that of her gunslinger shadow. Whispers began as the new arrivals' dress and social status was evaluated and found wanting.

Life as a social pariah was not going to be easy.

Reaching Auntie Madge's table, she curtsied again. The seated aristocrat bowed her head slightly. Her diamond tiara glittered in the sunbeams that poured down through the faceted glass roof. Her sky-blue lace dress and embroidered iris corset showed off her skeletal frame to perfection. The countess's gray eyes wrinkled into what passed for a smile in ladies of her age and social stature.

Next to Madge sat an unknown young man in a green-and-yellow paisley vest and bow tie. The youth was remarkable for his almost complete lack of a chin. He was pallid and skinny with an insignificant blond mustache that glistened with an overabundance of wax. His face lit up as he ran his eyes over Constance's curves. He caught her eye, flushed with embarrassment, and stood to bow to the new arrivals.

Constance curtseyed to the young man and glared at Trusdale. The American took her subtle hint and gave a bow made awkward by the overcoat and hat he carried.

The dowager countess reached for her opera glasses. She peered through the gold binoculars at the cowboy's attire. With a frown, she said in a ringing upper-class tone, "Good heavens, is the circus in town?"

"Lady Margaret," said Constance, "may I introduce Mr. Trusdale, of the Kansas Trusdales?"

He half-bowed, lost his grip on the hat, and dropped it at the dowager's feet.

The countess wrinkled her nose. "I see, an American. How unfortunate."

Truer words were never spoken. "Mr. Trusdale is a consultant on a security matter I'm investigating."

Madge's gossamer brows lifted. "Indeed? I never could understand the company either you or your father keeps. May I introduce Lord Pinkington-Smyth? His father will be with us presently.

Pinkie, this is my goddaughter Constance Haltwhistle, of the Northumberland Haltwhistles."

In a high-pitched nasal tone, Pinkie said, "I'm delighted to meet you, Miss Haltwhistle. What a very fetching hat."

The countess rolled her eyes. "Never mind all that. Constance, my dear, the word is that you are *persona non grata.* How could you possibly offend every noble simultaneously? Even your father had the good manners to insult only one peer at a time."

She cleared her throat. "Ah, well, Auntie, I'm so glad that you asked. You see, my coming out ball was going quite splendidly. I'm convinced that I was mere moments away from gaining a marriage proposal from someone or other, when suddenly—"

"Get to the point, girl. I'm seventy-three, time is of the essence."

A kidnapping was so far beyond the pale that she feared Auntie Madge would refuse to be seen with her. The less said, the better. "Um, to summarize, my exo-suit champagne dispensers flew off into the night."

The countess gasped. "Alas, my girl, that I was bedridden that evening with a case of acute languor. Perhaps I could have spotted the deficiencies in your party preparation. Why you chose to use flying drinks dispensers is a mystery for the ages."

"It was an error I shan't repeat."

"I should think not. Honestly, Constance, you should have asked for my help on the first day of planning this calamitous event. Mark my words, young miss, your independent streak will cost you everything. If it hasn't already."

Constance's lips committed a very un-British quiver. Even the Brass Queen didn't stand a chance against the dowager Countess.

Madge's gray eyes softened to a lighter shade of steel. "That said, no one actually died. Don't despair, my dear. I'm sure everyone will forget about the incident within a decade or two." She bestowed a royal wave upon the table's empty chairs. "Do sit, both of you."

A waiter pulled out a gilded bamboo chair for Constance. She settled her bustle onto the cushioned seat and pulled the chair closer to the turquoise tablecloth. She breathed in the meaty vapors of the lightly poached sloth kidneys perched enticingly close on a gold tasting plate. The servers swept in with whirlwind efficiency and set before her an array of blue-and-white Asian plates with a peacock theme.

A waiter appeared and offered a gilt-edged menu to Constance. Le Paon Pompeux celebrated the finest gastronomic delights from across the British Empire. With over sixty colonies, protectorates, and occupied territories to choose from, the restaurant's head chef never ran out of new and exciting cuisines to exploit. She ran down the alphabetical list of imperial conquests and their attendant entrées.

The countess said, "I think I'll take the pickled Ceylon junglefowl. Oh no, has the empire lost Egypt? I don't see it on the menu."

Pinkie said, "Oh yes, Countess. It was a dreadful war. The newspapers stated that all was lost at a massive airship battle over the Valley of the Kings. Both sides suffered major casualties—"

The countess shook her head. "Appalling. I used to love those baby Egyptian tortoises. One can only hope we invade again soon."

Pinkie said, "Oh, I'm sure we will. I've heard most of our foreign policy is based on sourcing gourmet goods. Spices, sugar, curries—why not tortoises? It only makes sense."

Constance said to the waiter, "I'll take the smoked Malayan river shark."

Trusdale frowned at the menu. "Mauritius flying fox?" He looked to Constance for assistance.

She smirked. "Tastes just like fried wombat kidneys in lemon soufflé." Trusdale stared at her. "I'm kidding, of course. It tastes like boiled badger in rhubarb jelly."

He turned an unusual shade of green and put down the menu.

A portly middle-aged man in a violet-and-white paisley vest and bow tie puffed up to the table from the rear of the restaurant. Pinkie and Trusdale rose to acknowledge him.

The countess said, "May I introduce Lord Newton Pinkington-Smyth, father of young Pinkie here?" The newcomer bowed and sat beside Madge. She sniffed. "So, late again, Newt? And I take it from your less-than-pleasant odor that you stopped by the snuff room before gracing us with your presence?"

"My apologies, Countess. A reprehensible habit, I know."

"Indeed. One can scarcely get through a meal these days without gentlemen running off to the snuff room every two minutes. Now, speaking of annoying gentlemen, Constance, have you heard from your father recently? Or is he still off chasing bizarre beasts and snatching ancient treasures from the dark heart of the uncivilized realms?"

"The last letter I received from Papa was about six months ago. He said he was traveling along the Yangtze River by steamship."

Pinkie asked, "Big-game hunter, is he?"

"He's a treasure hunter, of sorts. These days he hunts mostly for religious relics. He believes a handful of items scattered through the world possess sentience, perhaps even souls."

Her godmother smirked. "Well if it's sentient relics he wants, he should come here. I can see at least twenty from this very table." She nodded at a blue-haired lady at the next table, who smiled back.

Trusdale whispered to Constance, "Don't you mean the Congo?"

She blinked at him.

Trusdale murmured, "You told me he was in the Congo. The Yangtze River is in China."

"I don't need a geography lesson from you, thank you very much."

He grinned. "Anyone ever tell you that you're a rotten liar?"

"How dare you! I'll have you know that I'm an excellent liar!" Her voice rang out as clear as a bell over the strains of the string quartet.

The music stopped. Every musician, patron, and waiter turned to stare at the self-proclaimed fibber.

Constance groaned and hid her face in her hands.

The countess said, "And there we have it. The apple certainly doesn't fall far from the tree. Of course, it's not your fault, my dear. This is entirely your father's doing. He's left you alone for years on end, running around that huge house like a wild animal. With no company but the servants. It's positively a crime. No wonder you can't get a husband."

Constance squirmed.

The countess continued, "You need to get cracking, girl. How old are you now, nineteen?"

"I turned twenty-one in March, not that anyone noticed. Cousin Welli gave me a bottle of superb gin and a rather splendid hat, but otherwise—"

"Twenty-one?" her godmother said with eyes wide. "Good lord, then the bloom is definitely going off the rose."

Pinkie smiled at Constance from beneath his depressed mustache. "Oh, I think the bloom is still quite enchanting, Countess."

Constance demurely studied her water glass. It wasn't a proposal, but a compliment from a young lord not wearing a wedding ring was a start. *Perhaps Pinkie might be the savior of my estate? Yes, our children will be a tad chinless, but still . . .*

The countess fixed Pinkie with a withering stare. "What nonsense! She's an absolute wreck. There she sits, the descendant of an incorrigible line of baronial rogues on her father's side. Her mother, by comparison, was a virtual saint with an impeccable ancestry. Why she succumbed to Henry's bombastic charm, I have no idea."

Constance sagged and picked imaginary fluff off her sleeve.

The countess continued, "Now the wretched girl has instigated a social catastrophe. Even I might find it difficult to ensnare her a suitable husband after such a public disaster."

Constance swallowed hard. She slowly traced her initials on the tablecloth, C-A-Z-H.

Auntie Madge sighed. "Of course, I'd be willing to try and help you find a spouse, my dear. All you need to do is ask." She eyed Constance as one might examine an heirloom antique gathering dust in an attic. "A little cleanup is required. I've certainly seen less pleasing faces in my time, but we would have to introduce proper bouffant styling to your beauty regime. I mean, honestly, Constance, whatever have you been doing to your hair?"

She reached up and patted her tight auburn bun. "Ah, well I've been doing it myself. My lady's maid resigned three weeks ago. It was most inconvenient. Apparently, she got offered a place at the Italian court. An agency sent me a temporary maid to fill in for her, but the new one barely speaks English and can't style hair for the life of her."

"Indeed? Servants can be so self-centered. You give them a roof over their head and pennies in their pocket, and then poof. Off they go to Europe at the drop of a hat. There should be a law against it. Is this the same maid who put you in that awful white dress?"

"Well, no, I chose this—"

Madge shook her head. "My dear, you know full well that only pastels are proper for a spring luncheon. You really must pay more attention to these matters. A white dress cinched by a scarlet corset is suitable attire for institutional visits only. Unless you've visited a hospital or a police station this morning, you're completely underdressed."

"Well, I, that is, yes, I'm sorry, Auntie."

"And have you lost weight? My goodness, girl, you're positively wasting away. No wonder the men can't see you. You're practically wraithlike. Don't you agree, Newton?"

The portly man studied Constance's figure for far longer than was appropriate. "She seems pretty well padded to me."

"Nonsense, Newt. Waiter, bring this child a plate of pâté immediately."

With lightning speed, a porcelain plate of goose pâté with a silver fork appeared before Constance. At least, she hoped it was goose. In this restaurant, it could easily be emu, or aardvark, or polar bear.

The countess's eyes bore into her. Constance sighed and took a mouthful of the pâté. The silky mousse was smooth, savory, and delicious, with a taste not unlike well-aged bacon. She took a second bite, and then a third.

The countess gasped. "My goodness, dear child, that's quite enough. I said to eat something, not to develop gout right before our very eyes."

Constance pushed away her plate and glanced over at Trusdale. The American shot her a sympathetic look.

The gold curtains to the vestibule parted. Lady Pemmington, Lord Burdock, and two remarkably handsome gentlemen entered the dining room. Constance kicked Trusdale.

He winced and murmured, "I'm guessing Burdock is the older man? Or are you just feeling violent?"

She whispered, "Yes, and yes."

Lady Pemmington, a forty-year-old beauty in pastel-yellow lace, took a seat at her usual table. The two tall, dark, and dapper men sat either side of her. Constance could only assume they were Italian. No Englishman could ever look so polished. Lady Pemmington had a penchant for European collectibles, and it looked as if she had just procured a new set of trophies.

Lord Burdock remained standing. He was a short, middle-aged man with a protruding belly that strained the seams of his red-and-black paisley vest. A bushy gray beard enveloped his jowly face, and a gold monocle utterly failed to add distinction to the beady eyes beneath his receding hairline. Burdock appeared to be making his apologies to her ladyship, tapping his nose as he spoke.

"The dreaded snuff strikes again," the countess remarked. "What has the world come to when ladies must wait for men to indulge their vile habits before every course? There should be a law against that too."

Burdock adjusted his bow tie and gray morning coat. With a bow to his companions, he walked to a closed set of turquoise velvet curtains at the rear of the dining room, parted them, and disappeared.

Trusdale said to Newton, "I guess those curtains lead to the snuff room?"

"Why yes, my boy. Do you partake of the vile weed?"

"Just starting today. Excuse me." Trusdale stood and bowed to the table. Constance gaped as he strolled to the rear of the dining room with his coat and hat in hand. He pushed through the velvet curtains into the gentlemen-only world of snuff.

The dowager countess huffed. "What appalling manners. Now, Constance, let's return to your lack of a fiancé. Before word of your drinks disaster spreads any further, I strongly recommend that you secure an immediate engagement to the highest-ranked man who'll take you."

Hope flitted across Pinkie's pallid face. Constance held her breath. *Is he the one?* Why didn't she feel happier about sorting out the estate's problem's in one fell swoop?

The countess glared at the youth. "Pinkie, please note that she should aim for a husband who will significantly enhance her social status. That clearly disqualifies you."

Newt said, "Quite right, Countess. I'm planning for Pinkie here to head into the clergy. Best career for a second son, don't you think?"

For a moment, Constance met Pinkie's alarmed brown eyes. Apparently, this was the first the chinless youth had heard of his new career.

Poor Pinkie—only the firstborn sons got to have any fun.

Chapter 12:
The Vile Weed

TRUSDALE PARTED THE VELVET CURTAINS to reveal a propped open vault door. Crafted from six inches of solid steel with an intricate brass locking mechanism, the door of Le Paon Pompeux's snuff room wouldn't have looked out of place at the Bank of England.

His heart pounded. Interrogating Burdock was his best shot at finding Maya and her boys, but in a public setting? Tricky. The security systems of English snuff rooms surpassed those of most bullion depositories.

It was no secret the British Empire was spread thin across the globe. Redcoat regulars had been supplemented by conscripts, dragged from their homes to serve queen and country. Unsurprisingly, homesickness was rife. Ever efficient, the military had ordered the Steamwerks to find a portable solution. Maya's scientists had developed a unique way for troops to momentarily visit their hometown, no matter where they were stationed. The Geo-Sensual Memories (GSM) powder became known by the slang term of "snuff."

Inhaling a pinch of snuff gave soldiers a sensory experience of their birthplace so profound that morale and patriotism increased tenfold. Snuff kept a man going when all around him seemed lost, whether on the front line in Bechuanaland or in the backwaters of Bahrain. It was widely agreed that snuff, pomp, and hierarchy were the bulwarks of the British military machine.

Due to the powder's exorbitant cost, each soldier was issued only one small tin of snuff per campaign. Off the battlefield, GSM became a recreational experience for the ultra-wealthy. Elite gentlemen's clubs and exclusive restaurants had replaced smoking rooms with snuff vaults to accommodate the craze. Within these bastions of self-indulgence, enthusiasts snorted varieties of snuff such as the Essence of Halifax, the Spirit of Scunthorpe, and the ever-popular Tincture of Leeds.

For the affluent man-about-town, snuff provided relief from the tedium of long dinner conversations focused on etiquette, shooting sports, and the gambling losses of the rich and reckless. For the impoverished workers who couldn't afford a physical trip on a steam train or airship, a sniff of snuff was the only way to catch a glimpse of exotic climes. Black-market vendors of stolen snuff, known as, "snuff snatchers," created their own dens to cater to proletarian sensory tourists.

The steel vault was decorated to resemble a gentlemen's lounge. On the left wall, mahogany bookcases bore dozens of silver snuffboxes. Engraved copperplate script provided the name of the sensory destination within. Facing the shelves sat a pair of sofas upholstered in oxblood leather, and a freestanding brass candelabra cast a subdued light in the windowless room. The air was cool, with an earthy spice scent reminiscent of a Turkish bazaar. A Persian rug added a splash of red, gold, and blue to the riveted steel floor. Overlooking it all, a mounted lion's head gazed dourly upon Lord Burdock as he studied the snuff-boxes, torn between a pinch of the Air of Arundel or the Heart of York.

His paisley vest and gray morning coat strained at the seams, his bow tie was askew, and his black shoes were worn and unpolished. He appeared to be a man who needed money, or a friend, rather than an evil mastermind bent on exploiting the invisibility serum.

Time to get friendly.

Trusdale dropped his coat and hat on a sofa and reviewed the boxes of snuff. Maybe a Canadian accent might help him win Burdock's trust? After all, who doesn't love a Canadian?

He smiled at Burdock. "Good afternoon, sir. Looks like they have every type of snuff you could want aboot here. Could you be helping me out with any recommendations, eh?"

Lord Burdock's brows lifted skyward. "I take it you're not from around here?"

"You have a keen ear, sir. I was born and raised in the great city of Ottawa."

"A Canadian? Interesting. Always nice to meet one of our colonial cousins. As for recommendations, well, it's hard to say. You won't find a more comprehensive selection anywhere. Although, there always remains the eternal problem . . ."

"What's that, sir?"

"That these soldiers seem to come from such dreary places. Why can't they come from Tuscany or Italy? I'd personally like to experience the scent of a Swiss mountain range, not A Mélange of Manchester."

"I couldn't agree more."

Burdock smiled politely and continued to mull over his snuff choices. Evidently, he was in no rush to return to Lady Pemmington and her two Adonis lookalikes.

Trusdale wasn't in any rush to get back to the dining room either. The dowager countess had glared down her nose at him since the moment he sat at her table. Her badgering of Constance was downright vicious. Inexplicably, the countess's recommendation that her goddaughter should marry any peer with a pulse had turned his stomach.

Before him sat a silver box that offered the Soul of Sheffield. He reached out and flipped open the box. He'd never tried snuff, but he'd heard British soldiers say it was the best part of going to war. To his right, Burdock eyed A Smidgen of Stamford.

It might cement my cover to sample the snuff. Besides, what harm can a tiny pinch do to a full-grown man? He took a few grains of the tea-colored powder and rolled it between his fingers to release the compounds within. He put the snuff on the back of his hand and gave a gentle sniff.

An aromatic symphony tickled his olfactory nerves. The first scent was moorland heather, earthy and herblike, with an overtone of blackberries, hay, and horses. His mind conjured an image of a stone farmhouse, purple moors on the one side, hayfields on the other, horses in the barn, geese waddling across a cobblestone yard, blackberry pies cooling on a kitchen window. The scene dissolved into a woodland clearing. He breathed in the mineral scent of bluebells intertwined with dirt and leaves and ozone. A note of coal smoke drifted through the trees as the forest transformed into a metalworker's shop. He inhaled the coal smoke tinged with oil, metal, and the sweat of honest labor. He could taste the heather, blackberry pie, smoke, rainclouds, and a hundred other scents he couldn't identify. This was his home; this was a place worth fighting for; this was . . .

It wasn't Kansas. He snapped open his eyes. Gasping, he leaned forward and placed his hands on the shelves, holding on tight as his head swam with a confusion of sights and smells.

Burdock said, "That's why you're supposed to sit down." The peer gestured at the leather sofas.

"Thank you, sir, good advice." Trusdale wiped his brow. "That was a mighty odd experience. It seems to be my day for it. I thought I was going crazy out there, in the restaurant."

"The food here is enough to make any man's head spin. Some of those spices . . ." Burdock shuddered.

"I wish it had been the food. Can you believe, as I walked here from my table, I thought I heard disembodied voices discussing how best to assassinate some poor soul? Something about scientific journals, and serums, and side effects no one told them about. Maybe I'm hearing things? Or perhaps this place is haunted?"

Burdock gawked at him. "What's that?"

"I'm wondering if this building has ghosts in residence. I know I heard voices, but there was no one there. I swear on my mama's Bible, it sounded like there were three of them. One of them might even have been a woman. I've got quite the ear for foreign accents. Hers was melodious, singsong, with a touch of Wisconsin, maybe? Ah, now I think about it, her inflection was more pronounced. Kinda like a bouncy Plattdeutsch, with a northern lilt, eh?" He raked his hand through his hair. "Well, gosh darn it, sir, I must apologize. For the life of me, I can't remember what's north of Prussia."

"It couldn't be . . . you don't think it was Scandinavian, do you?"

Trusdale slapped his forehead. "That's it! And boy, did she sound displeased."

"Oh, my God." The color drained from Burdock's face.

"Why, sir, you're not looking so good. Do you need help?"

"I'm not sure, I . . ." Burdock edged toward the doorway, eyes fixed on the closed velvet curtains. "I've got to get out of here. They're killers. If they think I'm responsible, I'm finished."

"Responsible for what? What's going on?"

Burdock hesitated.

"If you tell me what's going on, maybe I can figure a way to get you out of here. Between you and me, I'm not exactly defenseless, eh?" Trusdale walked to the couch, put on his Stetson, and picked up his coat. He reached inside to a hidden holster and drew out a snub-barrel revolver, the Smallstack S50. The double-action revolver could be easily concealed in the palm of his right hand.

Burdock's eyes widened. "Good Lord."

"It's only for defense. There are pickpockets and worse on the streets out there. Here, you can have it. Sounds like you need it more than I do." He offered the man his gun, calculating the odds that Burdock would take it as low.

The nobleman shook his head. "No, thank you. I'm a rotten shot even when the target isn't invisible." Genuine gratitude shone from the portly man's eyes. Right now, Trusdale was the closest thing he had to a savior.

"Very well, sir, you let me know if you change your mind. Now, you're telling me I'm not hearing things, that there really are ghosts out there? Why do they want to hurt you?" He pulled on his coat. If Burdock made a break for it, he'd be ready.

Burdock's brow glistened. From his pants pocket, he pulled a black silk handkerchief. He wiped his forehead and blew his nose like a bugle.

Trusdale faked a smile. Burdock wouldn't run. If he kept him talking, all would be revealed.

Sure enough, Burdock slumped against the vault door. "Not ghosts; assassins. If you must know, I'm a dabbler in the sciences. It's just a hobby, you understand. I acquired a journal that contained a formula for a serum that confers invisibility."

"You don't say." Trusdale kept his tone friendly, but raised an eyebrow.

"I know it sounds like madness, but it's the truth. I spent two years and much of my fortune trying to create the serum. I thought I'd become as rich as Midas. Instead, I got pulled into—well, nothing good. I've cut ties with my former associates, but it seems they are out for my blood."

Trusdale let out a low whistle.

Burdock stuffed his handkerchief into his pocket. "To cut a long story short, a member of the royal circle persuaded me to hand the journal to a Steamwerks scientist. I was promised a substantial payoff if the serum worked."

"Which member, and who's the scientist?"

Burdock studied the floor. "I can't tell you. They'll kill me."

"Seems like that's already the plan, eh?"

Burdock blanched. "You're right, good Lord, you're right. I must escape. Will you really help me?"

"Yes, sir, any way I can. You know . . ." Trusdale scratched his ear. "This scientist—I'll bet I can guess who it is. I've had some occasion to work with those scientists, and I noticed that Dr. Maya Chauhan isn't a gal who likes to follow the rules."

"That's true, but no. My contact is her right-hand man. When the serum was administered to test subjects, it did induce invisibility. But within days, the poor creatures were consumed by a violent insanity. Imagine a world stalked by invisible madmen—no one would be safe."

Trusdale did his best to mimic Burdock's horrified expression. "You're right, that's just dreadful, and not something I'd expect of Dr. Chauhan at all. Truth be told, I wouldn't have expected it of *any* of those fine scientists. Which of them would be willing to overturn the laws of nature like this?"

Burdock shook his head. "I'm sorry. I just can't tell you."

The velvet curtain swept to one side, then dropped closed with a swish, but no one walked through.

Both men gasped. Burdock scrambled back, his face ashen.

"Who's there?" called Trusdale. No one answered.

Blood pounded in his ears and his wounded throat throbbed. Trusdale pulled back the hammer on his snub-barreled revolver and leveled it at the doorway. He moved between Burdock and the door, shielding the peer from his unseen foe. He should have guessed his assailant hadn't given up the fight.

Burdock whimpered, "It's not my fault, creature. I just gave him the journal. I am sorry for your plight." He hid behind Trusdale.

Trusdale stood tall, making himself as imposing as he could manage facing thin air. "Invisible person, I request you leave this man alone. He's not the one you want. He didn't make the serum." He glanced at Burdock. "Are you sure you can't let that name spill? If you tell our noncorporeal friend here who's to blame for their distress, it might calm their madness or—well." He dropped his voice to a whisper. "I hesitate to suggest it, but it might give them a different person to blame."

The curtain moved to one side again, dropping closed onto emptiness. While Burdock's whimper escalated to a moan, Trusdale cursed under his breath. Had the woman from the Pyrrho Club left, or were there now two assassins here? A second invisible assailant was all they needed. If he fired his gun within the vault, he might accidentally kill Burdock with a ricochet. "I don't mean to alarm you further, sir, but you really, *really* ought to volunteer what you know if this situation is as dire as you claim, or I'm not going to be much help to you in here."

Burdock sank to his knees and sobbed. "It's Dr. McKinley you want. He developed the serum. I didn't know about the risks to you, I swear."

Trusdale pulled Burdock to his feet. "Stay behind me—this way." He dragged Burdock through the doorway, braced for contact with an invisible body. As they approached the curtains, the outline of a person within the velvet folds moved. "Run!" shouted Trusdale to Burdock.

As Trusdale lunged for the shape, Burdock raced past. The curtain jumped out of Trusdale's grasp and swirled to a stop beside him. He yanked back the velvet, flailing his arm wildly to locate the invisible foe, or foes.

Constance ducked and blinked up at him. "I say, is this the cloakroom?"

He gaped. "What do you think you're doing? I might have shot you!"

"It's an old séance trick. You know, one person sits in a room talking about ghosts, and the other moves the curtains and makes noises, that kind of thing. This was the curtain part. Rather effective, don't you think?"

"I was getting the information we needed."

"Yes, but now you've got it faster. It's McKinley. The way you were droning on, this would have taken all night."

He groaned and dropped the velvet curtain onto her face.

"Well!" exclaimed the curtain in an offended tone.

He resisted the urge to say several ungentlemanly things and sprinted out into the dining room. No sign of Burdock, but the kitchen doors were swinging. He ran over and pushed through to see Burdock hurtle out the rear door into an alley bright with afternoon sun.

What else might the fleeing lord know?

Thanks to Constance's "help," there was only one way to find out.

Trusdale ran through the kitchen and out into the cobbled alley after Burdock, his smooth-soled Western boots slipping on the stones. "Wait," he called. "The coast is cl—"

Burdock rounded the corner at the end of the alley and fled onto the High Street with no signs of slowing down.

The chase was on. Trusdale sprinted as fast as he could after the fleeing nobleman.

He might not have a kingdom to give for a horse, but, lord, what he wouldn't give right now for a fast pony and a long lasso.

Chapter 13: Red Versus Blue

AN HOUR AFTER LEAVING LA Paon Pompeux, a solitary Constance lounged on the gold cushions of her dragon carriage. She was surrounded by the red and blue samurai armies that scrolled across the vehicle's walls. It seemed the blue army was about to be flanked by enemy archers. Above the High Street clatter of carriages, street vendors, and a distant brass band practicing for the Queen's parade, the town hall clock struck four. She glared at Trusdale's battered suitcase on the opposite bench. *Where on earth is he?*

His vanishing act had led to an unpleasant lecture from her godmother about the dangers of consorting with foreigners. Auntie Madge was against foreigners in both principle and practice, primarily because they just weren't English enough. She displayed particular acrimony toward foreigners who fled before the dessert course. She also proposed there should be a law against any person with the unbridled gall to wear a neckerchief to a luncheon.

Constance was with her on the neckerchief issue. *Is there any chance Trusdale carries a bow tie in his suitcase?* With this burning fashion question as a pretext, she moved to sit beside the case. The brass combination lock required the rolling of dials to spell out a six-letter word.

Her first attempt was obvious: K-A-N-S-A-S.

No luck. She tried O-R-E-G-O-N and N-E-V-A-D-A without success. Once the United States had failed her, she turned to more esoteric themes. What would a man such as Trusdale like? She tried L-A-S-S-O-S, H-O-R-S-E-S, and C-O-W-B-O-Y. Surprisingly, none of these words opened the case.

She recalled the family portrait within Trusdale's watch. What were the names of his siblings? Liberty, Charity, Freedom, Hope, Verity—

She entered the name V-E-R-I-T-Y. The lock clicked open. She grinned and pushed up the lid.

A pair of well-worn red woolen long johns greeted her. She screwed up her nose and pulled aside the underwear.

Her eyes widened. On top of a crumpled black shirt rested a solitary brass gauntlet adorned with a delicate labyrinth of copper wiring. The wires swept up into an exquisitely crafted electrostatic ray gun mounted directly on the forearm plate. Five dials indicated a range of shock levels from "Ouch" up to "Naptime." Engraved lettering declared the glove to be the Trusdale Perambulating Kinetic Storm Battle Mitten #003.

Her jaw dropped. Kinetic? Perambulating? Could this be an electric-shock gauntlet powered solely by the movement of the user's body? How on earth did a cowboy develop such a wondrous weapon?

She clutched her hand to her chest. Heavens, could his assertion that he worked with Nikola Tesla actually be true? Was Trusdale a genius? Was he so intelligent, that a mere amateur science dabbler like her couldn't recognize his brilliance, disguised as it was behind his down-home charm?

More importantly, would he sell the patent to the Brass Queen? If the electrical shock could be modulated down to a nonlethal strength, this could become the go-to weapon for anyone who wanted to protect themselves without causing permanent harm to their attacker. Perhaps—

"AHEM."

She glanced up to see Trusdale standing on the carriage step, blue eyes narrowed, face flushed, and lips pressed into a thin line.

Now he arrived, after all that time she'd spent *not* breaking into his luggage.

She snapped the suitcase shut and made a show of straightening the case on the bench. "There, that's better."

He fixed her with a glare so fierce it took her breath away. None of the servants ever glared at her. There was an occasional sigh, and a good deal of muttering, but never an actual glare.

In true British tradition, she pretended nothing untoward had occurred. Any impression that she had been caught red-handed rifling through his underwear was clearly the fantasy of a fevered brain. She moved back to the opposite bench and folded her hands primly. "Do hurry up and get in. To ensure that no one suspects that I'm secretly a debutante detective, I've decided it's imperative that I attend the Lord Mayor's council meeting at four. He sent me a personal invitation, embossed with the city seal. I think I'm finally making a positive impression—"

"So help me!" Trusdale stepped up into the carriage. He loomed over her, his face taut with tension. "You didn't see anything inside that case, do you hear?"

Heart thudding, she pressed her back against the seat, ready to kick him if needed. "Like I'm interested in your paltry gadgets and questionable underwear."

"Better make sure you keep it that way."

"Or what?'

His shoulders sagged.

Hah! All bark, no bite, thank goodness.

He scooped up his suitcase and sat opposite her, cradling the case as if it were a small child. *Goodness, how dramatic.* It was common knowledge that Americans were curiously attached to material possessions, but to actually hug one's luggage, well, that appeared to be taking attachment too far, mysterious glove or not. Did the glove mean something more personal to him than a miraculous invention? Or was Trusdale unnaturally fond of his drawers?

She called out to Hearn, "Drive to the town hall, as swiftly as you can." The carriage lurched as the four chestnut ponies sprang into a bone-juddering trot. Shoppers strolling along the flagstone pathways pointed out the dragon to their children. The pinafore-and-short-trousers set clapped with excitement as the mythical beast swept by.

Trusdale continued to glare at her. He seemed to be deliberating on what to say. To resist the urge to straighten his neckerchief for him, she sat on her hands.

When he spoke, his tone was carefully controlled. "Do you have any idea what you have done?"

This question could have covered a wide range of events, from early childhood to her choice of dessert at luncheon. "Could you possibly be a little more specific?"

"You interrupted me in the middle of interrogating Burdock. Thanks to you, he got away before I was finished."

Ah, that. "I believe that, thanks to my assistance, Burdock blurted out that he was working with a Steamwerks scientist called McKinley. He surely means Dr. James McKinley, Maya's colleague. Who else could it be?"

"The same Dr. McKinley who was just kidnapped, you mean."

"Well, yes, I suppose . . . ah." Her brow furrowed. "Yes, I see that could be problematic. Why would McKinley kidnap himself?"

He shrugged. "Maybe he planned the kidnapping and made himself a part of it so he can play the innocent when he shows up later. Or maybe someone kidnapped him to get their hands on the formula. Either way, we're no closer to finding the scientists."

"So if you think Lord Burdock had more information to give, why ever did you let him go?"

Trusdale snarled, "I didn't let him go. He got away. There's a subtle difference there. Can you see that?"

She could, but she didn't care for his tone. "You're not actually blaming me for the fact that you lost Burdock, are you? Heavens, you're the one who told him to run for it."

"I thought there were real invisible people there. You almost gave me a heart attack."

"Yes, well, that was the idea."

His eyebrows rose so high they vanished beneath the brim of his hat.

"Not *you*. Burdock. Séances are very scary to the feebleminded. Have you ever attended one, Mr. Trusdale?"

"You're trying to change the subject."

She folded her arms. "The point is that I was quite capable of interrogating Lord Burdock myself. If you hadn't blundered your way into the restaurant and interfered, at this point, we might well know more about McKinley's part in all this."

"Interfered? You think I interfered? Why, you . . . not that you ever asked, but maybe I have skills that could help us find the kidnappers. Maybe if you weren't so tied up in this secret 'Plan' of yours, we'd have already put together a strategy that made sense. It's time for you to step back and let me take control of this investigation. If you don't like that, I'll get out of this carriage right here, right now." He sat back on the bench cushion with his chiseled jaw set firm.

There was a sharp intake of breath from Hearn and Cawley, eavesdropping from the driver's seat. Whatever she said now would travel through the servants' quarters faster than a fox chased by hounds. If she asked Trusdale to stay, she would look weak. If she let him leave, her investigation into the kidnapping could grind to a halt. After all, with whom but Trusdale could she reasonably discuss invisible foes without sounding like a total lunatic?

Touché, sir. An Englishman would never have gone straight to an ultimatum. It was a bold move on the American's part. She didn't want him to leave, but on the other hand, she didn't want him to win.

She straightened her posture. She hadn't run a global arms operation without developing a few verbal combat skills of her own. "I'm sorry to hear that, Mr. Trusdale. Naturally, I'll be delighted to drop you off at the alley of your choice. As there isn't a single empty hotel room in the entire city due to Her Majesty's impending visit, no doubt even the alleys may prove a little crowded. But I'm sure you'll manage; you do seem to be the resourceful type."

His face fell.

"Of course, you're more than welcome to bunk with the Steamwerks refugees at Haltwhistle Hall. It might offer you the opportunity to question them about McKinley. Presumably, he's been utilizing the Steamwerks laboratories to create his loathsome serum. Purely your choice of course. I'll leave you to decide."

The carriage drew to a halt at the town hall. The gothic clock tower indicated that she was exactly twenty-three minutes late for her meeting.

"Do excuse me." She stood as Cawley came to the carriage door. "As the official decorator of the Queen's parade, I must attend the lord mayor's council. Should I not see you again, Mr. Trusdale, I wish you all the very best."

She stepped down from the dragon carriage, holding on to Cawley's gloved hand for support. The silence from her traveling companion was golden. It was clear that her red samurai had just shot down Trusdale's blue samurai in a classic flanking maneuver. Whether he was in the carriage or not when she returned, she'd had the last word.

After all, it wasn't like she *needed* his assistance; she was the Brass Queen. She had money, and minions, and contacts in places both high and low. His companionship had proven useful and at times stimulating, and true—he'd put them further ahead in their investigation with his invisible person connection, given that it had led them to Burdock, and thus McKinley, but still . . .

She stomped up the Town Hall steps.

Did she really want to ask him, ask anyone, for help?

She stopped at the top of the stairs and looked back at the carriage. Trusdale had stretched himself out on the golden bench. He was using his suitcase as a pillow, his Stetson was pulled low over his broken nose, and his muddy boots were up on the silk-covered seat.

Was he looking at her from under the brim of his hat?

This was no time to display weakness.

She jutted out her chin and strode into the town hall to face the lord mayor and his cronies.

The Brass Queen was ready for battle.

A haze of cigar smoke floated lazily in the air as she slipped through the studded oak doors at the rear of the council chamber. Cathedral-worthy stained-glass windows showed Sheffield's progression from farming community to cutlery crafting to the manufacture of Steamwerks armaments. Rays of sunshine through the jewel-toned glass dusted color over fifty dour council members seated opposite the lord mayor and his twelve aldermen.

The Crown-appointed "representatives of the people" consisted solely of stout, balding men in three-piece suits with a penchant for money and power. Not one held an aristocratic title, but with the Queen's visit pending, knighthoods were in the offing and tensions were running high. If Her Majesty enjoyed the visit, some of the assembled men might elevate their humble status to land ownership, paisley vests, and matching bow ties.

Lord Mayor Braithwaite's voice rang across the chamber as Constance tried to slink her way unnoticed to the rear bench's sole empty seat. The gray-bearded administrator paused midsentence and bellowed in a broad Sheffield accent, "Ah, Miss Haltwhistle, so good of you to finally join us. We were just discussing you."

She froze as a sea of middle-aged men turned to stare. Whispers flitted around the chamber and echoed up to the molded plaster ceiling. She curtsied to the councilmen and continued her progress to the seat. Before she could reach it, the lord mayor roared, "Do tell, Miss Haltwhistle, how go the decorations? Will our flowers rival the Garden of Eden in all its glory?"

Assuming the Garden of Eden bore an uncanny resemblance to a Northern industrial town covered in garlands, she couldn't see why not. "Yes, Lord Mayor."

"And should we be allowing for any attacks by cage-bearing airships during the event?" This brought a rumble of laughter from the assembly.

"I don't believe one is scheduled, my lord."

"Indeed? Can we assume the destruction of the Exhibition Dome was also not scheduled?"

Constance was in no mood for this. "What's your point?"

"The point is that this council has lost faith in your ability to represent our city in the matter of flowers for the Queen's visit. After all, it was the *Royal* Steamwerks Exhibition Dome you managed to bring down. To protect Her Majesty's sensibilities, we feel we have no choice but to hand over your responsibilities to a more suitable party."

"Who?"

"Well, my wife has always shown excellent taste—"

"Not from where I'm standing."

"Now, look here, Miss Haltwhistle—"

The chamber doors opened behind her. The lord mayor halted his outburst, his eyes wide with alarm. He stood, bowed, and stammered, "Y-your Royal Highness, what a delight to see you here. Please, all rise for His Royal Highness Prince Lucien Dunstan, the Third Duke of Hallamshire."

The assembly rose and bowed to the nobleman widely rumored to be the Queen's favorite grandson.

Constance's breath caught at her first sight of a royal. He was impossibly handsome, with slate-gray eyes, angular cheekbones, and an aquiline nose presiding over an impeccably curled handlebar mustache. His wardrobe was to die for. A purple velvet tailcoat tapered from his broad shoulders over a lilac ruffled shirt and a black silk vest decorated with a golden lion motif. White calfskin jodhpurs hugged his horseman's thighs above pristine riding boots polished to a mirror finish.

Fashion-wise, it was love at first sight for Constance. *Is there any chance I could persuade Trusdale to wear such an outfit?* Her heart fluttered unduly at a vision of the hulking American in lilac ruffles and tight white breeches.

In a plummy baritone, the Prince said, "Gentlemen, I do not wish to interrupt. I've reviewed the plans for my grandmother's visit. Excellent work. Now, please do continue with your business as if I were not here. I'm sure your parade will surpass the countless others she has witnessed."

The lord mayor cleared his throat. "Indeed it will, Your Royal Highness. To that end, I was just explaining to Miss Haltwhistle here"—he gestured toward Constance—"that her presence on our decorating committee is no longer required. A lighter floral touch will better enliven Her Majesty's parade route."

The Prince turned to study Constance. She fidgeted as he took in every aspect of her dress and posture. Her lack of a proper lady's maid was no doubt apparent. Why had she never considered carrying emergency ball gowns in the carriage on the off chance that she might meet royalty?

It was too late to change now.

The Prince finished his inspection, and to her astonishment, a smile of approval lit his face. Her surprise compounded when he asked, "Miss *Constance* Haltwhistle?"

She nodded, for once speechless.

"I must apologize for my manners. I was not aware that a lady was present." The Prince dipped into a supremely elegant bow. Constance gawked at the lowered lord before dropping into a hasty curtsey.

She peeked up at him as he straightened. He smoothed his waistcoat with a manicured hand. "Arise, my dear. Now, am I to understand that you are the same Miss Haltwhistle who has worked so tirelessly on our city's floral decorations?"

"I am she, Your Royal Highness."

The Prince stepped forward and took her right hand between his lily-white palms. "Then, dear girl, I have only one word to say to you about your choices for my grandmother's visit."

Every councilman in the chamber held his breath.

"Perfection. Absolute perfection."

A whoosh of relief emanated from the councilmen.

She decided not to point out that he had spoken three words, not one word. Though technically, it was two words, as "perfection" was used twice—

The Prince bent to kiss the back of her right hand. The scent of musk pomade drifted up from his perfectly coiffed dark locks secured with a diamond clasp. She gulped, stunned that her first kiss was from an actual prince, in front of an audience of men in appalling suits.

He smirked as her knees trembled. Gray eyes locked on hers, he gently released her hand.

Had the temperature in the chamber suddenly soared? It was so hard to tell through a chain mail corset.

His Royal Highness turned to address the council. "I can only assume that you gentlemen are in the process of giving this divine creature a medal as a reward for her sterling decorating efforts. Why, the rose arches across the main thoroughfares will sing their flowery poesy to all who pass beneath them."

What a very intelligent man. He was quite right; her rose arches were floral poetry of the highest degree.

The lord mayor spluttered, "Well, yes, Your Royal Highness. If you think that's required—"

"Oh, but I do," said the Prince. "And I am quite sure my grandmother will too, once she sees this young lady's impressive accomplishments."

She decided that the Prince was the most perceptive man she had ever met. She grinned at him, and he beamed back from beneath his handlebar mustache. Perfect teeth, almost continental in their whiteness.

The lord mayor pursed his lips. "I'll start work immediately on that, my lord. Councilmen, you are dismissed." He rapped his gavel on the oak bench. The men rose and shuffled their way to the rear doors.

Constance and the Prince stood to one side as they passed. She gazed up at him. "Thank you, Your Royal Highness. I'm thrilled that you appreciate my arrangements."

"Please, Miss Haltwhistle." He smiled. "Call me Lucien."

Chapter 14: Haltwhistle Hall

TRUSDALE AWOKE WITH A START as the dragon carriage rumbled over a cattle grid. He'd stretched out on the golden bench of the dragon carriage the moment Constance had flounced up the Town Hall steps. No sane man turned down the opportunity for a quiet nap when the opportunity presented itself.

He sat up. The dragon was traveling along a gravel road at the bottom of a wide, green valley. Ancient stone walls created a patchwork quilt of emerald pastures flecked with snowy sheep. The sheep grazed up to the top of the valley walls, stopping just short of sheer granite cliffs crowned by a brownish-violet smudge of moorland. The earthy scent of heather blew down from the moors on a bracing breeze. A waning sun hung low in the early evening sky.

Trusdale inhaled deep breaths of fresh country air. What a pleasant change after the coal smoke of the city. Sitting primly on the bench opposite, Constance was studying an etiquette book, *Babett's* something or other. Such rulebooks only existed to institutionalize judgement on others. *Who cares when a hat can be worn, or who precedes whom to dinner?* He folded his arms and studied his aristocratic ally. For all her concern with manners, she was happy enough to throw out the rulebook when it suited her.

Is she ignoring me now?

Sadly, no, she wasn't. "Awake, are we?" she asked, glancing up from the book. "We're on the Haltwhistle estate now, which means you'll soon be able to question the Steamwerkers to your heart's content. Which is not to say that I *need* your alleged skills, only that I will put them to good use."

"Oh, is that a fact now?"

He thought he caught a hint of embarrassment behind her cool façade, but it disappeared too quickly to be sure. "I have to admit that your roguish charm might draw information out of the engineers better than a formal interrogation would for this next step in the Plan."

"My roguish charm?" A grin slipped across his face.

She scowled. "I'm still in charge. I'm allowing you to offer a greater degree of assistance, that's all."

"Is that your way of asking for my help?"

"You may contribute at a higher level. Don't make a song and dance about it. I presume you think I should be flattered that you chose to sleep in my carriage over a dank alleyway."

"That's a decision I'm already starting to regret." He rubbed a crick in the back of his neck as she glared. Her eyes were as green as the meadows around them. What flaws did those emerald jewels hide? Deep down, did she care about more than her family assets? She claimed Dr. Chauhan was a dear friend, but Trusdale had yet to meet anyone who truly cared about Miss Haltwhistle beyond her own servants. And she was paying them to be with her. Always surrounded by people, she was nevertheless alone, sitting on her imaginary throne atop a pile of gold.

Deep in his chest, his heart ached for her solitude.

Everybody deserves to love someone who loves them back.

He took a deep breath. Lord knows, he understood the struggle to measure up to familial expectations, two weeks into pretending to be the older brother he had spent his whole life idolizing. And he admired her stubborn expectation that others could and should respect her.

He exhaled and closed his eyes. Constance was a riddle a man could spend a lifetime trying to solve. His heart had been trampled by the fairer sex before, but something about her innate self-possession beckoned to him. There's nothing more attractive than confidence. But Constance was something else . . . regal. Powerful. Unique.

If he didn't find some way to establish a truce between them, one day, he'd regret it.

Fortune favors the bold. Trusdale tipped up the brim of his Stetson and smiled his warmest smile. "I have to say, that . . . you . . . I . . ." He faltered beneath her stare. "That is . . . it's real nice grazing you got there, Miss Haltwhistle. Your sheep have lucked out, for sure. They may not know it, but I sure do. So, you live here on the estate year-round?"

She blinked, clearly surprised by his friendly tone. "Um, well, yes I do. We own additional land up in Northumberland, on the border with Scotland. The ruins of Haltwhistle Castle sit amidst five thousand acres of rugged moorland. I haven't visited there since I was a small child, but I'm told the grouse shooting is outstanding."

"Huh. You don't go down to London? I thought you aristocrats revolved around the royal court."

She shook her head. "We Haltwhistle's are relatively low on the peerage ladder—the bottom rung, you might say. Our estates aren't wealthy or prestigious enough to bring invitations to the court. Besides, Papa always insists that I stay cocooned here on this estate, safe from, well—everything, I suppose. I only started venturing out into the local environs over the past few months. As for London, Papa has forbidden me to even think about going there. He says that if I want to experience the Big Smoke, I should read Dickens."

"Seems a little closed-minded for an adventurer, or whatever he is."

She shrugged. "He just doesn't approve of London for me. It seems he can travel the wildest reaches of the universe with abandon, while I am fated to spend my life in the North of England. He claims the North is a more genteel environment for a young lady. Apparently, he hasn't read *Hard Times*."

"How do you feel about that?"

"A man's reading habits are his own business."

"I mean not traveling. Why doesn't he take you with him?"

Her eyes darkened. "Because that's how he lost my mother."

"Right. Malaria."

"The great equalizer. Disease cares not which rank we're born to. Papa lives in his own world now, far from me and the estate. He's found other things to occupy his time."

"Like what?"

"Oh, um, artifacts and whatnot. He used to send home all sorts of bizarre items to be cataloged for the family treasure vaults."

"Really? How bizarre are we talking?"

"You wouldn't believe me if I told you. It seems most of the wretched things carry curses of a diabolical nature, particularly the mummified bodies. Papa decided to try and communicate with the corpses telepathically."

He gaped. "Did it work?"

She snorted. "Of course it didn't work, they're dead."

"That's a shame. I wonder what ancient pharaohs would say?"

"Probably, 'what do you mean I'm dead?' Denial is not just a river that runs . . . never mind. Anyway, the hieroglyphics aren't even the worst of it. The steam pipes to the orangery run through the cellar where the mummies rest. The humid air provides an ideal breeding ground for fly larvae in their musty bandages. Those deceased pharaohs have spawned a vast swarm of flesh flies that have staked out territory in the lower billiard chamber, the great library, and the south end of the main dining room."

"Flesh flies?"

"*Sarcophagidae* is their Latin name. Bitey little beasts." She shuddered.

"Ugh. You got anything else besides mummies and bugs?"

"I'll say. Frankly, Mr. Trusdale, I own more relics than the British Museum. I know that for a fact because they secretly dump all the things they can't store or display into our cellars. Papa allows this so he can rummage through their junk to see if there's anything of interest to him."

"And what does interest him?"

"Sadly, just about everything." She sighed. "Now I'm stuck with thousands of curiosities, each more macabre than the last. I've no idea what to do with them all. Papa refuses to let me sell any of them in case one artifact is part of something larger. He thinks everything in the universe is connected, so nothing should be discarded."

He scratched his chin. "Perhaps you should open your own museum."

Her eyes lit up. "Why, that's an excellent idea. I can't believe I didn't think of it myself. Thank you, Mr. Trusdale. It's so good to see the famed American ingenuity at work."

He decided to take that as a compliment. "You're welcome. You know, if you need any help evaluating these items, I could check them out. I've been quite the world traveler myself."

"Really?" She steepled her fingers. "And where have you been?"

"All over the place—Mexico, Belgium, Alaska. You know, I could tell you stories of things I've seen, things that would turn your hair as white as snow."

She folded her arms. "Humph. I'm not that easy to scare."

"If you say so." He leaned back on the seat. Constance appeared simultaneously intrigued and annoyed. She clearly wanted to hear one of his stories but wasn't going to ask.

It was a small triumph, but he took his victories where he could find them. He didn't want to knock the porcelain queen off her self-imposed pedestal, but on the other hand, it wouldn't hurt her any to step down off it once in a while.

The valley widened dramatically. Stone farmhouses and outbuildings with slate roofs dotted the fields.

"These are some of the outlying farms," said Constance. "We have two hundred tenant farmers here, mostly tending sheep. The horses and pigs are kept in the stable block."

"No offense, but it's hard to imagine a fine lady like you as a pig farmer."

"A fine lady? Why, sir, that almost sounded like a compliment." She batted her eyelashes with vaudevillian flair.

"More an observation that appearances can be deceptive."

She gestured at his black attire. "Now, that comment makes me wonder what foibles you're hiding beneath your gunslinger garb."

"This ranks as normal where I come from. And I assure you, there are no foibles hidden here. Not a single one."

"What a dreadful shame. How very dull your life must be. I've always found that people's foibles are the most interesting things about them. For instance, my cousin Wellington has a penchant for what can only be described as filthy limericks. And Hearn, my driver, loves his ale perhaps a little too much for a man in charge of a coach and four. Alas, my only foible is an interest in pigs. I believe that producing high-quality pork products could prove to be the future of the estate. I'd love to replace some of my family's business lines with something a little less—well, let's just say, alternatives to some of our more esoteric dealings. If I am to hold the reins of this enterprise, I feel that it's only right that I should try a new road now and then, don't you?"

He shrugged. "I guess so, and what kind of 'esoteric dealings' are we talking about?"

She pursed her lips. "We aren't talking about them, and you're missing the point. I'm considering developing a new wave of epicurean bangers to complement our current products. In addition to porcine perfection, there are the horse lines, too, of course, from carriage ponies to draft shires. Like everything in life, it all boils down to the correct breeding. Some of my horses possess such rarefied genealogy that in human terms they would probably be royalty."

"Pah. One of the things I like best about horses is they don't give a hoot about such nonsense. A horse doesn't care whether humans classify him as a Thoroughbred or a Mustang. He just is."

"Perhaps some horses would find life easier if they tried to blend in with the herd a little more." She nodded pointedly at his Stetson. "Tell me, why don't you wear English attire during your stay on our sceptered isle?"

He bristled. "Excuse me? I'm dressed the way I always dress—it's practical and comfortable."

"Practical? Comfortable? It's as if you don't care about fashion at all."

"I don't." He pointed at her tiny bowler hat. "And while we're at it, any hat that doesn't cover your head is nothing more than an affectation."

A wave of magenta rose up her neck and swept across her cheeks.

He decided to press his advantage. "Excuse me for asking, but if you're so keen on fitting in with the herd, why are you wearing a chain mail corset? Oh yes, I see that glint of metal through your lace finery. You can't have it both ways, Miss Haltwhistle. Are you a dainty lady or—what? A knight? Are you planning on assaulting dragons like the warrior on your family shield? Won't your corset get in the way?"

"You'd be surprised what I can do in a corset if provoked."

"I'm glad to hear it. I'd hate to think my partner couldn't look after herself."

She blinked. "Partner?"

"It seems to me that you and I are both used to doing things our own way. Like when I tried to interrogate Burdock with a modicum of understanding about how men's brains work, and you pretended to be a ghost."

"An invisible assassin, actually."

"Nonetheless, if we both keep trying to overrule each other, we aren't going to get anywhere fast. So, how about a truce? We'll agree we both have an equal say. You know, partners."

She squinted at him. "What's in it for me?"

"Well, I won't make fun of your stunted hat, for a start."

"Pfft. As if I care what you think about my bowler." She reached up and tilted the offending article to an even jauntier angle.

He held back a smile. "So, it's a deal?"

"I suppose. As we're now partners, I'll consider upgrading your sleeping accommodation from the hay barn to the main house, at least for one night."

"That's most magnanimous of you. Are you sure you've got the room?"

"You tell me." She gestured down the driveway.

He leaned over the side of the carriage. Amidst formal gardens, a stoic Norman keep stood at the center of a rambling manor house. Each generation of the Haltwhistle family had expanded the original keep with wings and facades in different styles. An abundance of crenellation and honeyed sandstone skillfully unified the best elements of medieval, Gothic, and Baroque designs into a fairy-tale fantasy of turrets and towers, arched leaded windows, and an impressive glass-domed clock tower that doubled as an observatory.

Trusdale let out a low whistle.

Constance beamed. "Welcome to my ancestral seat, Mr. Trusdale."

Chapter 15: Cousin Wellington

TRUSDALE FELT LIKE A TIME-TRAVELER as he walked through Haltwhistle Hall's display of decorating taste through the ages. Elegant, mid-Georgian sitting rooms filled with Chippendale cabinetry nestled next to Baroque staterooms plastered with neo-classical murals that celebrated church and monarchy. Flowery rococo rooms led into medieval-style chambers with suits of armor, tapestries, and heraldic shields. Trusdale followed his new partner through the antique-stuffed maze, breathing in the scent of applewood fires long gone out and admiring the portraiture.

Constance said, "As you may notice, there's not a cohesive theme to the house. Every generation tends to do its own thing to a couple of rooms. We leave the rest as a testament to our forebears' taste, whether good or bad."

He studied the gold-framed oil paintings of her ancestors. The artistry was so exquisite that he could almost sense their disapproval of his attire. He pulled his duster coat together and loosely buttoned it. "You're related to all these folks? There are so many . . ."

"Yes, I am. Gloomy bunch, aren't they? Here, this chap is a little cheerier." She pointed at a painting of a short, stout man with a magnificent auburn beard in a redcoat general's uniform. The officer stood beside a pile of golf balls on a putting green. Far behind him in the distance, a shadowy city hoisted the white flag of surrender.

"That's my late grandfather General Horatio Hannibal Haltwhistle. He's better known as 'Hellfire Horace, the Scourge of Peebles.' Apparently, the town took issue with an increase in the royal wool tax and sealed their gates in protest. Queen Victoria isn't one to stand such nonsense, so she sent Grandpapa and the Brampton Bombardiers up to Scotland to lay down her law. Due to a mix-up in logistics, the troops arrived with ten cannons but no cannonballs. My grandfather overran the local golf club and pelted the town of Peebles into submission with a barrage of golf balls shot from the cannons. You might say he beat them at their own game. Peace and taxes followed shortly thereafter. You may have heard people quote his words from that day, 'a great leader uses any resources at hand to obtain victory.'"

"Even golf balls—an illustrious ancestor indeed."

"Sadly, you can't say the same about the rest of my forebears. 'Rogues, dilettantes, and thieves,' as my father used to say."

"And which would you be?"

She laughed, sending his heart into a series of flip-flops. "Heavens, do I have to choose? I suppose dilettante would be the least damning, although it would be difficult for me to pull off. I'm just naturally good at everything."

"We all have our crosses to bear."

A faint mechanical rumble sounded from outside the house.

Constance cocked her head. "From the sound of it, one of my many crosses is about to make an appearance." She sighed and headed for the floor-to-ceiling French doors that led out to the rose garden. Cawley darted to reach the doors before her and flung them wide open. He stepped back out of the way as his mistress sauntered through.

Trusdale followed the Baron's daughter out to a worn flagstone patio heavy with the scent of spring roses. The rumble grew louder. Over the top of the garden's gray stone walls, he spotted a lone horseman galloping toward the house. A cloud of smoke puffed out from the rear end of what was unmistakably a mechanical steed.

The steam-powered stallion approached at full tilt. The bronze beast shook its copper mane and charged directly at the garden wall. The rider pulled frantically at the chain reins to no avail. Trusdale gaped as the metal horse exploded through the wall with a deafening crash that threw rock shrapnel across the flower beds. The rider stood in his stirrups and hauled back on the beast's reins with all his might. The stallion reared up onto its piston-driven back legs, freezing midair as its chest engine shuddered to a stop. The machine balanced perfectly on its massive hindquarters, forelegs curled, its brass rib cage now visible beneath the bronze musculature, leather flanks, and power-cable arteries. Every element of the mechanical horse was crafted to echo real equine physiology, down to the chiseled veins, engraved hair patterns, and flowing mane and tail crafted from ultrafine copper wire.

A slender man in his mid-twenties with Byronic hair slid ungracefully over the backside of the horse. He pushed his multilensed sniper goggles up onto his black top hat, revealing green eyes sparkling with mischief. The newcomer shared Constance's pale skin, noble nose, and full lips, with a slightly more masculine jawline.

Embroidered gold peacocks preened on the burgundy velvet of his tailcoat, and his red silk shirt was partly open to reveal a chest that had never performed a push-up. Conspicuously tight black britches tucked inside scarlet hunting boots completed the ensemble.

How long would the man have lasted in Kansas City with an outfit like that? If not for the Sherwood S72 telescopic rifle strapped across the horseman's back, Trusdale would have assumed he was an artist or a composer. A low-slung belt of high-percussion rounds suggested that the new arrival was a somewhat flamboyant hunter with an eye for a kill from a distance.

Constance muttered, "My cousin Wellington. The man was born purely to make an entrance." She called out, "For heaven's sake, Welli, that's the third wall this month."

Welli grinned. "Sorry, old girl, can't quite get the jumping part down. You're supposed to kick down twice, but the ruddy thing won't respond. I swear it has a mind of its own."

Constance folded her arms as Welli sauntered up to the patio. The tall man kissed her on the forehead. He peered at her miniature bowler hat in pretend horror. "Good God, Connie, are you wearing that hat on a bet?"

"You're hardly one to critique another's fashion. To what do I owe this pleasure?"

"Several things: First, our delightful godmother is on the warpath again. Apparently, you're a disgrace to the family and so forth. Something about traveling with circus people and behaving like a madwoman in a restaurant?"

Constance groaned and glared at Trusdale. "The 'circus people' would be you."

Welli appeared to notice him for the first time. The aristocrat gave his outfit a once-over and grinned. "Well, hello, cowboy. Connie, have you hired yourself a gunslinger?"

She snorted. "I wish. You should see the size of his gun; it's minuscule. He whipped it out at Le Paon Pompeux to scare some imagined miscreants. If they had actually been in attendance, they would have probably died laughing at the length of his barrel."

Trusdale scowled. "Now, hold on there, missy. The Smallstack S50 is meant to be carried as a concealed armament; it's not designed to impress."

"Then you'll be delighted to know that it didn't."

Welli tut-tutted at Constance. "Really, old girl, never criticize the size of a man's weapon. It's just not done. This is why you're still single."

She rolled her eyes.

Welli dropped into a bow. "Lord Wellington Pendelroy the Third, at your service, good sir."

Trusdale bowed back. "J. F. Trusdale, at yours, Your . . . Lordshipness? Or is it—"

"Just call me Welli, everyone does." He smiled. "I say, Trusdale old boy, introducing oneself with initials—it's simultaneously mysterious and yet oddly specific. I'm officially intrigued, but first I must apologize for Constance's manners. Her lack of *savoir-faire* is most regrettable, I'm sure you'll agree."

Trusdale glanced between Welli and his cousin. "Well, I don't rightly know—"

Welli grinned. "Spoken like a true gentleman. You could learn a few things from him, Connie. Now, Trusdale, how did a fine man like you become acquainted with my poorly-hatted cousin?"

Constance butted in. "Mr. Trusdale is the gentleman who was kind enough to save my life at the Exhibition Dome."

Trusdale stared at her. She'd never admitted that he'd saved her life before—at least, not to him.

Welli clapped him on the back. "Well done, Trusdale, old man. You have my sincere gratitude. I didn't arrive at the party until midnight, and by then . . ."

Constance sighed. "All was lost."

Welli nodded. "A tad dramatic, but accurate. As for your reputation as a high society hostess, perhaps the loss isn't so great. I couldn't stand it if you turned into a clone of Auntie Madge, all manners and etiquette to the detriment of true happiness. That's what she's after, you know. She wants to build an army of bad-tempered old bats to police everybody else's fun."

"I'm guessing she caught you doing something you shouldn't be doing?"

"More like someone—two someones, to be precise. I doubt she'll be stopping by unannounced for a while. Fortunately, she was so irate at you, I got off with a relatively light tongue-lashing." Welli turned to Trusdale. "Have you had the pleasure of meeting our godmother, the Dowager Countess of Benchley?"

"Yes, at lunch today."

"Then I apologize for whatever nightmare she put you through. In case you were wondering, it never gets better. Now, Trusdale, have you been formally introduced to Connie?"

She said, "No, he hasn't."

Welli sighed. "Isn't it wonderful when Connie answers for you, Mr. Trusdale? I'm sure you don't find it annoying at all."

"I don't—well, not always," she muttered.

Welli cleared his throat. "As I was saying, Mr. Trusdale, may I formally introduce you to my delightful first cousin, Miss Constance Aethelflaed Zenobia Haltwhistle. Some say she's the last in a long line of she-wolves and scoundrels, save for my late, sainted aunt Annabella."

"My mother."

Trusdale nodded. "I got that."

"Constance would continue to rule both this rambling pile and the barony of Brampton-on-the-Wall, if my father hadn't brought in lawyers to force her to marry or quit the Hall. This petty war between our lines is getting completely out of hand." Welli pushed back his forelock and studied his petite cousin.

Constance rubbed her forehead. "All right, out with it. What's happening?"

The young lord twiddled with the pearl buttons on his cuffs. "My staff has found out that Papa is buying up wagons of salt to scatter on your lands once he's taken control. He's stated that he's going to burn this old dump down to the ground, with you in it, if possible."

She groaned. Trusdale fought a strong urge to put his arm around her. Instead, he addressed Welli. "With respect, my lord, there's no need to be so blunt. Can't you see you're upsetting the lady?"

"The lady is fine," said Constance. "Even if I wasn't, I'd still have to know my enemy's plans. Welli has been my spy in Uncle Bertie's camp over the last year. Fortunately, our blood runs thicker than his bile."

"A spy, huh? That's dangerous work," said Trusdale.

Welli shrugged. "It's worth it. Connie is, well, like family to me. Real family, not just what our bloodlines say we are." He grinned at her.

She gave the faintest of smiles back. "You're the brother I never wanted."

"You're too kind, my lady." Welli dropped into a mock curtsey. Constance swatted him.

Trusdale chewed on his thumbnail. "Can't you talk your papa out of this? It doesn't seem right for a family to turn on itself."

"Reason has long departed father's mind on this matter. He loathes the Baron with a passion and would love to see Constance ruined. I'm sorry to say such feuds are common amongst the great families that lord over this realm."

"Doesn't seem like a good basis for government."

"I'm sure the American government runs like a well-oiled machine."

"Kinda."

Welli guffawed. "And so it goes with all who seek to rule others, whether through birth or the electoral college." He turned to his cousin. "Now, don't despair. Your fairy godmother has heard you secured an invitation to the Royal garden party tomorrow. Auntie Madge has pledged she will parade you like a prize racehorse until an eligible bachelor bids for your hand."

Trusdale's stomach knotted.

Constance sagged. "Ugh. I'd hoped to have some choice regarding my husband, but I suppose I *have* no choice."

"Don't do this," Trusdale blurted. The two aristocrats stared at him. He coughed. "I mean, you shouldn't make the decision of a lifetime on the fly, and certainly not to hang on to some dusty old house." He gazed at the flame-haired woman before him. "You should follow your heart, not—"

"My heart is here." She gestured at the house, the rose gardens, and the fields beyond. "Nothing matters but keeping the estate safe."

He bit his tongue.

"It's only a plan, Mr. Trusdale," Welli said. "If it makes you feel any better, I'm sure Connie's personality will be proof against all but the most determined suitor."

Constance scowled. "How dare you. I am charm personified."

Welli smirked. "Yes, what man isn't drawn in by a timely observation on the weather?"

"*Babett's* says that's the correct way to open a conversation with a gentleman."

"Oh, well, if *Babett's* says so, it must be true."

"Exactly. Now, I'm loath to comment on your fashion unless absolutely forced, but it does appear that your tailcoat pocket is *wriggling*."

Welli stared down at the offending pocket. "Oh Lord, I almost forgot. May I introduce you to Boudicca?" He reached into his coat pocket and pulled out a tiny bundle of tan and black fur. A disheveled puppy with curious dark eyes peeked up from his hand. Welli held the puppy out to Constance, "I know you never turn away a stray. Here, take her. She's a Yorkshire terrier. Apparently, my horse master got her to keep the rats down in the barn."

She took the puppy and cradled it in her arms. The puppy squirmed and yapped as the woman tickled its furry belly. "And you were afraid she'd get hurt?"

"No, she finished off the rats, then started bossing around the bigger dogs, not to mention the staff. She's scaring them to death. Naturally, I thought of you as the ideal mother for the little troublemaker."

"Very funny. All right, I'll take her. Cawley, prepare a bubble bath for Her Royal Cuteness, Boudicca the Yorkie, warrior queen of all tiny terriers."

Cawley groaned and stepped forward to collect the puppy.

Constance gently handed over her new charge. "I'll call her 'Boo' for short. Do you like that name, Boo?" The puppy wagged her tiny tail. "Excellent! Cawley, please add 'puppy butler' to your many roles. Provide Boo with the finest ground steak, a blanket, toys, and anything else she desires. I'll look in on her later."

"Yes, miss," he said, clearly not thrilled at the prospect of spending the evening bathing a canine.

Welli said sternly, "And, Cawley, just make sure Connie here doesn't make the dog wear any hats. I'm counting on you, Cawls. Don't let me down."

The old man sighed as the puppy set to worrying his lace cravat into shreds. He shuffled away with the wriggling dog held close against his chest.

"Are you staying for dinner?" Constance asked Welli.

"No, sorry. My apologies to you and Mr. Trusdale. I have a card game to attend. Do you play, Trusdale? We'd be happy to set one more place. The boys and I will take it easy on you."

"That's very kind of you, but I'm a little bushed."

"Another time perhaps. You're staying here?"

He nodded.

Constance said, "I'm going to put him up in the Oak Room. He'll sleep better away from the servants' hullaballoo. You know how rowdy they get with townie visitors."

"Visitors?"

"I invited a few dozen Steamwerkers to stay here for a while. The Steamwerks has gone into a security lockdown due to the kidnapping. I'm on my way now to see what mayhem my industrial guests have brought to the ballroom."

Welli's eyebrows disappeared under his forelock. "Really? A cowboy in the family wing and proletarians in the ballroom. Whatever would Godmother say?"

"You'd better not tell her. It sounds as if tomorrow will be enough of a trial as it is."

"Mum's the word, my angel dove. Well, Trusdale, I hope you enjoy your stay at the Haltwhistle Home for the Displaced. Please remember, her bark is worse than her bite. That goes for the puppy, too. I look forward to our next encounter, hopefully over a card table."

Welli bowed with an exaggerated flourish. Trusdale bowed back. He got the feeling that Welli, for all his show, was shrewder than he seemed. The young lord probably won far more card games than he lost.

Constance grumbled, "Do make sure you ride that mechanical monstrosity out through the same hole you made coming in."

"No promises, my sweet, but I'll try. I'll see you at the Prince's party tomorrow. The countess expects you to arrive at Benchley Manor by noon. She said something about your hair being a national disgrace, and her need to take you in hand with curling irons and powerful pomades. Until then, farewell."

Welli strolled over to the rearing steam horse. He stared up at it. "You know, I've no idea how to get back up there. Mind if I borrow a carriage?"

Constance clucked her tongue. "You can take the picnic carriage, but so help me, if you lose it in the card game . . ."

Welli wafted himself with an imaginary fan. "Heaven protect me from your wicked slander. I'll have you know, young miss, that I never lose. I merely lull my opponents into a false sense of security."

"You lulled two carriages and ten barrels of my best blackberry cider at your last game."

"And I shall win it all back tonight, and more besides. Farewell, dear one." Wellington sauntered away, leaving his rearing bronze stallion as a garden ornament.

Trusdale watched him stroll toward the hole in the wall.

Constance tugged on his sleeve. "Don't worry, he can make it to the stable block. It will take more than a stalled steed to stop Welli getting to a card game."

He followed her back into the house. "So, your cousin calls you Connie?"

"He's done so since I was a toddler. I can't get him to stop. Incidentally, it was a very smart move of yours not to play cards. He and his gang of rakes are little short of cardsharps. You'd have been lucky to get out of their clutches with the shirt on your back, never mind your wallet."

Trusdale smiled. That was the closest he'd come to an actual compliment from the lady of the manor.

Chapter 16: The Steamwerkers' Ball

CONSTANCE HEADED FOR THE BALLROOM at what felt like a snail's pace. The normally five-minute walk had stretched to twenty as Trusdale stopped every ten feet to peruse portraits from her rogues' gallery of ancestors. *Why is this cowboy so fascinated by my forebears?*

She tapped her boot on the parquetry. "Would you mind hurrying up? The paintings aren't going anywhere in the next few hours." She tilted her head to listen as the merry toots of a steam organ drifted through the house. "Is that a waltz? Is sounds as if our old ballroom calliope is up and running. That instrument hasn't worked in years. In fact, hedgehogs have been nesting in the drum box for the last four winters."

The American strolled to her side. "I guess the Steamwerkers took a broken steam organ as something of a challenge."

They walked into the ballroom together. The chamber was more crowded than she had ever seen it. Freestanding candelabras sculpted to mimic silver birch trees cast flickering light over at least a hundred estate staff and Steamwerkers. A row of French doors had been thrown open to the rose gardens. The cool evening air drifted in with a breath of spring over sixty perspiring dancers. They whirled beneath a vaulted ceiling decorated with silver-leaf zodiac constellations set against a midnight sky. Thousands of cut-crystal stars scattered across the dusky blue walls twinkled in the candlelight.

With a sweep of her arm, she announced in the manner of a tour guide, "Welcome to the Celestial Ballroom, Mr. Trusdale. It was constructed in the sixteenth century by the eighth Baron Haltwhistle, Edwin the Stargazer. He also built the clock tower observatory, considered a radical departure from common sense and good architecture at the time. From within its glass dome, you can see for ten miles across the estate. The heavenly view goes even further—'to the edge of forever and back again,' as Papa used to say."

Trusdale stared up at the constellation of Aries above his head. "I'd sure like to see forever. Will you take me there?"

"I didn't mean . . ." The observatory was her own personal hiding hole. Within its crystal dome, she could gaze out at the world, or retreat to an entirely different one through the pages of a good book. "That is, I should warn you, the stairs are a little rickety . . ."

"I don't mind."

"Well, isn't that lucky? How are you with heights?"

"Terrific."

She sighed. "I suppose I could take you up there later for a few minutes. The stars come into their own the closer you get to midnight."

He gazed down at her and murmured, "It's a date."

Her breath caught sharply. She drank in the flecks of violet in his far-too-blue eyes.

His lying eyes.

She folded her arms. "Speaking of dates, April the twenty-first is an excellent date, don't you agree?"

He frowned. "What's that now?"

"Honestly, Mr. Trusdale, can't you remember your own birthday?" She raised her eyebrows in mock surprise. "And you seemed to be nearly sure of it as we left the Pyrrho Club."

Confusion clouded his almost-handsome face.

In a governess-worthy tone, she said, "You categorically stated that April the twenty-first is your birthday. If so, then your star sign is Taurus." She pointed to a muscular bull snorting down from the ceiling next to Aries. "Yet your pocket watch is engraved with the constellation of Leo." She gestured toward a roaring lion leaping over the French doors. "I believe Edwin the Stargazer would concur with me that either you have stolen another man's watch, or you are fibbing about your birth date."

He groaned. "Don't tell me you've been waiting this whole time to bring this up?"

She smirked. "I wouldn't dream of telling you so. Lies fascinate me, Mr. Trusdale. I do so love a good story well told. Why don't you tell me yours?"

He pursed his generous lips. "You won't get any tales out of me, Miss Haltwhistle. Now, if you'll excuse me, I've got work to do."

"I don't excuse you, and what work?"

"Finding out if any of the Steamwerkers can shed light on Dr. McKinley's experiments. If he was whipping up invisibility serum at his laboratory, somebody might have seen something."

"Or not. Invisibility, you know. Hard to see."

He stared at her. "The process, not the end result."

Her cheeks burned. "Oh, right, of course. I knew that."

Trusdale turned to study the dancers. The distinctive break in his nose didn't entirely detract from the perfection of his chiseled jaw. Constance's head grew oddly light.

From a lack of food, perhaps? The luncheon at Le Paon Pompeux had been high on drama and low on sustenance. As Trusdale dawdled his way through the Hall's ancestral portraiture, she'd taken a moment to send word to her kitchen staff to prepare a sixteen-course dinner for two. It would be a nice welcome to aristocratic life for her newly minted 'partner,' while affording her the opportunity to bring out the good china.

Butterflies fluttered in her stomach at the prospect of seeing the main dining room staged for company. She could barely wait to see the one-hundred-foot polished mahogany table set with the Louis XIV dinner service. The golden plates would shine in the light thrown from the silver candelabras swiped from a Venetian palace by Papa. After a rigorous swatting at the hands of the housemaids, the swarm of flesh flies that roamed the south end of the dining table was unlikely to attack. Trusdale would be her first formal dinner guest since the day her father had abandoned her for good.

There were dozens of estate workers milling around the edges of the ballroom. Footmen in their green Haltwhistle livery mingled with the brown-and-white-uniformed Steamwerkers. Black-taffeta-gowned maids with frilly aprons and white mini-bowlers perched jauntily on their heads shooed grubby stable boys away from the punchbowl on a laden buffet table. Farmhands devoured pork pies and turkey legs washed down with hard cider in stoneware jugs. At the far end of the room, a line had formed to carve slices off a whole roast pig turning on a spit in the stone fireplace. Earthenware plates piled high with pork, buttered potatoes, and savory sage stuffing were held in the hands of happily munching proletarians.

Constance's mouth watered at the forbidden working-class fare. Her sixteen-course banquet would be a strictly French affair. *Babett's* asserted Parisian haute cuisine was mandatory for a lady hosting her first grown-up dinner party.

With her first grown-up guest.

Trusdale was at her heels as she worked her way through the crowd toward the thirty-two-pipe steam calliope. The Steamwerkers and estate staff bowed and curtsied as she swept by. Usually, Constance barely noticed such acknowledgments. With Trusdale right behind her, the traditional display of servility seemed rather stiff and stuffy.

She hoped he didn't think she enjoyed this.

Not that she cared what he thought.

But if she did, she wouldn't want him to get the wrong idea. This was just the way things were done in England. Did he know that?

Her concern about his level of ignorance left her as the crowd around the organ parted. A raven-haired Steamwerker was playing the calliope. Her oil-stained fingers danced across the keyboard, to the delight of a circle of onlookers. Beside the musician's boots, a basket held a family of hedgehogs lapping from a saucer of cream. Two maids sat beside the basket and cooed over the adorably spiky mother and babies.

Constance mused, "I wonder if the Steamwerkers know anything about plumbing? The kitchen staff have been asking for a pipe down into the well for ages."

Trusdale stood beside her. "You'd need a pump, not just a pipe."

"Really? Maybe you *are* the engineer I think you're not."

He scowled. "Again? You need to be more trusting."

"Of you?"

"Well, maybe not me, but somebody, someday. It's hard going through life alone." He stared almost wistfully at the jolly crowd cheering the Steamwerker's earsplitting waltz. "If these folks keep drinking at this rate, I'll be able to coax a few secrets out of them before midnight."

"That's a rather underhanded approach. I thought you'd use your natural charm, not alcohol."

He shrugged. "I use whatever works best. You don't need to approve of my methods."

"Good, because I don't. Perhaps you should offer a monetary incentive for information?"

"You can't bribe a loyalist. I'm guessing every engineer here loves the Steamwerks and all it stands for. Best just to get 'em talking about how they play a small part in the imperial machine. A little flattery here, a touch of guile there, and I might gain a few insights into what's going on in Her Majesty's laboratories."

"It sounds sneaky."

He glanced at her sideways. "I'm sure a woman with your impeccable integrity might be offended by covert actions, but the ends justify the means. We can't all skate through life on good looks and old money."

She spluttered, "Skating? More like drowning. You have no idea—"

She stopped as the nearby servants stared. Years of yelling for tea across vast rooms largely unequipped with servant bells had developed her lungs to an impressive capacity, and her voice had carried despite the cacophonous calliope.

Trusdale didn't step away. He studied her as if she were a rare butterfly, or a misprinted postage stamp.

She glowered. "Why—you're deliberately trying to goad me."

"I'm just wondering what secrets you hold so close to your corset that you can barely breathe."

"Nothing you'll find out, Mr. Trusdale."

He chuckled. "Calm down, I'm only teasing. You know, for the first time in my life, I kind of envy farmers and the like. I always wanted to get away from the land, make my way to the big cities, see the world. I wanted adventure and excitement, maybe more than a little risk. It looks to me like these folks may have had a better idea. A cottage in a valley, a woman in your arms, beer in your belly—seems like they made all the right choices in life."

Constance's heart felt as brittle as sugar glass; one tap, and she'd shatter. "They had it all, until I took charge. Fifteen generations of Haltwhistles protected this land and the people on it. Now the fields will be salted, the house razed, and everyone here will be cast out into the wilds because of my lack of a husband."

"I wouldn't count Yorkshire as the wilds exactly."

"I'm starting to think all those wretched mummies Papa dragged back from Egypt really are cursed. And not just with fly larvae. This ridiculous inheritance law is the bane of my existence. A stupid, outdated piece of nonsense that should have been struck down years ago. The Queen has a lot to answer for."

"I reckon most of the world agrees."

Their eyes met. A moment of sadness shared amidst the raucous crowd. Worry lines etched his forehead below his Stetson. She wasn't the only one holding sorrows close to the chest.

The steam calliope burst into a rousing rendition of the folk favorite, "The Ilkley Gallop." Constance stepped aside as Steamwerkers rushed by her, eager to reach the dance floor. The estate staff hurried to join the engineers. Milkmaids and shepherdesses in floral cotton dresses linked arms with lady metalworkers. The ladies formed a single line, as did the men. Stout farmers in their Sunday-best suits, liveried footmen, and welders faced their female counterparts. With the sexes organized into their respective battle lines, the top couple grasped hands and side-stepped their way down the center aisle as their fellow dancers cheered.

Trusdale said, "Maybe we both need to enjoy what we have, while we have it." He held out one black-gloved hand toward her and smiled. "Miss Haltwhistle, may I have the pleasure of this dance?"

She gaped at his outstretched palm as if it might well explode. "Surely you jest? I couldn't possibly."

He frowned. "Why not? It's your party, isn't it? Your palace, your rules?"

She imagined her heart pounding as she sidestepped down the aisle with him, his holding her hands tight, his blue eyes crinkled into a grin, as the staff roared with delight.

She shook her head. "*Babett's* makes it perfectly clear that one cannot dance with one's servants. It's just not done."

His gaze darkened, and he dropped his hand. "I'm not a servant."

"No, but they are, and you're not exactly . . ."

"Not exactly what?"

She didn't need to say it.

His mouth set into a hard line. "Forget I asked. I'd hate to upset the natural order of the classes."

"Well, quite. There are rules of propriety that one can't . . ."

He stared across the ballroom, spine as rigid as a redcoat sergeant's.

She stammered, "I don't mean to—it's just that the time and place are—I mean, I really do love to dance. Maybe one day—"

"Forget it. Let's eat." He strode toward the roast pig turning in the fireplace and stood at the end of the line of farmhands, waiting to pick up a plate.

She scurried after him. "What are you doing?"

"What does it look like? I'm gonna get dinner."

"But—I mean, you're staying in the Oak Room, as my guest, you can't just muck in here with the—you know—the—"

"With the what?"

Behind him, the line of farmhands noticed the newcomers. One by one they dropped into bows and curtsies toward her.

She set her face into a marble mask—Artemis, untouchable, implacable. "Enjoy your evening, Mr. Trusdale."

With her heart heavy but her nose held high, she swept from the ballroom and entered the glittering grandeur of the main dining room. In the romantic light cast by a dozen stolen candelabras, Constance nibbled through a sixteen-course dinner. Aside from the swarm of flesh flies that lazily circled the room, she was utterly alone.

A single tear ran down her cheek.

And dripped onto her plate of gold.

Chapter 17: The Die Is Cast

TWENTY MILES NORTH OF HALTWHISTLE Hall, Prince Lucien Albert Dunstan was unimpressed with the beauty of his nymphs. A dozen nubile maidens in togas lolled around his gold-plated chariot. The two-wheeled vehicle stood in the center of his Versailles-inspired mirrored ballroom, lit to perfection by a dozen crystal chandeliers.

Two snowy Lipizzaner stallions stomped impatiently before the chariot. Their steel-shod hooves rang off the white marble floor as blue-liveried grooms soothed the fretting beasts. Lucien held their driving reins loosely in one hand as he addressed the room. John Waterhouse, England's foremost portrait artist, stood red-faced before a dozen early party guests, a legion of servants, and three love-struck duchesses the Prince had already tired of.

The duchesses eyed the splendor of his regal frame clad in an imperial purple cloak, a gold breastplate, a scandalously short leather battle skirt, and sandals. A golden laurel wreath rested upon his long dark curls, a precursor to the crown he would soon snatch from his silver-haired granny's head. He'd look magnificent in it. Certainly, he'd cut a more aesthetically pleasing figure than Waterhouse's models-turned-nymphs.

"And this one." Lucien pointed at a raven-haired muse who had taken the London art scene by storm the prior season. "I wouldn't allow her to muck out the stables, for fear she would terrify the horses. Waterhouse, I insist you bring me better-looking women. Beauty is a gem these tawdry trolls will never wear. Such a gaggle of dowdy geese has no place being seen outside of a farmyard or a nunnery. I swear every mare in this herd must have seen at least twenty-three winters. They're well past their prime, such as it was. Some of these snaggle-toothed crones should be out on a heath stirring cauldrons, not littering up my ballroom with their putrid flesh."

Two of the offending nymphs burst into tears, sobbing onto each other's shoulders like paid mourners at a slumlord's funeral.

Lucien wrinkled his nose.

The bearded artist wiped his brow and bowed low next to his easel. "Your Royal Highness, my apologies. I see the greatest beauties of London are not fit for your royal eyes. I shall search for more personable young goddesses to decorate your—"

"And make sure the next boatload of tarts has flaming auburn locks. Redheads, every one of them, with Cupid's kettledrums I could beat a tattoo on. He cupped his hands on his chest. "I'm in the mood for some plump, pre-Raphaelite spice. Have I made myself clear?"

"Yes, my lord." The artist clapped, and the terrified nymphs fled the room.

The Prince sneered at their scantily-clad stampede. "You see what I put up with?" he bellowed, "a herd of heifers in togas. Why am I the only man in this kingdom with true taste and discernment? Why am I served tripe when I demand truffles? Why—"

A loud knock sounded from the closed French doors. In the courtyard outside, Gunter Erhard beckoned and pulled back into the shadows. Lucien's lip curled. Erhard was ruining his favorite historical artifact by his uninvited presence. The priceless mosaic the servant skulked upon had been recovered from the sunken ruins of Julius Caesar's summer villa in Stabiae, Italy. The eruption of Mount Vesuvius in AD 79 had sent an enormous tiled image of Mars, the god of war, to the bottom of the Bay of Naples. Lucien had brought it to England. Emperor Caesar's sandals had marched across the very mosaic where Erhard now lurked.

Lucien gritted his teeth. Once he took control of the throne, Erhard's head would be the first to roll in his new royal court. Who needs a badly dressed servant who keeps showing up without invitation?

He snapped his fingers, and three servants scurried to the rear of the chariot. They dropped their backs into a flight of living steps. He stomped his sandals down upon their spines as he descended to floor level.

The portrait artist bowed so low his nose almost brushed the marble floor. The Prince snapped, "I shall await your return with flame-haired nymphs, Waterhouse."

"I assume ginger wigs will suffice?"

He shot the artist an icy stare. Waterhouse paled. "My apologies. I shall send an immediate telegram to Scotland—"

"Spare me the details. I need air. Do not follow me."

He strode out of the ballroom to join Erhard. Goosebumps rose on his bare legs from the chilly night air. "Well? Is there a problem?"

"Oh no, Your Royal Highness. Everything is going precisely to plan, except—"

"I knew it. What?"

Erhard cleared his throat. "It appears that the Haltwhistle woman has allied herself with Chauhan's mysterious colleague from the ball. To find out the stranger's identity, I attempted to 'persuade' Dr. Huang to share—"

"Remind me which one is Dr. Huang?"

"The Hong Kong-born scientist. He told me—"

"Stop. What kind of persuasion?" Was there anything more interesting than the latest torture techniques? Ground glass in the eyes, wild bees in the pants, toenails ripped out as the victim turned on a spit over a low flame . . .

"I'm afraid it was merely a mild whipping with a balled rope. We'd learned our lesson from attempting to interrogate Dr. McKinley. He passed out within seconds of holding a lit candle to his feet. So, we decided to take it easier on Huang. Even so, the old goat didn't blurt out the intel we required until we threatened to break Chauhan's fingers in front of him. It seems he's fond of her. Naturally, we'll exploit that."

The Prince grimaced. "Chauhan, Huang. Couldn't the Queen hire English scientists to run the Steamwerks?"

"I believe Dr. McKinley is Scottish."

"As I said, *English* scientists. What's the point of ruling the world if we allow colonial hangers-on to squirm their way into every facet of our society? Victoria's growing tolerance for upstart crows is yet one more symptom of her senility. Do you know she even has Indian servants at Buckingham Palace? Running around, wearing pants, like they own the place."

"You'd prefer them not to be wearing . . . ?"

"I'd prefer them to stay over there, not over here. Bloody foreigners."

The Austrian flushed.

"You don't count, Erhard. You're, well, mine."

"Yes, your highness. Utterly. Completely. Nothing gives me greater pleasure than serving your illustrious personage to the best of my—"

'Yes, yes. Enough of that. Pray tell, what intelligence did the Chinaman share?"

"Ah, it seems Chauhan's mysterious companion at the ball was an American . . ."

"Ugh."

"Indeed, my Prince. He booked into the Pyrrho Club under the name 'Justice Franklin Trusdale.' Apparently, he's a noted electro-engineer who used to work with Tesla. The item Chauhan passed to him during her kidnapping is a small, triangular power source called the Enigma Key. The Swedes believe the key's energy is being harnessed by Chauhan to drive the Steamwerks GSM project."

Lucien frowned. "GSM?"

"Otherwise known as soldier snuff. One pinch can transport you to a sensory realm—"

"For God's sake, man, I know what snuff is. Why not call a spade a spade? If you mean snuff, say snuff."

Erhard cringed. "May I please offer my deepest apologies, Sire? As ever, your keen mind overtakes my humble oratory skills."

"Just get on with it."

"As you wish, Your Royal Highness. The Swedes have assured me that King Oscar's only interest in the artifact is to create an army of Swedish super-soldiers with which to support your own military expansion into the Americas."

"Hmm. I suppose we can always use more cannon fodder during the invasion. I assume we have stockpiles of snuff to keep our own boys happy?"

"A thousand acres of storage sheds, by my estimation. Enough to keep the British troops dizzy with desire to fight for their homeland for years to come."

The leather battle skirt chafed his belly. Lucien tugged at the gold-studded waistband to loosen it a couple of inches. "Then let Oscar have this Enigma Key, for now at least. Once I'm emperor, I can reclaim it at my leisure, if needed."

"Solomon could not have devised a wiser strategy."

"No doubt. I presume that you already have this wretched key safely in hand?"

Erhard shifted his weight from foot to foot. "Ah. Well, it appears that Mr. Trusdale is quite adept at keeping things under his hat. Literally. One of our assassins almost retrieved the artifact from him at the Pyrrho Club, but failed. We later attempted to fit a bomb to the bottom of Haltwhistle's carriage when she entered the glassworks, but . . ."

"Let me guess, utter failure on the part of your operatives."

Well, yes, her driver chased our men away. He's built like a brick . . . wait, how did you know the bomb wasn't planted?"

"Because I met the far-too-alive Miss Haltwhistle at the town hall this very afternoon. She was remarkably whole for a bombing victim."

"You've met her?" Erhard's mouth fell open. "The Swedes say she's a nightmare. She's paranoid, trained to avoid any and all assassination attempts, and she's never alone. Those rustic servants of hers trail her everywhere. They say—"

Lucien held up his hand. "As I said, I just met her. She's a mere slip of a girl. Apart from an unhealthy obsession with flowers, and hair that could stand a comb through it, she appears devoid of any trait that should give a professional killer pause. Have you found out why Oscar wants her dead?"

"Not yet. It appears to be a personal vendetta against her line."

Lucien chewed his lip. "Most curious. What did the Haltwhistle family do to draw a king's ire?"

"Apparently, their ability to offend is quite well-known on an international level."

"Indeed? Hmm." He rubbed his chin. "She did hold my gaze for longer than one would expect for such a low-ranked maid. As sharp as cut glass, her eyes were, greener than a . . ."

"Meadow?"

"Billiard table."

"Most poetic, Your Royal Highness. I assure you, her emerald eyes will be closed permanently by dawn, or by tomorrow lunchtime at the latest, should my agent on her estate fulfill the assigned role."

Lucien sighed. "I seem to have heard this refrain before. On the off chance your assassin fails, I've had the presence of mind to invite Constance Haltwhistle to my party tomorrow. A garden soiree should provide plenty of opportunities to end her young life."

Erhard's eyes widened. "A brilliant move."

"Naturally, and I want you to make sure that her death is spectacular enough to draw the attention of the London papers. If Baron Haltwhistle still lives and breathes upon this earth, surely, he will read the London *Times* over his morning tea. An Englishman abroad still requires the comforts of home. If his only daughter's demise doesn't bring him out of hiding, we can assume that he's deceased. That should satisfy Oscar's vendetta."

Erhard looked suitably impressed. "Such genius. I would never have dreamed of inviting her here."

"Everyone knows I enjoy the rough with the smooth. Lowborn or highborn, I find many different types of women to my taste. A girl with her natural assets could conceivably draw my eye enough to warrant a party invitation. Her death can play a part in the afternoon's entertainment."

"As you wish, Sire."

Lucien bestowed a thin-lipped smile. "My faithful Erhard, once I gain the crown my first task shall be to reward you. Why, I can almost see the coronet of an earl shining upon your brow. Great wealth, lands, and power will be yours to command."

The Austrian licked his lips. "Thank you, my lord. My ascension has been a long time coming."

"That it has. I promise you will get everything you deserve, and far more besides."

"Your Royal Highness is too kind."

"I know. It's my curse. That will be all."

Erhard bowed low. Lucien turned and strode into the ballroom. As the three brunette duchesses batted their lovelorn eyes toward him, a short, voluptuous redhead danced through his mind. Miss Constance Haltwhistle was going to make a very pretty corpse indeed.

It was such a waste.

She would have made a truly outstanding nymph.

Chapter 18:
The Morning After

TRUSDALE AWOKE IN A DARKENED room to see wooden angels glowering down from the carved canopy of a four-poster bed. His skull pounded like an angry circus bear on a big bass drum, the sure sign of a night spent drinking. In his travels. he'd many a time awoken with a hangover and unfamiliar bed companions, but angry angels were a first.

The embers of last night's log fire glowed red in a Gothic stone fireplace facing the end of the bed. The scent of burnt applewood hung in the chilly air. Velvet curtains were drawn tight over the windows. Darkness shrouded what appeared to be an oak-paneled room.

Tudor-y. Tudor-y wood. Where on Earth—?

He groaned. Haltwhistle Hall. Home of the world's strongest hard cider. The blackberry and apple brew kicked like an ornery steer. After the first five pints, he'd kind of lost track of himself.

What the heck happened last night?

He vaguely recalled asking the servants to show him to Constance's room. He almost remembered banging on her door, so that he could tell her about the information he'd gained from the Steamwerkers. Then there was a vision of Constance in a white silk dressing gown holding a brass blunderbuss and a little black-and-tan terrier yapping . . .

He shook his head. Must have been a dream. Why would he share mission intelligence with Miss Haughty Drawers after her performance in the ballroom? She reckoned she was too fine a lady to dance with him. Why, she wouldn't even take a bite of supper by his side.

To heck with her—and her little dog too.

The bear in his head drummed out a military tattoo and his cracked nose ached. He gingerly touched his neck. The knife slice that had almost ended him was crusted over and slightly itchy. *Good, it's healing nicely.* Temples thudding, he rolled onto his side and pulled a thick quilt up over his shoulders. He snuggled into the soft mattress and closed his eyes. Maybe he would feel better in a few hours. Or days. Perhaps a week of peace and quiet was exactly what he needed.

There was a knock at the door.

He uttered words unsuitable to be heard by even wooden angels and sat up. His eyes adjusted to the dull glow from the fireplace embers and he blinked, owl-like, at his clothing strewn across the floor. His boots were nowhere to be seen.

Except for his threadbare woolen socks, he was as naked as a newborn.

The knock sounded again. He rolled to the edge of the bed and stood, thumping his skull on the four-poster's solid frame. Biting his tongue, he padded across the frigid flagstone floor, scooping up his red long johns on the way. After a one-legged dance to pull them on, he opened the door.

In the limestone hallway stood two adolescent footmen in mint-green pantaloons bearing silver breakfast trays. Rays of colored light shone on the straw-haired twins through a stained-glass window ending the corridor on the left. Trusdale winced at the bright image of a rearing unicorn mare. The mythical beast, free of chains and rider, balanced upon a Tudor rose amidst a green frame of entwined ivy.

He shielded his eyes from the unicorn's light and peered around the door frame to his right. Four additional footmen stood in the hallway holding buckets of steaming hot water. Cawley served as a surly rearguard to the pantalooned parade. The footmen reviewed his choice of long red underwear with mild disdain. The straw-haired twins snickered.

Trusdale waved. "Morning, fellas."

The servants advanced. Trusdale backed into the room as they marched in. The twins set a breakfast table by the curtained windows. The other footmen made their way over to a section of Tudor wall paneling. A knothole was pushed, and the door to a hidden bathroom opened. The servants poured water from their buckets into a clawed copper bathtub. Cawley headed to the fireplace. With the breakfast table set, the straw-haired boys drew back the velvet curtains.

Trusdale blinked as morning sunlight poured into the room through the leaded windows. The view on one side of the chamber was of extensive lawns, mature trees, and a walled rose garden. Through the adjacent window a two-hundred-foot-long white-framed orangery led to a sandstone stable block. Beyond the stables, a massive bronze airship hangar stood empty. Edwin the Stargazer's clock tower bell tolled eight.

As if on cue, the boys pushed open the windows, and a fresh breeze scented with grass and a hint of roses blew into the room. Trusdale shivered in his long johns as Cawley struck a flint to light the fire.

Trusdale cleared his throat. "Thank you, Mr. Cawley, much appreciated. You know, I think you may have got the wrong impression about my taste in engravings back at the print shop. I wasn't really looking at the lady on the swing. I mean, I saw her, but I wasn't—"

Cawley creaked his way out of the room without a glance or a word.

A lanky footman pulled out the chair from the breakfast table, standing at attention behind it like a grenadier. Trusdale sighed, padded over to the chair, and sat. The footman whisked a white linen napkin onto his lap and asked curtly, "How does sir take his tea?"

"You got any coffee?"

The footman's snort confirmed the likelihood of receiving coffee was as high as finding Queen Victoria's crown hidden in the teapot.

Trusdale picked up a single fork in his right hand to begin eating. The servants studied him, apparently fascinated by his table manners. He transferred the fork to his left hand, cut with his knife in his right, then switched the fork to his right hand, ate a mouthful, and repeated the process. So adept was he at the star-spangled fork flip that in less than two minutes, he'd shoveled down every morsel of the fried eggs, lean bacon, pork sausages, baked beans, black pudding, sliced tomatoes, and sautéed mushrooms.

The servants seemed impressed at his speed. Or amazed. Or bemused. English faces seemed to hold a unique ability to freeze into a faint smile that camouflaged all emotion that lay beneath. No wonder the Queen's spies were the best in the business.

He pushed back his plate, satiated by a week's worth of protein. "So, is Miss Haltwhistle up yet?"

The lanky footman said, "Yes, sir. Apparently, she had some 'trouble' sleeping. She called for her chestnut Arab to be saddled at five and was last seen galloping across the moors by the estate gamekeeper."

Trusdale could envision the red-haired woman, her long mane streaming behind her as she raced a horse of pure fire across the heather. But he didn't care for the way the footman said "trouble" and glared. That image of Constance in her night attire armed with a blunderbuss, and a little dog yapping. It had only been a dream, right?

His left ankle hurt. He reached down, running his hand over a grazing just behind the bone. It felt like a series of tiny dog bites.

He frowned.

And where exactly were his boots?

Twenty minutes later, he stood in his socks outside Constance's bedroom, debating whether to knock on her door. The stained-glass unicorn window cast a rainbow of light over the hallway's yellow limestone walls. Beside the iron-studded Gothic door hung a muted tapestry of mounted female archers chasing a stag across a field of flowers. The tapestry looked familiar, as if he'd studied it in some detail before.

He leaned his throbbing forehead against the thick, dark planks of the door.

He'd never drink again.

Or at least, he'd never drink Haltwhistle Hall's hard cider.

Not on a Wednesday, anyway.

There was no sound within. The servants had been unsure whether Constance was inside her room or still out riding the moors. He'd sent them all away. If he owed Constance an apology for waking her in the night, he'd rather not have to make it in front of an audience.

It occurred to him that he'd never spent a single moment alone with the Baron's daughter. Even on their long carriage rides together, Cawley and Hearn had no doubt eavesdropped on every word between them. Maybe she'd warm up a little if it was just the two of them? Perhaps they'd laugh about the night before?

He straightened his Stetson. On the other hand, maybe she'd shoot him with her fancy blunderbuss. She could have his body dumped in a ditch within the hour. Who would ever betray her out here, in the middle of her own personal kingdom?

There was a faint rustle within the room. He knocked, yanked the knot on his neckerchief straight, and tugged down his best silk vest. In his cleanest shirt, black cotton frock coat, and gray woolen pants, he was a proper American gentleman from the ankles up. Save for the holes in his socks and the cold sweat running down his spine, he'd have caught the eye of any fine lady in Boston with a taste for a Western-styled man. Especially with his majestic black Stetson pulled down firmly on his head.

It was a matter of national security that he rarely took off his hat, no matter the social etiquette about wearing a hat indoors. It was an easy task for the average cutpurse to pick a man's pockets, but no one could ever steal a hat from his head without his noticing. It was his favorite hiding place for secret codes and Maya's curiously tingly artifact. The triangle had started to vibrate gently against his skull from the moment he'd entered Haltwhistle Hall. It was more of a tickle than a sting, and not altogether unpleasant. At times it was almost a whisper, melodic and soothing. It sure felt a whole lot better than his headache, which was starting to take on a life of its own as a malevolent force in his skull.

A metallic clunk sounded within the room.

So, she was in there. Maybe she hadn't heard his knock? Or maybe she was pretending not to have heard?

The tension was killing him. It was now or never.

He pounded on the door, jittering the latch loose. The door swung inward with a creak that set his teeth on edge. As a host of servants didn't come running to defend their mistress's chamber, he peered around the door.

The bedroom was flooded with sunshine streaming in through the leaded windows. There were none of the dark-stained oak panels that dominated his room. Here, a riot of floral wallpaper exploded across the walls with splashes of gold, red, and blue. A four-poster bed sprouted a plush green quilt. On the mirrored bedside table, a vase of orange blossoms cast a sweet, exotic scent. A neat pile of books beside the vase revealed Constance's interests in gardening and modern farm techniques. A white marble fireplace bore a jumble of golden trophies topped by pigs and ponies, proof of her success in the show ring.

A wallpaper-covered door to a bathroom stood ajar, but there was no sign of Constance.

On the bed lay a scattering of untouched dog toys and one very well-chewed Western boot.

How did the new puppy get ahold of my boot? Trusdale strode into the room to claim his footwear, halting at a rustle inside the bathroom. Probably the puppy, Boo, destroying something else. Maybe the tiny terrier was gnawing on his other boot?

He tiptoed to the bathroom door. Inside the white marble chamber, a blond maid, built like an Amazonian, was barely contained in her black-and-white uniform. She poured white powder from a green box into a silver claw-foot bathtub filled with steaming water. A dozen empty water jugs stood next to the tub on the polished marble floor. He read the words on the maid's box of powder: *Ablethorpe's Super-Concentrated Arsenic. Beware! Poison!*

Admittedly, Constance was a bit of a pill, but still . . .

He drew back. The maid might have heard him knock on the door, but if so, she'd most likely have assumed that with no response from within, he'd moved on. In which case—

The dull whine of an illegal incendiary pistol came from the bathroom. He threw himself face-first at the floor, jarring his cracked nose.

A sizzling foot-wide flame ray exploded through the door with a thunderous boom. Smoking splinters rained down on his back, burning hot through his coat. The smell of scorched wood filled his nose as the flame ray blasted through the opposing wall into the adjacent rooms.

Ears ringing from the explosion, he scrambled across the Persian rugs and took shelter under the bed. There, he found the grisly remains of his other boot. The Yorkshire terror, Boo, had struck again.

Black ankle boots clattered out of the bathroom. The maid headed for the stone corridor holding her gun in one hand and her voluminous skirts up in the other.

He rolled out from under the bed and bounded for the hallway. As he burst out the door, the whine of the pistol kicked in, and an orange blast of heat shot past his head. The flame ray seared down the corridor and shattered the stained-glass unicorn window into a thousand colored shards.

Trusdale cringed, shielding his eyes from the glass splinters. He didn't know how attached Constance was to her Tudor windows, but he guessed an unscheduled demolition would to do little to improve her disposition toward him.

He scrambled back into the bedroom and slammed the door. Behind the door was a wall-mounted gun rack that held five exquisite brass blunderbusses. Each weapon was styled as a different trumpet-flared flower: honeysuckle, fuchsia, lily, foxglove, and petunia. A maker's mark of a crown on a cog by the serial number 001 was stamped on each polished barrel. The sleek lines of the weapons made the high-end Orphanator firearms look as old-fashioned as wooden clubs.

He whistled and grabbed the petunia. It was light and balanced, the brass as smooth as glass to his fingertips. On the right of the rack, a shelf that should have held buckshot for the brass blooms stood empty, save for a crystal bowl of white rock-salt pellets. Constance seemed to like fine guns and nonlethal ammunition. *How curious.* Rock salt wasn't much of a defense. *Heck, I may as well head out there with a pillow and hope the maid has a colossal feather allergy.* Still, beggars couldn't be choosers.

He poured the salt crystals into the petunia, cocked the hammer, and yanked open the oak door. As the dull whine of the incendiary pistol began to build, he stepped out into the corridor and pulled the trigger.

Chapter 19: Heads Will Roll

AFTER A SLEEPLESS NIGHT, EXHAUSTED by a new puppy and a tipsy American, Constance was not in the best of moods. Her mother had always told her that a lady never showed anger. Presumably, that lady had never met one J. F. Trusdale, if that was his real name, which she doubted. Hopefully, the telegrams she had sent from the Pyrrho Club to her American contacts would soon reveal the truth about Mr. Tall, Dark, and Almost Handsome.

She stomped through the long glass orangery in her most severe black riding habit. Her no-nonsense top hat and veil, straitlaced corset, and baronial ermine shrug should warn the world that she was not one to be trifled with. The effect was somewhat ruined by Boo pouncing on her long silk skirt as it brushed along the slate floor.

Morning sunshine shone down through the glass panes of the white-framed hothouse. A gentle hiss of steam pipes filled the humid air with moisture and warmth. Ten neat rows of Valencia orange trees in terra-cotta pots seemed to stand at attention as she swept through their ranks. She adored the sheer competence of an orange tree. Few trees could produce glossy evergreen foliage, fragrant white blossoms, and sweet, juicy fruit simultaneously. They epitomized nature at the very top of her game.

As far as her corset allowed, she took in a deep breath of the citrus-perfumed air. The scent was so pleasant, she wavered for a moment on the cusp between bad temper and good humor.

An explosion from the family wing tipped the scale firmly to the negative. Her jaw dropped as a sizzling, foot-wide ray of flame exploded through the sandstone wall of the second floor of her home. The flame ray faded into the sunshine as it reached the edge of its range.

What on earth?

A second flame ray blasted through the stained-glass unicorn window that had been a gift to her family from Queen Elizabeth I.

The dull boom of a blunderbuss followed.

If the servants have got drunk in the gun room again, so help me, heads will roll. She was in no mood to deal with the estate staff, or the people who chose to eat with them.

The gunfire continued, making its way through the house. Servants screamed damage reports to each other in increasingly hysterical tones, and the ding-dong of the fire bell rang out across the estate.

Constance sighed and pulled an orange off the closest potted tree. She began to peel the ripe fruit, its thick, dimpled skin weighing heavily in her palm.

Whatever was going on, she could wait until the shooting stopped before wading in. She'd learned the hard way that terminating the employment of an armed servant rarely went well. Being shot in the backside with rock salt for the third time this month was a fate worth avoiding. It was to prevent more serious injury to her person that she'd banned metal ammunition from the estate. Somehow, the move assuaged her occasional guilt about designing the world's finest weapons as the Brass Queen. It was the ammunition that caused harm, not the guns.

Most days, she almost believed this was true.

Her new lady's maid—*Astrid? Agnes? Enid? I really should pay more attention to these things*—sprinted into the orangery as if chased by an angry pack of Mr. Orwell's Security Sheep. Flocks of the vicious sentry sheep guarded the outskirts of the Haltwhistle estate against poachers. *Surely the sheep haven't got into the house again?* The staff had been traumatized for weeks after the last woolly assault. Commando sheep had holed up in the music room for the best part of a week until coaxed out with a wagon of fresh lettuce. The sheep had been unbearably smug since their victory.

Fortunately, no sheep appeared on the maid's heels. The blonde servant sprinted across the slate floor. As she ran, her long black skirt flew up, showing an indecent amount of white petticoat. The maid raised one arm and pointed what appeared to be an incendiary pistol at Constance. A power dial glowed red on the side of the weapon.

I'm almost sure that maid is called Edith . . .

An empty click sounded, and the servant hurled the spent pistol at Constance's head.

Confident of the gun's exact weight, mass, and trajectory, Constance made the barest of sidesteps. The pistol narrowly missed her cheek and rattled across the floor as she stepped back into the orange trees and pulled out her trusty stiletto hairpins.

Of all the nerve! She could barely believe King Oscar was using a Brass Queen original against her. She'd designed the Värmedöden pistol so that Oscar's personal guard could clear escape routes through walls in an ambush situation, not for use on people. She'd been absolutely clear on that matter in the contract. Did he have no shame?

Astrid, Edith, or Agnes shot right by her and headed for the trapdoor that led down to the treasure vaults beneath the orangery. Boo ran after the fleeing maid, yapping fiercely and snapping at her ankles.

Constance's small amount of patience evaporated into the humid air. Falling cages, carriage bombs, incendiary guns. Just how many indignities must she suffer to get through this week alive?

She had just stepped out of the orange trees when a heavy body slammed into her and sent her flying. She crumpled into an inelegant heap with her top hat pushed down over her eyes. Before she could catch her breath, a man's hand dragged her roughly to her feet.

Trusdale lifted her hat and stared down at her with annoyed concern. "Sorry, I'm after your maid. Whatever you do, don't bathe."

With that, he sprinted after her attacker, down through the vault trapdoor, with Boo barking at him the entire way.

Oh yes. So help me, heads will roll.

Chapter 20: Dead Egyptians

TRUSDALE SPRINTED ALONG A NARROW stone passageway after the maid. The light from the trapdoor soon dwindled, and darkness closed in. He slowed as the maid's footsteps began echoing loudly, indicating she'd entered a larger chamber ahead. Then her footsteps stopped. Maybe she was waiting for him in the darkness, gun in hand.

No point in rushing up there to get his head blown off.

He walked slowly, tracing his right hand along the rough limestone wall. The passageway was scored with centuries-old chisel marks from workers long dead. Through the holes in his woolen socks, the rock floor was as cold as a tombstone. An odd smell permeated the air—embalming fluid? Rotting books? Something metallic, something—wrong. He shivered, pulling his frock coat tight.

An odd tingle of heat pulsed through his hatband. He took off his Stetson and slipped out the one-inch triangle of Maya's artifact.

The smooth, black metal warmed his palm. A tickle in his mind murmured to him. He peered at the triangle, lifting it close to his eyes as a blue light flickered from its core. That was a new trick.

Footsteps came up behind him. Trusdale turned, holding the metal triangle up as a light source in the dark. The dim blue glow showed Constance, in a dented top hat and carrying an orange, glaring at him.

She said, "Hearn and Cawley are on their way. The maid can't get out of the treasure chamber, so we may as well wait for their assistance. May I ask, where did you get that?" She pointed at the glowing triangle.

Any sane person would have asked what it was, not where he got it.

That said, honesty was probably his best policy, for now at least. When you were chasing a homicidal servant down a dark, creepy passageway, even a snooty Englishwoman was better than no backup at all. "It belongs to the Steamwerks. Maya Chauhan passed it to me in the middle of the kidnapping."

"But where did she get it from? My father traveled half the world to find the Enigma Keys, and he never managed to find a blue one. They're beyond rare. He started to think they were a myth."

Trusdale gaped at her. "You know what this is?"

"Of course. The keys are fragments of ancient technology that was once used to tear the veil between dimensions. They're scattered throughout the deepest, darkest places of the Earth."

His headache upped its game to a pounding migraine. "Ancient what now? And who exactly made these—keys?"

"Ah, well, that's the mystery, isn't it? Ghosts? Creatures that live far beyond the range of any telescope? Superintelligent aardvarks from the core of the earth with a taste for interdimensional travel? My father believes they were made by humans, perhaps even alternate versions of ourselves. There are entire worlds that live in the same space we inhabit, separated from us by the merest whisper of time and circumstance. Perhaps in one of those worlds, you're asking a better question while wearing more suitable attire."

"Such as?"

"Perhaps a nice tweed cloak and a deerstalker?"

"I mean, which question should I—"

"Oh, right. Tweed-cloaked Trusdale would probably ask, 'What are the Steamwerks doing with an Enigma Key?' Is it the snuff? I always suspected a hint of dimensional shenanigans there. You take a pinch of this world, add a dash of its mirror realities, and poof! Mental transportation without physical movement. Child's play, really. You'd think they'd—"

Her eyes widened as he leaned down close to her. She took a step back.

"Miss Haltwhistle, I beg you, focus. Is the key dangerous? Could it be used as a weapon? Could it power something that might invade or destroy the US?"

"Yes, definitely, but why would the Steamwerks want to invade or destroy the US?"

"Empress Victoria's ambitions are legendary."

"Pfft. So's her ability to keep what she has. Maya was always talking about how Victoria's resources were stretched wafer-thin across the empire. Of course, she might have just been angling for a better price on my—umm—farm goods. The Steamwerks are one of my best customers."

"But this key—with it, Victoria could, I don't know, do something awful?"

She tapped her chin. "Power tends to corrupt even the best of us. To be safe, you should give me the key. I guarantee I can put it somewhere Her Royal Highness will never find it."

"I don't think so." He slipped the triangle into his left vest pocket. Blue light pulsed through the silk, as if he'd captured a lightning bug from another world. "You seem to have a knack for attracting trouble. Speaking of which, any idea why your maid just dumped a box of arsenic in your bathtub?"

She shrugged. "Who knows what goes on in the minds of maids? Her apparent animosity toward me does explain the acid in my soup last week. Then she 'accidentally' stabbed me with a letter opener, but my underwear got the better of her. I ask you, is there anything worse than an incompetent assassin?"

"A competent one?"

"Well, yes. Good point."

He gazed into her emerald eyes. She looked away. He said, "Please, tell me the truth. Why is this woman trying to kill you?"

Constance scuffed the ground with her boot. "Fine. Not that it's any concern of yours, but I believe it relates to a misunderstanding over a delivery of farm goods to one of my European customers."

"Farm goods? Really?"

Her right eye twitched. "Um, I think it was sausages. Rather than accepting my explanation, my customer thought fit to seize another customer's shipment. Let's just say it would take more than a poorly equipped expeditionary force to steal my sausages."

"You're not making much sense."

"When does war make sense? Needless to say, I retrieved most of my—sausages, and Oscar has been sulking about the matter ever since. He thought he could do as he wished because he's royalty, but no one cheats a Haltwhistle."

"Wait—are you talking about King Oscar of Sweden?"

"Oh, do you know him?"

He blinked at her. "Ah, no, we don't run in the same social circles. But the woman who tried to kill me at the Pyrrho Club spoke Swedish, and your blond maid sure has a Scandinavian look to her."

"I hadn't noticed."

"You're not much of a people person, are you?"

"It depends on the people." The scent of oranges drifted up from her hands. She finished peeling the fruit and popped a segment into her mouth before noticing his stare.

She flushed. "Oh, I'm sorry, would you like a piece? They call the Seville 'the King of Oranges,' you know. They're a touch bitter but quite marvelous for the digestion."

He shook his head. The Enigma Key was officially no longer the strangest thing in the corridor. That prize went to Constance.

Back toward the trapdoor, a tiny flame flickered in the darkness. A faint hiss of gas echoed along the rock passageway.

Constance commanded, "Let there be light." Gas lamps burst into life along the passageway, one golden sconce at a time.

Trusdale blinked as the rough stone passage came into view. Cawley and Hearn walked up, faces grim. Cawley carried the petunia blunderbuss Trusdale had dropped in the house when it ran out of shot, along with a bag of rock-salt pellets.

Their mistress said, "Well met. Let's see if we can find this murderous maid, shall we?"

Trusdale led the way. The passageway opened into a vast cellar with a Gothic rib-vault ceiling. Sparse pools of golden gaslight exposed the shadowy outlines of hundreds of wooden crates, both large and small.

Dark mounds of ancient history spilled around the crates. Mesopotamian statues of naked winged gods lay next to Sumerian pottery and Babylonian shields. Gold Aztec altars were strewn with Viking helmets and Tibetan monastery bells. Books and scrolls in unknown languages were half-buried in mounds of gold coins, jewels, and caskets of ivory and jade. A life-size golden chariot of Ramses III was drawn by three silver-winged horses ornamented with ruby eyes. Egyptian sarcophagi were stacked along the stone walls; some were partially open to reveal their colorfully painted interiors and the drab mummies within.

Constance said, "My father's junk room. The only thing worse than the mess is the dust. None of the maids will clean in here. They're afraid the mummies will attack them. Total hogwash of course." She kicked a gold death mask across the flagstone floor with a clatter.

The riches of a thousand lost civilizations. Trusdale blew out his cheeks. "I guess one empire's junk is another empire's treasure."

Constance screwed up her nose. "The important artifacts are locked safely away in Papa's personal vaults, not here. These are just souvenirs from his early dimensional travels. Back before Mother died and he got obsessed with the Enigma Keys. Incidentally, yours hasn't spoken to you, has it?"

He gaped at her. "How could it possibly—?"

"Ah, of course not. Takes proper training to hear them. Mind you, gin helps."

"What on Earth are you—?" Trusdale stopped as he heard the unmistakable whine of an electrical pistol deep within the shadows of the cellar. One of J. F.'s old designs, if he wasn't mistaken. He yelled, "Watch out!" and pulled Constance with him into cover behind a stone sarcophagus. The two servants scurried behind another sarcophagus.

"All safe? Good," he whispered. "All right, I'm gonna make a commotion and draw her fire. Hearn, you see if you can work your way down and get behind her."

Constance said, "Who made you king all of a sudden? If it's me she's trying to shoot, I should be the one drawing fire."

"Trust me, I know what I'm doing."

Constance pursed her lips. "I doubt that—and where's your tiny gun?"

"It's in my room, and it's not tiny, it's a concealed weapon. I—"

The sarcophagus exploded as a blast of white lightning punched through it. The force blew him to the ground in a cloud of stone dust and burning mummy fragments. The taste of ancient bandages filled his mouth, ashy and dead.

He pushed himself up from the cold floor and tried to shove Constance into better cover. She resisted him, straining to reach the downed Cawley. Hearn dropped to his knees and cradled the elderly man's head in his hands.

Cawley was prone but unhurt. He croaked to Trusdale, "Excellent judgement on the cover, sir."

"You're welcome." Trusdale gently pried the petunia blunderbuss from Cawley's grasp, jostled Constance firmly behind some stacked crates, and took off sprinting toward the dull whine of the recharging electro-gun.

He leaped over a golden Byzantine casket fit for an emperor. Behind the casket, the maid was ready for him, her back pressed against a stack of brightly painted mummy coffins.

She fired. As he suspected, the gun took a full second to release its lethal electrical charge. He dropped and rolled away as the lightning blasted into the vaulted ceiling.

For a moment, the electrical storm danced along the Gothic ribs of the cellar roof. Then the ceiling shuddered, and centuries-old architecture collapsed in a thunderous explosion of rock and dust on top of the maid.

Trusdale covered his head as rubble thudded onto his back. He lay still, trying not to breathe in the stone dust. When all was quiet, he staggered to his feet.

The maid had been crushed beneath the rock.

Constance picked her way over to him through the debris of the fallen roof and the orangery above. She studied the mound of fruit trees and rock that marked the grave of her former attacker, then glanced back at her servants. They were dusting off each other's coats by the cellar entrance.

She murmured, "It's so hard to hire the right staff these days, isn't it?"

Chapter 21: Rough Brute

AN HOUR LATER, TRUSDALE SAT in the driver's box of the dragon carriage, sandwiched between Hearn and Cawley. Four chestnut ponies snorted steam into the chill morning air as they trotted away from Haltwhistle Hall. The clop of their hooves on the gravel driveway drew curious stares from snowy-white sheep grazing in the rolling green meadows. A bracing breeze laced with the earthy scents of heather, sheep, and grass threatened to blow away his hat. He pushed the Stetson down tight. The tingle from the artifact tucked inside the lining diminished with every passing mile.

Constance had "suggested" that he travel in the driver's box, while she sat alone in the rear of the carriage, surrounded by trunks and hatboxes. Only his suitcase and Boo, the puppy, shared her solitude. Ostensibly, there was no room for him in the rear, but he knew the real reason why he was up front with the servants.

The Baron's daughter was not pleased with him.

Not pleased at all.

He'd assumed that if truly angered, she would bellow a few insults his way. Instead, her order to ascend to the driver's box had put him firmly in his place. Then she'd ordered Hearn to drive to the Steamwerks Exhibition Dome—the very spot where she'd first ran into him. *What's her plan—to dump me there and drive off? Where's her gratitude? Haven't I just saved her from a murderous maid?*

Admittedly, he'd destroyed priceless heirlooms during his gunfight with the maid, and brought down the roof of her family treasure vault, but she'd claimed she didn't care about the hoard of riches anyway. So, other than all that, everything was peachy.

He cleared his throat.

Hearn shot him a warning glance. "Hush, best keep your voice down. We don't want to annoy Miss Constance. Cawley says we're all in trouble as it is."

Trusdale muttered, "Why?"

Hearn said, "Apparently, me and the old man are incompetent, and you're a rough brute. She said you shoved her about in the cellar without so much as a by-your-leave. And she wasn't too thrilled about you poking around her bedroom when she wasn't there, never mind touching her petunia. Now, keep it down, or she'll hear us."

"I had good reason to touch her—never mind. Why does she think you're both incompetent?"

Cawley muttered, "That maid had weapons stashed in the vault. We didn't find them when we searched down there last week for a ruby tiara Miss Constance wanted to wear about the house. Loves a fancy hat, she does. No special occasion required. Anyway, the maid must have hidden her guns well, because we never saw them."

Hearn added, "Hopefully, we'll see no more assassins on Haltwhistle lands. I tell ya, it's lucky Miss Constance don't get scared too easy. An attempted poisoning or shooting don't worry her none. Mind you, if you leave a waistcoat button unfastened in town, she'll throw a blue fit."

"So, she's not easy to work for?"

To his surprise, Cawley chuckled. "Nay, lad, I wouldn't say that. It's all relative with the bluebloods. She's the best of the Haltwhistles I've served by far. Less temper than her father, more sense than her mother. The estate would have done a lot worse without her taking the reins. She's risen to the challenge like a, well, like something that rises to a challenge."

Hearn nodded. "Aye, well said."

Cawley continued, "I won't say she's a gentle soul, but there's a warm heart beneath that tough exterior."

Hearn nodded. "Poor lamb, all alone in the world, save for her cousin Welli. Lord Pendelroy isn't a bad fella, for a rake, a fop, and a poet."

"And where exactly is her father, the Baron?" asked Trusdale.

Cawley and Hearn exchanged glances. Hearn said, "Buggered off, that's all we'll tell you. And none of us servants want her to wed a stranger for our sakes."

Trusdale rubbed his jaw. "I don't see why the local lords aren't lined up around the block to marry her. She's prickly, it's true, but—"

"The problem is, Mr. Trusdale," said Cawley, "fiery gals aren't too popular with the gentry. I don't just mean her hothead temperament, although that doesn't help; I mean her hair. Some folks don't want red-haired offspring running underfoot. It's all a bit too 'Celtic barbarian' for the fancy set."

Trusdale shook his head. "There's no accounting for taste. I love the way her hair glints brighter than a new penny in the sun—"

He stopped, aware that Cawley and Hearn were both staring at him. "I mean to say, it's a shame some people judge others by such things as hair color or style."

Hearn twirled the end of his walrus mustache with one meaty hand. "Oh, I dunno. I know I've had much better luck with the ladies since I grew this mustache. The bigger it is, the more irresistible I become."

Cawley snorted. "That's not what I've heard. Now, Mr. Trusdale, I've got to tell you something. All that nonsense in the vault with the assassin was a rum do, and no mistake. It gets a man to thinking—" The old man stared off across the fields, his rheumy eyes misty. He murmured, "You're not all bad, Mr. Trusdale. Not the sort of person we'd usually want around Miss Constance, but you did all right against that lightning gun. If you hadn't got us into cover behind that stone coffin, we'd be as crispy as battered cod."

"True," said Hearn. "And all that leaping about like a madman—"

"Oh aye, the leaping was grand. And Hearn and me wouldn't have charged face-first at an assassin unarmed and outgunned. It takes a real hero to be so daft. We both agreed, you did well back there, lad. Far better than we could ever have expected from a non-Yorkshireman."

Trusdale bowed his head to what was clearly a heartfelt compliment. Cawley smiled toothlessly.

Hearn whistled. "Well, blow me down, Cawley. You aren't being pleasant to a foreigner, are you?"

"Sod off, you bald turnip."

Hearn laughed. "Aye, that's more like it. Thought you were getting as soft as that puppy Miss Constance started carrying around."

"That damned dog's bitten everybody in the house except herself," said Cawley gravely. "Gawd knows what it would be like if it was an inch or two bigger. And talking about soft, I saw you chatting up that engineer woman in the rose garden 'til all hours."

Hearn grinned through the gap in his front teeth. "Master Welder Emily Lambert. Ah, Emily, a rose any other name would smell as sweet. Or is it a nose? A nose by any other name . . . either way, I talked her into stepping out for a walk with me sometime. She said she's curious to see whether my personality gets any better when I'm not drunk."

Trusdale chuckled. "So, that sounds . . . promising?"

"Oh, aye, very promising I should think."

Cawley sniffed. "It won't last. These things never do."

"Oh shut up, you old trout," Hearn said to Cawley. He whispered to Trusdale, "He's been down on love since the cook dumped him two months back."

Cawley glowered. "She did not. We had a parting of ways."

"I heard she threw a roast pheasant at your head."

"Aye, well, that was the end of it. You don't throw a man's dinner around like that. Very unprofessional kitchen behavior, that is." The old man folded his arms and glared across the meadows.

Trusdale said, "While we're on the subject of poor behavior, I didn't do anything . . . embarrassing, last night, did I?"

Hearn and Cawley burst out laughing, then shushed each other.

Trusdale frowned. "Really? I was that bad? I swear I don't remember much of anything. Did I wake up Miss Constance?"

Hearn said, "Aye, you could say that. She had half a dozen maids in there with her helping her sort through her old dresses. She was set on stitching together a costume for that garden party she's going to this afternoon. You wanted to speak to her alone, which wasn't going to happen. When the servants refused to leave, you got into an altercation with that dog of hers, fell facedown on the rug, and started crooning. Apparently, you're quite the songbird when drunk."

Trusdale groaned. Lord help him, he'd tried to serenade her. He'd done that before when a lady caught his eye, but in Kansas, no one thought twice about a little serenading after a night out on the town. The gals there kinda liked it.

He put his head in his hands. He couldn't imagine Constance appreciating a down-home tune. No wonder she'd pulled out her blunderbuss. His shoulders sagged as the carriage rumbled on.

Hearn clapped him hard on the back. "Don't worry, son, Miss Constance rarely sulks for more than a day, even with a list of crimes as long as yours. By tomorrow, she'll no doubt be talking to you again, whether you like it or not. By the way, I reckon I owe you an apology, Mr. Trusdale."

"How's that?"

"I should have stopped you from downing that tenth pint of blackberry cider last night," said Hearn. "Our purple nectar is far stronger than it looks. We grew up on it, but for an out-of-towner, it's nothing but trouble. Seems all warm and mellow, then bang! You're off playing the bagpipes nude on top of one of the turrets."

Cawley said, "Oh, shut up. That was only because it was Christmas." He leaned close to Trusdale. "I only play the bagpipes at Christmas."

Hearn guffawed. "It wasn't the bagpipes people objected to."

The carriage rolled to a stop outside the Steamwerks Exhibition Dome. The dome was partly shrouded by tarpaulins. Scaffolding supported a dozen workmen who toiled to repair the damage caused by the airship attack.

Cawley whistled. "Oh, it looks far worse in the daylight."

Hearn nudged Trusdale in the ribs and said, "That's what they said about him playing the bagpipes."

They all jumped as Constance yelled from the back of the carriage, "So, I'll just climb down by myself, shall I?"

Cawley almost flew off the driver's seat to open the door for her.

Hearn pushed Trusdale to get out of the carriage.

Trusdale said, "Wait, Hearn, why are we here?"

"Didn't she tell you? Apparently, you lot are breaking into the Steamwerks."

Chapter 22: A Foolproof Plan

CONSTANCE'S PLAN WAS FOOLPROOF. THE only problem was that the fools she needed to help her carry out the plan had their own opinions, and that just would not do.

It was almost ten, and the sun glinted off the crystal architecture of the Royal Steamwerks Exhibition Dome. They stood at the entrance to one of the dome's eight display halls, which splayed out like tentacles on a giant crystal octopus. A steady beat of workmen's hammers, with an occasional crash of falling glass, filled the air. Birds sang sweet melodies from the pine forest that bordered the glass hall. The chestnut ponies stomped impatiently in front of the dragon carriage as Constance squared off against Trusdale, Cawley, and Hearn.

Trusdale stood his ground in puppy-chewed boots, his Stetson tilted low and arms folded.

Cawley had a new addition to his livery, a wicker basket strapped against his hip. The basket was filled to the brim with three-inch

Christmas baubles in a rainbow of colors. Each snowflake-painted glass ornament held a secret cargo of gentian violet and ink, in case of invisible attackers.

Hearn held the carriage ponies' harness, his shoulders hunched as if he were trying to make himself invisible through sheer will.

Constance faced the trio with her head held high. They'd have to capitulate to her rank and mission-appropriate fashion sense. She'd chosen the perfect ensemble for a spot of industrial espionage. Her purple top hat provided a sturdy platform for mirrored-lens brass goggles with built-in thermometer, barometer, altimeter, and compass. A violet silk gown with puffed sleeves, a high frilled neck, and a voluminous skirt provided ample protection against ink splatters from Cawley's baubles. A jet-black corset cinched her waist and camouflaged the bulk of her chain mail underwear.

Sadly, the two smoke grenades she had stuffed into her bustle bag were far heavier than she'd anticipated. The grenades were part of her defense array which included stiletto hairpins, steel-toed boots, and her brass blunderbuss. A black wicker hip basket on a low-slung belt held her supply of rock-salt ammunition. The Brass Queen was fully prepared for battle, once she'd put down the revolt in her own ranks.

She roared, "This isn't up for debate!"

The men gaped at her. To keep them off balance, she switched to a softer tone. "Mr. Trusdale, I apologize for breaking your confidence in public, but you said Maya had a secret passage running from her laboratory to the Exhibition Dome. We're going to pop into the passage, enter the Steamwerks labs, and search for any clues McKinley might have left behind. Simple, quick, and easy. It's a splendid plan, and it's what we're doing."

She waited for the trio to concede. For some reason, everyone was remarkably unsupportive of her brilliance today.

Hearn and Cawley studied the ground, as all servants did when they felt their employer was officially off the deep end.

She glowered at them. They'd spent one hour in the driver's box with Trusdale and now were practically republican rebels. "Look, I'm heading to the Duke of Hallamshire's garden party this afternoon. Everyone who's anyone in high society will be there. Some local wag is bound to bring up the kidnapping. It would be nice if I could honestly say that concrete progress has been made toward apprehending the villains responsible. Then all I have to do is change the subject, dazzle everyone with my scintillating conversation, and before you know it the lords will be lining up to propose to me. I've researched local weather predictions for the next ten days, so I'll have plenty to talk about. Everyone here should be cheering this bold step forward in my perfect Plan."

The men remained silent. She shouted, "For heaven's sake, don't you want to find the scientists? Dr. McKinley may be wrapped up in this invisibility serum nonsense, but Maya and Huang are guiltless. And we have all morning to search McKinley's laboratory. I mean, honestly, gentlemen, how hard can this be?"

"Nope," said Trusdale.

She scowled at him. "What do you mean 'nope'? That's not even a word, never mind an argument."

"It means no. Now, I realize that's not a word you've heard much of in your highfalutin' life."

Hearn and Cawley groaned and fidgeted with their harness and baubles respectively.

Trusdale continued, "But there is no way I'm gonna break into the Steamwerks. Absolutely no way."

She set her jaw. "Who said this is a break-in? We'll just take a quick look around McKinley's laboratory. Nothing will be broken, I assure you."

He shook his head. "Do you understand that the Steamwerks produces primarily military hardware? That means guards, security systems—"

"Oh for heaven's sake, no one is there. The Steamwerkers were evacuated in the lockdown. Many of them are sleeping off hangovers in my ballroom right now."

"They are not the guards. Do you think a lockdown means they just put a big padlock on the gate and sent everyone home?"

Actually, that was exactly what she thought. Trusdale's logic was added to the list of things that annoyed her about him today. She tapped her boot on the gravel driveway and contemplated the reflection of clouds in what remained of the Exhibition Dome.

Trusdale turned to Hearn and Cawley. "You two can't possibly think this is a good idea?"

Her face burned hotter than a Madras curry, a popular delicacy at Le Paon Pompeux. "Oh, Britain is a democracy now, is it? Everyone gets a vote? *Vive la république.* Isn't that what that Parisian mob shouted right before the French king had them all hanged?"

Hearn and Cawley cringed.

She grinned. Clearly, the only way to stave off a peasant revolt was by putting her foot down with a firm hand, as the old Yorkshire saying went.

Trusdale prompted the men. "Well?"

They wouldn't dare stand against me, would they?

Hearn cleared his throat. "It's a grand idea, Miss Constance, but Mr. Trusdale may have a point about there being guards, probably redcoats."

She fixed him with a scorching glare. "Really? And what about you, Cawley?"

Cawley croaked, "Mr. Trusdale's not completely wrong, miss."

"Hah!" Trusdale's chin jutted skyward.

Apparently, it would take more than force to crush this rebellion. "We'll be back here in an hour," she said.

"In an hour, we'll either be shot, pinned down, or on our way to be hanged," said Trusdale. "You're crazy to even think about it."

She huffed. "I am not insane!"

Cawley agreed. "That's true, sir. We've had doctors up to the house and everything. They say she's just high-strung. That Freud fella was quite adamant about the matter."

"See?" said Constance, thinking fast. "Plus, you said last night that you would do almost anything to get your hands on the original invisible man's journal, and McKinley's too, if he kept one."

"When did I say that?"

"Shortly after you collapsed on my bedroom floor and started singing a song about mermaids."

Trusdale flushed. "Well, I don't recall—"

"In fact, now I think about it, this is mostly your plan."

He shook his head. "It's a horrible plan. I would never have come up with this—just waltzing in there in the broad light of day. I mean, if the Steamwerks was open as usual, and a single operative could slip inside a lab for a quick reconnoiter, that's one thing. A bunch of amateurs breaking in on a security lockdown is quite another."

"Yet here we are, all ready to go. You said something about the formula being too dangerous to be in the Steamwerks' hands. That an invisibility serum would be misused by the 'imperial warmongers.' But that can't be your true opinion of the Steamwerks, can it? Not with you consulting for them? A man of your impeccable integrity would never accept remuneration from imperial warmongers—isn't that right, Mr. Trusdale?"

The American scowled.

She smiled. What he'd actually said was that despite being the unwitting tools of imperial warmongers, individually, the

Steamwerkers were some of the nicest people he'd ever met. That would teach him to talk politics on a belly of Haltwhistle cider.

Trusdale rubbed his temples. "If there is a journal or two there, and I could take them, well, that could stop the formula from falling into the wrong hands—"

"So, we've decided to go." She gestured toward the display hall's entrance. Through an arched doorway, the glass gallery led directly to the central dome. Ten decades of scarlet military uniforms stood at permanent attention on display dummies along the corridor.

Trusdale held out his hand. "No, not you. Not any of you. It's too dangerous. I'll go by myself."

She had to admit he was brave. Easily manipulated, perhaps, but brave. She gave him the nod to proceed.

Trusdale grabbed two handfuls of Cawley's Christmas baubles and thrust them into his pockets. He tipped his hat. "Miss Constance, it's been a real delight getting to know you."

"I would imagine so. Do you have enough baubles?"

"To take on the British army? Sure." He strode toward the dome, shoulders hunched in his duster coat, Stetson pulled down tight.

If Trusdale was right, and her plan was terrible, this was the last time she would see him alive. Constance's throat tightened.

For the first time in her life, she was almost sorry she'd won an argument.

Chapter 23: The Steamworks

AFTER AN ARDUOUS JOURNEY THROUGH Maya's secret passage, Trusdale pushed open the swinging bookcase into her laboratory. The second-floor science lab backed onto a hillside that sloped down to the Exhibition Dome. He blinked, his eyes adjusting to the daylight cast through the grimy glass roof of the lab. The walls and floor were made of riveted bronze plates. A glass-paneled door, which led out onto an iron balcony that overlooked the Steamwerks, allowed the patrolling redcoats to keep an eye on the empire's finest scientific mind.

When he'd first entered the facility two days before, his ears had rung with the roar of the blast furnaces and the discordant din of a thousand metalworkers' tools in action. Now, beyond a distant hiss of boilers, there was only the faint rumble of the underground waterfall that powered the Steamwerks' reaction turbines and steam presses.

Trusdale exhaled. The air was warm and laden with the taste of smoke and oil. Despite the Steamwerks' evacuation, the huge furnaces that drove the armaments factory would need to be stoked by a skeleton crew. Each furnace took a full month to reach the blistering temperature required to melt the Steamwerks supra-alloys. The bronze and brass produced by the Werks bore names the Romans might have recognized, but the alloys' capabilities were far beyond anything the ancient world could have imagined.

A pink wicker folding screen separated Maya's meager living space from the main laboratory. In the center of the lab, four steel workbenches arranged in a square allowed the scientist to flit between her latest projects. The benches were piled high with blueprints, machine parts, and scale models of her impressive creations. Two dozen foot-high bronze-and-brass armored exo-suits in action poses faced off against their brethren. The bulbous mechanized infantry suits each held a different weapon, from a massive medieval-style mace to a heavy-bolt cannon.

A miniature troop transport, designed to resemble a medieval castle on a flatbed wagon, was drawn by sixty steam-powered warhorses. The artificial shires were the military version of Cousin Welli's sporting steam horse. The troop transport was shadowed by a scarlet-ballooned airship hanging from a filigree cast-iron roof bracket. The dirigible dreadnought with its armored gondola and twin turret cannons swayed gently in the warm air.

The imperial machine, in miniature.

His enemy.

He closed the fake bookcase behind him. The illusion of ordinary shelves filled with scientific journals was convincing. Above the bookcase, a gold-framed portrait of Queen Victoria hung on the laboratory wall. The rotund seventy-seven-year-old wore her customary bejeweled goggles, a petite diamond crown, and a black leather battle corset over her gown. In her right hand, she held the golden blunderbuss of war; in her left, the crystal globe of domination. As with all Victoria's portraits, her steely eyes seemed to follow him across the room.

He wouldn't be much of a spy if he didn't capitalize on an opportunity to find enemy intel. If he were Maya, where would he stash his secrets?

Behind the pink wicker screen stood a single bed with an embroidered rose coverlet. Two personal bookcases stuffed with romance novels, a side table with a tasseled lamp, and a yellow velvet armchair appeared to be the only creature comforts Maya required. Such was the focus of the scientific mind.

He dropped to his knees and peered under the bed. A pink blanket almost covered a metal lockbox the size of a large suitcase. Immediately, fantasies of documents inside detailing top-secret bases, new armaments, and the formula for soldier snuff danced through his head. With a grunt, he dragged the lockbox from under the bed and drew a bone-handled pocketknife from the depths of his coat. He picked the padlock with a jiggle of his mirrored blade and cracked open the lid. Dozens of cheap dime novels with tawdry true-crime covers filled the box, but there were no fat folders marked "Top Secret" he could share with his US handler to keep his job secure. Why was luck never on his side?

With a sigh, he pushed the box back under the bed, stood, and crept over to the windowed door that led out to the balcony. If he remembered correctly from his brief site tour, McKinley's laboratory was two doors down the metal gantry. His mission was to slip into the lab without being shot dead—or even worse, taken alive—by the redcoats.

Easier said than done. He pulled the door ajar and slipped his mirrored knife through the crack. Reflected in the blade, a redcoat sentry leaned on the balcony rail sixty feet to his left. The skinny, ginger-haired youth gazed down at the factory floor. He was a freckle-faced kid, probably no more than seventeen years old. His brass pith helmet with built-in sniper goggles dangled from his hands by the chin strap. His rifle was propped against the railing, and a half-empty gin bottle stood beside his black riding boots. Apparently, the lad was not anticipating anyone coming up here, certainly not his commanding officers.

Trusdale pulled back his blade and pushed the door closed.

A metallic click sounded behind him, and the false bookcase started to swing open. Trusdale shot behind a workbench and crouched, the blade grasped tight in his hand. He couldn't risk using his snub-barrel S50 revolver. Even a single gunshot would alert every redcoat in the Werks that skullduggery was afoot. Only a lunatic would think of using a firearm on a stealth mission.

He narrowed his eyes as the flared barrel of a brass blunderbuss poked around the edge of the bookcase. So help him, if that gun was attached to a flame-haired woman . . .

A female voice whispered, "I think we must be in the servants' quarters. I can see a rather shabby bed. Stay here, I'll go and reconnoiter the situation."

Constance was brave, he'd give her that.

He took off his Stetson and held it out past the bench to quietly draw her attention.

Stealthy she was not. The rock salt in her hip basket clunked with every step, and her mirrored goggles flashed in the sunlight beneath her lurid purple top hat. She only needed a bulls-eye pinned to her bustle to become any sniper's dream target.

She whispered, "We thought you might appreciate a little assistance."

He peered behind her to see Cawley standing in the passageway behind the open bookcase. The elderly servant looked particularly depressed in a set of shiny brass goggles. No doubt, she'd made him wear them.

He muttered, "If you were bringing anyone, you should have brought Hearn. This is hardly the place for an elderly footman."

She pushed up her goggles. "Hearn is strictly outdoor staff, while Cawley is indoor. There are conventions to be observed. Besides, Hearn is far too bulky to be stealthy. He could no more skulk silently than a very angry elephant in a very well-stocked china shop. And Cawley isn't merely my footman. He's my bodyguard, head butler, and chaperone. He's been specially trained to—"

"Since when does violating a government facility require a chaperone?"

Her eyes widened. "Don't be absurd. I'm a single lady under thirty, and from your consistently poor choices in attire, I assume you're a single gent. So, to avoid any suggestion of impropriety between us, we must have a chaperone. *Babett's Modern Manners* is quite explicit on the point."

"You should mention all that to the judge at your espionage trial. Maybe you can get off with an insanity plea."

Her brow furrowed.

Trusdale gestured at the door onto the balcony. "There's a redcoat sentry outside. If he sees us, we'll be shot, or arrested, slapped about, and hanged. That's what they do to spies."

The woman bit her lip. "But we're not spies."

"You think they'd believe that? Which is exactly why I came here alone. There's no point in us all risking our necks."

She pouted. "Incidentally, you didn't mention that the passage was full of traps. We had a dreadful time getting here. Cawley requires new pantaloons—trust me, you don't want to know why."

"I told you before, Maya likes her fun and games. You're lucky I turned off most of the devices as I came through. That's another reason you two shouldn't have come. You're just an accident waiting to happen, the both of you."

"Just to be clear, my ideas are usually excellent. However"—she blushed and studied the floor—"I can see that to the untrained eye this plan could seem to be a rare exception to that rule."

He snorted. Did she ever just admit that she was wrong?

She leaned back against the workbench and took a long, slow breath, closing her eyes. He caught a fleeting glimpse of an exhausted young woman. She murmured, more to herself than him, "I had to do something. I can't lounge around in the carriage whilst Maya and the others . . ." She opened her red-rimmed eyes.

He said, "I must lose myself in action lest I wither in despair."

She tilted her head. "Tennyson?"

"I read."

A hint of a smile played across her lips. "You're full of surprises, Mr. Trusdale."

"You're not exactly predictable yourself, Miss Haltwhistle." He felt a tic in his cheek jump as Cawley slunk into the room and closed the bookcase behind him. The aged retainer's knees creaked as he tiptoed to the workbench. His hip basket of Christmas baubles tinkled like jingle bells as he crouched exactly three steps behind Constance.

Trusdale winced at the noise. "I reckon you two should quietly go and wait behind the bookcase. If I make it back here safely, I'll escort you through the passage, but if an alarm sounds, head straight for the carriage and don't look back."

Constance said, "Well, I think . . ."

Trusdale glared at her.

". . . that's an excellent idea," she finished lamely.

Cawley nodded enthusiastically.

Great. *Now* they wanted to listen to him.

Outside, the sentry's boots echoed on the iron balcony as the redcoat marched toward the lab. The porcelain queen and old silky britches stared at Trusdale.

He whispered, "Hide."

They scurried behind the pink wicker folding screen and crouched next to the bookcase. The men held their breath, motionless, as the sentry's boots rang ever closer. Constance eyed the spines of the books beside her. Apparently unable to resist the siren call of a new novel, she drew a dusky pink volume from the shelf. She flicked through the pages of a romance novel entitled *The Duchess and the Sky Pirate*, stopping as Trusdale glared.

Flushing, she shelved the book.

The sentry stopped by the windowed door.

Trusdale readied his blade. If the sentry came in, he'd have to take him out quick and quiet. Lord knew he didn't want to hurt the lad. Maybe he could knock him out?

One beat, two.

The soldier walked on. His footsteps faded into nothingness.

Trusdale exhaled and hurried to the door. He pulled it open a crack. The sentry entered the bathroom at the far end of the balcony. He'd left his sniper rifle and half-empty gin bottle at his post, next to the iron stairway that led up to the rooftop airship pad.

Trusdale took a deep breath, held it, and listened. It was hotter out here; the air stank of smoldering coal and tasted like iron filings. Against the dull rumble of the underground waterfall and the hiss of steam boilers, voices murmured.

Motioning Constance and Cawley to stay put, he crept out to risk a glance over the edge of the balcony. A half mile long and five hundred feet wide, the glass-roofed Werks shed was so enormous it required an internal rail system. Steam locomotives ran on a three-track oval that swept around the inner walls of the shed. Within a hundred yards of his vantage point, two steam engines stood idle. In their attached freight cars, around fifty redcoat soldiers slept, read, or played cards.

On-duty patrols marched around the train tracks. Trusdale counted eight patrols of six men dotted along the rails. Each patrol kept time by the massive clocks that hung from the roof every hundred yards.

The square bronze clocks were open-faced masterpieces of cogs and gears, with gaslit numerals and hands. Each clock bore the Steamwerks insignia of a shield set with a brass cogwheel and two crossed hammers. Below the hammers ran the motto "Progress, Power, PEACE." The latter was an acronym for the Werks' five divisions: Propulsion, Evolution, Armaments, Calculation, and Energy.

Under each clock stood a forty-foot-high Brightside Converter Furnace. The iron egg-on-legs design allowed the melting of standard alloys with secret compounds to create the super-high-density metals used for Steamwerks military hardware. Copper steam boilers and heavy press machines flanked each Brightside.

In the space between the rail tracks and the furnaces stood a thousand tool-strewn steel workbenches in orderly rows. There were no assembly lines here. Each Steamwerker created a unit of military hardware from start to finish. Every exo-suit, warhorse, and cannon bore the individual maker's mark. Should the unit fail in the field, the Steamwerker would be held personally responsible. Serious failure resulted in an unbiased court-martial followed by the inevitable hanging. The failure rate of Werk's armaments was extraordinarily low; this led to the worldwide acknowledgment of the supremacy of British engineering.

A semi-completed exo-suit towered over every one of the hundred or so benches closest to Trusdale. Some of the suits stood as skeletal frames, others were fully armored. A few clutched weapons in their metal hands. He frowned at the brass flamethrowers that graced the closest row. *What is Victoria planning to do with so much firepower?*

Now was not the time to wonder. He took a shallow breath and tiptoed along the iron balcony to McKinley's laboratory. The glass-paned door was unlocked.

Quietly, he slipped inside.

Chapter 24: McKinley's Lockbox

THE AIR IN MCKINLEY'S LABORATORY was saturated with the bad-egg stench of chemicals. Trusdale pulled his neckerchief up over his nose like a bank robber and tried not to gag. He took shallow breaths through the cotton as his eyes teared from the acerbic fumes.

Now, this was a place where brass goggles would actually come in handy.

He slipped his knife into one of his inner coat pockets for safe-keeping. After a thorough rummage through his twenty hidden pockets, he drew out the tin case that protected his hexagonal-framed, blue-lensed goggles. He snapped the goggles on his nose, wincing as the rubber sealed with a smack around his eye sockets. Now he could swim in toxic chemicals, and his eyes would be the last body part to dissolve.

Sunbeams shone through the transparent roof onto hundreds of brown chemical bottles stored on shelves bolted to the bronze walls. As in Maya's lab, a square of steel workbenches dominated the center of the room. The benches held dozens of glass beakers and test tubes suspended in midair by delicate brass stands. A few beakers of red, sapphire, and indigo liquids puffed colored smoke, without any observable heat source.

Was this where McKinley made the invisibility serum? If so, how much could he have made? The lab was hardly a large-scale plant. Perhaps he'd only made a handful, or even just the three doses used by the kidnappers to steal the exo-suits.

He could only hope that was the case. The last thing he needed was to face an invisible army. The redcoats were more than enough trouble for his taste.

Trusdale strode behind the blue wicker folding screen that separated McKinley's living space from the lab area. A single bed with a rumpled green blanket stood behind the screen. Under the rumpled blanket was the same squared-off shape he'd found in Maya's room. He walked over and pulled back the cover to reveal a padlocked steel lockbox that bore the telltale scratches of attempted forced entry.

Still locked. Looks like somebody left in a hurry, unless . . .

He reached into his pocket and pulled out three of his weaponized Christmas baubles. Keeping the ornaments hidden in his hand, he leaned closer to the lockbox.

A soft footfall behind prickled the hairs on the back of his neck. He spun on his heel and hurled the baubles at a crowbar seemingly floating in space. Two shattered midair on the forehead of an invisible attacker.

The violet dye revealed the shocked face of a wild-haired, bearded male. The liquid ran down his neck in purple rivulets, each line tracing a thin stripe of naked flesh. The man blinked from eyes that were nothing more than voids surrounded by inky lashes. The surreal portrait gaped down at his violet-striped chest. He let out a thin, high wail that dissolved into a manic cackle.

Trusdale's skin seemed to shrink until it was two sizes too small, stretched tight over frozen bones. A whisper inside his brain told him to move, to run, to fight.

But he stood, mesmerized by the half-human face before him. Foam on the female assassin had shown him disjointed body parts, legs, curves, but to see such monstrous eyes . . .

Nausea rose into his throat.

The creature raised his crowbar and sprang toward him. Trusdale swung for an unseen jaw, missing as the muscular arm of a second invisible foe clamped around his throat and jerked him back into a wrestler's chokehold. He gagged, clawing at his attacker's forearm. The wrestler tried to crush his windpipe, as Trusdale writhed and thrashed like a rattlesnake caught by a coyote. He twisted to face the wrestler and punched wildly, connecting his fist with an invisible nose that crunched beneath the blow. Something warm and wet splattered across his face, and his nose filled with the iron tang of blood.

The man exhaled with a grunt, but didn't cry out. No doubt, the assassins didn't want to bring the redcoats running any more than he did. Trusdale punched again and felt the delicate bones of an eye socket shatter below his fist. Knocked back, the creature released its grip, just enough so Trusdale could wrench his way free. As he did, the first attacker swung violently at his head with the crowbar.

He jerked away from the iron bar and snap-kicked where he suspected the assailant's knee would be. The heel of his boot connected with a satisfying crunch, and Mr. Crowbar staggered.

Trusdale took his chance, reached into his pocket for Christmas ornaments and threw a handful in the direction of Mr. Chokehold. Three smashed in midair, revealing the face of a bald man with a thick wrestler's neck and an unkempt beard. Behind the wrestler, the dye splattered across a pair of invisible legs.

He'd have known the shape of those legs anywhere. It was the female assassin from the Pyrrho Club.

Three madmen to one Trusdale.

The odds were gonna kill him.

Heart pounding, he backed to the edge of the bed and faced his attackers with fists clenched and jaw set. There's only one way to win unarmed combat against a group—improvise, stay on your feet, and initiate the attack.

Trusdale rushed the wrestler. Startled by the move, the man failed to block his solid punch to the throat. He gagged as Trusdale threw his full force into a sternum palm strike, sending his energy straight through the wrestler's torso. Mr. Chokehold went flying backward into the woman. Both fell as Trusdale dodged a swing from Mr. Crowbar.

Trusdale grabbed the beard of the thug and yanked with all his might. His foe's purple-stained face twisted into a grotesque mask of hatred, punctuated by rolling tears. Trusdale shoved the man back toward the wrestler, who was now staggering back into the fray. Miss Legs had disappeared out of his line of vision . . .

Trusdale sensed a movement behind him and spun as the female assassin threw a brown chemical bottle at his face. He lurched backward, tripped, and sprawled on the bed as the open bottle sailed over him and shattered against the riveted bronze wall. There was a sizzling sound as a shower of liquid—some kind of acid?—pelted his hat. The wide brim saved him from all but a single drop that bit into his chin, creating an instant dimple. He hissed, but kept his howl inside.

The two male assassins scrambled out of the splatter zone, whimpering as stray drops of acid burnt their naked flesh. The woman must be nuts to fling chemicals so close to her own men.

You can't beat crazy. He pushed himself up from the bed as Messrs. Chokehold and Crowbar gained their feet. His three opponents moved into a semicircle, poised to attack as one.

This was it. A fight to the death with three barely-visible professional killers in a Steamwerks laboratory guarded by half the British army.

He'd never imagined his death would be so . . . bizarre.

A hanging, yes. A bullet through the brain, yes. But torn apart by invisible madmen?

He shuddered.

The distinctive clunk of a blunderbuss being cocked came from the doorway. His attackers turned as Constance strolled into the lab, her mouth set in a determined line. Cawley followed her in and closed the lab door. He held Christmas baubles in his hands, ready to be launched.

Trusdale's eyes widened. Here was his exit, as long as Constance had the common sense not to fire the gun. If she did, the redcoats would be on them in a flash.

He and Mr. Crowbar both whispered, "Don't shoot!" The two enemies glanced at each other, momentarily bonded against a greater threat.

"So," said Constance to Trusdale. "How are things going?"

Miss Legs launched herself at Constance, sprinting straight at the lace-bedecked redhead. Trusdale, Mr. Chokehold, and Mr. Crowbar all gasped at the assassin's recklessness.

Constance twirled her blunderbuss around and struck out fast with the stock of the gun. She hit Miss Legs soundly in the stomach. With a groan, the assassin staggered back out of range.

The men blinked. Constance was surprisingly fast for a lace-and-corset-wearing young lady. In fact, Constance was pretty fast for a Royal Navy marine.

"Could we please move this along?" Constance said. "I have a luncheon engagement."

Confuse the enemy. Nice.

Mr. Crowbar said to his female associate, "*Det är Haltwhistle-kvinnan—stoppa henne.*"

Trusdale's Swedish wasn't perfect, but he knew he'd just heard an order to kill Constance.

The redhead peered down her nose at the assassins. "I must say, Oscar is really scraping the barrel, using invisibility as a weapon. You can tell him from me, he's officially off my customer list."

"I shall pass no message, daughter of the devil," said Mr. Crowbar.

Constance's voice dropped to a dangerous growl. "I assure you, minion, I control the business now, not my father. And it will be a cold day in hell before Oscar sees another case of Haltwhistle goods. I may even send his enemies a few thousand cases of my more specialized product lines if he doesn't call off this ridiculous vendetta."

Outside the laboratory, the sound of a lone soldier's boots rang along the iron balcony. Trusdale could only guess that the young, hopefully inebriated sentry was heading back to his sniper post.

Without warning, Chokehold dived for Trusdale's legs as Mr. Crowbar lunged for the metal lockbox on the bed. He swung his crowbar at the damaged lock. The lock broke open with a loud, metallic clang.

The time for caution was over.

Trusdale leapt sideways as the wrestler charged, avoiding the brunt of his attack. Focused on the purple stain of the man's neck, he thudded a full palm-strike into his spine, driving him to the floor as Mr. Crowbar wrenched open the lockbox.

Inside were two brown leather journals and a gas mask.

Trusdale and Mr. Crowbar both dived for the journals.

The soldier's footsteps reached Maya's lab.

Trusdale grabbed the journals in his right hand as his opponent smashed an elbow strike into his ear. Trusdale reeled, stars in his eyes, clutching the journals. Mr. Crowbar raised his weapon to strike the death blow. Trusdale dodged, slamming his knee hard into the rising wrestler's ribs, then stuffed the journals into a coat pocket as he ran to help Constance.

Miss Legs had backed Constance up against the steel workbenches and prowled in a semicircle before her. She stood a good foot taller than her red-haired foe and was attempting to maneuver into kicking range. Constance kept her at bay with jabs of her gun stock. Cawley had thrown ink baubles at the Swede, but his poor aim had so far revealed only a hint of her torso and her feet. Every step she took, the woman left a purple footprint upon the bronze floor.

The woman made a feint, then stepped in to roundhouse-kick Constance. Constance jumped sideways to avoid the blow, but her bustle thumped into the steel workbench behind her.

Trusdale's mouth dried.

As if in slow motion, the array of brass stands, glass beakers, and test tubes on the workbench teetered, then fell to the floor.

The crash of glass on metal was deafening.

Chapter 25: A Dirigible Too Far

CONSTANCE HAD CHOSEN HER LINGERIE well. A chain mail under-corset and three layers of ruffled silk petticoats provided full protection from the flying glass of the fallen experiments.

The unclothed female assassin scrambled to escape the dagger-like shards, colliding with the approaching Trusdale. As the assassin spun toward him, two macabre violet-streaked faces leered behind the American. Apparently certain that he was theirs to destroy, one of the monsters raised a crowbar, preparing to swing it at the back of Trusdale's skull.

Constance knew that if she didn't act now, Trusdale was a dead man.

A young, freckle-faced redcoat appeared at the doorway, gaping into the laboratory.

Three assassins, one redcoat.

Decision made, she yelled, "Duck!" at Trusdale and Cawley, flipped around her petunia blunderbuss, and fired. The brass gun boomed, shooting out a fantail of rock salt. Five people howled to a greater or lesser degree, depending on their level of clothing.

Constance winced at their pain. In retrospect, perhaps she should have thought her action through a tad more thoroughly. "Sorry," she said to the group, none of whom looked particularly pleased with her.

Trusdale shared several colorful words with the room at large. He bounded for the door, focused on grabbing the gawping sentry.

A bullet from the factory floor below whistled past the American's head and shattered a large pane of glass in the roof. He cringed as the glass shards rained down, cutting into his coat.

The sentry threw himself backward to avoid the glass, hit the balcony rail, and started to tip over. In one feline movement, Trusdale rose from his crouch, lunged for the lad's bandoliers, and pulled the shocked soldier back to safety. For a moment, he and the wide-eyed youth stared into each other's eyes.

Her heart glowed at the touching moment. Two enemies, bonded by—

The sentry hollered for his troopmates even as Trusdale shushed him. Men shouted orders at each other as the soldiers started to organize. A volley of bullets whistled by Trusdale's Stetson as he ducked for cover. A hundred combat boots started to thunder up the iron stairs. Trusdale glanced over at Constance, his brow furrowed over his blue-lensed goggles.

He'd blame her for all this nonsense.

Life was so unfair.

Trusdale drew his minuscule revolver out of his coat. The single sentry put his hands up. Ignoring him, the American snapped at Constance and Cawley, "Head for the stairs to the left. Get to the roof, there's an airship dock up there."

Trusdale stepped out onto the balcony and fired several high shots at the oncoming redcoats, causing them to retreat. The assassins decided to abandon the journals and raced by Trusdale, heading for the roof. The cowboy squeezed several shots off toward the factory floor to scatter the assembling troops.

"Go!" said Constance to Cawley, pushing him out the door. The retainer sprinted after the invisibles with her close on his heels. Trusdale brought up the rear. She glanced back to see the American pull a handful of brass ball bearings from a pocket inside his coat. He flung the balls over his shoulder onto the balcony's metal-plate floor, to hamper the pursuing soldiers.

One has to give credit to a man with brass balls.

She glanced down at the factory floor and the hundreds of exo-suits in various stages of construction. A handful of them held her Phoenix F-451 flamethrowers in their metal grasp. The Brass Queen's finest work, and yet . . . nausea swam through her at the realization that her creations were on their way to the battlefield. She'd never thought too hard about sending armaments she never saw to customers she never met, but imagining the weapons opening fire on living, breathing human beings . . . Her stomach churned. Distracted, she stumbled, and was caught by a strong hand that yanked her upright.

"Hurry up, will ya?" said Trusdale, shoving her in the small of her back. "Stop daydreaming, start running."

She'd opened her mouth to state that she'd like to see him run wearing a bustle, when a bullet ricocheted off the balcony rail twenty feet ahead and disappeared into the right temple of the brawnier invisible man. His partially visible skull exploded like a dropped pumpkin, spraying jigsaw pieces of purple-stained flesh across the iron gantry. The headless corpse ran on for one step, two, before pitching over the railing, landing with a wet thud on the skeletal frame of an exo-suit below.

The unfinished behemoth tipped and smashed into the suit behind it, which fell with a crash into its two neighbors, who tumbled into theirs. The suits fell like dominos in a thunderous wave of destruction that fanned across the factory floor. Redcoats dodged the falling mechanicals, shouted fresh curses, and shot wildly at the balcony.

A bullet dinged her bustle, and black smoke began to pour from her rear end. One of her smoke grenades had joined the party. A sooty cloud engulfed her as she scurried up the stairs to the roof, catching her boots on her petticoats with every step.

A heavy hand thumped onto her bustle. She gasped and half-turned. Trusdale pushed her up the stairs, swatting at her behind.

"Do you mind?" she said indignantly.

"You're on fire."

"No, I'm not—it's just a smoke grenade. I like to be prepared for any emergency."

"Dang, you're plumb loco. Cut dirt, will ya?"

"I beg your pardon?" It appeared that when stressed, Trusdale started to use phrases from a foreign language she was not familiar with. Flemish, perhaps?

"You have to move faster, get gaited, giddyup." Trusdale propelled her forward, hoisting her skirts up high above her ankles. She put her outrage on hold as the impropriety helped her ascend the stairs faster. Her lungs burned from the acrid smoke, but it camouflaged the group from the irate soldiers below. Shots from the factory floor whistled by them as the soldiers tried to find targets in the black fog.

The invisibles and Cawley stopped at a padlocked iron door at the top of the stairs. Mr. Crowbar whacked the lock, which sparked, but didn't break.

Now she was going to die alongside the assassins who wanted to kill her.

Oh, the irony.

Trusdale dropped her skirts, pointed his minuscule revolver over her shoulder at the padlock, and shouted, "Duck!"

Cawley and the invisibles ducked.

Before she could protest, Trusdale fired the gun over her shoulder. Her ears rang like church bells as the padlock exploded.

Even deafened, Constance admired the shot. Accurately firing a double-action revolver, one-handed, was quite a feat. She doubted even Cousin Welli could have made that shot, and he was the best marksman she knew.

Cawley rose and pushed open the door, flooding the stairs with bright sunlight. The two invisibles rudely shoved him aside and sprinted down a metal-plate path with waist-high railings that ran over the tempered-glass roof.

Constance took one step up, then flinched as a bullet blasted through the brim of her top hat.

The next shot was even closer. She screamed as a bullet seared along her scalp just above her right ear. Pain exploded through her skull. Hot tears ran down her cheeks and the scent of burnt hair and flesh filled her nose. Disbelieving, she touched the fingertips of her right hand to the fresh, wet wound as Trusdale shoved her through the doorway. As she stumbled out onto the roof, he turned and slammed the door, then reached inside his coat and pulled out a green rubber doorstop. She watched, confused, as he shoved the wedge of rubber into the crack beneath the door.

"There. That should hold 'em for a few minutes." He moved to her side and examined her wound. "You were lucky. Just a scratch." His voice sounded like a whisper from a distant mountaintop, close, yet far. "You'll live. Shouldn't even scar, if you leave it alone."

She blinked up at him. Her head felt curiously light, and her belly fluttered like a caged hummingbird.

He frowned, and he snapped his fingers in front of her eyes. Displeased with the results of his scientific inquiry, he stooped forward, encircled her waist with his right arm, and hauled her over his shoulder like a sack of grain.

She squealed in anger and thwacked him across the spine with her blunderbuss.

"Quit it, missy." Trusdale sprinted after Cawley and the invisibles. He panted, "You've got dilated pupils. Which is serious. Besides, you're too dang slow. This ain't no promenade."

Even as clammy dizziness swept over her, she was annoyed. She huffed, bouncing uncomfortably on his shoulder as he ran. She reluctantly dropped the blunderbuss to grab hold of his coat. It felt and smelled like a well-worn saddle, soft and smooth with a hint of horse.

Admittedly, this was a faster, if incredibly inelegant, way to travel.

The steel-plate path flew by under Trusdale's boots. The plates were bolted directly to the filigree struts that held the glass roof panels in place. Far below on the factory floor, hundreds of redcoats milled around like ants on a picnic blanket. Constance ignored them, particularly the ones who were pointing incredulously at her still-smoking bustle.

Trusdale said, "Dang, you weigh a ton."

"How dare you. It's my chain mail corset and bustle. I can assure you, underneath it all, I'm as light as a feather."

"Could've fooled me. You feelin' better?"

"Yes," she lied. Shots rang through the jammed iron door as the redcoats tried to shoot their way through. Bullet holes blossomed into metal bouquets through the riveted panels, but the door held fast.

"Uh-huh. Hang on, we're nearly there."

Trusdale's long legs ate up the distance to the dirigible dock in less than a minute. As he ran by empty winches, Constance craned her neck to see which airships were tethered. She spotted several two-person mini-dirigibles, five freight barges, and two enormous red-ballooned troop carriers bobbing at the end of steel cables. Trusdale headed for a mini-dirigible with a yellow-and-black striped gasbag that resembled a giant bumblebee.

A stick of dynamite blew a hole through the door behind them. Startled by the blast, she glanced up as two scarlet-coated soldiers raced through the smoke. They dropped to one knee on the charred metal path and aimed their long rifles her way.

An officer in a rather fetching ostrich-plumed hat appeared behind the two soldiers. He shouted, "Make ready . . . present . . . fire!"

The soldiers emptied their rifles with a crash like Vulcan's hammer.

Bullets whistled through Trusdale's flapping coat mere inches from her head. Still dizzy, Constance watched in horrified fascination as the rounds scorched through the leather, narrowly missing his torso. She studied the battered coat and noticed numerous bullet holes, knife slashes, and acid burns. So that was why the American wore the shabby coat in public. It was yet another tool in his repertoire of escape tricks.

Trusdale's breath came in heavy gasps as he sprinted toward Cawley, who was frantically cranking the winch handle to pull down the dirigible from its hundred-foot-high mooring. The cigar-shaped balloon ran about thirty feet long, with a two-person gondola hanging below. The semi-invisible people winched down an orange dirigible not far beyond.

Constance noted, "The invisibles—they're leaving."

"So what? Let 'em run. We got both the journals, not that it matters if the redcoats shoot us dead."

Goodness, Trusdale is such a defeatist for a man with so many bullet holes in his coat. She'd have thought he'd feel invincible.

Cawley's face bore more lines than the Great Northern Railway as he locked the winch. He grabbed the lowest rungs of a rope ladder that dangled from the dirigible. The airship's oval copper gondola hung thirty feet in the air above the platform. It wouldn't be the easiest climb for any of them, even without the nuisance of being shot at by redcoats.

The retainer said, "I don't think I can get up there. You two best go on without me."

Trusdale roared at him, "Git on up there, you old coot, fast."

Cawley jumped and practically flew up the ladder. His buckle shoes were a blur of activity.

Constance gasped at his septuagenarian agility. Old age was clearly just a state of mind that could be remedied by a firm tone from a man in a dodgy hat.

Trusdale said to Constance, "You too, missy, git goin'. No excuses."

He swung her off his shoulder directly onto the ladder. She grabbed ahold of the twisted rope tightly, the harsh fibers cutting into her palms. She scrabbled to get her feet onto the rungs, but her boots caught on her skirt and petticoats. For a moment, she hung by just her arms, her feet pedaling furiously for a hold. Trusdale yanked her skirts aside and pushed her boots onto the rungs, guiding her feet and helping her climb.

Surely, no gentleman would take advantage of a life-or-death situation to peek at a lady's lingerie, would he?

Admittedly, she had seized the opportunity to review Trusdale's credentials at the Pyrrho Club when he threw himself naked at her feet. But still, that was an entirely different scenario—wasn't it?

As she scrambled up the ladder with bullets whizzing by her head, she acknowledged to herself that the whole Steamwerks situation had spiraled out of control. She felt more like wayward baggage than a bold adventuress. Dizziness and the pitching movement of the ropes caused her stomach to turn. She longed to stop climbing, but Trusdale kept guiding her feet onto each rung, urging her on in his deep baritone: "Come on, you can move faster than that, I know you can. Look up, not down. You're almost there." Though his tone encouraged, she inherently resented being told what to do. She had no issues with authority, as long as she was the one giving the orders.

Finally, she reached the side of the gondola. Cawley disappeared headfirst into the rear. This left her with the front driver's seat, and Trusdale with no seat at all.

She shouted down to Trusdale, "Cawley and I can't fly this thing. We don't know how."

"Quit yappin' and get in there."

She hesitated, debating how to swing her way into the front seat. This was why she hated mini-dirigibles; there was just no elegant way to get in and out of them without risking life and limb, or the accidental showing of far too much ankle.

A bullet flew into the balloon above her, and a hiss of escaping hydrogen added to the sound of gunfire and shouts from the soldiers now reaching the edge of the dock platform.

Trusdale shoved her bustle upward and forward.

Constance shrieked and tipped headfirst over the pilot's seat. She landed on the soft burgundy leather in a crumple of petticoats. Trusdale scrambled in after her, pulling her backward onto his lap. She surveyed the mahogany flight-control panel's dozens of complicated gauges and switches. A right-hand wooden steering stick with a left-hand chrome throttle dominated the center of the panel. Three brass foot pedals stood out against the plush maroon carpeting. The contraption looked like it would be a beast to fly.

A bullet hit the side of the gondola, blowing a neat hole through the metal and passing out the opposite side.

"Guess the Steamwerks didn't build this bucket. Your underwear provides better armor than this cheap copper." Trusdale punched the controls. "I need you—"

He ducked as a bullet whistled a fraction of an inch over his Stetson.

He needed her? What did that mean? Was this American courtship? His timing was remarkably poor. "I'm very sorry, Mr. Trusdale.

You are a very attractive man, of course, but the social gulf between us is too great," she shouted over the cracking of gunfire.

"Very attractive, huh? Darlin', I'm flattered, but right now I need you to push the throttle forward. I can't reach with you in the way. Grab the chrome handle and push it forward five seconds after I step on the coal-gas pedal."

Her cheeks burned. "Oh, I thought you were . . . never mind."

"Boy, the sooner we get you to a doctor, the better. You're losing it."

"I am not in shock. Probably." She grabbed the chrome handle, ready to act, as Trusdale stomped on the center brass pedal.

The dirigible shot up like a champagne cork as hydrogen replaced air in the gasbag's ballonets. Trusdale flicked up a long row of switches, igniting the motor that drove two propellers at the rear of the airship's balloon. The motor buzzed into life with a sound like an overgrown bee. It was a fitting match to the black-and-yellow striped balloon overhead.

Constance pushed the chrome handle, and the airship lurched forward like a sailboat caught by a fast-moving wave. They swept away from the Steamwerks toward the city.

Trusdale said, "Keep it at full throttle. We'll hightail it into town, ditch the ship on a rooftop, and try to hide. We'll never outrun the big troop ships. As long as they don't hit us with an incendiary round, we've got a slight chance of making it."

A blue tracer bullet flew by the hydrogen balloon.

Constance blinked. "Wasn't that an—?"

"Incendiary round."

Her stomach churned.

Out of the frying pan.

Into the inferno.

Chapter 26: Time to Fly

THE MINI-DIRIGIBLE BUZZED ITS WAY through the azure sky. Ahead, the city's smokestacks stood like turrets in a castle built on the sturdy backs of generations of metalworkers. Seven majestic emerald hills surrounded the dark cauldron of industrial might. Agriculture and industry had fought for control of this valley, and industry had clearly won.

Trusdale glanced over his shoulder. Two scarlet-ballooned military airships pursued them like sharks after a minnow. Every few minutes, a blue-trailed incendiary round would fly toward them, falling just short of the ship's hydrogen-filled gasbag.

His hands were full keeping the mini-airship in line, overtaxed as it was with three passengers and a hydrogen leak. And he, personally, was overtaxed with the nonstop barrage of helpful comments from an agitated Constance. It appeared medical shock amplified her natural belligerence and need for control.

"You're flying far too straight, Mr. Trusdale. Let me take over. I can handle it."

"Absolutely not. You don't know how to fly an airship."

"But I do know how to serpentine, which, apparently, you don't." She lunged for the control stick, but he fended her off by dropping his left knee fast, tumbling her into the side of the gondola. She struggled to sit back up in a flurry of petticoat lace and ill temper.

"An airship can't 'serpentine' fast enough to avoid incendiary bullets, so keep your hands off my stick! Which is more important to you here, being in control of the situation, or living?"

There was a pause while she appeared to seriously consider the question.

"Are you crazy?" he snapped. "The answer is living. The answer should always be living."

"But they're getting closer." She pointed back at the troop carriers. The sun glinted off the brass pith helmets of the redcoat soldiers milling about on the open decks. Good thing they were only light transport ships. If they'd been armored ships with cannons, he'd never have made it off the Steamwerks roof.

"That's why we have to keep going as fast as we can in a straight line. One slow turn and we're done for. We're only just out of their shooting range."

Constance folded her arms and did her best to glare at him. He caught sight of his own eyes reflected in her mirrored goggles. They were the wild, red-rimmed eyes of a crazy man. That was the effect she had on him. Death was rapidly starting to lose its sting.

"Miss Haltwhistle, will ya just listen? Three hundred yards is the maximum range of their incendiary shells. At most, we're forty yards beyond that range, and they're eating up that space faster than a pack of wolves on a jackrabbit. Once we lose that distance, one direct hit, and we'll be on the ground in ten seconds in the middle of a blazing inferno—in the midst of townsfolk, I might add. Now, I thought they would've had more sense than to shoot at us above the town, but that's the redcoats for you. Military intelligence ain't got nothin' to do with it."

Cawley spoke up from the back. "What if we lightened the load, sir? Would that make the ship go faster? I'd be happy to step out, as needed."

Constance barked, "Don't be ridiculous, Cawley. If you think I'm going to go home and explain to the other servants that I let you jump out of an airship, you're quite mistaken. Stop being so selfish, will you? I'm trying to think."

Trusdale said, "That's your problem right there. The only thing you should be trying to do is pray. Right about now, we need a miracle."

Constance pushed up her mirrored goggles, her eyes wide. "You don't think we're going to make it, do you?"

He sighed deeply, at peace with whatever his fate should prove to be. He could almost reach out and touch the firmament from the airship. He was halfway to heaven, halfway to hell. Except for the drone of the motor, the chilling breeze on his face, and the unremitting helpfulness of Constance, this was a relatively serene setting for his final moments. There were worse places to meet eternity.

Constance punched him hard in the ribs. "You can knock that off right now. What with you giving up and Cawley jumping out, it's a wonder we're getting anywhere. You're both just doing this to vex me, I know it."

The force behind her punch was impressive. She was much stronger than she looked. He said, "You'd better start sweetening your tone, young lady, or I've a good mind to make you walk the rest of the way."

Constance stared at him wide-eyed—then her expression softened into a charming smile. "Well, in that case . . ." She leaned in close. Her warm breath touched his cheek, chilled by the smoke-scented breeze from the city sprawl below. He became hyper-aware of her soft weight on his thighs, the curves of her corset. Her perfume of orange blossom and honeyed rose filled him with sweetness. Her glossy red hair brushed across his throat like silk as she gazed deep into his eyes. "I'd be ever so grateful if you could give me the time?"

He swallowed hard. "Time for what? Wait, I mean, yes, of course I can. That is, ah, your bustle's blocking my pocket watch."

Constance slipped her right hand over his waistcoat, feeling for the watch. Her hand reached inside the vest pocket containing the Enigma Key.

"Wrong pocket." He moved his attention from the airship controls to her eminently kissable lips.

A bullet skimmed through the rudder on the airship's tail, causing the ship to drop hard to the left. He yanked the steering stick right and struggled with gravity for control as the gondola bucked like a bronco.

Constance shrieked and slipped her arms around his sides, burrowing her face into his chest, as the gondola lurched.

He hoped it wasn't just the lack of a seat belt that caused her to grab hold of him so tight. Now that he thought about it, hadn't she said something about finding him attractive, back there when they took off?

Another bullet slammed into the motor of the dirigible. The engine stuttered—as did his heart—then spluttered back to life with an unseemly belch of oil and smoke.

Constance sat up. "Pfft. So much for forty yards."

He sighed. There she was, the acerbic aristocrat. Where was the woman who'd asked for the time so nicely? How could he get her back? "We're forty yards outside the range of incendiary rounds, but regular shells are faster and go further."

She rolled her eyes and slipped her hand into his other waistcoat pocket to draw out his pocket watch. She flipped open the silver case, and he glimpsed the family portrait inside. Homesickness swept through him. What was he doing here, risking his life so far from his family? Hadn't they lost enough?

But all Constance cared about, apparently, really *was* the time. "Twelve thirty. I'm late for my luncheon with Auntie Madge. The old bat will crucify me."

"That's what you're worried about right now? With imperial airships on our tail? Darlin', you need to get your priorities straight."

"Mr. Trusdale, if it comes down to a choice between a fiery death at the hands of the redcoats and being late for lunch with the dowager countess, believe me, the redcoats are the soft option."

She slipped the watch into the wrong pocket on his waistcoat. Trusdale sighed. He'd fix it later, should they live.

They were now flying over the city center. The grimy air of industry enveloped the dirigible and provided some cover from the pursuing ships. Brick chimneys grew like stalagmites from the slate roofs below as he weaved the airship around the taller smokestacks and airship cargo cranes.

Constance asked, "And why didn't we land in a field?"

"Snipers. Snipers in airships love to shoot people running in fields. They get medals for it. Apparently, it's their favorite part of the job."

The closest docking platforms were dotted with redcoat soldiers. The redcoats pointed at the airship as it sailed into view. Trusdale guessed that the military's famed semaphore signalmen had been hard at work waving flags to alert every lookout post of the stolen ship's flight. No country on Earth produced better flag-wavers than the British. If there was a message to be passed, a celebration to be made, or a country to be claimed, it was usually a British flag-waver who got things started.

Sunlight flashed amber from a set of sniper goggles on a rooftop.

Constance tensed on his lap. She'd seen the same sniper.

Trusdale slammed the control stick to the right, pitching the ship into an ungainly lurch that dropped his stomach into his boots. He held his breath as a lone incendiary round smoked a blue trail up from the roofline.

He prayed it would miss the gasbag. The shell curved at the apex of its range. As if in slow motion, the smoking projectile dropped and punched a neat hole into the hydrogen-filled balloon of the airship.

The icy chill of the grave swept through him.

Their life expectancy could now be measured in seconds.

Chapter 27: All Fired Up

IT WAS AN AIRSHIP PILOT'S worst nightmare: a terrible choice of the best way to die. Which was worse—burning alive in the air, or crashing into the ground with the flaming balloon on top?

Blue smoke snaked out of the bullet hole in the balloon. An orange flame licked around the hole and began to eat its way across the striped black-and-yellow fabric.

Every muscle in Trusdale's body tensed, and he sweated in places he hadn't known he could sweat. Time slowed in the way it does when eternity is on the line. He became hyperaware of everything around him: Constance, warm and frilly on his lap, her orange blossom and rose perfume sweetening his soul; Cawley praying in the rear seat; the buzz of the airship engine; the cool breeze on his face; the blue sky and snowy clouds of a perfect spring day.

Twenty seconds. He had less than twenty seconds to land the ship.

Constance kept one hand on the throttle, the other gripped his knee. Her breath came short and fast. He was sure she knew the score. Redcoats one, Renegades zero.

He squinted down at the roofs, looking for any location remotely flat and not covered in soldiers. Acres of slanted slate roofs, red-brick chimneys, and cargo cranes stretched in all directions.

Between warehouses to the northeast, he spotted the thin blue line of the Sheffield Canal. The waterway moved goods through the city on narrow boats pulled by heavy horses on the towpaths. If he could line up a straight run at the water . . .

He ordered, "Slam the throttle back, *now*."

Constance, rigid as a board, complied without argument. Her face was a shade whiter than snow. The mirrored goggles she'd pushed up onto her forehead reflected the flames above.

He prayed, *Dear Lord, please, let this work . . .*

With a sudden roar like a furnace, the fire took hold of the balloon. The flames spread across the painted material like lava. Black smoke belched out of the gasbag as it disintegrated. The hot cloud burned his nostril hairs, and the bitter taste of charbroiled paint filled his mouth. Trusdale, Constance, and Cawley all cringed as embers dropped down onto them.

Ten seconds left.

The motor stuttered, and the ship dropped, sending Trusdale's guts into somersaults. He wrapped his left arm around Constance's shoulders, pulling his leather coat over her head. She held him close, her heartbeat thumping against his chest—or was it his heartbeat? He couldn't tell the difference between them. He steered for the canal as the balloon blazed above and bullets whistled by from the rooftop redcoats.

He shouted, "We're going in the drink, hold on!"

The canal came up fast—too fast. The straight line of water glistened peacefully between the iron warehouses. He turned the ship hard, dragging the final second of compliance from its fiery frame.

There was a moment when the inferno above was reflected in the cool water of the canal below. Then the falling gondola slapped hard onto the water's surface, skipping like a stone up to an iron bridge.

It began to sink.

Cold water surged around his legs as the wreckage from the burning balloon collapsed toward him. He took a deep breath of acrid air and pushed Constance and himself down below the waterline as the gondola sank beneath the flames.

The water wrapped him like a heavy cloak, pulling him into the murky depths of the canal. He held onto his hat with one hand, Constance with the other, waiting for his moment to rise. The light from the burning balloon on the surface cast a fiery glow through the darkness. As the heat and light from above dissipated, he pushed Constance upward. He followed her, breaking through the balloon debris, taking a gulp of steamy air that made his chest burn. The airbag's metal frame was hot to the touch as he splashed through its charred skeleton.

Constance picked her own way through the frame before plunging into the deep water beyond. She disappeared for a moment underneath the gloomy waters, then broke the surface with a gasp. She splashed frantically, trying to dog-paddle in place as the weight of her chain mail began to drag her down into the depths.

She can't swim. Why didn't she mention that on the way down?

Trusdale plunged over to her, threw his right arm around her waist, and endeavored to drag her on her back toward the banks of the canal.

She struggled against him all the way.

With a longsuffering groan, he heaved her out onto the muddy canal bank and collapsed on the dirt as Cawley crawled up beside them.

Trusdale asked, "Anybody hurt?"

They didn't answer, gasping like beached fish on the mud. Cawley's livery was covered in oil from the rear motor. The elderly man seemed to have aged at least a decade since breakfast.

Green algae had woven through Constance's red tresses like Medusa's snakes. Her violet dress was splayed around her like a sodden handkerchief tossed aside by a giant, but she didn't complain. He didn't know many folks who, in the space of a few hours, could handle an assassination attempt by a maid, a grazing with a bullet, and a near-drowning with such equanimity.

Or was she still in shock?

He stood and offered Constance his hand. She took it without so much as an eye roll. He pulled her up to standing. "Why didn't you tell me you couldn't swim?"

She raised one eyebrow. "I had no idea whether I could or couldn't. I mean, animals swim, and they don't get lessons on how to do it, so I sort of assumed—"

"You should learn."

"Yes, very helpful, thank you. At which point of my almost drowning did that occur to you?"

"No need to get snippy. And you're welcome, by the way, for my saving you. Again. So, Cawley, why can't she swim?

"She refused to wear the outfit, sir. She said her woolen bathing suit was too ugly."

"Cawley, you blaggard," she said indignantly. "That's personal information. He's not family."

The servant pulled a strand of algae out of his ear. "Yesterday you let him stay as a guest in the family wing. Doesn't that almost make him family?"

Trusdale said, "If you two have enough energy to bicker, you have enough to move. The redcoats will be here any minute. Come on,

Cawley, up and at 'em." As soldiers' shouts rang out over the roofs, he tugged Cawley to his feet. "We need transport, or a safehouse, or—"

Constance said, "I instructed Hearn that if we ran late at the Steamwerks, he should drive the carriage to Pinder's Print Emporium and await further instructions. It's all part of my—"

"If you say Plan with a capital 'P', so help me, I'll toss you back into the canal," said Trusdale.

"Well!" She looked genuinely affronted.

He tilted his head and tapped water out of his ears. "All right, it's not a great option, but it's better than staying here to get shot. You two got your breath back?"

They nodded.

"Good. Crashing was the easy part. Now, we run for our lives."

Chapter 28: Run Like a Girl

CONSTANCE KNEW SHE DIDN'T RUN like a girl. She ran like a woman who'd read about running in a book but had never had the time or inclination to try it for herself. This was precisely the case, as she'd decided at an early age that running was best left to servants, preferably to fetch tea and cakes.

It was her new least favorite activity except for swimming. Her legs ached, her sides hurt, and she panted like a hunting dog after an errant bird. She couldn't recall being forced to exert herself to the point of perspiration at any time in the last few years. Since Papa had left, she'd been able to be as sedentary as she wished. Long hours of martial arts training with foreign tutors had once kept her in shape, but now she had to admit that not all her bulk came from her chain mail underwear. A few extra pounds, armored corsetry, and skirts laden with canal water did not aid her velocity along the cobbled back streets.

Cawley raced ahead while Trusdale loped at her side. Three-story red-brick tenement blocks towered over them. Colorful laundry flapped on peg lines strung across the alley. A band of ragged children chased a cat amidst piles of horse manure and foul-smelling puddles. The scent of working-class cooking drifted out of open windows—boiled cabbage, roast pigeon, and the ever-popular rat-and-kidney pie. The sound of babies crying and couples arguing drifted through the smoky air.

She longed for the heather of the open moors, or at least the golden cushions of her dragon carriage. She'd never visited the back streets of the city before and was shocked by the lack of civilized amenities. After twenty minutes of scuttling through the alleys, she hadn't seen so much as one decent tea shop.

Trusdale kept glancing behind, checking for pursuing soldiers. He offered a nonstop stream of helpful comments, such as, "Hurry up," and, "Come on, will ya? Any slower and you'd be going backward."

"Go on without me." She hoped this sounded like a noble sacrifice on her part, rather than an excuse to sit down on the cobbles and await her fate in a less tiring way.

"Nope, I'm not leaving you alone in an alley to face a troop of regulars. They're not too far behind us. Get your scurry on."

She strongly suspected that the only reason the American hadn't physically picked her up again was to avoid drawing attention from stray pedestrians. As it was, the few people who had taken a second glance at them appeared more intrigued by Trusdale's hat than her own bedraggled state.

The tenements gave way to the back entrances of tradesmen's shops. Many of the rear doors to the shops stood open, allowing her to glimpse vignettes of proletarian life as she trotted by. A cobbler hammered a sturdy work boot on a wooden shoe form. A cutlery polisher worked a carving knife on a pedal-operated buffing machine.

A red-faced laundrywoman stirred a steaming copper cauldron of unmentionables with a wooden paddle. Piles of soiled clothing encircled her like an angry sea.

Perhaps life for the working class was less idyllic than she had imagined? She'd always felt a twinge of jealousy toward her employees with their simple lives, boisterous families, and ale-fueled celebrations of everything from lamb season to the harvest. She'd assumed that poor townsfolk would have a similar life, albeit with less livestock. However, it seemed that several of the workers she had passed in the alley looked downright depressed, and not the sort of melodramatic sadness that society ladies were obligated to display at least once a week.

Melancholy was a skill that she'd worked hard to master. For three weeks she'd diligently followed *Babett's* recommendation that a true lady should display palpable gloom every Sunday afternoon. The practice consisted primarily of writing dreadful poetry, usually focusing on a metaphor of a lone bird trapped in a gilded cage. After an hour of sonnets and sighs, she would judge herself fashionable enough to cease. She'd then read a more exhilarating book about sky pirates or other colorful sorts.

Now that she'd traveled the back alleys, actual misery amongst the poor seemed to be widespread. She resolved to add to her widows-and-orphans charity contributions additional funds to aid the working-class poor.

The middle class, however, could sort themselves out.

Cawley sprinted to the end of the cobbled alley like a prize whippet, then stopped to wait for his companions. Beyond him, a stream of bourgeois townsfolk flowed along the paved promenade. Some were clad in fashions barely three seasons out of date. If not for the cheap materials and lack of escorting servants, one could almost have mistaken them for aristocracy.

Beyond the promenade, the Gothic basilica of the town hall towered over the formal flower beds of the Victory Gardens. The public park was created to celebrate the defeat of the Dutch airship fleet off the Isle of Wight in 1889. By day, the garden's benches were a haven for weary shoppers and courting couples. The latter were always accompanied by ever-watchful chaperones. At night, the benches served as beds for the scores of aging war veterans allowed by royal charter to beg for change within the confines of the park.

Trusdale slowed to a stroll as Constance scurried up to Cawley's side. She pointed across the square, past a life-size white marble statue of Britannia in Grecian garb driving a chariot, to the green frontage of Pinder's Print Emporium. The dragon carriage snarled in red-and-gold splendor before the store's long window.

Constance grinned at her companions. "As promised, gentlemen, there's our transportation."

Trusdale was watching the redcoat patrols that marched along the white gravel paths crisscrossing the park. The soldiers scanned the townsfolk for anarchists, suffragettes, and other troublemakers—present company included. He said, "All right, then all we need to do is get over there without drawing the redcoats' attention. Mr. Cawley, do you have any money on you?"

Cawley drew out a soggy roll of pound notes from his pantaloons pocket and handed it to the American.

"Stay here." Trusdale shot down the alley and disappeared through the back door of the laundrywoman's shop.

"And he was never seen again," said Constance.

Cawley sniffed. "Not if he knows what's good for him."

Hmm. Cawley seems to be suffering from an even greater deficit of joy than usual. Could it be related to the fact that I shot him with rock salt? "Um, may I offer my sincere apologies for the shooting incident, Cawley. It appears that may have been a miscalculation on my part."

The servant's rheumy eyes widened in shock.

She placed one hand on her hip. "Heavens, it's not as if I've never apologized before, is it?"

"Actually, miss, it is."

"Oh." She dropped her hand. "Well, there's no need to make a fuss about it."

"No, miss."

She scuffed her boot on the cobbles. "I hope it didn't hurt too much."

"Like a swarm of bees stung my belly."

"Heavens. Then I really *am* sorry."

His lip quivered. "Thank you, miss."

"I mean it. I'll never shoot you again, I promise."

"Not many employers would be so considerate."

"I do my best."

"We all know that, miss. We really do."

The tears welled up before she could stop them. A blurry Cawley reached into his tailcoat pocket and drew out a red-and-white polka-dot handkerchief. He offered it to her. "Now, miss, don't concern yourself about me. If you ever point a firearm my way again, I'll be sure to duck."

She smiled. "That's the spirit, Cawley. Papa used to say there's nothing more exhilarating than dodging enemy fire."

"Ah, well, it takes all sorts, miss." He studied the wound above her ear. "Are you feeling better now? Not quite so dizzy?"

"Much better. There's nothing like a crash landing in a chilly canal to clear one's mind."

He nodded. "Glad you're back to being yourself, miss."

"Me too," she said, ignoring her aching skull. The protector of the barony of Brampton-on-the-Wall was not going to be vanquished by a mere bullet searing her scalp. The Haltwhistles were made of stronger stock. If Trusdale could walk around with a scabbed throat, a black eye, and a swollen nose, she could certainly handle a gunshot wound with equanimity.

Trusdale burst out of the laundrywoman's shop and sprinted toward them. Over his arm, the American carried three jute cloaks in the full-hooded style favored by local shepherds, more patchwork than original garment. "Right, look sharp. We're gonna disguise ourselves before splitting up. Meander your way on over to the print shop, and try not to look conspicuous."

Constance screwed up her nose. "I refuse to wear to wear such an item. Benedictine monk is out this season."

"Really? So, what's your plan, Miss Adventure? Are you just gonna sashay on over there, hoping that every soldier is shortsighted? How many soaking-wet redheads in violet gowns do you think are in this town right now? I'm guessing there aren't too many. Take my advice: put on the cloak, sneak into the carriage, squat on the floor, and you might just make it home."

She scowled. "Squat? I think not. At most, I shall recline elegantly on the floor. You know, I think you're trying to make me look bad on purpose. Was there no other choice of outerwear?"

"This beats what they'll give you in prison, although a few months in there might do wonders for your attitude. Here, this one has fewer patches."

He held out a cloak that was marginally less disgusting than the other two. She snatched it from his hand and wrapped the coarse cloth around her shoulders. It emanated the medicinal smell of carbolic soap with a hint of mouse.

Trusdale grinned. "You're welcome. And if I was trying to make you look bad, believe me, you'd be wearing something a lot worse than an old cloak. Consider yourself lucky. Now, flounce on over there, missy. Stay along the edge of the square if you can, and don't bat your eyes at the soldiers. I know how you ladies love a man in uniform."

Constance shot him a glare she sincerely hoped would send him straight to hell.

Trusdale's grin grew even wider. He stepped in close to pull up her cloak hood, then yanked it down as far as it could go over her face. "There, that's the best look I've seen you in yet. Very fetching."

Constance bit back an unladylike phrase and skulked away. She kept her head down as she wended her way between the shoppers on the promenade. It seemed every redcoat in Yorkshire watched her as she headed for Pinder's Print Emporium.

Chapter 29:
The Duchess and the Sky Pirate

CONSTANCE MADE HER WAY AROUND the edge of the square under the watchful eye of Britannia. The statue thrust a trident triumphantly to the sky. The marble maiden personified imperial power on sea, land, and air at every memorial park throughout the British Empire—from Anguilla to Zaire.

Bold pigeons perched on the goddess's plumed helmet, adding their own small decorations to the sculpture. Papa had always said there were few creatures in the world more patriotic than British pigeons, though unfortunately their contributions to art in their limited palette of white were rarely appreciated. Pigeons were the most misunderstood of all of nature's *artistes*.

Constance pulled close her tatty brown cloak and tried to look inconspicuous. It was the first time in her life she had dressed to evade attention rather than to attract it. Blood pounded in her ears, a fast tattoo that dulled the street noise to a background rumble. Her breaths came fast and shallow, and her damp clothes seemed as heavy as Britannia's stone robes. Curiously, her head felt light, as if she'd been sampling the estate's notoriously alcoholic blackberry cider.

She fluttered between the pedestrians, homing in on Pinder's store as surely as any pigeon. It was almost like the flying sensation she remembered as a toddler, being carried down the staircases at Haltwhistle Hall by her mother. Mama had always said she wasn't really flying, but Constance never truly believed her. Like all children, once upon a time, she'd flown.

Deep in her bustle, Trusdale's triangular artifact added its own electrical tingle to her physiology. She knew she had done him an enormous favor by liberating the Enigma Key from his vest pocket. Whether he would view it that way remained to be seen. Hopefully, he'd assume he'd lost the key in the canal. If instead he suspected she'd stolen it, it wasn't as if he could search her. Propriety would never allow it. What was put in the bustle stayed in the bustle.

She could feel the artifact licking around the edges of her brain, sampling her, tasting her. She kept up her guard, maintaining a polite distance from the probing shadow. Hopefully, this key was a quiet one. The chatty keys could fast become a nuisance. And she had quite enough problems to deal with at the moment, thank you very much.

Constance kept her eyes down as she hurried by the redcoats close to Pinder's store. Despite the dreadful feeling that a hand would descend upon her shoulder at any second to drag her off to jail, she reached the side of the dragon carriage without arrest. The driver's box was empty, and a street boy stood holding the chestnut ponies' heads.

The ponies munched on sweet oats in nose bags embroidered with the Haltwhistle shield. The golden shield's image of a tiny knight kicking a red dragon up the backside illustrated the demise of the Dragon of Wantley, a popular local legend. It was the tale of a Haltwhistle ancestor who discovered a dragon's only vulnerable spot and took advantage of the situation wearing a suit of Sheffield armor with sharp-toed boots. The story of the arse-kick of doom was the subject of two operas and a host of ribald drinking songs in the city's most raucous taverns. It was also the reason for the Haltwhistle family's reputation as no-holds-barred fighters.

Rogues, dilettantes, and thieves. With the theft of the Enigma Key, Constance now knew which family category she fell into. She was a thief.

Was becoming a thief a stepping-stone to achieving the title of rogue? Or were they separate career paths? *Babett's* didn't cover such matters.

Hearn's bulky frame appeared through the poster-plastered window of Pinder's Print Emporium. She strolled by the glass in her shepherd's cloak, then, turning with a speed any pickpocket would have envied, she darted for the emporium's door.

She pushed it open and a wave of warm air, heavy with the scent of ink and books, swept over her. The massive steam-powered printing press hissed in standby mode. Hearn stood at the long oak counter, talking to Eli Pinder. Pinder was showing the liveried driver something behind one of the countertop privacy screens.

What can Hearn be studying so intently?

She strolled over to see.

Pinder snapped, "Oi—you, out. No beggars in here, thank you very much."

She turned to look for the beggar. There was no one else in the shop. *Is Pinder drunk, again?*

Trusdale walked into the store and threw back the hood of his cloak.

Pinder's gaunt face brightened. "Ah, hello again, sir. I'm glad you're back. I've a series of lithographs of a very specialized nature, involving a see-saw. I'm sure they'll be right up your peculiar alley."

Trusdale's cheeks reddened. "Ah, no, thank you. I'm not here for any—art."

"You should see it before you make that determination. It's quite the sauce."

Hearn leafed through a small book on the counter, *A Beginner's Guide to Writing Love Sonnets.* Constance blinked. *Goodness. Surely Hearn's party trick of bending an iron bar around his neck was more than enough to woo the local shepherdesses. Is he now trying to impress the milkmaids too?*

Hearn noticed her and stuffed the book inside his coat faster than a steam train on a downhill gradient. He slapped a handful of coins on the counter and said loudly, "Miss Constance, thank heavens you're here. I was getting worried."

Pinder laughed. "Good one, Hearn. She does have the same coloring as herself. Mind you, this hay bag looks like she's spent the morning in a sheep dip. Go on, out with you. You won't get any pennies in here. Try the park."

She spluttered with indignation, heat rising in her cheeks.

Cawley walked into the print shop and pulled back his cloak hood.

Pinder whistled. "Well, Cawley, what happened to you? You look almost as bad as this wretched—" He glanced back and forth between Cawley and Constance.

The penny dropped. Pinder chuckled. "Well, well, well, how the mighty have fallen."

Constance snapped, "We're wearing these cloaks for a bet. Now, have you received any response to my kidnapping poster? Surely someone wants the reward?"

"Aye, as a matter of fact, someone does."

"Oh, thank heavens. I've been so worried."

"Have you now? Well then, before we go any further, let's discuss my finder's fee. I'm thinking fifty pounds."

"Mr. Pinder, lives are on the line."

"Make that sixty pounds."

Constance put her hands on her hips. "My offer is five pounds, and I don't allow Hearn to beat you up for your exploitation of the situation."

"Thirty, or I pop on outside and ask the redcoats who they're looking for." Pinder smirked. "I'm not daft, Miss Haltwhistle. You wouldn't be walking around the city center like a vagabond unless you really did the naughty."

"You're an absolute villain, Pinder. Very well, thirty, if the tip proves to be good."

"All right then. Seems a certain dancer in Attercliffe has some news about airships that go bump in the night. She works at the Wiggle Room, and she only takes hard cash, if you know what I mean."

She frowned. "I don't."

Hearn said, "I do. I'll handle it, Miss Constance."

"Does this place serve whisky?" Trusdale asked Hearn.

"Oh, aye, sir. They stock all the fancy liquors, at a decent price too. There's a rumor crates of alcohol regularly fall off the back of wagons in that part of town."

"I'll come with you," said Trusdale.

"And so will I," said Constance.

Cawley cleared his throat. "Sorry, miss, but don't you have a prior luncheon engagement, and the royal garden party to attend?"

She stared blankly, then slapped her forehead. "Crikey, yes, Auntie Madge will be furious. This headache is driving me to distraction."

Trusdale managed to look both guilty and worried at the same time. "Maybe I should come with you instead?"

"To lunch with my godmother? I think not. You've made enough of an impression on her to last a lifetime. And you certainly won't be welcome on her airship. It's a tempered-glass galleon. Everyone would be able to see this." She waved a hand at his damp, black ensemble.

Trusdale slapped both hands to his cheeks and said in a high-pitched tone, "Heaven forfend."

She growled, "How dare you—?"

Hearn interjected, "I'm sure you don't want to keep the countess waiting, miss. If you'd like to head out, I'd be happy to interrogate the dancer for you, honest I would."

She took a deep breath. "You're a treasure, Hearn. Very well, interrogate away. Mr. Pinder, my telegrams, if you please."

Pinder handed her a thick stack of yellow telegrams. The top four bore the thrilling red stamp of "International Wire: USA" across their sealed envelopes. The telegrams from her American contacts. Now she would find out if Mr. "J. F." Trusdale was exactly who he said he was.

She beamed at the tall American. He regarded her warily. She said, "Cawley, you'll drive me to Auntie Madge's estate. Hearn, please find out what you can from the informant. Mr. Trusdale, I would tell you where to go, but I'm far too much of a lady."

Trusdale scowled.

She smirked. "Hearn, is Boo still in the back of the carriage?"

"Aye, miss. That little Yorkie's been doing a grand job guarding all your trunks and hatboxes. Someone so much as looks at that carriage the wrong way, and she yaps loud enough to wake the dead. I let her have a good run around the park, and she curled up as pretty as a picture on that pile of old ball gowns you've got in there."

"Old . . . I'll have you know that's my costume for the garden party. Everyone's required to wear floral attire. I'm going as arrowhead."

"The waterweed?" asked Hearn.

"The aquatic spring blossom, yes. Cawley, we'll stop by a few bogs on the way over to Auntie Madge's to see if you can find a few live arrowhead blooms to adorn the dress."

Cawley's shoulders sagged. "Nothing would give me greater pleasure, miss."

"Good man." She paused, trying to recall the title of the novel she'd leafed through in Maya's laboratory. At that time, she was not yet a thief, and had placed the pink volume back on the shelf where she found it. Now, what was it called? *The Countess and the Gamekeeper*?

She furrowed her brow. No, not a gamekeeper. The inside plate had shown a striking image of an airship pilot. He'd been a muscular man in a tricorn hat who inexplicably didn't wear a shirt while flying his ship. But he did wear an eye patch. "Mr. Pinder, before I go, do you happen to have a copy of a novel called *The Duchess and the Sky Pirate*?"

Pinder's jaw dropped. "You're kidding, right? I wouldn't have thought you were one for the romances, Miss Haltwhistle."

"It's for a friend. A maid—no, a shepherdess. You know what they're like. Just give me the book."

Pinder scrabbled under the oak counter and drew out a thick novel bound in a dusky pink leather. "Here you go. You might want to tell your 'friend' there's a whole series of these books. Apparently, the duchess has quite the travel schedule."

"That will be all for now, thank you." She ignored Trusdale's raised eyebrows and snatched the novel off the counter. Yanking up the hood of her shabby cloak, she turned and stormed toward the door with her nose in the air and cheeks burning.

She heard Pinder whistle and say, "Well, who'd have thought it? She's as depraved as you are, Mr. Trusdale. Right, gents, I'm closing for lunch. Who wants to head down to Attercliffe and see some saucy ladies?"

No one turned Pinder down.

Chapter 30: The Wiggle Room

After a morning packed with assassins, redcoats, and Constance, Trusdale reckoned he'd earned a few drams of whisky at the Wiggle Room. His damp clothes were drying nicely in the warm, beer-scented air of the underground club. The shepherd's cloak had proven invaluable in a tense game of hide-and-go-seek with the redcoats through the back alleys of Sheffield. With the cloak now bundled by his feet, he sipped the Scottish ambrosia, truly glad to be alive.

As the invisible assassins were probably still in their dirigible heading for the hills, maybe he could breathe easy for a little while? Lord knows, he could use a reprieve from the unfolding disaster that was Constance's Plan with a capital 'P.'

On the cogwheel-shaped stage before him, eight voluptuous ladies high-kicked a Yorkshire version of the can-can. Their brass goggles glinted in the gaslight as they danced. Their costumes bore an uncanny resemblance to the Steamwerks ladies' uniforms of white shirts, brown bloomers, and high-laced boots. A full brass band accompanied the performers with an enthusiasm bordering on mania. Two blond, bosomy Valkyries in horned helmets and leather armor swung on trapezes bolted to the vaulted cellar roof. The immortals casually tossed axes to each other over the heads of the dancers.

Hearn nudged him in the ribs. "Now, there's a sight for sore eyes, eh? Welcome to *Freya: The Musical.* This show has it all: men dressed as women, women dressed as men, songs, jokes, jugglers, magicians, fire-eaters, swordplay, and a chariot pulled by blue leopards. Best entertainment in Sheffield, for less than the price of two fish-and-chip suppers. Now, that's value in entertainment."

The brawny driver clinked his mug of warm beer against Trusdale's whisky tumbler and Pinder's absinthe goblet. He quaffed down a half pint of malted goodness in one hearty gulp, white foam cresting the wave of his walrus mustache. Hearn slammed his mug down hard on the round oak table and belched with gusto.

Pinder took a sip of absinthe and leaned over to Trusdale. The gaunt man raised his voice over a rousing tuba solo from the brass band. "Aye, it's a grand play all right. The Viking goddess Freya makes a bet with Odin that love can overcome war. She casts a spell on the Steamwerkers of Sheffield, so they all fall in love with each other. Then the Steamwerkers declare love on France and build automaton poets. The poets fly over to France and spout sonnets until everybody there falls in love too. Then there's a dancing cow that symbolizes the end of war. For the finale, there's a fan dancer. He's amazing, he is. Ends up in just his breeches, suspenders, and flat cap, if you can imagine that. We still can't figure out how he gets his shirt off without buttons flying all over the place."

Trusdale nodded. It wasn't quite the burlesque he'd seen in Paris, but he could appreciate a leather-clad Valkyrie on a trapeze as well as the next man.

He took another sip of whisky from his tulip-shaped tumbler. The caramel elixir warmed him with the taste of peat-grown heather, briny meadows, ancient oak barrels, and a deep, lingering finish. With every sip, he appreciated the dour men of the Highlands who took the time to develop their distilling craft to such sublimity.

Rotgut, it was not.

The former brewery cellar, now converted to Sheffield's largest theater, provided a surprisingly sophisticated array of vintage liquors. Hundreds of workmen sat around oak tables, smoking cigars and downing shots and ale. Most of them wore Steamwerks uniforms and took particular delight in the similarly attired dancers. The audience almost kept time with the trumpets, trombones, and drums of the rousing score as they cheered, clapped, and stomped their steel-toed boots and clogs on the cobbled floor.

"So, you two come here often?" asked Trusdale.

"Aye. We get in free, because Hearn works here," said Pinder.

Trusdale goggled at the liveried driver. "You're a . . . dancer?"

The driver chuckled. "Nay, lad. Every Friday night they have a boxing match. I'm the main attraction. I take on anybody who's daft enough to step into the ring. I've never been beaten."

The lights dimmed, and the dancers produced blowtorches. With a hiss of gas, each torch burst into blue-flamed life. The dancers pirouetted through an intricate pyrotechnic choreography that just stopped short of burning down the theater.

The cellar grew noticeably warmer. Trusdale glanced around to see if there were any fire exits other than the steep steps that led up to the street.

There were none. His eyes lingered on a mirrored bar manned by a brunette in a green fairy outfit. The all-female serving staff of the theater each wore the same alluring uniform. With their long hair pinned up into fanciful styles, the women flitted between the tables in emerald tulle gowns, tightly laced over-corsets, and gossamer wings. It was a very adult fairyland as the alcohol, dim lighting, and thundering music vibrated patrons into an advanced state of relaxation.

The brunette behind the bar winked. She ran her hand down the side of her corset and wiggled her wings.

Hearn nodded toward the barmaid. "In case you're wondering, Mr. Trusdale, that's Ethel Cartwright, or Lucretia, as she likes to be called. She'll dance on your table for ten shillings, and will drink you under it faster than you can blink. She's a dab hand at lifting wallets. I'd keep an eye on her, if you go that way."

Pinder leered. "From what I've seen, Mr. Trusdale here prefers redheads. Short, cantankerous redheads, to be precise."

Trusdale spluttered his whisky, spraying the precious liquid over the oak table. He wiped his mouth on the back of his hand. "No, not at all. Why would you say that?"

"I'm a keen observer of the foibles of others. Keeps me entertained. If you want my advice—"

"Which he doesn't, Pinder. No one does."

"—you'll run back to America as fast as your legs can carry you. That Haltwhistle woman is a winsome siren, luring you into a whirlpool of lunacy. Escape while you still can." Pinder waggled his eyebrows as he took another sip of absinthe.

Hearn glowered. "Don't make me slap you, you daft pillock. Ignore him, Mr. Trusdale. Pinder is clearly barmy for saying such a thing. He knows well and good that a gentleman such as yourself would never think of a fine lady like Miss Constance that way. It's ridiculous to even joke about it."

"Of course it is," said Trusdale, "because of . . . ?"

"Land, money, titles, breeding, tradition, her father—need I go on?"

Trusdale ran his fingertips around the top of the whisky glass. "Reckon you hit all the points why she would never—"

"Like any sane man would fancy that red devil," Pinder spat. "She's a shrew of the first degree. She's made the printing of the Queen's parade programs an absolute nightmare. The things she's said about my dangling participles keep me awake at night."

Hearn wagged his finger at Pinder. "I'm warning you right now, you leave Miss Constance alone. She's got enough on without you badmouthing her to all and sundry. She's not a bad lass, mostly, and she's dealing with matters strange and unusual."

"I'm glad to hear it—ow." Pinder flinched as Hearn slapped his arm.

"Shut it, or else. 'Ey up—looks like Freya's about to make her grand entrance."

The crowd exploded into cheers as the dance reached a fiery climax. The dancers formed into two lines facing each other, creating an honor guard to the rear of the stage. The ladies held their blowtorches high as the crowd whooped and hollered as loud as the patrons of any Wild West bar.

Hearn bellowed over the din, "Pinder said that the goddess Freya is the one who responded to our poster. Her stage name is Arianna, and her real name is Betty Harbottle. She might be able to give us a tip about the kidnapping."

The dancer's blowtorches flared to create an ethereal blue gateway to Asgard. The stage curtains opened, and two rare blue leopards, as big as Shetland ponies, stalked out. The cobalt spotted cats drew a golden mini-chariot through the flaming arches. Standing tall in the chariot, the goddess Freya surveyed her cheering devotees with a warm smile. She was a full-figured woman in her early thirties with wild blond tresses falling to her waist. Worn over a flowing gold tulle gown, a leather breastplate enhanced her ample charms to epic proportions. A cloak of falcon feathers draped from her broad shoulders.

She brought the blue leopards to a halt at the front of the stage. As the brass band rose to a crescendo, she heaved her impressive bosom once, then sang of love as only a goddess could.

Trusdale was enchanted from the first perfect note. Her soprano voice filled his body with heartache. Loves won and lost flashed before his eyes. *Am I destined to always be alone?*

He glanced around the table. Hearn's eyes glistened in the dim light. The big man reached into his pocket and pulled out a white handkerchief. He blew his nose with the passion of a trumpet solo, then drew a small book out of his tailcoat pocket and mumbled sonnets to himself.

Pinder stared glassily at the stage, slack-jawed with rapture. Tears slid down his lean cheeks and soaked into his wispy mustache. He ran his scrawny hands through his greased hair and sighed.

Around them, men forged in the heat of steel furnaces wiped their eyes on their shirtsleeves. As Freya finished her song, the workmen gave a standing ovation that rocked the foundation of the underground theater.

The blue leopards glowered at the sea of workers. At Freya's command, they drew the chariot once around the stage, then stalked back through the curtains.

After that, the spell was broken. The brass band switched to a lively jig. A troop of male clog dancers clattered onto the stage to toss large metal cogwheels at each other with surprising grace.

Hearn said, "Now's our chance, gents. We'll head backstage and see what Arianna has to tell us about this kidnapping." The liveried driver stood and gulped down the last of his beer. "Willful waste makes woeful want."

Trusdale agreed. "Waste not, want not." He downed his whisky, savoring the warm peat finish. He followed Hearn and Pinder toward a hidden door set into the oak-barrel wall. Trusdale straightened his damp neckerchief and took off his hat as he strode backstage.

This would be his very first meeting with a Viking goddess.

Chapter 31: The Goddess Sings

THROUGH THE HIDDEN DOOR, A world of pleasures awaited any workingman with extra coin burning in his pocket. Three female fire-eaters, splendidly outfitted in brass chain mail corsets over orange tulle gowns, performed a private show for a group of miners. The men sat on a wooden bench enthralled as the ladies tossed their fire fans in a fearless pyrotechnic display.

Trusdale paused, mesmerized by the dancers' grace.

He sure did love fire-eaters.

Hearn tugged at his sleeve. "Come on. Miss Arianna has her own private hidey-hole in the back."

They walked between the wooden screens that separated the miners' area from the open dressing room. Two standing gas lamps cast a golden glow over a half-dozen buxom ladies as they laced each other into red silk corsets. Their costumes were completed by knee-length white bloomers and blue, high-laced boots. Other troupe members slathered makeup onto their faces at the mismatched collection of antique mirrors splattered across the cavern wall.

Two blond Valkyries in leather armor polished their swords and encouraged a male Steamwerks dancer as he practiced tossing ostrich-feather fans high in the air. He caught the fans and swept into a passionate, swan-inspired dance in his wooden clogs.

Impressive. Not quite as good as the fire-eaters, but still . . .

The cloying air was filled with the scent of tallow-based greasepaint, cheap lavender perfume, and a hint of smoked spices that Trusdale couldn't quite identify.

Pinder said, "Ooh, look, Hearn, they've set up a snuff room. Or at least, a snuff area." The printer pointed at a well-worn green sofa pushed against the cellar wall. Beside the sofa, a glassy-eyed stuffed fox stood guard over a shelf that held twenty brightly colored tea caddies. A postcard glued to the front of each tea caddy named the snuff inside. Trusdale recognized A Glob of Glasgow and A Dab of Dublin from Le Paon Pompeux's snuff room. Mysterious new blends included A Longing for Lolita and Saucy Bugle Boy.

"Right, gents," Pinder said. "I'll leave you here. I'm going to make sure the snuff is up to snuff."

Hearn scowled. "Haven't you learned your lesson? Absinthe and snuff? Isn't that a quick way to spending a night in the gutter?"

"I'll be all right."

Hearn continued, "It can't be the real thing. The Steamwerks wouldn't hand out Lolita and Saucy Bugle Boy to the armed forces. That powder could be made from anything—old tea leaves, opium, who knows?"

"I'll be fine, you old worrywart. I know what I'm doing. Oh, and give my love to Betty."

"That's Miss Arianna to you, and I'll do no such thing. Let's go, Mr. Trusdale; we should be able to catch our songbird before her next number."

He followed Hearn to the end of the cavern. Behind a rose-painted screen, the goddess Freya waggled a feather duster to amuse the two blue leopards, now secure inside a large iron cage. The leopards yawned as Trusdale and Hearn rounded the screen.

"'Ey up, Miss Arianna. How's tha doin'?" said Hearn.

Betty beamed. "Harold. How do? I haven't seen you for a few weeks."

"Aye, I've been busy."

She narrowed her eyes at Trusdale. "Who's the offcumden?"

Trusdale guessed that meant stranger, or foreigner. He smiled at Betty.

She didn't smile back.

Hearn said, "Nay, lass. Don't mind him, or his outfit. He's a right good sort and a friend to my employer. Miss Arianna, may I present Mr. J. F. Trusdale, from America."

Trusdale bowed low to the Viking goddess with the voice of an angel.

"Ooh, fancy with your moves, aren't you?" She curtseyed pretty nimbly for a woman in a leather breastplate. The movement fluttered her falcon-feather cloak, to the fascination of both leopards.

"Do sit down, gents." She indicated a wooden bench opposite a sagging beige armchair. On the chair rested a ball of red wool, skewered by two knitting needles, and an almost complete child's scarf. She moved the knitting to one side of the chair and sat in a swoosh of feathers and tulle.

Hearn and Trusdale took a seat on the wooden bench and stared in awe at the cobalt leopards. Betty said, "Don't be afraid of these two dears. They're long past their prime and as tame as tabby cats—rescued years back when the old Sheffield zoo closed. They're fed the best diced mutton, and a farmer friend of mine lets them run loose through his cornfields when they're not performing. He says they're the best scarecrows he's ever had. I call them Dido and Aeneas."

"From the opera?" asked Trusdale.

Her eyebrows raised. "That's right. You like Henry Purcell, Mr. Trusdale?"

"Yes, ma'am. And may I say, you've got as beautiful a singing voice as any opera singer I've ever heard."

She blushed. "Aww, bless you. I reckon Love herself reaches out to us through music. No matter the risk of heartache, my advice is to roam this earth until you find your true love. Once you do, sing a duet until the stars are eclipsed by the light you shine on each other's soul."

Hearn nodded. "Aye, that's what I always say. Well, perhaps not in those exact words, but close enough in meaning. Now, a little bird told me that you might know something about the disappearance of three scientists."

Her face fell. "I might; it depends. Who's offering this reward?"

"The Haltwhistle family. And the reward's a thousand pounds, cash. That should pay you and your son's way for the next ten years."

Betty gave a low whistle. "Blimey. With that much money I could give him everything I've never had. All right, Harold, that's enough for me to talk. But you must keep this between the three of us. This is a dangerous business."

"I give you my word."

She hugged herself and rocked, her face tight with tension. "All right then. I'll share my tragic tale. It all started innocently enough. A few months back, the troupe put on a private show for a bunch of toffs over at Poncenby's Gentleman's Club."

Hearn said to Trusdale, "Poncenby's is an upper-crust club, very exclusive."

"That's right. After the show, I chatted with a young lord from Handsworth with a keen ear for singers. A week or two later, he introduced me to Prince Lucien Albert Dunstan."

That name sounds familiar . . .

Hearn gasped. "Oh my gawd. The Queen's grandson?"

"The same, and he fancies himself a patron of the arts both high and low. He offered me a fair amount of money to serenade him with an operatic performance while he took his morning bath."

Hearn's jaw dropped. "His morning bath?"

"Yes. He has this huge bathtub, big enough for twenty people. Solid gold it is. Every morning he's in there with his houseguests. Different women most every day, and stark naked, the lot of them. Ooh, I've seen some things . . . mind you, it's the chamber orchestra I feel sorry for. Fancy having to play your instrument in full evening dress with all that soapy nonsense going on."

Trusdale raised an eyebrow. "He has an orchestra in his bathroom?"

"Yes, he has a stage permanently set up. Sometimes, he invites a troupe of open-minded actors to perform Shakespeare in the buff. He claims this allows true art to shine, without the artifice of costumes and props. He's ever so cultured, so it must be true. And talk about sophisticated. Why, I must have heard him swear in ten different languages. I can't say I wasn't a little in awe of him when we met. He can be absolutely charming when he's not being a complete brute. He's a real-life Heathcliff, all bad temper and brooding good looks. The girls go mad for him."

She sighed. "Anyway, of course, one thing led to another, and before I knew it, I was being paid to do things that had nothing to do with singing. Now, that's all part of being a full-service entertainer, and I won't say I wasn't willing, but I didn't know that he was the jealous type. It seems the Prince couldn't have cared less if I had a dozen regular clients, but lord help me if I ever fell in love. And the trouble is, I did, with Alan, one of our cogwheel jugglers."

Her blue eyes brimmed with tears. Hearn reached into his waistcoat pocket and offered her his white handkerchief.

Betty took it and dabbed her eyes. "Bless ya, Harold." She balled the handkerchief in her hands and stared down at it. Her voice dropped to a whisper. "So, Alan and I started talking about getting married and moving down to London. He reckoned I should try to get onto the vaudeville stage. He said I should be a proper singer, respectable like. He had a cousin who could put us up, and he'd got himself a decent job lined up at Covent Garden Market. It was going to be wonderful."

She sniffed and dabbed at her eyes once more. Hearn leaned over and patted her knee. "It's all right love, you can tell us."

"It's hard. So hard." Her voice broke. "But I've got to tell someone. Don't ask me how, but Erhard, the Prince's right-hand man, heard about our plans to elope. He told His Royal Highness, who got all riled up about me leaving. On Tuesday evening—the same night those scientists were taken—the Prince got blind drunk and sent his men out to pick up Alan and me. Deep in the woods on his estate, he forced Alan to face him in a duel. Of course, Alan didn't know anything about dueling with pistols. They handed him a gun, telling him that was the one he had to use. They said it was all set to fire, all he had to do was pull the trigger."

Hearn said. "Bloody Nora."

"I know. Dueling's a regular occurrence for the toffs, but Alan barely knew which end of the gun was which. Anyway, Erhard called for the duel to start. That Austrian devil dropped a handkerchief onto the ground. The Prince and Alan took ten slow paces away from each other as Erhard counted. Alan was gazing at me the whole way. They both got to the tenth step, turned, and fired. But Alan's gun just clicked. It wasn't loaded. Then the Prince's gun rang out. He shot poor Alan right between the eyes. Alan was dead before he even hit the ground."

Hearn clenched his fists. "Poor blighter, he never stood a chance. I'd like to get my hands on the whole bloody lot of them. I'd show them what it's like to be on the wrong end of an unfair fight." He opened his left palm and punched it with his right fist. "No messin' about. They'd rue the day they took one of our own."

She sobbed, her body racked with grief. "You ain't even heard the worst of it. The Prince, Lucien, devil incarnate that he is, roared with laughter and strolled away from Alan's corpse, as cool as a cucumber. Like he could murder an innocent man any day of the week and not even care." Her eyes lit with fury. "Then Erhard, that scar-faced bastard, had the nerve to saunter up and say this was just a warning, and I'd better not leave town without the Prince's consent. He said I should watch myself, or they'd come after my son next. The boy's only five years old. Who threatens a child like that?"

Only a swine, that's who. Trusdale gritted his teeth. "This Erhard, he's—"

"Ex-Austrian military. Got drummed out for some dark reason. He dresses shabby, but always carries an antique officer's saber. He fancies himself quite the sergeant major, giving orders whenever the Prince's back is turned. Anyway, there's me wailing over Alan's body, with thugs standing over me, telling me it's time to go. Erhard starts talking to midair, paying me no notice. He's telling someone I literally can't see to set up lights in the woods near that old tin mine the Prince's father turned into a folly. He made it a point to this ghost that the lanterns must be visible from the sky."

Trusdale nodded. "Maybe guiding in an airship?"

"Exactly. It wasn't until later that it hit me how odd him having a conversation with empty air was. I've been playing back every detail of the evening over and over again in my mind, wondering if I could have said something, done something, to stop it all turning out as it did. If only I could have—"

Trusdale shook his head. "Don't blame yourself. The fault lies with the Prince, not you."

"Aye. But I got took in by his fine words and manners. He's a devil. Pure and simple. And Erhard talks to ghosts. For all I know, Alan's death was some sort of sacrifice to dark forces beyond my ken."

"Sadly, evil men don't need a dark force to drive them to murderous acts," said Trusdale. "And now we've heard your story, it seems clear that you need to get out of this place. Sooner or later, the Prince will start to clean up loose ends. Right now, he thinks you'll be too scared to talk. But he could change his mind. You and your son should leave this town, maybe even this country."

She blew her nose loudly into the handkerchief. "I don't know where to go."

Hearn sucked air through the gap in his front teeth. "Baron Haltwhistle has a town house in London he never uses. You and your boy can travel down there today. Stay for as long as you like while you get yourself set up. There's a live-in butler there who can help you travel to the continent if you think it's necessary."

Betty sniffed and rubbed her eyes. "The Haltwhistles won't mind?"

"The Baron's in no place to disagree, and his daughter wouldn't say no, I promise you that."

Betty smiled weakly. "She sounds like an angel."

Hearn gave a wry grin. "That she isn't, but she has her moments. She'll see you right."

"Thank you, both of you. You're true gents." Betty's red-rimmed eyes glanced up as a Valkyrie popped her horned helmet around the wooden screen.

"Sorry to interrupt," the Valkyrie said. "Betty, they're adding two new numbers so you can fill in for the fan dancer. He's had a bit of a mishap. Apparently, he decided to switch his ostrich feathers for the fire fans."

Betty sighed. "He never learns." She stood. "I'd best get out there and see what they want me to sing. The show must always go on, even for the broken-hearted. Thank you for listening to me, gentlemen. I owe you more than you know." She curtseyed and swept sadly away in a flurry of feathers.

Hearn whistled. "Poor lamb. And who would have thought that Prince Lucien was kidnapping scientists in his spare time?"

"Where have I heard the name Lucien before?" Trusdale struggled to dredge up the right memory from the swirl of events over the past two days. "I don't exactly keep up with all of Victoria's royal relatives."

"Prince Lucien is the biggest landowner around here. His estate, Wedgeworth Warbling, is a good thirty thousand acres. In fact, Miss Constance is on her way to—" Hearn blanched.

Trusdale's heart plunged into his boots. "His garden party? Dammit, Hearn, if Lucien is the one behind all this, she's in serious danger!"

Hearn blew out his cheeks. "So is the Prince, if she finds out he's the one who ruined her party. As the estate staff say, 'Hell hath no fury like a Haltwhistle armed.' She'll have his guts for garters, if he's not careful. What time is it?"

Trusdale reached for his fob watch, recalled Constance had put it in the wrong pocket, and drew it out. He flipped open the case. "It's almost two."

"The party starts at two thirty. She's probably on her way there now. She hates being late for anything."

"Her cousin Wellington was invited to the same event."

"Lord Pendelroy? Well, he's always late to everything. With any luck, we can hitch a ride on his airship out to Wedgeworth Warbling."

Trusdale slipped the watch into his waistcoat's left pocket and patted the right. He expected to feel the triangular shape of Maya's artifact but didn't. He turned his pocket inside-out and checked for holes. He ran his hands feverishly up and down his waistcoat, searching for the metal triangle, then sprang up and started pulling items from every pocket on his person.

Hearn stared at him slack-jawed as a pile of oddities dropped to the floor: a box of revolver shells, a bunch of skeleton keys, a brass telescope, a knuckle-duster, a map of the Netherlands, three pairs of goggles, a flint and steel, a pair of handcuffs, a bottle of India ink, fishhooks and twine, a harmonica, a compass, a lady's lace handkerchief, a knife, and a dozen other items including McKinley's journals. The caged leopards were particularly captivated by an ostrich-feather quill stuck into the paper casing of a stick of dynamite.

Hearn cleared his throat. "You lost something, Mr. Trusdale?"

"My trust in humanity, and a key I was keeping for Maya Chauhan. Damn that woman."

"Maya?"

"No. The thief." He sighed and stuffed his belongings back into his pockets.

The artifact was gone.

Only one suspect came to mind.

Chapter 32: Unnatural Selection

ON A GRAND AIRSHIP TWENTY miles away, Constance perched on a footstool as her hair was tugged into an elegant updo by two of Auntie Madge's sturdiest maids. A breeze whistled across the deck and tested the styling skills of the servants. As they labored, they whispered to each other about the fabulous impression the countess's crystal dirigible would make when it landed at the Prince's garden party. The eighty-foot long galleon was a welcome upgrade for Constance after the cramped conditions aboard the bumblebee mini-dirigible. Her wooden stool was a far more suitable seat than a cowboy's lap, although admittedly, it wasn't quite as comfortable.

Auntie Madge reclined in poisonous splendor upon a golden chaise longue. The Countess of Benchley, à la Miss Deadly Nightshade 1845, had outdone herself with her floral costume. Her silver hair was pinned into a pompadour, ornamented by an exquisite diamond tiara. An emerald sari, decorated with black-onyx nightshade berries, wrapped her bony frame. She peered down her long-handled opera glasses at a thick stack of yellow pages resting upon the albino mink throw that covered her lower extremities.

Similar throws lay across the laps of Madge's noble guests as they lounged upon silver thrones arranged in a circle. Lord Pinkington-Smyth and his chinless son, Pinkie, held on to their top hats as the wind picked up, ruffling the scarlet roses sewn onto their vests. The eighty-year-old Earl of Pembroke made a bolder floral statement with yellow greasepaint caked across his wrinkled face, giving the sour-tempered peer an almost sunny disposition. The Duchess of Courtland was a living icicle in a blue hyacinth gown and white pompadour wig.

Despite the chill breeze and her lack of a throw, Constance was in heaven. It was her maiden voyage on a first-class dirigible, and she didn't want to miss any nuance of the experience. She gazed through the tempered-glass deck at the rolling hills below. The glass was partially etched with cheeky harp-playing cherubim flying amidst billowing clouds. They peeked down with her at a patchwork of lush, green pastures and fresh-plowed fields. The view from heaven was enhanced by the music of a slender brunette harpist in a snowy Grecian robe, to which Constance listened in rapture.

Sharp pins needling her scalp interrupted her daydream. The maids apologized as they struggled to affix her mother's emerald tiara to her updo.

"It doesn't have to be on there permanently, you know," said Constance.

"Begging your pardon, miss, but if it slips off kilter—your godmother—"

"Will throw a blue fit. Proceed."

In *Babett's* exhaustive list of social sins, an off-kilter tiara was practically a hanging offense. What could be the punishment for showing up to a royal garden party in a homemade costume?

Constance smoothed out the skirts of her off-the-shoulder ball gown. In one night, she had transformed the gown into a billowy representation of the waterweed arrowhead. Ten layers of ragged silver chiffon cascaded over a navy blue taffeta underskirt. Silver fringe ripped from the main dining room curtains evoked sunlight sparkling on pooled water.

Cawley had grumbled his way through moorland bogs to gather real arrowhead plants to complete her ensemble. Her silver bodice bore a trim of dark green leaves shaped like an arrow's point. White blooms dotted her skirts, and a silver Persian recurve bow and a quiver stuffed with white-fletched arrows completed her personification of *Sagittaria vulgaris*.

The weapon partially offset her lack of armored underwear. Upon arrival at her godmother's estate, Auntie Madge had ordered the maids to dispose of her canal-sodden clothing as she bathed. Despite her protests that her chain mail lingerie served as a posture-improving necessity, she was cinched into a traditional whalebone corset that Madge had sported barely fifty years before. The whalebone did wonders for her feminine curves but would not protect against an assassin's blade.

By the skin of her teeth, she had managed to persuade the maids to allow her to keep wearing her hidden bustle bag. Sadly, the bag now only held one unused smoke grenade, the Enigma Key, and her romance novel. Whether any of these items would help protect her against attacks by Swedish cutthroats remained to be seen. With Cawley sent packing back to Haltwhistle Hall by Madge, she was entirely alone. If only Hearn were here, or perhaps even—

She shook her head, and the maids chorused a groan.

No. She wasn't desperate enough to wish for Trusdale. Her telegrams from Bobby Two-Fists, Tesla, and the West Point academy proved he was not the man he claimed to be. She couldn't wait to see the look on his face when she exposed him as an imposter. Mr. J. F. Trusdale was nothing more than a—

"Don't you agree, Constance?" said the countess.

Every eye on the crystal airship was trained upon her.

She sat up straight. "I'm sorry, Auntie, I missed that."

The countess frowned. "Am I to understand that you haven't been listening to one word I've said?"

"Oh heavens, no."

"Then you agree that the situation is best resolved before the party's end?"

"Absolutely." *What situation?*

"And I trust that you will keep your opinions on any subject other than the weather to yourself. The last thing a man wants to hear is a woman's opinion. Am I right, Newton?"

Lord Pinkington-Smyth glanced up from his hunting periodical and considered the matter. "Well, yes, I suppose—"

"Also, make sure you stand next to the least attractive woman in attendance. A swan shines brightest amongst the pigeons, don't you agree?"

Unsure if a response would count as expressing her opinion, Constance remained silent.

The countess nodded. "Finally, you're learning. Rest assured, young woman, your future lies safely in my hands." The society maven tapped the yellow pages upon her lap. "I have here the entire RSVP list to the Prince's party, with every eligible bachelor highlighted for my attention."

Constance's eyebrows almost hit her tiara. "How on earth did you get that list?"

"Apparently, the artisan who printed the party invitations accepts donations for such information. Ten pounds, I believe, was the sum requested of my social secretary. Despite my general distaste for contact with the seamy underworld of local business, I purchased a copy of the list. The only name not on there is your own, given that you received a personal invitation from the Prince."

"Might this printer's name have been Eli Pinder?"

"I believe so. Why?"

"He would've charged me fifty pounds for such a list. I knew he was a scoundrel."

"For heaven's sake, child, do try and focus on the larger picture. I've arranged for the local vicar to conduct your wedding ceremony directly after party's grand finale, a polo match."

Ask not for whom the wedding bell tolls, it tolls for me.

Madge scanned the list. "Now, do be quiet. I'm trying to narrow down your potential beaus to an even fifty."

Constance gasped. "Fifty?"

"Indeed. I'm eliminating all foreigners, of course. There's an inordinate number of European counts on here, most unsuitable." Madge ran her liver-spotted hand down the list, then tapped her finger on a name. "Ah, now, this one is interesting, the Earl of Doncaster. Married twice, widowed twice . . . hmm, that doesn't bode well. What do you know about him, Newton?"

Lord Pinkington-Smyth glanced up from his newspaper. "He owns the most splendid pair of matched hunting hounds."

"Excellent, we'll put him down as a maybe."

"But . . ." Constance rubbed her temples. "I have a stellar plan of my own. I read a magazine article last night that stated the best way to capture a gentleman's interest is to giggle and coyly bat a feather fan. I shall approach the handsomest, eligible peer at the party . . ."

"Are you carrying a fan?"

"Well, no, but I do have arrows. I could waft a few of those around—"

"Absolutely not. I shall not be known as the godmother of the woman who stabbed her potential fiancé in the eye."

"But—"

"Honestly, Constance, anyone would think you didn't really want to get married."

Constance wrung her hands. "It's just that I'd assumed I'd have a modicum of input on my future husband. It's not as if I expected true love or anything—"

"I should hope not. Fairytales are for children, not an heiress in immediate need of a spouse."

For the good of the estate. What choice did she have?

And yet . . .

Was it wrong to wish for a little romance? A stolen glance. A moment of understanding. Maybe, even an adventure or two? Constance sighed as the maids clipped surprisingly heavy emerald earrings onto her earlobes. She jiggled her head at the unfamiliar weight.

One more burden to bear.

The servants looked to their mistress for approval. Auntie Madge ran a discerning eye over the jewelry. "Good," she said with a shadow of a smile. "The stones intensify the green of your eyes. Most becoming. We'll make a silk purse out of your sow's ear yet."

Constance reached up to touch her gunshot graze. A flesh-toned medicinal paste disguised her wound. Fortunately, Auntie Madge believed her claim that she'd been nibbled by a flesh fly. At last, she'd found a use for the nasty, biting beasts.

She sneezed as the maids set to powdering her face into a whiter shade of pale with pulverized pearls. Soft wax colored with ruby dust was dabbed onto her lips and cheeks. With a steady hand, one maid painted her eyelashes with a thin line of soot and wax to give the Egyptian look so favored by fashionable ladies this season.

The countess said, "Not too much. She's attending this event to secure a husband, not to dance a burlesque. Just a hint of coquette should do."

Constance clutched the arm of a maid as her head swam and the Enigma Key burst into a melancholy wail about dead oceans and ancient foes . . .

The countess barked, "Is she airsick? Bring out the smelling salts. For heaven's sake, we're almost there. We don't need her passing out in full sight of the other guests."

The wail inside her head faded, as did her headache. *Thank you for taking away my pain*, she thought at the Key. *I know you didn't have to do that.* The Key didn't answer her.

She'd never felt more alone.

The airship sank into a steady descent as they approached the royal estate of Wedgeworth Warbling. Constance stared down at the ancient canopy of oaks, birch, and beech through the glass deck. Twenty-foot-high fences encircled the estate. No escape on foot then, should she turn into a runaway bride. She might have to marry, but did she really need to stick around for the honeymoon?

She sat up straight. "I'm feeling more myself, now. The movement of the ship was a little bouncy and . . . never mind. I'm curious, is it normal for a royal park to be so thoroughly fenced in?"

Lord Pinkington-Smyth peered at her freshly painted face and broke into a toothy grin. "Not on this scale, my dear. It's a safety precaution. The Prince doesn't want anything getting out of the park."

"You mean, *into* the park, like poachers?"

"I mean *out* of the park, like lions."

"Lions?"

He nodded. "Prince Lucien is a big-game hunter, but he doesn't care to travel to get his thrills. He imports exotic creatures by airship from all over the world. The chaps at my club say that he holds the most splendid shooting parties for tigers, elephants—you name it. I hope to secure an invitation someday, but it's very exclusive. If you're not within twenty heartbeats of a throne, the odds of an invite are small."

Constance peered down at the ground with greater interest. "He transports these poor beasts by airship?"

"Bypasses customs that way. You know the royals, they're a law unto themselves. Who else could fly an elephant in a cage over the Yorkshire hills without causing an outcry over public safety? You think it's bad news when a pigeon drops a gift on your shoulder? Imagine an elephant dropping a load of—"

The countess interrupted. "Thank you, Newt, we get the picture. Now, tell me truthfully—does she look like marriage material? Constance, stand and give us a twirl."

She dutifully stood and pirouetted. Even the Duchess of Courtland looked momentarily impressed.

Lord Pinkington-Smyth lowered his reading glasses. "She cleans up a treat. It's a shame about the hair color, but even so, she might draw a few glances."

"Oh, Miss Haltwhistle—I think you look like an aquatic princess," said Pinkie.

Auntie Madge sniped, "With the substantial midriff of a country woman. Gertrude, Winnie, avail yourselves of her corset laces and pull her into shape. If a rib breaks, so be it."

The two maids closed in. Gertrude held a mink throw in front of Constance to act as a changing screen. Winnie unbuttoned the rear of Constance's gown and grabbed the laces. Constance took a final breath of freedom before the corset crushed her into stylish shape.

The pain was excruciating.

Chapter 33: Armed and Fabulous

TWO HOURS LATER, TRUSDALE AND Hearn awaited the pleasure of Lord Wellington Pendelroy in His Lordship's townhouse kitchen. Trusdale walked slowly back and forth in front of the open red-brick fireplace large enough to roast an ox. As he walked, he gently peeled back the soggy pages of the leather-bound journals he'd snatched from McKinley's laboratory. Although the pages were close to disintegration, he counted his blessings that the practical minded scientists who wrote of the invisibility serum had chosen to do so in waterproof ink. Not invisible ink, as might have been done by writers with a greater sense of humor. Such ink, typically citrus juice or milk, would never have survived a dip in a Sheffield canal. But Trusdale could read the scientist's shellac ink as clear as if it had been written that very morning.

As the pages dried, so did Trusdale's damp clothes. His new cologne was a musty mix of industrial canal and coal smoke. Behind him, Hearn sat at a laden farmhouse table, munching on thick slabs of bread topped with pork and chutney. The driver's shirt sleeves were rolled up, displaying enough swirling, spiral tattoos to raise a demon or scare a pickpocket straight.

Thumps from the floors above marked Lord Wellington's progression toward party readiness. His butler had passed on the message that Constance was in danger, and apparently, Welli was dressing as quickly as a lord of the realm could. Which was far too slow for Trusdale's liking. But as Welli's airship was his only shot of reaching Constance before something dreadful happened . . .

Trusdale ground his teeth and focused on the journal.

Without a codebook, deciphering McKinley's secret scrawl was tricky, but the letters were finally falling into place. McKinley had accidentally created the invisibility serum when he sneezed a pinch of soldier snuff into a cup of Darjeeling tea. Aware of the explosive nature of his discovery, he'd contacted the royal family directly, through the most important local peer, namely Prince Lucien Albert Dunstan. McKinley had given the Prince fifty samples of the serum, but kept the formula secret. He'd hoped to share his findings in person with the Queen herself, thus securing himself a peerage.

Hearn brushed fallen crumbs off his breeches. "Anything interesting in that journal?"

"The end of life on Earth as we know it."

"Blimey!"

"McKinley wouldn't share the formula for the invisibility serum with Prince Lucien. Apparently, His Highness didn't take too kindly to that. I'm guessing the kidnapping of Chauhan and Huang is to leverage the formula out of McKinley. If he gives it to the Prince, that swine could create an army of invisible assassins. No one on Earth would be safe. Paranoia would spread like wildfire."

"Lord, and there's only us to stop him!"

The world is surely doomed. Trusdale snapped the journal closed as a stately Indian servant, his uncut beard frosted with silver, entered the kitchen. He was immaculately turned out in a blue turban, a white collarless shirt, and loose gray pants. A curved dagger in his blue sash belt and an iron bangle identified him as a Sikh warrior.

Hearn stood. "'Ey up, Mr. Singh. This gent is J. F. Trusdale, a friend of our young Miss Constance. Mr. Trusdale, may I introduce Mr. Ajeet Singh, His Lordship's personal valet and right-hand man."

The valet bowed gracefully. Unsure of the protocol and impressed by the dagger, Trusdale bowed back.

With only the slightest hint of his native accent, Mr. Singh said, "I am honored to meet you, Mr. Trusdale. Lord Pendelroy has been alerted to your concerns regarding the safety of Miss Constance. Be assured that the airship will be here momentarily. Please follow me to his lordship's closet."

Trusdale shadowed the valet up the stairs as Hearn brought up the rear. The steps led to a hallway lined with gold-framed portraits of green-eyed aristocrats. An open archway allowed a glimpse into a parlor decorated with the trappings of numerous grand tours. Gazing over the opulent parlor with a look of disapproval was a huge albino yak head mounted on a teak shield. The unfortunate shaggy-haired bull wore a set of brass goggles and a red bowler hat.

Mr. Singh seemed to anticipate his curiosity in the bull. "His Lordship's nemesis, Dorjee, the great white yak from Tibet. His reign of alpine terror has finally ended."

Interesting. It seemed that, unlike many bachelors whose parlors were decorated with the spoils of empire, Welli had actually traveled to foreign climes. "Mr. Singh, if you don't mind my asking, how did you come into His Lordship's service?"

"We served together in Burma. Lord Pendelroy was captain of Her Majesty's Fifth Foot and Mouth Brigade."

There must have been more mettle to Welli than his rakish lifestyle suggested. Welli's former regiment were Britain's finest diplomatic shock troops. If negotiations failed, the Fifth Foot and Mouth subtly reminded stubborn locals that Victoria's rule was absolute via a kick up the backside from their steel-toed boots.

Mr. Singh continued. "We fought shoulder to shoulder against Boxer insurgents who were persecuting religious minorities. Upon completion of my service, I contacted His Lordship requesting employment in his household. He was kind enough to provide excellent positions for me and my wife."

Hearn said, "Mrs. Singh used to be an airship pirate. They called her the 'Curse of the West China Sea,' isn't that right, Mr. Singh? She's retired now of course. She can't very well fly around Yorkshire pirating from the *Lady Penelope*, can she?"

"Alas, she cannot. However, Lord Pendelroy does allow her to sail the airship north to raid the Scots when his gambling funds are low. This keeps her happy."

Trusdale said, "Ain't no one happy if the wife ain't happy."

Mr. Singh nodded. "Very true, sir. Even more so when the wife in question is a dab hand with a cutlass."

Trusdale chuckled, following the valet up the second flight of carpeted stairs to a hallway festooned with pink floral wallpaper. A mahogany door ahead opened, and out stepped a devilishly handsome medieval knight.

Trusdale's jaw dropped.

Wellington's silver breastplate glittered through a blue gossamer tabard embroidered with white water lilies. A delicate chain mail, more jewelry than armor, glittered across his slender limbs. A blue silk cape hung debonairly from his slim shoulders, and his green leather sword belt was fashioned to represent intertwining lily leaves. An impressively bejeweled Norman sword hung by his side.

Welli said, "My costume isn't as heavy as it looks. I'm actually quite mobile." He gave a twirl to show off his armored flexibility. "Ta-dah! Mind you, my diamond-studded boots are a little too tight. I've removed them for now."

Welli's embroidered stockings bore his family coat-of-arms. Two rearing badgers supported a blood-red shield bearing a silver fan-tailed peacock. A tiny earl's coronet topped the shield beneath a flamboyantly plumed helmet.

Trusdale blinked. "So, you're an earl?"

"Heavens, no. That would be my foul-tempered father, the Earl of Pendelroy. I remain a humble viscount surviving on a pittance of a trust fund set up by my late grandfather."

"And a redcoat captain too, so I hear."

Welli brushed back his forelock and grinned. "Ah, so understandably you believe I may well turn you in? See if there's a huge reward for locating England's most wanted cowboy, Steamwerks burglar, airship destroyer, and apple of my young cousin's eye?"

"Apple of—?"

"Now, believe me, Trusdale . . ." His eyes darkened, and Trusdale caught a glimpse of the soldier beneath the silks. "Under any other circumstances, if I knew a man had broken into the Steamwerks I would turn him over to the redcoats in a heartbeat. However, as Constance was your accomplice, I'll let it go. She's family, and as such, I'd rather she didn't get hanged by the Crown. The social ramifications could be grievous. I'd also miss the little troublemaker."

Mr. Singh said to Welli, "My lord, with your permission, I will head to the roof to prepare for the airship."

"Carry on, Sergeant."

Singh bowed and headed for a paneled door to Trusdale's far left. He pulled it open and disappeared up a flight of wooden steps, with Hearn close on his heels.

Welli said, "I'm going to bring you into my closet, Trusdale, to get you properly attired. The theme of the Prince's party is 'Les Fleurs Animées.'"

Trusdale hated theme parties. "What's Les Fleurs—"

"Everyone will be dressed as a flower or plant. The word from my printer is that there was only one guest, the Belgian Count du Flange, who declined the party invitation. It seems the count suffered a hunting accident and is unable to travel. You will adopt the count's identity to slip past the guards."

"But if he's injured—"

"You made a last-minute recovery. For a frankly outrageous fee, Mr. Singh persuaded Pinder to print up an exact copy of Du Flange's party invitation. Your disguise will cover your face, so with any luck, we should just glide right in without raising so much as an eyebrow."

"Should?"

"Relax, Trusdale. My tailor, Francesco, has your disguise well in hand. Hearn will remain in servant's garb. I'll send him to locate my godmother's airship in case a quick exit is required for the old dear."

Trusdale stopped. "Hold on now—a tailor? Your servants might be loyal, but how do you know you can trust an outside man?"

"If a gentleman can't trust his tailor, then all hope for civilization is lost."

"If you say so."

"I do. Now, if Constance were here, she could probably whip up a truly fabulous costume for you. She's quite the seamstress. As a child, she used to create the most delightful military uniforms for the Egyptian mummies stored in her father's vaults."

"She made costumes for—"

"Mummies, yes. I dread to think what she's going to make that new puppy of hers wear. Poor little Boudicca. No Yorkshire terrier should have to wear a hat. It's against the breed standard."

Trusdale grimaced. "That damned dog almost ate my boots."

"Be glad it wasn't your whole leg. Boo terrorized the staff at my family's estate. You wouldn't believe the damage one small Yorkie can unleash."

"I think I would. I believe she bit me as I tried to sing a love song after one too many ales."

Amusement flitted across Welli's face. "We're still talking about the puppy, right?"

"Yes. Why?"

"Just checking. Shall we?" The armored water lily swept into his closet. Trusdale shook his head and followed.

Light poured into the twenty-five-foot square room through a Georgian multi-paned window, illuminating a closet decorated in the style of a Moroccan palace. The ceiling was tented in red silk that flowed down the walls like hot lava to pool on a red-and-white mosaic floor. A series of mahogany shelves and a brass rail that ran around the closet displayed Welli's sumptuous wardrobe, from flamboyantly colored shirts and pantaloons to a staggering array of footwear. Trusdale marveled that any man could own so many impractical items of clothing.

In the center of the closet, a white-haired, olive-skinned man who looked to be about sixty glanced up from his sewing. The tailor sat on an ottoman piled high with bolts of silk cloth in a dizzying display of hues. He gave Trusdale's Western dress a professional once-over and continued sewing with a snooty sniff.

Welli said, "May I introduce the fabulous Francesco. He's thrown together a little something for you to wear. I had to make some assumptions about your size, but I'm sure you'll be able to pass for a Belgian count. From a distance, at least."

Trusdale gasped at the outfit laid across the tailor's lap.

"Oh, hell no—I'm not wearing that. Not in a million years. Not in a month of Sundays. Not for the Queen of England, if my head was on the line."

Welli frowned. "But surely, for Constance?"

Mr. Singh appeared at the closet doorway. "My lord, the airship has arrived."

Welli said, "Decision time, Trusdale. Are you with us?"

The newly minted Count du Flange groaned and took off his Stetson.

Chapter 34: A Party to Die For

PRINCE LUCIEN MARCHED ACROSS THE front lawn of Wedgeworth Warbling, lord of all he surveyed. Around him, two thousand nobles dressed in the finest floral costumes waltzed to the joyous violins of Strauss's "Voices of Spring." Not one of their bejeweled costumes outshone Lucien's own, inspired by the sword-leafed gladioli. The House of Fabergé had created for him a bejeweled version of the plant's military namesake, the gladius. His sword's scabbard bore faceted emerald foliage with purple-sapphire blooms. The sword's pommel held a goose-egg-sized diamond pried from the crown of a conquered maharaja.

Lucien knew from experience that nothing impressed the ladies more than a diamond-laden sword. In more ways than one, he was dressed to kill. A Tyrian purple cloak cascaded from his broad shoulders, a majestic backdrop to his silver Roman breastplate. A scandalously short black leather battle skirt hung from his hips. His muscular horseman's thighs were on full display above his gladiator sandals.

He scanned the bowing crowd for attractive flora worthy of joining him at his private after-party. Once he'd won the upcoming mechanical-animal polo match, he would draw the lucky few away to his Baroque boudoir. Aside from deposing Victoria, it was his life's calling to spend as much time practicing procreation as the day allowed. To pass on his title and estate to a legitimate heir, one day he'd have to marry.

But not this day.

A brunette beauty with violet eyes and a curvaceous body sheathed in blue iris blooms curtseyed before him. His smile slipped into a smirk. He'd spent so much time pursuing world domination lately that he'd overlooked the simple pleasures of social sovereignty.

He bestowed a pointed sneer that drew a gasp of horror from nearby guests. A ducal sneer could ruin a woman's standing to the point that she would be forced by her family to enter a nunnery, or even worse, to emigrate to America to marry new money.

The brunette wilted into a subpar faint. Her bustle hit the lawn he'd ordered to be sprinkled with lavender blooms, sending out a puff of fragrance. He took a deep breath of the heady perfume, stepped over her prone body, and strode on. He rated that faint a six out of ten. One used to be able to tell a highborn lady by the gracefulness of her fall. What was the world coming to when a faint was simply a faint?

He resolved to make daily fainting practice mandatory for every woman over the age of eleven directly following his coronation. It would be the first of many laws he would pass, including forbidding women to read any work beyond the King James Bible, barring any female from ascending to the British throne, and ensuring that ladies over the age of thirty were banned from entering public venues, including theaters, parks, and government buildings. Was there anything worse than seeing a woman past her prime, well, anywhere?

Better to keep them invisible, or at least out of sight and mind. After all, Paradise was built for a single man, and fell because of woman. It was time for men to assert their dominion over the fish of the sea, the birds of the air, and every living thing that moved upon the earth. Especially women.

He plucked a glass of raspberry champagne from a passing butterfly waitress. Five hundred servers flew between his guests on mechanical wings. They hovered a few inches from the ground, flapping their stretched-silk wings to provide cooling wafts of air to guests unused to the heat of the afternoon sun. British aristocrats studiously avoided the glare of the sun to keep their complexions fashionably pale. England's reliably rainy weather was lauded as a sign that the good Lord favored the English upper class over their Continental neighbors, who were regularly cursed by Mediterranean sunshine and clear blue skies.

He sipped the brut rosé as he watched the waltzing dancers. Between the whirling blooms, Gunter Erhard beckoned furiously from the shadow of the orchestra's stage.

Lucian grimaced. *Am I now subject to the summons of my own servant?* Irritated, he grabbed the arm of an orange-and-black-winged waitress and yanked her to his side. He took his time sampling the hors d'oeuvres laid out on the hovering woman's silver tray. He savored the petite perfection of three Stilton-and-pear canapés, a tiny crown-shaped blackberry jelly, and a glass thimble of chilled mint-and-pea soup. A meal fit for a Lilliputian king.

Erhard's face turned a satisfying shade of magenta beneath his dueling scars. The servant's gestures grew more frenzied, and he waggled his eyebrows like a madman. Lucien smirked at the Austrian's discomposure. The butterfly server mistook his glee for personal favor and smiled up at him shyly. Her dark brown eyes held no trace of the fear usually displayed by his servants.

She must be new. The Prince resolved to publicly flog the woman before the day was out for daring to look him in the eye. Such impertinence was intolerable. Ah, how she would scream. Alas, the lesson on proper subservience had to wait. Erhard's eyebrows were clearly in need of attention.

Lucien sauntered across the lawn and slipped into the stage's shadow. "Erhard, did I not state that you were banned from walking among my guests unless you wore a floral disguise? Where the devil is your costume?"

"I'm wearing it, Your Royal Highness, see?" The Austrian pointed to a small white flower pinned to his blue tailcoat lapel. "Edelweiss."

He glared at the blossom and his right-hand man with equal distaste. "Erhard, you don't have an ounce of whimsy within you."

Erhard beamed. "Why, thank you."

"I assume there is a reason behind your wild gesturing?"

Erhard nodded. "The Haltwhistle woman arrived with her godmother. I set three of my best men upon her cunningly disguised as insect servers. Their mission was to stab her, poison her, or trip her so that she would break her neck, without causing undue disruption to your guests."

Alas, the untimely end of his red-haired nymph. It was a tragedy such a fine body was wasted before he could take his pleasure from it. More than her natural assets, she had created surprisingly elegant decorations for tomorrow's parade. Her use of decorative floral arches to grace the Queen's route through Sheffield was truly inspired. When his carriage passed beneath the first floral arch in the morning, he would bow his head in respect to the late Constance Haltwhistle.

Lucien sighed. "The end—did she suffer?"

Erhard reddened. "Ah, well, that's the thing. Her wretched godmother batted all food and drink from the girl's hand to save her figure from ruin. Hence, we could not poison her victuals. Blow-darts of poison got caught in the vast netting of her skirts. The cutthroat assigned to trip her down any and all steps took a terrible tumble himself due to her ill-placed foot. She backed into our knife man with her bustle and caused him to stab himself in the thorax. At this point, I sent in two reserve killers. She seems to have accidentally kicked one with enough force to break his kneecap. The other managed to fall into an arrow she was waving around. Either she's incredibly lucky, or she's the devil in bloomers."

Lucien gaped. "You mean to tell me that five grown men couldn't take down one petite girl? Where did you hire these incompetent thugs?"

"Your Royal Highness, I assure you, they are all highly skilled—"

"Apparently not. Send in the invisible Swedes. Surely they can choke her without drawing too much attention?"

"Ah. We lost one of the transparent Swedes to a bullet at the Steamwerks. The other two returned safely, but they are becoming more addled in their mental faculties by the hour. I sent them to patrol the perimeter of the folly. They should still be able to handle such a basic task. I fear asking them to launch another attack upon Miss Haltwhistle would only speed up their mental decline. The late assassin maid we had placed in her home believed the girl possessed an innate ability to stir chaos and confusion in the minds of those around her."

"I find that hard to believe."

"The ability becomes more apparent when one tries to do her physical harm. Mayhem is her best defense. To prevent her from once again circumventing certain death, perhaps Your Royal Highness could invite Miss Haltwhistle to stand on the front line of spectators at the polo match? If you could 'accidentally' ride your mechanical mount right over her—"

"And take out who knows how many other guests? I think we can do better than that. Where is the girl now?"

"The Countess of Benchley is displaying her to a plethora of gentlemen of advanced years and poor fortune."

"An engagement auction? Interesting. Show me."

Erhard slipped into the costumed crowd. Lucien followed the Austrian at a discreet distance.

The auction for his future victim's hand was almost over. He glimpsed her red hair at the center of a circle of champagne-swilling octogenarians. They poked at her with bony fingers in the manner of men used to fine horseflesh and finer women.

The sari-clad Countess of Benchley shooed the suitors back from her goddaughter. "Really, gentlemen, enough. To return to the bidding. I've already addressed your concerns as to the girl's unfashionable hair color, excess weight in the bustle area, and diminutive height. She can solve all three problems by wearing a high-stacked pompadour wig and unloading the . . ." She glared at Constance. "*Items* she is carrying in her bustle. The woman can be taller, blonder, and lighter by nightfall. I am open to final bids. What do you say?"

The men muttered to one another. Their intended bride stood in the center of their circle in all her short, red-haired, bustle-heavy splendor.

Lucien blinked.

The bare-faced woman of yesterday had transformed into a blush-cheeked water nymph. Her long auburn hair had been tamed into a sophisticated fiery swirl. She was crowned with an emerald tiara fit for an empress. Her porcelain face was set into a mask of languid boredom, but her eyes blazed with untamed fury.

The Prince's toes curled with excitement. He'd never seen feminine rage before. He had certainly deflowered, derided, and devastated countless women. He was in the process of dethroning the most powerful woman in the world. Yet, not once, in all his encounters with the fairer sex, had he witnessed such pure, unabashed ferocity as he saw in Constance's eyes.

His heart pounded beneath his Roman breastplate.

Constance gave a theatrical yawn and gazed over her wrinkled suitors' heads toward the polo field. Below her smooth alabaster shoulders flowed a torrent of silver and blue fabric embellished with startlingly realistic white silk arrowhead blooms. In any other context than a high-society party, he would have sworn they were fresh-plucked flowers.

He would have to find out her supplier.

An aged daffodil announced, "Lord Barrowmore here. I can offer Miss Haltwhistle the title of viscountess and an excellent sewing room at my Plymouth estate. Can she darn socks? The servants can't seem to make such repairs to my liking. It would be her primary role within the household."

Constance glowered. The countess shot a warning glance at her goddaughter. "I'm sure she'd be delighted to darn away her days."

The daffodil nodded thoughtfully.

A corpulent daisy with a yellow-powdered face and a ruff of white petals stepped into the fray. "Earl Snedley of Cork. I can offer the girl the title of countess and a home at Swamply Manor in Ireland, provided that she has all her own teeth."

The countess asked Constance, "Do you, child?"

"Indeed I do. In fact, if it is teeth you're after, I have an entire collection gathered in the Congo by my father. The tribes there create the most splendid panoramas of jungle life from their fallen enemies' teeth. They also produce rather striking furniture from their bleached bones. I have a banqueting table and twelve chairs laid out in the morning room created entirely from the remains of one unfortunate tribe."

Earl Snedley blinked. "Good Lord."

The matchmaker glared at Constance. "Yes, thank you for that, my dear. I do apologize, gentlemen. The girl's mind has been somewhat addled due to reading too much fiction."

The daisy smiled toothlessly. "We'll soon put a stop to that. No woman reads in my household. First a book, then an idea, and then where will we be?"

"Up to our ears in women with ideas," said the daffodil.

The daisy nodded. "I had to raze the library at my estate to keep my last wife out. The little fool threw herself into the blaze to save a medieval copy of *The Canterbury Tales*. Apparently, she had a passion for Chaucer that she never had for me. Fortunately, this galling incident leaves me free to marry this young thing."

He set his rheumy eyes upon Constance's ample bosom. "We can honeymoon in the west wing of Swamply Manor. Countess, once your vicar has performed the ceremony, my airship can take us directly to the bridal chamber. I trust you will prepare her properly for our nuptials. Where exactly are those blond wigs you mentioned?"

Constance blanched ten shades of pearl. Her right hand slowly slipped to her back quiver and drew out a single arrow. She casually laid the shaft upon the bow.

Lucien frowned. It would be a dreadful inconvenience to send killers after the girl to Ireland.

The countess said, "Then we stand at the final offer, gentlemen, for the hand of Miss Constance Haltwhistle. The closing bid for the sole heir to the barony of Brampton-on-the-Wall, a magnificent Yorkshire estate, a London town house, and a ruined castle on the Scottish border goes to—"

The Prince bellowed, "I offer the title of Princess, access to the royal hunting grounds, and the creation of offspring in line for the British throne."

Every peer within earshot gasped in astonishment.

"Sold!" barked the countess.

A stout body thudded onto the lawn. Amidst the jewel-encrusted footwear of the party guests lay a comatose man in worn brown-leather riding boots.

Erhard had fainted.

Lucien rated the faint a solid three out of ten.

Chapter 35: Blood, Sweat, and Gears

LORD WELLINGTON PENDELROY WAS TRULY in his element at a royal costume party. Trusdale followed the armored water lily as he wove through the florally-bedecked attendees that encircled the polo field. With an elegant bow here and a touch of flattery there, Welli had brought them within thirty yards of the sidelines. Their goal was to reach the front row to scan the spectators for Constance and her godmother, neither of whom would ever settle for a back-row view.

Trusdale turned a largely deaf ear to Welli's constant chatter. The young lord seemed to think that a nonstop flow of trivial prattle would make them fit in with the aristocratic crowd.

The water lily said, "Now, Du Flange, I'm sure you're familiar with the rules of Prussian polo. There are only seven hundred and thirty-seven, so it's much easier to understand than cricket. The field is circular, with four A-shaped goalposts and four teams of four riders. The mechanical mounts are about the size of a shire horse. They range in styles from mundane animals, lions, tigers, and bears—"

"Oh my." Trusdale narrowly avoided trampling a comely begonia that dropped at his feet. More ladies were fainting by the minute, presumably due to the combination of corsetry and too much champagne.

"—to wyverns, griffins, and so on. Each team is allowed one substitute rider to be brought in to cover any fatalities. The teams hold together until only four players remain, then it's every player for themselves. The last mount standing wins the grand prize upon scoring the final goal. So, the trick to winning is to work with your team in the early stages, and then turn upon them viciously as soon as your opponents are downed."

Welli bowed his way around a group of pink peonies. "Some say the game is an allegory for shifting aristocratic allegiances. Others say it's a damned fine way to win some truly gloat-worthy prizes. The main prize today is a replica of the Queen's crown."

From the polo field, three plumes of black smoke rose into the sky. They drifted toward the gray clouds gathering ominously above.

"Thank heavens that wretched sunlight is fading," Welli said. "It looks like we can expect a shower soon. Rain is an obligatory guest at any English outdoor event."

Trusdale growled, "Forget the weather. You've got this covered, right? Once we find the ladies, you escort them home, while I head into the woods to search for the folly. I need to know I can count on you. Lives are on the line, not least our own."

"Heavens, who's a grumpy little flower then?"

Trusdale huffed into his yellow petal ruff and remained silent. His disguise was perfect. A deerskin respirator with mirrored brass goggles hid his face. A green velvet doublet stretched tight over his chest, and a puff of pansied hose swelled around his hips. Green silk stockings hugged his legs down to the emerald-encrusted slippers that had replaced his Western boots.

He was a six-foot-two sunflower, and he was not beaming.

Welli nodded. "That's better. No offense, dear chap, but try not to talk too much. You're an accent waiting to happen. Remember, you're a Flemish count."

A crash of colliding metal exploded from the polo field. The spectators roared with delight as a gleaming copper tiger head soared up into the overcast sky. The three-foot sphere of feline ferocity arced over the crowd, heading straight for Wellington. Trusdale launched himself at the unsuspecting water lily's back. Welli stumbled and fell as the tiger head dropped like a kitty comet.

The head thudded six inches deep into the lawn behind Trusdale's emerald-studded heels. The beast's gaping jaws snarled in primal fury, its fangs glinting like assassin's daggers. Vicious puncture wounds dotted the creature's skull, and black oil oozed from within.

The aristocrats had scattered like mice before the great cat's attack. They drifted back into place as Welli groaned and pushed himself onto his knees. "For heaven's sake, man, do be careful. I could have broken my neck, and then how would we find Connie?"

Trusdale grabbed Wellington's shoulder and pointed toward the polo field. A steam-powered unicorn danced upon the carcass of a mechanical tiger. The unicorn's silver horn dripped with oil from its feline victim. The mythical beast's form was crafted from silver scale armor draped over a skeleton of gears and pistons. Sitting sidesaddle upon the prancing beast was a red-haired beauty in a gown of tumbling silver-and-blue waves. Her cheeks glowed, and a smile lit her painted lips. She brandished a riveted bronze polo mallet with such natural ferocity that a cave troll would think twice before giving offense to the mounted maiden.

The trampled tiger sank into the turf mere inches from its comatose rider. The wrinkled lord's yellow-powdered face was toothlessly agape within a ruff of white daisy petals.

Constance pulled the silver unicorn up into a rear. As the equine masterpiece reached for the clouds, she held her war mallet high and bellowed at the prone rider, "Know this, villain, a man who burns books is a monster of the first degree. Your poor, brave wife deserved far better. May the ghost of Chaucer haunt you to the end of days!"

The crowd roared with appreciation for the woman's enthusiasm. Trusdale wondered about her sanity. The unicorn surged into a gallop and raced away.

Welli said, "Constance does so love her Chaucer. Her mother used to read her *The Canterbury Tales* as a bedtime story. She left out the bawdy parts, of course. You know how filthy the classics can be. Geoffrey Chaucer puts even Organzia Prodworthy to shame."

"Who?"

"The author of *The Duchess and the Sky Pirate*, *The Duchess and the Gamekeeper*, *The Duchess and the Third Regiment of Royal Dragoons*. No? It's a very popular novel series."

"I think Miss Haltwhistle has one of those books on her person."

Welli raised both eyebrows. "Good heavens, does she indeed? That's hardly recommended reading for a well-bred young lady."

A thunder of hooves shook the turf as a torrent of metal stampeded after the silver unicorn. The daisy rolled into a ball as the steam-powered beasts charged by him. A copper-scaled wyvern, a brass-and-bronze patchwork giraffe, a bronze hippo, and a brass centaur raced by. The daisy whimpered as a massive gold lion ridden by a gladiator soared right over him and shot after the herd.

"Speaking of ladylike pastimes," Welli said, "Prussian polo isn't the best sport for our young Constance. I know that it's open to a wider range of players these days—lords, ladies, even liberals—but still . . ." He furrowed his brow. "The violence, the swearing, the unsportsmanlike behavior."

Trusdale pulled Welli to his feet. "You don't think the menfolk will take it easy on her?"

"You misunderstand, it's Constance I'm talking about. She's a poor loser and a worse winner. She's creating enemies on that field that will last the rest of her life."

"It could be a real short life unless we get her out of here. The only positive is that she's out in the open. The Prince can't harm her in plain sight of the crowd."

"I'm not sure you understand the finer intricacies of Prussian polo. It's supposed to be a bloodbath. That's all part of the game."

"Then we need to get to her, fast." He pushed by Welli and roughly shouldered his way through the crowd.

Welli followed in his wake, bowing apologetically to offended peers. "Sorry, everyone. What can I say? He's from Belgium, you know."

By the time they reached the front row of spectators, two members of Her Majesty's Auxiliary Nurse Global Emergency Levitation Service—known colloquially as Angels—were fluttering on bronze wings toward the downed daisy. It was an indication of the Prince's royal rank that he could commission the British military's crack airborne automaton medics to serve at his polo match.

Chinks in the wings' metal plumage revealed steel cables that snaked through gold skeletal frames. White steam billowed from the medics' engine backpacks. The personal steam engines were powerful enough to carry the Angels across any combat zone. Over a chain mail battle suit, each automaton wore a white tabard bearing the bloody cross of Saint George. All Angels bore the utility belt of medical salvation and the dual daggers of permanent anesthetization.

They administered either first aid or a *coup de grâce* as necessitated by their patient's injuries. For this reason, British soldiers both loved and feared the winged medics. The final vision of many a wounded soldier was an Angel hovering above him.

The daisy appeared to be well aware of the medic's kill-or-cure treatment options. He struggled to rise, staring at the approaching automatons with undisguised terror.

Trusdale muttered, "Isn't anyone going to help him up?"

Welli snorted. "I doubt it. No one in their right minds interferes with an on-call angel. Their bedside manner leaves much to be desired."

The daisy rose to his knees, clutching his ribs, pain etched across his face.

The crowd muttered expectantly as the angels increased their speed, daggers drawn.

Trusdale found himself charging through the crowd, knocking silk-clad blooms flying in all directions. He burst through the front line, racing to put himself between the daisy and the angels. As they approached, he flapped his hands at the metal medics. "Go on now, shoo!"

Welli called from the sidelines, "Um, du Flange, perhaps you shouldn't . . ."

Trusdale never found out what he shouldn't do. The angels' silver crusader helmets turned to regard him. Medically dispassionate, they evaluated his physical state.

His black eye, his cracked nose, the blood-encrusted wound across his neck . . .

The daisy struggled to his feet. Cradling his ribs, he jogged off the field.

Trusdale's throat dried. If the medics answered to the Prince rather than to God or the Queen, they likely had been programmed to be even less than merciful than usual. He backed away from the angels, his hands held out before him, palms exposed, nothing to see here.

They swooped in like eagles on a three-legged rabbit.

Trusdale leapt backward, stumbled on tiger debris, and fell. Heart pounding, his fingers closed on a long, bronze rod.

The daisy's war mallet.

The angels' struck him with a tornado of knives. He rolled on the turf, blocking their blows with the handle of the mallet like Little John guarding a bridge. Their blows didn't pass. He lurched to his knees then onto his feet, swinging the mallet with all his might at the nearest angel.

The blow connected, clipping a wing and sending the angel spinning into his comrade. Their cables tangled, and sparks cascaded from one angel's left wing. It wrenched itself free, molting bronze feathers onto the turf as its wing slowed. Its intact companion's helmet rotated between Trusdale and his wounded colleague; adding, subtracting, generating damage reports.

The wounded wing stopped beating. The angel plunged to earth, sinking ankle-deep into the mud. It stabbed its knife tentatively at its malfunctioning wing.

Its colleague reached a diagnosis, and attacked the fallen angel.

Trusdale counted his blessings and retreated. He scanned the polo field for Constance. A mounted melee was underway an acre down the field. A menagerie of metal mounts tore one another apart for the glory of winning a replica crown. In the center of the mechanical mayhem whirled a single-horned silver steed.

Leaving the battling angels to taste their own medicine, Trusdale sprinted down the polo field as fast as his emerald slippers could carry him.

It was time to catch himself a unicorn.

Chapter 36: The Lion and the Unicorn

TRUSDALE WAS NO STRANGER TO the brutal realities of a cavalry battle. At age twenty-one, he'd seen his share of action against a company of Canadian mercenaries in Montana. The polite yet deadly Mountie Mercs had caused mayhem during their successful annexation of the northwestern states. But the bloody battle for Chief Mountain paled against the spectacle now before him.

The wyvern writhed on its back as the hippo reared and crashed its stumpy legs down through the creature's metal ribs. With a shriek of gears torn asunder, the wyvern shuddered into stillness. The hippo's daffodil-costumed rider raised his war mallet in triumph as the spectators cheered.

The centaur attacked the hippo from the rear, leaping fifteen feet to close on its prey. The brass half-man clasped its cable-articulated arms around the daffodil's waist and reared, yanking the hapless flower from his saddle. Legs dangling, the daffodil swung his mallet back over his shoulder. He caught the centaur a blow to the temple that sent it careening into the hippo.

Sparks flew as the two mounts' armor plates caught fast, and each beast became both captor and captive of the other. As they thrashed together, metal plates sheared off and cogs spewed onto the turf. The spectators screamed with pleasure as the mashed-up mechanicals wrestled their way down into the mud. The hippo exploded in a fountain of oil and machine parts. The daffodil and tulip riders flopped like dying goldfish in the debris.

Trusdale sprinted by the fallen flowers. Fifty yards ahead, the lion, the unicorn, and the giraffe fought for possession of a red egg-shaped ball.

Constance's riveted war mallet clipped the egg. It soared through the air and clanged off the muzzle of the bronze giraffe. The giraffe's chinless young rider blanched beneath his red-rose-festooned top hat.

The silver unicorn surged after the egg with the golden lion on its heels. The lion's rider wore a Roman breastplate, a flowing purple cape, and a sneer beneath his handlebar mustache. Trusdale gasped as the lion clawed for the unicorn's rear end. He shouted a warning to Constance, but his cry was drowned out by the crowd's bloodthirsty howls.

The giraffe stumbled and fell into the feline's flank, causing the lion to miss its mark. It pounced again. As it leaped, the gladiator stood in his stirrups and swung his war mallet with venom. He aimed not at the ball, but directly at Constance's emerald tiara.

Trusdale's heart clenched.

Lightning flashed from the dark clouds above. For a split second, the three combatants seemed frozen in time and space as the white light carved their metal skeletons into grotesque statues. The gladiator's war mallet sliced through the air as Constance ducked her head low. Thunder crashed as the mallet brushed by her auburn hair.

A fanfare of trumpets rang out, and the mechanical mounts halted instantly. The unicorn was caught at full gallop with only one rear hoof and one foreleg touching the turf. The beast balanced perfectly on two metal hooves. One out-flung foreleg reached toward the egg, which rolled and stopped ten yards ahead of its mythological pursuer.

The lion reared in a petrified pounce. Two hind legs held the giant beast steady while its golden forepaws clawed for the unicorn's derrière. The six-inch claws hovered two feet above the unicorn's white silk tail.

The giraffe's brass-and-bronze head gazed sightlessly up at the darkening sky. The heavens rumbled ominously, but no rain yet fell.

The three players relaxed their grip on their brass-chain reins. Constance sat back on her sidesaddle and stretched out her arms.

Welli shouted to Trusdale, "Tea break. This is our last chance to catch Constance before the game turns really nasty."

Only the British would pause a pitched battle for a cup of tea. Even the Canadian mercenaries held off on teatime until the battle was won.

Trusdale ran on. A wave of costumed peers swept onto the field to stomp divots into the ground and to pick up souvenir cogs from the downed mechanicals. Six blue-and-gold-liveried engineers surrounded the unicorn. Each wore a tool belt stuffed with spanners, wrenches, and hammers. With brass oilcans, they squirted oil into the metal mounts' joints.

A skinny ostler scurried to the rear of the unicorn and gawked up at the rampant golden lion. Cautiously, the ostler slipped into the narrow gap between the two beasts. From a pouch on his belt, he drew a handful of supra-coal spheres. He pulled aside the unicorn's silk tail and unceremoniously shoved the coal up the creature's fuel chute. Shoulder-deep inside the mechanical wonder, he turned aside his face as black smoke belched out of the steed's behind. He coughed into the silk tail as tears welled in his eyes.

Constance wrinkled her nose as the acrid smoke wrapped around her like a sooty shawl. Without calling for a mounting block, she slid down from her sidesaddle in a flurry of silver and blue ruffles. She made a perfect landing on the turf to a smattering of applause from the crowd. She dropped into a gracious curtsey, and the applause swelled in volume.

The gladiolus gladiator dismounted from the lion with far less panache.

The giraffe rider slumped over his mount's neck and wiped his tear-stained cheeks on his sleeve. Trusdale recognized the chinless youth as Lord Pinkie from Le Paon Pompeux.

A butterfly server approached Constance, who scooped a pink porcelain teacup and saucer from the woman's silver tray and gulped down the tea in two hearty swigs.

Trusdale could have sworn she grinned into her teacup as she studied the lion.

"Connie!" shouted Wellington.

Her rouged face lit up as her cousin approached. "Welli! Where on earth have you been? You've missed everything." She didn't give Trusdale a second glance. He hung back, not wanting to give himself away, for now.

The Roman gladiator sauntered over to join Constance and Welli. Waves of costumed nobles dropped into bows and curtseys before his strappy sandals, but he seemed oblivious to the groundswell of subservience.

The gladiator studied Constance with the air of a well-fed hawk reviewing a flea-bitten rabbit. A scar-faced servant in a dusty tailcoat trailed at his heels. An officer's saber hung at his hip. Trusdale recalled

Betty's description of the Prince's right-hand man and guessed this must be Erhard. The servant stared at Constance with fear etched across his craggy face.

What has she done now?

The butterfly server offered the silver tea tray to the gladiator. He batted her away with a snarl.

Wellington dropped into an elegant bow. "Your Royal Highness, I must congratulate you on the success of your soiree. Your garden party is without a doubt the most splendiferous affair in the history of floral celebrations."

"I know," said the Prince. "Pendelroy, isn't it? I believe you almost fleeced me out of house and home at our last card game."

"That was purely beginner's luck, Your Royal Highness."

"There appears to be a lot of it about." The Prince eyed Constance. "Now, my dear girl, I believe that you stated you'd never played Prussian polo. Yet here you are, alive and kicking in the final chukka."

Constance said, "You asked if I had played the game. I have not. However, I have endured a few private lessons on how to ride mechanicals from Baron von Cronberg."

Lucien's square jaw dropped all the way to his sandals. He spluttered, "You mean Baron *Adler* von Cronberg?"

"The same. Do you know him?" asked Constance innocently.

"But, well, he practically *invented* Prussian polo. How did a slip of a girl like you—"

"He lost a bet to my father. Papa forced him to visit our estate to show me a few tricks. Apparently, this entire game is based on a rather violent croquet match the two of them had in their college days."

Lucien fumed. "Good lord. If I'd known that, I might have put you on my team. Does no one tell me anything?" He scowled at Erhard. The stocky man avoided the Prince's glare and twiddled with the white bloom pinned to his lapel.

Constance grinned. "It's too late now, my Prince. The crown is mine."

The Prince smirked. "Not so fast, oh light of my life. It appears that my lion is about to tear you limb from limb."

"On the contrary, I have you precisely where I want you."

"Pfft. Pendelroy, how *exactly* do you know my overconfident fiancée?"

Wellington cocked his head. "I'm not sure that I do, Your Royal Highness." The crowd tittered.

Constance squealed, "It's me, Welli. I'm going to be a princess."

Nausea lurched up from Trusdale's stomach. He barely stopped short of launching his lunch into the respirator.

Wellington said to the Prince, "I'm sorry, Your Royal Highness, I don't mean to offend, but, Constance, *this* Constance, is to be your bride? I mean, good Lord, *why*?"

A tremor of shock ran through the crowd.

Constance scowled at Wellington. She said to the Prince, "Welli is my cousin; please feel free to ignore him."

"As you wish, my frilly fancy." Lucien glanced at Trusdale. "And is this still-upright sunflower also part of your delightful family?"

Trusdale realized with a start that he was the only member of the crowd who had not bowed to the Prince.

Idiot. He dropped into a low bow that ended with an ominous tearing sound from his backside.

Lucien curled his lip.

"Ah, may I explain, Your Royal Highness?" Welli said. "This is the Count du Flange. I must apologize for both his manners and his hose. As you may be aware, he recently suffered a terrible hunting injury that has somewhat addled his senses."

"I'd heard he'd broken his leg."

"Oh no, it was a blow to the head. Nasty business. His face is ruined."

"Is that so?"

"And his vocal cords, damaged beyond repair. He can't speak, can barely see. The physical devastation has been—"

"And why is he taller?" interjected the Prince. "The count I knew stood no more than five foot eight in riding boots. This sunflower must be at least—"

"Modern medicine," stated Wellington somberly. "They have a pill, serum, or tonic for everything now. You wouldn't believe some of the recent scientific advances."

The Prince nodded. "You're right, it's getting out of hand. Some of the things I've seen of late—they're just horrifying. One might almost start to think that playing God is a bad idea." Erhard coughed. The Prince shook himself. "But I digress. Can Du Flange still ride?"

Welli blinked. "Well, yes, I suppose so."

"Excellent. I invoke the extinction clause. The Count du Flange shall be my dodo."

The crowd cheered.

Constance pursed her lips and glared at Trusdale.

Welli shot him a worried glance and announced loudly, "Just in case there are newcomers to the sport here today, a dodo is a substitute player who can ride during the final chukka in place of a deceased team member."

Lucien said, "In this case, alas, the poor Duke of York, I knew him well. I was going to ask Lord Talbot to ride in his place, but the fool appears to have passed out on top of Lady Wirral."

Sniggers ran through the spectators. An engineer drew a yellow flag from his utility belt and held it in the air. Within seconds, the crowd parted to make way for the substitute mount. A bronze dodo as big as a plow horse waddled onto the field, with a liveried engineer holding its brass-chain reins. An ornamental sapphire bridle adorned its vulture head. Polished jet eyes glittered through the tendrils of smoke that drifted from its prodigious black-and-gold beak. Layers of bronze feathers covered the bird's body beneath a burgundy velvet saddle with gold stirrups. A tail of white ostrich feathers bobbed wildly with each swaying step.

Welli said to Trusdale, "As dodo, your main job is to stop the rival team's players from shooting at the goal. You guide the bird with the reins and stirrups. Kick down twice to jump. And whatever you do, don't—"

"Pendelroy," Lucien snapped, "there's no need to explain the obvious to the count. Everyone knows he's one of the preeminent players of Prussian polo in all of Europe. Isn't that right, Du Flange?"

He was what now? A polo player? Did the gods laugh when they did these things to him? With all eyes upon him, Trusdale nodded.

A trumpet fanfare rang out. The Prince said, "Ah, there's our five-minute warning. Let the battle commence. Du Flange, mount your dodo." He turned to Constance. "And you, my beloved bride, try not to break your pretty neck."

"Ditto." Constance slapped her unicorn's ribs with unnecessary gusto. She slipped her opera-gloved hand into the innards of the beast directly behind the saddle. A crackle of blue electricity danced over the unicorn's coat. Constance smiled sweetly at the Prince.

Lucien frowned at her. He strode to his lion's side. Three engineers dropped to the ground to provide their backs as a sturdy mounting block.

Constance clambered up her metal mount under her own steam. Using the brass reins as a climbing rope, she walked her white ankle boots up the side of the beast and slid her ruffled bustle onto the saddle.

Of all the spectacles Trusdale had seen this day, this was his favorite by far.

A whisper of disapproval ran through the crowd.

Welli said, "Connie, wait."

"I'm not talking to you."

"But, I must tell you, the Prince—"

Constance's voice rang out. "Can someone *please* clear the field of noncombatants?" As if summoned by a spell, a troop of redcoats materialized and shooed away the crowd.

Trusdale gaped at the redcoats. Where the heck had they come from? The tunnel vision of his goggles was gonna be the death of him.

Wellington evaded the redcoats with a dancer's twirl and flounced to Trusdale's side. "Tell me you know how to ride a mechanical."

"Well, I've never—"

"Then tell me you understand the game."

"I wasn't really listening—"

"Think of it as mounted rugby."

"What's rugby?"

Welli sighed. "Then for God's sake, just stay away from Constance. Remember, the odds are always in her favor."

"Why's that?"

"Because the little minx cheats."

Chapter 37: The Extinction Clause

IT TOOK A TRUE CAVALRYMAN to mount a mechanical dodo with style. Trusdale swung himself up onto the bird's saddle with a panache the real Count du Flange would have envied. The crowd cheered his ascent; new blood was always welcome on the Prussian polo field.

The rhythmic hiss and clank of ratchet-and-pawl gears filled his ears, and the bird's bronze rib cage shuddered against his calves. The heat of the coal furnace within the bird's belly warmed his hose. His mouth parched, he licked his lips behind the leather mask. The automaton's innards might have been a scientific marvel, but as a cavalryman, he balked at riding a steed without sight, sentience, or soul.

Years spent riding a horse across the hills and grasslands of the Great Plains had taught him a valuable lesson. There was nothing like the view from a saddle to give you a clear perspective on your problems.

Three problems stared him in the face:

The first was the looming lion poised to destroy Constance's silver unicorn.

The second was the line of redcoat soldiers guarding the tree line beyond the polo field.

The third was the most serious: Miss Constance Haltwhistle.

Any sane woman would have taken one look at the metal lion towering over her rear end and admitted defeat. Instead, Constance lolled back on her sidesaddle as if it were a drawing room fainting couch. She'd thrust one gloved hand down into the unicorn's insides behind her saddle, and her brow was furrowed. Her pink tongue poked indecorously from the side of her mouth as she fiddled with her steed's innards.

He thumped his heels into his bird's bronze ribs. Several jewels dropped off his slippers and tumbled to the turf, but the dodo didn't budge.

Constance glanced at him with one perfect eyebrow raised. He kicked again. She collected her chain reins into her left hand. With her right, she swung her war mallet with a little more menace than Trusdale cared for.

He held a mallet of his own, but would have preferred a gun to better effect Constance's escape. If only he'd not let Welli talk him out of sticking his Smallstack S50 down the front of his hose. So what if it ruined the cut of his jib?

He guessed his stirrups might control the bird. He leaned down on the left and felt the weight of the beast shift to the port side. He leaned on the right, and the beast swayed to starboard.

But how did you make it go forward?

Maybe if he kicked down?

He dropped his full weight into his slippers. Sensing no immediate response, he dropped his weight down again.

With a metallic shriek, the dodo hurled itself ten feet into the air. He clutched for a horse's mane that wasn't there as hot steam billowed around him. The bird plunged back down to earth. It thudded its claws into the turf alongside the unicorn as he yanked on the chain reins. The dodo's head flew back and slammed into his chest so hard his breath whooshed into his face mask. His goggles steamed instantly, blocking his view of Constance's astonished face.

As his fogged lenses cleared, he realized his dodo now stood in the shadow of the rearing lion, out of the Prince's line of sight. The clanking hiss of four mechanical beasts in standby mode created a racket that could cover a discreet conversation with the unicorn's rider.

Constance proclaimed in a ringing tone, "If that leaping spectacle was supposed to intimidate me, Du Flange, you are barking up the wrong unicorn."

The spectators whooped, presumably impressed by her bravado. Constance bestowed the restrained smile of a fledgling princess upon her newfound fans. Keeping her lips taut, she leaned toward him. The hair rose on Trusdale's neck as she growled, "I warn you now, Du Flange, if you get in my way, I shall put an end to your polo-playing career, permanently. That crown is mine."

She sat back and whirled her riveted war mallet in a perfect circle. The studied venom within the swing was breathtaking.

It was by far the most thrilling death threat Trusdale had ever received.

He shook himself. "Miss Haltwhistle, it's me, Trusdale."

Constance narrowed her eyes. She glanced over her shoulder at the rearing lion and muttered, "Must you invade every party you're not invited to?"

"Your life is in danger. You need to leave the polo field, right now, and go on home."

"Oh heavens, good sir, well, if you say so." She fumbled with her reins as if about to dismount.

"Really?" *Who would have thought she'd be so reasonable?*

She scowled. "No, not really. For your information, my life is constantly in danger, and I see no reason why that should ruin my afternoon. Now, I'm about to win this match, take a fabulous crown as my trophy, and marry the most eligible bachelor in England. I suggest you leave before I expose you as an uninvited interloper."

"Please, trust me—you can't marry the Prince."

"I think you'll find that I can. At seven o'clock, directly after the conclusion of this match, to be precise. You and Welli are *not* invited to the ceremony."

"But—"

"And furthermore, I'm horrified at Welli's barbarous behavior. How could he embarrass me so publicly? By questioning Lucien's decision to choose me as his bride, he insulted us both. You can tell Welli that any man would consider himself lucky to marry me."

"Well, maybe, but for how long, I'm not sure. The point is your fancy fiancé over there is—"

"What do you mean, 'maybe'?"

"Damn it, woman, listen. He's trying to kill you."

Constance snorted. "Well of course he is, you fool. This is Prussian polo, not afternoon tea with the vicar."

"No, I mean, we think he might be behind the cage that crashed into your party, the invisibles, the kidnapping, everything. We believe he might have stashed the scientists in an old mine right here on this estate. All we need is proof—"

"Who's 'we'?"

"Arianna—that is, Betty, a singer at the Wiggle Room, heard the Prince's man—"

"Mr. Trusdale, it's bad enough I have to marry a stranger. But the Prince is the best, and frankly the only, option I have. Unless you have specific evidence of your claims . . ."

"But, you don't want to marry him, do you?"

She stared down at the unicorn's neck, absently stroking it as if it were a real pony. "What choice do I have?"

His heart ached for her. "I'll bet no one on the Haltwhistle estate wants you to marry a murderer just to keep a roof over their head."

A bugle flourish sounded across the field.

Constance squared her shoulders. She half-turned and stuck her gloved hand once more into the unicorn's behind.

He frowned. "You should never put your hand inside a mechanical—"

A single cannon shot boomed, and a crackle of blue light danced over the unicorn's hindquarters. The rear hoof of the stallion shot up and smashed through the lion's left front paw, sending it flying straight up into the ethersphere.

As the paw waved goodbye to the Earth, three steam-powered steeds fired into motion.

Constance's unicorn shot like a silver bullet from beneath the lion and thundered down the field with its white silk tail waving like a war banner. Pinkie's giraffe lurched after her.

The lion stumbled onto the stump of its severed front limb. Prince Lucien was launched from his saddle over its shoulder and tumbled into the dirt. The Prince staggered to his feet, spat out a mouthful of mud, and shook his fist at his departing fiancée.

Constance glanced back over her shoulder, and drove the unicorn on.

Chapter 38: Endgame

AT HEART, EVERY WOMAN DESIRES a crown.

Diamonds glitter in the mind's eye of scullery maids and duchesses alike. From the pyramids of Egypt to the vast ice palaces of the Arctic wilds, the sun never sets on an unspoken desire for regal headwear. Most ladies, conscious that ambition is frowned upon for the fairer sex, relegate such grandiose dreams to their secret diaries.

Constance was no such lady.

She pressed the unicorn into a charge and swung her mallet to send the egg soaring through the east goal. The crowd roared.

That was the team prize secured. To win the crown, all she needed to do was dismount Pinkie and Trusdale. Then, she would be the last beast standing.

Is it too early to take a victory lap?

The unicorn rolled like a moonlit sea beneath her. She thrilled at the steam power that throbbed through the sidesaddle. Her thighs squeezed the saddle's dual pommels to keep her seat stable as she slammed her left foot down into her single stirrup. The unicorn bore down on Pinkie's giraffe. Once the giraffe was eliminated, she had only to take down Trusdale's dodo and it would be game, set, and a dazzling diamond hat to the future Princess Constance.

Surely Lucien didn't mind that she'd sent him tumbling into the mud? Judging by his insistence that she play in the match, he didn't want a limp wallflower as his bride.

Still . . .

Down the field, the Prince stood alone, glaring at her as a team of liveried engineers scrambled to repair the damaged lion.

Constance gulped. Now she was dreading her wedding night for more reasons than the typical Victorian bride. Lie back and think of the estate. At least their children would be handsome.

Midway between the Prince's lion and her unicorn, a dodo lumbered her way. It would be midnight by the time Trusdale reached her. She had plenty of time to take out Pinkie in her last few moments as a single woman.

She braced for impact as the unicorn's horn slammed into the giraffe's left shoulder and skewered the bronze beast. With her struggling victim caught fast, Constance inflicted a barrage of targeted mallet strikes. The giraffe staggered like a newborn calf and flung its rider into the mud. Grateful that his ordeal was over, Pinkie rose from the mire, tipped his top hat, and scampered for the sidelines as she bashed in the giraffe's head with her mallet.

Satisfied that the beast was beyond an in-match repair, she pressed the unicorn into a collected walk over the debris of her fallen foe. With the barest shift in her weight and a firm feel on the right rein, she requested a dressage turn on the forehand. As the unicorn's forelegs paced in place, its hindquarters swung in a perfect half-circle. She surged the beast into a showy canter to applause from the equine-savvy crowd. Sitting deep into the rolling stride of the canter, she focused her gaze on the egg-shaped ball.

The egg had landed fifty yards behind the goalposts and now rested on the turf just short of the woods. A handful of redcoat soldiers leaned upon their rifles and heckled the designated egg catcher. Ignoring the taunts, a shuffling servant in a red dragon costume approached the egg with a large butterfly net. The dragon was one of her father's contributions to Prussian polo, recalling the family's heraldic shield. As a child, she'd watched Cawley play the original dragon on the front lawn of Haltwhistle Hall. Like his forebear, the Prince's venerable retainer scowled out of the gaping jaws of his papier-mâché dragon head. Motorized wings flapped slowly upon his spiked suit of scarlet scales. The servant had decided not to avail himself of the two-foot lift that could be gained from the mechanical wings. He dragged his scaled tail across the turf with the apathy usually displayed by those who work in the service of aristocrats.

Constance mused, *Even when given wings, not all men dare to fly*. She knew if she suddenly sprouted wings, she would soar to the heavens and beyond without hesitation. Deep inside her mind, the Enigma Key whispered to her, *Be careful what you wish for.*

Ah, now it spoke English. How utterly marvelous. And its voice reminded her of both mama's and Maya's, warm and gentle, with a musical tone that ebbed and flowed like an ocean. Logic told her that she'd met the key mere hours ago, but somehow, it had always been a part of her. The key was her confidant, her muse, her partner.

With a friend like this, her enemies best watch themselves.

She concentrated every ounce of her being on projecting an air of benevolent warmth toward the tiny triangle. Telepathic communication with extradimensional artifacts was not a subject she'd excelled at. Papa had spent numerous hours trying to school her on the complexities of biologically accessible thought, but the lessons usually ended with cultural misunderstandings and an occasional aether explosion. Fortunately, Papa always managed to direct any resulting time and space anomalies into the less fashionable alternate dimensions. Thus, the universes closest to her own lived a comfortable life unpolluted by the seamier side of cosmic chaos.

She focused her thoughts, painstakingly writing each word in white chalk on a mental blackboard. She spelled out, *It's so hard to know what to wish for, sometimes.*

The Enigma Key filled her mind with a vision of interlocking cogs and gears enveloping her like a cage. *Wish for liberty.*

She thought, *Of course, I must apologize for my insensitivity. I should have removed you from my steed's posterior following your release of the aether fire. I do hope we can still be friends?*

The Enigma Key dropped into her mind a yellow sea bobbing beneath a scarlet moon. Two giant purple kraken waved their tentacles at her as they drifted by on the ocean swell.

Is that you? Two of you? Gosh, I'd never thought of you as having actual bodies. I presume you're on a planet in a different dimension?

The kraken nodded, as best as kraken could. *We are trapped here for eternity.*

Constance thought, *How dreadful. Well, I appreciate your efforts to humanize our interaction. Other non-human beings from alternate worlds that I've chatted with have been far less polite. I applaud your sensitivity to my lack of tentacles. Please, be patient for a moment, and I'll pop your physical protrusion into my universe back inside my glove.*

Constance thrust her right arm inside the unicorn's innards, finding the one-inch key lodged within. She slipped the triangle inside her kidskin glove. Her father had forbidden her to speak to strange artifacts and beings without his direct supervision. They could be manipulative and dangerous. But Papa had selfishly abandoned her, and there was a crown on the line. And what self-respecting woman wouldn't use every power at her command to gain a fabulous crown?

The crowd burst into a thunderous round of applause.

The dodo had broken into a brisk trot toward the east goal. Trusdale's pansied posterior bounced like a beach ball on his padded saddle. His sunflower ruff quivered like an angry lion's mane around his brown leather respirator. His left hand held the dodo's chain reins high above the bird's bronze-feathered neck, and his right held the polo mallet aloft.

The dragon egg catcher shuffled up to the sidelines. The egg hung heavy in his butterfly net.

Trusdale's going for a goal. The nerve of the man! She stomped her left foot down into her stirrup and charged the unicorn toward the dodo.

Trusdale thrust his emerald slippers twice into his own stirrups. The dodo launched into the air with the elegance of a rabid frog. The egg catcher hurled the egg onto the field and broke for the safety of the crowd.

Trusdale pulled back his arm to swing at the egg.

Constance pushed the unicorn to its full bone-shaking velocity. She grazed the dodo close enough to brush Trusdale with her petticoats. She didn't have time to blush. Her eyes were fixed upon the egg not ten feet ahead.

A blur of hurled bronze mallet flew through the unicorn's forelegs, causing it to stumble. Shock burned through Constance as her bustle lurched off the saddle and headed for the clouds. The world tipped upside down as she flipped over the bowed unicorn's left shoulder. She glimpsed her white buttoned boots dancing indecorously across the somber sky. A flurry of silver and blue skirts billowed over her head as she thudded bustle-first into the mud.

She blinked away tears of anger and punched her way out of her chiffon chrysalis. She emerged from her skirts and glared at her assailant.

Trusdale peered down at her from the back of the dodo.

What manner of brute throw's a polo mallet at a lady's unicorn?

The brute growled, "For the last time, Miss Haltwhistle, you need to get out of here. Trust me, the Prince—"

"Trust you?" she spluttered. "You're not even who you say you are. I have telegrams from America that prove you're a liar and a fraud and a—"

He groaned. "And a lot worse besides. You're right, I'm a liar. But I've got an inkling that you are too. We might not be the best of people, Miss Haltwhistle, but the Prince is an absolute devil."

"Who exactly are you?"

He glanced around at the crowd, then leaned down and whispered, "Call me Liberty."

"Why would I—"

"That's my real name, Liberty Trusdale. J. F. is—that is, *was* my older brother. I stepped in to fill his place at the Steamwerks when he died in a carriage accident. The reason why I did this isn't important, but I'll thank you to stop prying into my affairs. Now, if you'll excuse me, I'm about to carry out my own plan with a capital 'P'. I'm gonna go find a folly in a forest. And you, Miss Haltwhistle, can consider yourself rescued."

"I don't need to be—"

He pushed the dodo into a waddle toward the egg. She gasped as the bird kicked the egg up and through the goalposts. The crowd erupted into a cacophony of cheers at the last bird standing.

Trumpets blared out the official confirmation. Trusdale had won the crown.

Two thousand spectators applauded. She glowered at the dodo's swaying white tail feathers, taunting her as the bird waddled toward the redcoats guarding the woods.

The crowd surged toward their new champion, stopping short as the dodo exploded into a bouncing corkscrew spin. Aristocrats scattered like wedding confetti as the Count du Flange howled, "Look out! It's gone plumb crazy!" The bronze mount launched into a series of spine-cracking jumps as Trusdale flopped like a rag doll in the saddle.

As subtle as a tiger in a henhouse. Would it have killed him to attempt a Belgian accent? She stood to gain a better view of the dodo rodeo. *Is he actually enjoying himself?*

Trusdale flung his right arm up in the air and whooped as his two-ton bird pogoed across the turf. Five redcoat soldiers blocked his way as he approached the tree line. One ashen-faced private held up his palm to halt the dodo's dance.

The dodo flew into a whirlwind of hysterical hops. Her Majesty's finest dove into the forest undergrowth as the frenzied fowl spun in a deadly pirouette. Birch branches broke against the bird's metal frame as it gyrated into the greenery.

Leaving their dignity on the forest floor, the redcoats gave chase.

Applause broke out behind her, and she turned to see Lucien climbing aboard his newly repaired lion. Engineers and floral well-wishers eddied around the metallic king of beasts. The mud-drenched prince planted his warrior's skirt upon the lion's saddle and scowled at her. His handlebar mustache trailed like rat tails beneath flushed cheeks.

A crash that surely indicated a large metal dodo running through a large metal fence rang out from the woods. A smattering of red-coat gunfire drew an angry tiger's roar, followed by the trumpeting challenge of a bull elephant.

A murmur ran through the nobles closest to the tree line. The silk-clad blooms moved as quickly as propriety allowed toward the house as the jungle cries intensified. Gunshots rang out from the forest, and sweat broke upon Constance's spine. *Are they aiming at Trusdale? Or the other exotic beasts?*

Heart thudding, she tugged at the unicorn's reins. It clanked to its feet beside her. She placed one boot in the stirrup and hauled her muddy bustle back into the saddle.

Behind her stood her royal fiancé, ready to whisk her away to a life of gilded glory.

Before her, a dishonest cowboy danced with death.

Duty demanded that she wed. But her heart cried out for . . . *Liberty.*

Constance slammed the unicorn into a gallop and followed the dodo.

Chapter 39: Enemy Mine

THE MIDNIGHT MOON WAS CLOAKED by storm clouds as Trusdale approached the coal mine. Welli's ordnance survey map and his compass had proved invaluable in finding his way. He'd led the redcoats on a wild dodo chase through the woods before ditching the bird as close as he dared to his target.

Rain volleyed down through the branches of wizened oaks. He took a deep breath of cold, peaty air tinged with ozone. Earlier, the forest had seemed determined to kill him with bevies of lions, tigers, and elephants. Now, Mother Nature wished only to let him catch his death the old-fashioned way—through freezing rain followed by pneumonia.

He hunched his velvet-clad shoulders against the deluge as he trudged. Broken branches spoke of a hurried flight from the clearing he suspected had served as an impromptu airship landing field. He didn't need to be an expert tracker to find the square indentation in the mud where a large metal cage had once rested. No surprise, it was the same size as the one that almost crushed Constance the first night he met her.

He lost an emerald slipper in the mud. Too bushed to care, he plodded on.

Not that she knew it, but the fiery redhead now held a piece of his heart in the palm of her hand. *Dang, if she's gonna marry for all the wrong reasons, the least she could have done was pick a man who hadn't tried to drop a cage on her head.*

Lightning flickered, painting the trees silver as thunder crashed across the sky.

He gazed up between the swaying branches at the angry heavens. He said to the great beyond, "Lord, I'm not much of a religious man, but if you're listening, be straight with me. Am I being punished for stepping into my dead brother's shoes?"

The thunder rolled for what seemed to be an eternity.

He chewed the inside of his cheek. "I know I've made mistakes. When the MIC told me that J. F. had died, I should have rushed to tell my family, not agreed to take on his identity. I wish I'd done things different. I wish I'd been stronger. I wish I'd been bold enough to tell Constance that I . . ."

He sighed. "I guess it's too late for all that now. Lord, please, keep Miss Haltwhistle safe. I swear, I'll set things right back home with my family if you can just keep her safe. While we're on the topic, I wouldn't say no to a touch of safety myself."

A lightning bolt smashed into an oak tree not thirty yards ahead. He flung himself face-first into the mud. The tree split asunder with a bone-jarring explosion.

He lifted his face out of the dirt. "Too much to ask? Please, just look out for Constance then. I'll get by on my own."

The rain seemed a little lighter from that point on.

It took him less than an hour to reach the edge of the tree line. Ahead of him rose the forest folly. The two-hundred-foot-high obsidian volcano loomed dark against the night sky. Carved into the black stone was an imposing relief sculpture of the brawny Roman god, Vulcan. The bald, bearded metalworker glowered down at the sword he was forging on his anvil through riveted goggles. Rain glistened on his bulging biceps as he held his hammer high, preparing to make the next strike in his eternal labor.

The relief was lit by slow streams of golden, phosphorescent sludge that oozed down from the volcano's cratered top. The streams framed Vulcan like a portrait before pooling beneath him in a glowing moat that surrounded the volcano. *Aurumvivax*, Latin for "lively gold," was a glow-in-the-dark, non-toxic liquid metal used in high-end military lanterns. Trusdale had never seen it used for decorative purposes. The effect was eerily beautiful.

A white marble road swept over a bridge that spanned the moat and continued through an arched tunnel into the heart of the mountain. A handful of flickering electric bulbs lit the tunnel yellow.

Trusdale stole through the trees until he reached the ghostly flagstones of the road. Although pocked with weeds, the thoroughfare must once have created a grand approach to the folly. There didn't seem to be any sentries. Would he survive a stroll up the bulb-lit tunnel?

He flitted over the bridge and slid along the tunnel's red-marble walls traced with golden veins. His single slipper made no sound on the coal-black onyx slabs that paved the passageway.

Ahead, the rising walls of the hollow volcano were lined to the roof with crimson marble. A ten-foot-wide glass pipe that ran like a tree trunk up the folly's center carried the Aurumvivax to the volcano's decorative faux crater. An iridescent glow danced up the walls as the sludge made its ascent, adding an otherworldly luminescence to the vast cavern.

On the cavern floor beside the sludge pillar, three bronze-and-brass exo-suits rested on their knees. Their transparent chest doors stood wide open. In each titan's right hand, a brass flamethrower glimmered in the lava light. Around the suits, maybe fifty young men lounged on camp cots. Most seemed to be sleeping, while a handful chatted with their neighbors as they cleaned their rifles. All had blond hair cropped close in military style and wore gray cloaks, sweaters, combat pants, and polished black boots. No insignia marred their uniforms, but Trusdale would have bet his last dime that he was staring at Nordic commandoes.

Amidst the troops, eight galvanized-tin bathtubs were filled with standing bunches of long-stemmed red roses. A ninth tub was filled almost to the brim with a violet liquid, next to a large mound of empty vodka bottles. At the far end of the cavern, four men sat around a folding card table playing cards. Two officers and a scar-faced man in a blue tailcoat watched their hooded comrade deal.

Erhard—the Prince's right-hand man.

Trusdale gritted his teeth. Three prisoners sat behind the card players. Still dressed in their fancy attire from Constance's party, the scientists Huang, Chauhan, and McKinley rested upon blanketed gun crates. Ankle shackles tethered them to one another. All three were disheveled, with the two men displaying the bruised eyes of a rough questioning.

Trusdale balled his fists. The Prince and his lackeys would pay for such brutality.

Behind the sofa, three tunnels ran into the darkness. Golden signs above each entrance stated the passageways ran to the Main House, the Bottomless Pit, and the Devil's Cavern. None sounded like a safe exit, but his options were limited. If he could just reach Maya without being seen—

The hairs on the back of his neck prickled. He turned, too late.

A gun butt smashed into his jaw.

Pain exploded through his skull as darkness took him.

Chapter 40: War of the Words

PRINCE LUCIEN THREW BACK THE hood of his borrowed cloak as two burly Swedes dragged the unconscious sunflower toward the card table. The troops gathered in a circle to stare at the rain-soaked Count du Flange.

One of the troops reached down and pulled away the Count's leather respirator to reveal . . .

"Who the hell is this?" demanded Lucien of his troops, eyeing the comatose bloom.

Erhrad cleared his throat. "From the description given by our invisible assassins, I believe this is the infamous Trusdale, Chauhan's latest hire. Private Astrid Falk wrestled with this man in his bathtub. If we were to remove his hose, Falk said she noticed a distinctive birthmark upon his—"

Maya interjected, "Before we start de-hosing anyone, I can confirm that is Mr. Justice Franklin Trusdale, or J. F., as he prefers to be known. Please don't harm him. By reputation, he's a great scientific mind, an expert on all things electrical, and a—well, that is . . ."

She stuttered as Erhard reached for the prisoner's hose.

Lucien snapped, "For heaven's sake, Erhard, Chauhan's confirmation of identity will do. It seems your assumption that this fool didn't ride into the woods by accident was correct. Find out why he's here."

Erhard obligingly kicked Trusdale in the ribs. The prisoner groaned and muttered, "Dang, my head's throbbing like a bee sting on a bear's butt. Who let a mule into the tent?"

"Does he speak English?" asked Lucien.

Erhard drew his officer's saber and placed the tip against Trusdale's throat. The dazed American opened his eyes and blinked up at the weapon. Erhard snarled, "If you want to live, speak the Queen's tongue."

Soon to be the king's tongue, thought Lucien.

The sunflower flicked his eyes around the assembled group and said in a mock British accent, "Prince Lucy, old boy, how delightful to see you again. Erhard—still servanting, I see. Doctors Chauhan, Huang, McKinley, are you quite well?"

Lucien felt the familiar warmth of rage sweep through him. *Who does this foreigner think he's playing with? He should be shivering in his single slipper at facing my wrath.*

Dr. Huang said, "We're as well as can be expected, Mr. Trusdale. It seems they wish to airship us to Sweden at dawn. They're swapping us out for a second troop of commandoes. The poor blighters will become unsuspecting guinea pigs in their mad science experiments."

Trusdale dared to look directly at him. "More invisible soldiers, Prince Lucy? Whatever is the point?"

Ah, excellent, an opportunity to show off my strategic brilliance to a captive audience. Lucien puffed out his chest. "I'm glad you asked. My ultimate plan involves creating an invisible army of assassins who will eliminate—"

"Your Royal Highness, please don't waste your wisdom on this guttersnipe," Erhard said. He soundly kicked the sunflower in the ribs. "Tell me Yankee Doodle Dandy, where have you stashed McKinley's journals and the Enigma Key?"

Trusdale stretched back on the onyx floor and rested his head on his hands. A lazy smile crept across his tanned face. "A place where you'll never find them, unless I decide to help you. Now, I'm willing to cooperate, provided we can come to an understanding. As a show of good faith, first, you'll release the scientists unharmed."

"You're in no position to make demands," sneered Erhard. "And what use is McKinley's journal without his chemical expertise?"

"I assure you, Mr. Erhard," said McKinley, "my invisibility formula is simplicity itself. Alas that my aged memory has failed me on the specifics, or I would jot it down for you right now."

The Austrian scowled at McKinley. "It's curious that your amnesia kicked in the moment we kidnapped you from the party. I'm sure it could be cured by dripping hot candle wax directly onto your—"

"Dammit Erhard, we're not here for sport," said Lucien. The fool's ineptitude would be the death of him—today, if he didn't watch himself. "There are faster ways to make a man talk." Lucien wagged his finger. "You forget your place. I'm in charge here. I'll decide who speaks and who doesn't, and what forms of punishment are applied. Have I made myself clear?"

Erhard bowed. "As crystal, Your Royal Highness."

Lucien glowered at the cocky American. "I'd rather begin the proceedings by tormenting this miscreant. Trusdale—I will order Erhard to start removing your body parts in the order I find most amusing unless you betray the location of all things that I desire. Topping that list is the exact location of my flighty fiancée."

The sunflower raised his unkempt eyebrows. "You've misplaced Miss Haltwhistle? Before you two tied the knot?" His smile stretched to a full-on grin.

The scientists exchanged glances. "A redhead marrying the Queen's grandson? Has the world gone mad?" asked McKinley.

"If that's not the first sign of the apocalypse, I don't know what is. Miss Haltwhistle must be thrilled," said Huang.

Trusdale let out a low whistle. "Not thrilled enough to stay for the wedding, apparently. Tough break, Lucy, old boy. She didn't leave you standing at the altar, did she? Not in front of all those guests?"

Heat flared through Lucien's cheeks. "Why, no, she—"

"Didn't even have the decency to walk down the aisle," said Erhrad. "That woman is a villainous rogue, like every Haltwhistle before her."

Lucien's temples throbbed. "Rogue? That woman makes rogues look like hopeless amateurs. She's an unnatural beast. To leave a man, a prince, her fiancé, in front of the cream of society . . ." His heart hammered, sending his blood pressure soaring. "Death's too good for her!"

"And you *were* going to kill her, right?" asked the sunflower.

Lucien leered, "Not until after the wedding night, I wasn't."

He enjoyed the look of horror on Trusdale's face. The American spat, "Why you filthy—"

"Silence!" Lucien roared. "Another out-of-turn comment from any one of you, and I'll order the Swedes to start shooting kneecaps."

A hush fell over the grotto. The Swedes stared at him in what he could only presume was admiration. Lucien drew a deep breath. "That's better. Now, unless one of you can tell me the exact location of Miss Constance Haltwhistle—"

A crackle of blue lightning flared out from the volcano's entrance tunnel, causing the yellow bulbs of the passageway to flare to white-hot intensity. Sprinting mere meters ahead of the lightning, the ghostly silhouettes of the two invisible assassins, still speckled with purple ink, fled for the sanctuary of the grotto. They didn't make it. A kaleidoscopic whirl of colored light swept up the tunnel and devoured them. The tunnel's lightbulbs exploded in a brilliant flash.

Temporarily blinded, Lucien blinked until the darkened tunnel swam back into focus. A hissing metal canister flew out of the shadow and bounced to a stop on the black onyx floor. Smoke billowed from the canister as Erhard screamed at the troops, "Fire!"

With the speed of an Olympian, Lucien dove under the card table. His ears rang like a dinner gong as the troops let loose their rifles in a thunderous salvo through the smoke. The emptied shells ricocheted off the cavern walls, and the soldiers scattered to avoid their own bullets.

The Swedish soldiers regrouped and charged for the tunnel with bayonets glinting. To Lucien's right, Trusdale grappled with Erhard for control of the sword. The scientists gaped at the unfolding spectacle, flinching when a loud clang rang out from the exo-suits. The glass door on the center exo-suit had slammed close. The armored mech's steam engine rumbled into life as the titan rose to tower over the troops with its brass flamethrower raised. A woman's voice crackled through the suit's speaker grille, "The party's over, gentlemen. I suggest you all take a seat."

A thirty-foot stream of fire erupted from the flamethrower. The blaze of fire lashed across the cavern as the Swedes flung themselves to the floor. For three long seconds, the scent of paraffin filled the air as the troops cowered. The sudden heat caused sweat to course down Lucien's spine. It chilled on his skin as he recognized the exo-suit's pilot.

Safe inside the bulletproof glass cockpit sat a red-haired siren in a silver-and-blue ball gown. Constance said, "Do stay down, gentlemen, or else—well, I'm sure you get the picture."

The troops stayed low.

Constance appeared to notice him for the first time. "Is that my darling fiancé under the table? Sorry I left the party so abruptly, Lucien. I knew a certain sunflower would only get himself into trouble without me."

Trusdale stood, holding Erhard's sword in his hand. "Hey now, I'm doing pretty well, in case you hadn't noticed." He pointed the sword at the scientists. "I'm right in the middle of rescuing these folks."

One of the Swedes fumbled for his fallen rifle. Constance swung the flamethrower his way. "Hold it right there! Perhaps I should educate you all about the world's finest portable incendiary weapon, the Brass Queen Phoenix F-451 multi-fuel flamethrower. This exquisite armament is not only beautiful to behold—please note the fabulous firebird engraving along the weapon's stock—it can deliver a sizzling swath with astonishing accuracy up to a range of seventy-five feet. In other words, gentlemen, no one moves an inch, or I'll roast your chestnuts to a hue of my liking."

An unusual warmth stole through Lucien's heart as he studied his shapely enemy. Constance was as mad as a bat in a box, but she did know how to make a point. Her emerald tiara twinkled in the control panel's light as she studied her cowed opponents. With her aquatic-inspired gown and the bulbous armor's similarity to a deep-sea diving suit, she evoked a martial mermaid out to storm Neptune's palace.

She would have made a fascinating wife, if only for a single night.

Fortunately, he had a gift for handling women. He poked his head out from under the table. "My darling Constance, I'm so delighted that you could join us, although I'm not convinced that armor plating is suitable attire for my bride-to-be."

The exo-suit dropped into an almost-dainty curtsey. "My apologies, Your Royal Highness. I would have sheathed myself in white silk, but that didn't convey the fact that I could kill a man with quite the same force."

"You wouldn't dare, you godless harpy," said Erhard.

Constance narrowed her eyes. "Why don't you ask your invisible assassins if I'd dare? Oh, that's right, you can't. Sadly, they've departed this world for the next."

Erhard flushed. "You're the worst kind of devil, Haltwhistle."

She raised her eyebrows. "Why, that seems a little harsh. I certainly don't see anyone better than me in this cave—liars, lechers, mercenaries, misogynists, traitors, and tinkerers in all things unnatural. You can decide amongst yourselves which title fits each of you best. I'd probably be doing the world a favor by sending every single one of you to your eternal rest."

Surely a woman couldn't be so violent? But then again, Grandmama had her moments. "My sweet Constance," soothed Lucien. "Please, stay calm, take deep breaths. No need to get hysterical."

Her mouth hardened. "Call me hysterical again. I dare you. You will allow the scientists to leave this place immediately."

Erhard shook his head. "They're staying."

Lucien's breath caught in his throat at the servant's boldness. "I'll decide who stays and who goes."

"My apologies, Your Royal Highness." Erhard gave the shallowest of bows. "Your agreement with King Oscar is that you send the prisoners to him. To aid your imperial expansion, he needs a Swedish version of soldier snuff. The troops will, of course be yours to command."

Hmm. Why use British lads as cannon fodder, when foreigners could fill the breach? That did make sense . . .

"Erhard, you bad boy," said Constance. "Why don't you tell my fiancé the real reason Oscar covets the scientists? It's not for snuff. He wants them to crack the secrets of the Enigma Key."

Erhard's scarred face paled. "Your Highness, I've no idea why Oscar wants the key—"

Constance chuckled. "Oh, Erhard, such a fibber! Lucien, your servant's backstabbing thoughts are transparent to the kraken who have recently moved into my mind. King Oscar is driven by the same desire as the Steamwerks—to open portals to primitive worlds in other dimensions."

The three scientists gasped.

"Not that they've managed it yet," she continued. "You need more than one key to open those doors. And to transport an entire army without casualties, you'd need to understand the true nature of Aurumvivax. This golden slop is all that remains of the giant bubble craft that once brought visitors from another dimension to our world. Upon arrival, the ships melt, and the creatures emerge, ready to—" She shook her head. "Really? Heavens. How bizarre. One would have thought they . . . but we'll discuss that later."

She fixed Erhard with a Medusa stare. "I'm frankly appalled, sir, that you would conceal such an innovative strategy for empire-building from my beloved fiancé. Shame on you. What other secrets are you hiding?"

Erhard stuttered, "She—she's quite insane, my lord."

She grinned. "The kraken in my head say otherwise."

Lucien's own head swam. *Kraken? Other dimensions? What madness is this?* More importantly, was he merely a pawn in Oscar's larger ambitions? He clenched his fists. "She may be insane, Erhard, but she has a point. You never were particularly forthcoming about Oscar's plans."

"His only plan is to make you king of England and bathe in your glory and friendship. We promised him the scientists, the journals, and the key in hand. As we have yet to locate—"

Constance said, "Oh, I can help you out there. You mean this key and journal?" She held up a glowing blue triangle and a dusky-pink book.

Lucien barked at Dr. McKinley, "Is that your journal?"

The Scot frowned at the leather-bound volume. "Well, I, um—"

Erhard blustered, "A pink journal? It seems unlikely that a grown man would—"

"Why, Erhard, haven't you ever seen a map?" said Constance. "What color designates the British Empire?"

The scientists chorused, "Pink."

She smiled. "Exactly. Now, to smooth matters over with Oscar, I offer this journal, which contains the formula for the invisibility serum. I'll also throw in the Enigma Key, which provides access to untold power across an infinite number of dimensions. I'm feeling generous today, so I'll even forgive Oscar his attempts upon my life. Surely, that's an excellent deal for all concerned?"

Erhard shook his head. "Oscar wants the formula and the elimination of your family line. No deal."

A vein pulsed in Lucien's neck. "Once more, you overstep your bounds, Erhard."

"My apologies, Your Royal—"

"Shut up." He turned to bestow his most charming smile upon Constance. "My dear, sweet, calm girl. I agree to your terms. Please, step out of the suit so we can discuss how best you may serve me as your future king."

Erhard slapped his forehead with his palm.

Constance's eyebrows raised. "Future king, is it? Why, I'd be delighted to chat about your impending reign, once the scientists are heading for Haltwhistle Hall. I assume that the exo-suits are not vital components in your plan to depose the Queen. I see a few tubs of roses here, so I presume you intended to camouflage the suits with flowers and take a few potshots at Victoria during her parade tomorrow."

"Actually, they were just part of the backup plan in case—"

Erhard spluttered, "Prince Lucien, I beg you, tell her nothing. She's fishing for information."

"Why, the very idea! My Prince, are you taking orders from your servant, or are you the future English emperor, bold in thought and deed?"

The latter, definitely. He crawled from beneath the table and stood as tall and proud as any general in his history books. "Release the scientists."

Erhard blinked. "But—"

Lucien held up his hand. "Enough. It's not as if they can raise the alarm. I own the ear of every redcoat, police officer, judge, and courtier from here to London and back again. If Oscar wants them so badly, he is welcome to put forth his case in writing once Europe is mine."

Erhard said, "The agreement—"

"Has changed. Chauhan, Huang, McKinley—take the suits. We shall keep Mr. Trusdale as collateral against your silence."

The Swedes studied Erhard. The servant sighed. "Very well, Your Royal Highness."

Two soldiers approached the prisoners and knelt to unlock their ankle chains. The trio rose stiffly and walked toward the exo-suits.

The Enigma Key flashed in Constance's hand.

Lucien asked, "My dear girl, how exactly are you doing that?"

Constance studied the blue triangle. "The kraken raises an excellent point—two suits, three scientists. Dr. Chauhan, it's decision time. Surely you must know that Huang and McKinley are infatuated with you?"

The male scientists flushed.

Constance continued, "So I ask you, Maya, given your choice—would you rather ride alone in an exo-suit, or would you prefer to snuggle with one of your colleagues?"

Chauhan glanced between the two men. "Is she correct? Do you love me?"

Both men nodded sheepishly.

Chauhan clucked her tongue. "Forty years we've worked together—and neither of you could say a word?"

Huang said, "Well, the thing is, you're just so . . . you. How could we even hope to . . . ?"

McKinley added, "It would take a bold man to drum up the courage to say—"

"I love you," Huang finished.

Chauhan placed her hands on her sari-clad hips. "You're both useless, you know that?"

Constance asked, "But do you find one marginally less useless than the other?"

Chauhan studied the two. Then she clambered into one of the suits and patted her ample lap. "Come on up here, Zhi. Let me show you how the levers work."

Huang beamed and clambered in. A deflated McKinley settled into the other suit. The doors closed, and the suits' engines rumbled into life.

Constance shouted over the din, "Kindly run to the end of the white marble road and head southeast for twenty-three miles. Turn right at The Hateful Baker pub, go past the village station, and you should see the Haltwhistle shield cresting a pair of gilded gates. Follow the driveway up to the Hall and ask for Cawley. He'll set you up with tea and cake."

The suits saluted and clanked out of the volcano.

As their metallic footsteps faded, Constance grinned at Trusdale.

Lucien's stomach churned. *Surely she should only have eyes for me?*

The American scowled at Constance. "So, now I'm collateral?"

"I can think of worse words for you."

Lucien said, "Enough. I've fulfilled your request, dear girl. Step out of that suit and bring me the key and the journal." He glanced at the Swedes. Did they realize he intended to capture the woman alive? Once she surrendered, he'd dispatch an army of redcoats to recapture the scientists. Should they reach the sanctuary of Haltwhistle Hall, his troops would overrun the estate and eliminate all who stood against him. *And maybe those who didn't. Dead farmers told no tales.*

Constance's grin faded. "Alas, Lucien, we're still not quite even. First, as you have attempted to murder me on numerous occasions, I must regretfully decline your marriage proposal."

He gaped. "What? That offer is no longer—"

She held up her hand. "No, please don't beg, it's most unbecoming. Next, I recall that my coming-out ball was going quite splendidly until you shattered the roof and rained down shards of glass upon my guests." She swung the flamethrower up to point at the two-hundred-foot-high glass Aurumvivax tube.

Trusdale groaned. "Ah, hell no. Don't tell me you're gonna—that's a horrible Plan."

She pursed her lips. "The punishment fits the crime. I'm nothing if not fair."

She wouldn't . . . would she? "Wait!" shouted Lucien.

Perhaps he should have said please. A plume of fire burst from the F-451 and hit the tube half-way to the roof. The glass glowed orange, then exploded beneath the flames. A torrent of gold mud and glass shards rained down on the cringing men. The tsunami of mud fell upon Lucien like a two-ton weight, slapping him to the cavern floor and holding him there for what felt like an eternity. Almost numb with shock, he clawed his way up through eight feet of thick, choking, shimmering sludge.

He broke through the surface, heaving for air as the exo-suit waded through the mire toward him. Constance fixed him with a steely eye through the glass. "Now, Your Royal Highness, we're even."

He spat out a mouthful of metallic mud. "You, you—" His heart almost burst with lust and hatred. *My, what a woman!*

He bobbed impotently as the suit strode by him and plunged its hands deep into the golden sea. Constance hoisted up a sunflower as gilded as a sports trophy and tossed the spluttering man over one massive shoulder. She said smugly, "There—consider yourself rescued. Again."

The bloom muttered, and Constance laughed. "Language, Mr. Trusdale. There is a lady present." Holding the F-451 aloft, she strode out of the folly on her mechanical legs.

She didn't even spare her former fiancé a second glance. That insult was the final straw. Lucien bared his teeth.

No more Prince Charming.

Chapter 41:
Lady's Choice

CONSTANCE LEANED UPON THE IRON balcony that ran around Edwin the Stargazer's clock tower observatory. The rising sun cast a blush of pink over the charcoal line of the moors, warming the pastures and rose gardens, before lighting the honeyed sandstone of Haltwhistle Hall. A chill wind cut through her silver-and-blue ball gown as she surveyed her estate for the very last time.

Within the observatory's glass dome, Boo chased dust bunnies around a cannon-sized brass telescope. The oak floor vibrated with each ticktock of the clock mechanism below. For six hundred years, the pendulum had swung through the highs and lows of her family's history. Now it counted out her final moments as mistress of the hall.

A cough caused her to turn. Cawley bore her favorite bluebell-painted teacup and saucer upon a silver tray. "One for the road, miss?"

She went inside and closed the dome's glass door behind her. "Do you know if everyone got away safely? The farmers, the tenants, the shepherds, the swineherds, the house staff, the gardeners, the stable boys—"

"Everyone, miss. All laden down with enough gold and jewels to set them up in style in brand-new homes."

"I'm glad my father's treasure vaults came in useful at last." She took the tea and smiled. "I don't see your pockets lined with rubies and pearls."

"Don't you worry about me, miss. I've got a trunk stashed on your cousin's airship right next to Hearn's. We've got enough trinkets to keep us in featherbeds and fine brandy for the rest of our days, if we're so inclined."

She sipped the tea. "Has Welli stopped pouting about loading piglets, ponies, and exo-suits onto his ship?"

"He says you'll pay for the damage to his fancy teak planking, but he'll get over it. Mind you, you should have seen your godmother's face when Hearn ran the rest of the livestock onto her glass airship. She kept spluttering on about how people would see, but your cousin told her quite sternly that this was her penance for almost marrying you off to a murderer. That abashed her enough that she offered to take all our shire horses too. They'll have a lovely time of it on her estate in the South of France. Rolling meadows, clear streams, and a promise from Her Ladyship to keep them comfortable until you can pick them up again."

"*If* I can pick them up again," she sighed. "Oh, Cawley, I've made a royal mess of everything. All I had to do was marry. Now I have not only Uncle Bertie to contend with but Lucien's redcoats, too."

"He's a spiteful bugger and no mistake."

"I mean, since when is running out on an engagement a capital offense?"

"Since the man you ran out on can sign death warrants, apparently."

"And now Welli and Auntie Madge are guilty by association. And the staff. I've ruined their lives and lost everything that matters to me."

Boo yapped and pounced upon her silver chiffon overskirt. "Well, not everything, I suppose." She picked up the wriggling black-and-tan puppy and snuggled her against her breast. "Did the Steamwerkers leave for the city?"

"Aye, including that lass Hearn had his eye on. I called that one, didn't I?"

"Poor Hearn. How's he taking it?"

"Like the giant baby he is, badly. Drs. Chauhan and Huang accepted your offer to travel with us to France. Having seen how they lived at the Steamwerks, I'm not surprised. I couldn't find Dr. McKinley. Apparently, he disappeared a few hours ago."

She frowned. "Not literally, I hope? We never did account for that batch of invisibility serum he made."

"The cook said he mumbled something about 'redeeming himself,' before hitching a ride with a shepherd heading for the city."

"Oh dear. Is there anything more dangerous than a broken heart and a guilty conscience?" She cleared her throat. "Now, are you certain that *everyone* has evacuated the estate? No exceptions? Perhaps an out-of-towner who failed to heed the call to depart?"

Cawley pursed his lips. "Mr. Trusdale took a hot bath before riding off toward the village train station. On your father's stallion, no less. We haven't seen him since."

"So, now he's a horse thief? Marvelous." She heaved a sigh. "I suppose I shouldn't be surprised. Why would he stay? He's had a steamship ticket burning a hole in his pocket all week. And he made it perfectly obvious that he loathed bouncing along on the shoulder of my exo-suit for twenty-odd miles. You'd think he'd appreciate my daring rescue, but no, it was all, 'Why don't you let me drive for a while?' and, 'Can't I sit in there with you?' and, 'Are you sure you're going the right way?' I mean, the nerve of the man. As if I couldn't find my own way home by starlight."

"He is clearly an ingrate, miss."

"That he is." What had she expected? A marriage proposal? A handshake? A melodramatic goodbye? Trust him to be difficult. Selfish brute. Why wasn't he thinking about *her* needs?

He might at least have waved to her before heading back to America.

She drew herself up to her full height. "Well, he's gone, and that's that. There's no point lamenting the lack of gratitude in this world. It's time for us to depart. Cawley, to the laboratory."

Her loyal retainer stepped aside and followed her down the iron spiral stairs. Would that all men were so compliant. How much easier her life would be.

Located a hundred feet below the clock tower foundations, the laboratory bore little resemblance to the dank Norman dungeon it had once been. Rusting shackles had been replaced with tasseled gas lamps that threw a cheery glow over the twenty-foot-wide cavern. On the left side of the room, a brass console bristled with levers and dials in the golden light.

A penny-farthing bicycle on a wood-slat treadmill stood beside a copper bathtub. The tub held a trunk-size contraption crafted from cogs, gears, and chain drives. The makeshift kinetic generator was hooked to the brass console via a black telegraph cable that snaked across the gray flagstones.

A red wire ran from the console across the cavern and up the leg of a round, mahogany dining table. The wire wrapped around the base of a large copper birdcage standing in the center of the table. Nine silver candlesticks of varying sizes were placed around the cage. Wedged into the top of each candlestick sat a small metal triangle that glowed either red or green in the gaslight.

The Enigma Key tingled in her bustle. She reached back and drew out the blue glowing triangle. She concentrated on the blackboard in her mind and wrote out the words, *As promised, your friends within the other keys are here. I beg your indulgence for just a few moments more.*

In her mind's eye, two giant purple kraken wiggled like jellies. *But of course.*

Thank you, she thought. *I have to deal with a minor family emergency. Do you understand the concept of family?*

The kraken quivered, and to her surprise, each split itself into two smaller kraken.

Goodness. Congratulations on your bouncing baby selves. Please excuse me a moment.

She placed Boo on the stone floor. The puppy bounced to investigate the dark corners of the former dungeon. "Open the portal, Cawley."

He dutifully shuffled to the bicycle, clambered up, and started pedaling. The wooden treadmill rolled beneath the wheels, and the kinetic generator hummed into life. The black cable powered the brass console as the red wire electrified the copper birdcage.

A ball of blue energy appeared within the birdcage. It swirled to display an image of a red-faced man with a large ginger mustache glowering through a monocle.

She smiled. "Papa."

He scowled. "Don't 'Papa' me, young lady. Would you care to explain why two naked amnesiacs appeared from the void in the middle of last night's dinner party?"

"Oh, yes, I forgot about that. They are two Swedish assassins. To cut a very long story short, they took an invisibility serum which trapped their physical forms halfway between this world and the next. Naturally, they were losing their minds. I took pity and decided to kick them over to your dimension with the help of an Enigma Key. I threw in a healthy bout of amnesia to keep their mental demons at bay."

Baron Haltwhistle sighed. "You and your waifs and strays. What am I supposed to do with them?"

"With training, they're sure to make an excellent butler and lady's maid."

"Your mother won't like it, but I'll make sure they have a home."

She clenched her teeth. "She's not my mother."

The Baron rolled his eyes. "Not this again, Constance. The poor woman lost her husband, an alternate version of me. I lost an alternate version of her. If we can't tell the difference from our original spouses, who are you to judge who's who?"

"And the alternate version of me—how is *he* doing?"

"Constantine is fine. Why, you'd like him if you got to meet him." He chuckled. "Mind you, he's a bit of a hothead—a real chip off the old block if you will."

"I'm the chip, not him."

"Oh, Constance—"

"Don't. Incidentally, Uncle Bertie made good on his vow to hire lawyers to take the hall."

"As I said before, dear girl, simply marry and be done with it."

"I tried, but things didn't work out too well."

"Those tiny hats you wear do you no favors at all. I tell you, a large floppy chapeau and your Prince Charming will—"

"I don't need a Prince Charming; I need the laws changed so I can inherit this pile. Or an army. Or both. But that's neither here nor there, as I've managed to bring down the wrath of the Crown upon my head."

The Baron's monocle popped out of his eye. "Good Lord, Constance. Haven't I told you to stay well away from the royal court?

You know our history with them isn't exactly salubrious. By covenant, they turn a blind eye to us, and we don't—"

"I accidentally became engaged to the Queen's grandson."

"How on earth did you manage to—?"

"Auntie Madge."

He groaned.

"Exactly. Between Lucien's redcoat army and Uncle Bertie's determination to raze the hall, I fear drastic measures are required."

"You're raising an army? Well, I suppose you do have enough gold, and the Brass Queen is nothing if not well armed. You could clear out the warehouses and—"

"Neither Miss Haltwhistle nor the Brass Queen are ready to spill blood just to keep this house in the family. But listen well, papa, for I am far more than the roles I play to please others. This hall, and I, we both deserve a fate better than destruction at the hands of men too petty to appreciate our value. I will have to struggle through this world alone, but this house shall make her grand escape."

"The entire house? You're not burning her down?"

"Better. She'll disappear into thin air."

"That's the same—"

"I'm going to open a dimensional rift large enough to send the Hall to a world without humans to rest her ancient bones in peace. She'll decay over the centuries, but doesn't everything turn to dust in time?"

"My darling girl, what an interesting plan—"

"That's Plan, with a capital 'P'."

"Oh, just like your mother used to have. But her Plan's usually revolved around creating the perfect dinner party seating arrangements or introducing two single friends that she believed were fated to fall in love. She never—"

"Well, I have. And I'm going to continue to do so."

He cleaned his monocle on his waistcoat. "Do be practical, Constance. You can't possibly open a fractal chasm that wide, not unless you have a blue—"

She held up the blue Enigma Key.

Papa's eyes widened. "Good Lord, you have been busy."

She gestured at the red and green glowing triangles atop the candlesticks. "I'm breaking all the keys to release the beings within."

"Is that your idea? Or the keys?"

"Mostly mine."

He scratched his nose. "Hmm. I hope that's true. Have you truly thought this release business through? The consequences could be . . . far-reaching."

"I know what I'm doing. Are you aware that these poor creatures were originally trapped in these dimensional prisons by their enemies? They're essentially enslaved, forced to provide power at their master's behest. If they refuse, their planetary prisons are turned into nightmare worlds. It's all quite horrific."

"I'd advise against getting embroiled in interdimensional politics."

"I'm not. I'm just doing the right thing."

"With their help, to their benefit." He sighed. "My dear girl, are you quite sure—"

"It's the moral principle that's at stake here. I don't believe that sentient, living beings should be forced to power other creatures' dimensional devices."

He chuckled. "Tell me, is Cawley the one riding the penny farthing today? Or is it Hearn?"

"That's different. Cawley has a choice as to whether he pedals the bike."

Cawley's pace on the penny farthing slowed. "Do I, miss?"

"No, keep pedaling."

Papa smirked.

She said firmly, "That doesn't change my Plan, papa. I'm offering you one last chance to come back to me."

"A return journey is doubly dangerous. You should come to me."

She chewed on her lip. "I belong here, with the people I've sworn to protect. They . . . need me. And I need them."

She ignored the gasp from Cawley on the penny-farthing.

Papa folded his arms. "Then we are at an impasse. I just don't know where you get your stubbornness. It must be from your mother's side."

"No doubt."

He fiddled with his monocle. "So, this is really goodbye?"

"It is."

He wiped his eyes and replaced his monocle. "Very well. As a both a scientist and a father, I'm curious—what's your Plan?"

She checked off on her fingers. "Open a fractal chasm with an overload of aether energy, warn the Queen that her grandson's out to take her throne, and then take Welli's airship off on a grand world tour, starting with Paris."

"Does Welli know that?"

"Not yet."

The Baron sat back. "No offense, my dear, but that's a spectacularly horrible Plan. You could accidentally create a fractal chasm so large that it swallows the entire world, or get shot by the Queen's bodyguards, or—"

She exploded, "Why don't more people appreciate my vision? First Trusdale, now you; why do only the servants trust that I know best?"

"You're paying the servants to trust you. Who's Trusdale—is he a new hire?"

"No, he's an American horse thief and professional liar."

Cawley added, "Who stayed a whole night in the Oak Room."

She snapped, "Less talk, more pedal, Cawley."

The Baron raised one eyebrow. "Stayed in the Oak Room, eh? Heavens, Constance, are you blushing?"

"Certainly not. I'm just furious that he rode off on Beelzebub. Why couldn't he have taken a carriage pony, or walked, for that matter?"

"Hmm. This 'professional liar' sounds like a man with an eye for a fine horse. Cawley, who is this fellow?"

"An alleged engineer and possible cowboy, my lord. Brave, bold, but not exactly a gentleman."

Papa snorted. "Who is these days? Still, it's a shame you lost him, Constance. His offspring would have been truly outstanding."

Her jaw dropped. "Papa!"

He said innocently, "I'm talking about the stallion, my dear. Why—what did you think I meant?"

She muttered, "Nothing."

"And you're absolutely set on this fractal chasm idea?"

"I am."

He sighed. "Well, I won't waste my breath arguing with you; that way lies madness. I wish you joy in the years ahead. Remember my words—stay sharp, look your enemy dead in the eye, shoot them in the back if you can. The only high ground worth taking is that which allows you to throw rocks onto your opponents. Use any resource at hand to obtain victory, and never, ever, forget that you're a Haltwhistle. Continue the bold tradition emblazoned in the family motto. *Nos calce abjecistis inimicos nostros per medias usque ad nates.*"

"'We kick our enemies in the arse.' I must say, it sounds a lot more refined in Latin."

"Doesn't everything?"

"*Sic verum est.* Do send my love to—let's say, my new 'stepmother' and 'brother,' Constantine. I hope you'll all be reasonably happy together."

He grinned. "You'll always be my favorite child, Constance."

"I should bloody well hope so."

He guffawed as the image of his face flickered, shrank to a tiny spot, and disappeared.

The empty birdcage blurred as her tears welled. She blinked at the cage, half hoping Papa would reopen the connection, half glad that she'd got in the last word.

The Enigma Key popped images into her mind of sixty redcoat cavalrymen trotting by The Hateful Baker pub. Once they passed the train station, they'd be on her land within minutes.

She set her jaw. "Our foes grow closer. Pedal faster, Cawley. It's time to open the void."

Chapter 42: Horse Feathers

TRUSDALE FIDGETED IN THE TINY village train station just beyond the Haltwhistle estate. If he'd thought he could forget about Constance once he'd left the Hall, the architecture of Whirlow Junction said otherwise. The Haltwhistle shield was emblazoned at every corner of the crown molding that ran around the oak-paneled waiting room. Behind the counter, the snowy-haired, green-uniformed stationmaster tapped out his carefully worded telegraph message to his family back home in Kansas. *Tap, Tap* . . .

Trusdale chewed his inner cheek. Was there any good way to tell your parents and siblings that one of their own is dead? And that you've known for weeks, but are only just sharing the news? How about the fact that his brother was interred under the pseudonym Charles Clifford in a New York city graveyard? Not to mention that he'd been pretending to be J. F. . . . No, that part he'd have to share in person. There's only so much you can land on a family at one time.

Putting his own career and a little matter called national security above his family's needs wasn't a choice he'd made lightly. He'd have a lot of explaining to do once he got home.

Tap, tap, tap-tap . . .

But for now, it was good to get at least some things off his chest. Within the next ten minutes, he'd board the train to Liverpool. If he dashed, he might just make his steamship back to New York. A few more days travel, and he'd see his family in the flesh.

He should be happy to be leaving this crazy country. And yet . . .

Deep in his heart was a wound that would never heal. She'd never know it, but she'd marked him for life, as clear as if she'd shot him point blank with rock salt.

His life was gonna be a whole lot duller without a certain flame-haired aristocrat and her extended family of oddballs. But it was time for him to move on, time to . . . let go of a dream he'd never had a chance of making real.

Through the open doorway, Beelzebub stomped and tossed his ebony mane, testing to see if the reins tied to the hitching post would give way. The reins held tight, but the post wobbled. Beelzebub whinnied his disgust.

The stationmaster said, "He's a fiend, that horse, sir. Usually, he only lets the Baron or Miss Constance ride him. You must have a way with animals."

"He almost tipped me into a ditch or two on the way here, but we reached an understanding."

The stationmaster tapped on. "I'd rather walk for the rest of my life than go near that beast. Give me a steam train any day. The 7:48 will roll up here any second now. You could set the town hall clock by our trains' respect for the schedule." He finished tapping out the message. "That's it, sir. I'm sorry for your loss of your brother." He respectfully dipped his gold-braided cap.

"Thank you kindly. I have one more message to send. This time address it to Lieutenant Godfrey Gillingham, care of International Exports, Inc. New York City, USA. Dear God . . ."

Trusdale took off his Stetson and felt inside the brim. A strip of leather bore this month's code for communicating with his handler. The true identity of God was a mystery. Perhaps she was a woman, or a committee, or maybe even an old man in a flowing robe sitting on a throne. But if he didn't check in with God at least once a week, his paycheck would cease to be sent to his family.

But how do you tell the US Government that your simple spy mission has turned into an interdimensional incident involving telepathic kraken, invisible assassins, and a plot to overthrow the Queen of England?

He was gonna need a bigger code book. "After Dear God, say . . . nice weather here. Stop. A little blustery. Stop. The local flora and fauna are something to see. Stop. Maybe I'll take a few clippings to bring back home . . ."

The stationmaster ceased tapping out the message. "Clippings of fauna, sir?" He tilted his head. "What, like a rabbit's paw, or a deer's ear?"

"Um . . . I guess?"

The stationmaster stood and shuffled over to the counter. He murmured, "This particular message wouldn't be in code, would it, sir? Because you might be using the wrong one. There's been a bit of a kerfuffle at the Hall, as I'm sure you're aware." He nodded meaningfully at Beelzebub. The stallion stomped and glared, tugging back once more at the reins. The post swayed but held fast.

Trusdale put his Stetson back on. "You have a point. I didn't think to check up at . . . the Hall . . . what code I should be using." *What mess have I stepped into now?*

The stationmaster nodded. "We don't want another sausage incident, do we, sir?"

"Lord, knows, we don't."

"When in doubt, resort to flowers. We never mix up the orders involving flowers."

"Right. Good point."

The stationmaster smiled and went back to his desk. He unlocked the drawer and drew out a dusty book imprinted with a gold crown inside a cogwheel.

Why would Constance use code to talk about sausage deliveries? Was industrial espionage a problem in the British pork and bacon community?

The stationmaster opened the book and ran his finger down the page. "She sent three-dozen daffodils to Rome last week, to thank a certain priest for a special blessing." He wiggled his eyebrows meaningfully.

"Ah, yes, of course she did."

"And she usually informs her friend in France what's growing in the orangery when that happens."

"Yup, that she does."

"So, I'm thinking last Thursday's code should still work."

"I'll mention to Miss Constance how helpful you've been."

The man beamed. "Why, thank you, sir! It's a delight to work for the Haltwhistles. Their grandfather built this station, you know. There's not a person in this village whose life they haven't touched in some way. Usually for the better, as long as you mind your p's and q's. He tapped the side of his nose.

"Gotta watch those p's, or else. Between you and me," Trusdale leaned in and murmured, "she's got a bit of a temper on her."

The stationmaster laughed. "I'm not surprised. Running a global arms empire from an early age will toughen you up. But beneath it all, even the Brass Queen is flesh and blood. She looks after us locals like family."

Trusdale nodded in what he hoped was a sage manner. *Brass who now?* "There's nothin' more important than family."

"Well said, sir. So, will she be sending ten dozen roses, or a bunch of petunias to her great aunt in Bengal?"

"Um, definitely the petunias."

"We'll keep the rabbit's feet until next week."

"Good choice."

"And what would you like to send to God at West Point?"

Trusdale licked his lips. "You know what? I think we've sent him all he needs for now."

Beelzebub whinnied. A rumble of hooves approached, growing louder by the second.

Trusdale shot to the open doorway.

Redcoats. Lots and lots of redcoats. Maybe six-dozen cavalry, with a platoon of foot soldiers tight on their heels. Fixed bayonets glinted in the morning sun and the gold lion standard of Prince Lucien flapped in the breeze.

Blood pounded in his ears. Were they coming for Constance?

In the distance, a train whistle tooted. His last chance to get to his steamship on time was fast approaching.

His choice was clear. Duty versus . . . love.

Love. It always had to be love.

He sprinted to Beelzebub. There was no time to untie the stallion. He flicked out his knife, slashed loose the reins, and grabbed hold of Beelzebub's mane as the stallion reared. He swung himself up into the English saddle as the horse bucked. Shouts from the redcoats filled the air as he turned the prancing stallion toward home.

Let loose, Beelzebub burned like the devil through the sleepy village. His hooves flung gravel back at the army geldings as they gave chase. Trusdale clenched his teeth and rode low on the galloping stallion's neck. Back to Haltwhistle Hall.

Back to the Brass Queen.

Chapter 43: Leap of Faith

CONSTANCE STEADIED HER EMERALD TIARA as an unnatural wind howled across the raised stern of Welli's airship, the *Lady Penelope*. Above, the pink, cigar-shaped gasbag was buffeted by the aether gale. Far below, a gigantic ball of blue lightning consumed her hopes of saving the Hall stone by stone. Centuries of family history disappeared into the fractal vortex, heading for a plane of existence far beyond the reach of angry men with guns.

Her fingers were numb from gripping the edge of the airship's broad teak railing. Was this her cosmic punishment for trading in arms too long? Should she have focused more on pinching pennies and firing aged staff members?

No, that wasn't her way. Besides, designing aether weapons had thrilled her far beyond the mere monetary gain. Giving beauty, poetry, and magic to brass, copper, and wood had filled her heart with joy. Not to mention the satisfaction of hitting center target with perfect accuracy from ranges beyond the ken of any other designer. This was her gift to the world.

Then why do I suddenly feel . . . guilty? Firing the flamethrower over the Swedes heads had been satisfying. But in the hands of a villain, the same weapon would have reduced the men to ash and bone.

Now that the Hall was gone, was this to be her legacy?

She released the rail as the howling wind increased. Above, the pink camouflage cover ripped to reveal a six-foot gash of the black interior gasbag. This was the true heart of the *Lady Penelope*. The ship's whimsical pink-and-gold façade disguised her pirate heart. Hidden beneath the ship's gilded exterior lurked the armored hull of the almost notorious pirate vessel, *Bad Penny*.

Mrs. Singh occasionally flew the airship north for a spot of light plundering. Constance had loved to ride along and watch the former pirate queen at work. First, Mrs. Singh would assign two lookouts to the foredeck's handrail-mounted telescopes. Once a laden merchant vessel had been spotted, an ingenious chain-and-pulley system drew back the pink camouflage cover to reveal the black main balloon, emblazoned with the skull and crossbones.

At the pull of a lever, the pink side panels of the ship flipped to reveal black armor plating. Eight concealed cannons could be brought to bear upon an enemy ship's defenses, although they had yet to fire more than a warning shot at their prey. The surprise of being stalked by a pirate airship over the Scottish border had been more than enough to ensure a bloodless takeover of target ships. Looting was achieved quickly and politely by Mrs. Singh and her transient crew, mustered as weekend pirates from the Sheffield canal's vibrant pub scene.

The airship had been one of Papa's most prized possessions until the day Welli caught him in a bad bluff at the poker table. Constance added to her to-do list the need to win back the vessel at her earliest opportunity. Once more, the Haltwhistle flag would fly from the stern, replacing Welli's peacock standard.

She turned to watch her cousin, still fabulous in his water lily costume, pick his way across the lower deck between her hastily gathered belongings. Like her, he had balked at changing out of his costume into something more sensible. If they were to flee the country, branded as traitors, at least they could do so with style.

The teak boards were littered with trunks of her clothing, *objets d'art* from the Hall's treasure chambers, and five barrels of blackberry cider. Three exo-suits knelt on the deck as Cawley, Hearn, and Mr. Singh struggled to tie a flapping green tarpaulin over the behemoths. The oilskin cloth ripped from their hands and blew into the clouds as Welli climbed up the ladder onto the stern. The lightly armored knight nodded to Mrs. Singh at the steering wheel, resplendent in her scarlet sari with a curved gold cutlass at her hip. Welli joined Constance at the stern and peered over the handrail at the electrical storm below.

He gaped. "Good lord, Connie, did you leave the gas on?"

"Not exactly."

A sonic boom rattled her teeth as the last remnants of the hall vanished with a blinding flash of kaleidoscopic light. She blinked, leaning once more over the railing to watch a three-hundred-foot-deep crater race out from the former site of her home. The crater devoured the rose garden and the manicured lawn beyond.

Welli gasped. "What did you do? Did you plant dynamite? Tell me you didn't."

"I didn't. Don't worry, this is merely a reaction to raw aether. The crater will stop expanding before it reaches the stables."

She held tight to the rail as the wind picked up. Cawley and Hearn hurried to her side. Hearn whistled tunelessly as the pit below swallowed the empty stable block whole.

Constance said, "It will definitely stop before it reaches the airship hangar."

Picking up speed, the crater wolfed down the huge bronze structure and gobbled through acre after acre of green pasture, heading for the moors.

Constance pursed her lips. "Cawley, I fear you may have pedaled too hard."

"I'm sorry, miss."

Welli squinted toward the estate's entrance gates. "Look. Isn't that Beelzebub?"

A black stallion galloped down the gravel driveway toward the abyss. His rider crouched over the beast's neck with his Stetson pulled down low and his duster coat flapping. Constance's heart simultaneously lifted and sank. She groaned. "Our horse thief returns. His timing is simply intolerable. There's nowhere safe to land."

"Looks like the entire redcoat army is on his heels," said Welli.

Barely a hundred feet behind the black rider, sixty scarlet-coated cavalrymen charged at full gallop with their sabers drawn. Hundreds of foot soldiers followed at a brisk pace.

Constance's breath caught. Trusdale was finished.

Before I ever got to tell him that I . . .

She slammed her fist on the handrail. "Typical. He never thinks about anybody but himself. Take the ship in fast and low."

"But we can't—"

"Now!"

Welli jumped. "All right, keep your hair on." He shouted to the helm, "Mrs. Singh—we're taking on a passenger. Head for the gravel drive."

The pilot spun the steering wheel, and the ship banked hard left. Mr. Singh ran to help his wife steady the helm as the gale lashed the airship.

Constance yelled, "Full speed ahead."

"Aye, aye, miss," shouted Mrs. Singh.

Welli pouted. "I could have told her that."

"I've saved you the trouble. You can thank me later." Constance leaned over the rail and studied the rider. "I fear we may be too late." She yelled, "Make haste!"

"I don't think he can hear you."

"I'm talking to Mrs. Singh." She shouted over her shoulder, "Dive! Take this bucket down!"

"With pleasure, miss." Mrs. Singh plunged the airship into a fierce descent.

Constance's trunks of clothing skidded across the teak boards. She barked at her servants, "Clear the decks."

They stared at her, unfamiliar with the buccaneer parlance she had picked up in her cursory reading of *The Duchess and the Sky Pirate*. As she lacked a more swashbuckling crew, she pointed at her belongings strewn across the lower deck. "The trunks—get rid of the damn trunks."

Cawley and Hearn sprinted to the ladder, slid down it in an almost pirate-worthy fashion, and grabbed the nearest trunk. They hauled it to the side of the ship and flung it over the handrail.

Welli murmured, "Oh, Constance, your wardrobe."

She roared, "Throw everything over the side. We need to clear a space." She tugged at Welli's sleeve. "Come on, we'll help."

They climbed down the ladder and launched her autumn boot collection over the rail. The wind whipped her skirts into a chiffon tornado as she grappled with a bevy of unruly hatboxes.

The ship screamed down toward the earth.

Cawley picked up Trusdale's battered black suitcase with its sturdy brass combination lock. Constance slapped it out of his hands. "Not that one—everything else."

Cawley headed for a trunk of cloaks. With Hearn's help, he cast her most cherished velvet outerwear over the ship's side.

Mrs. Singh dropped the airship into the belly of the abyss. Walls of dirt, stone, and coal rose around them as they raced along the crater bottom toward the oncoming riders.

The chasm stopped expanding. A cliff wall of sandstone rock solidified before them.

Constance tossed a bundle of petticoats into the crater. "Side-on, Mrs. Singh, and rise, fast, as close as you can to the top of the cliff."

The ship swung sideways and rose.

A black horse reared at the edge of the precipice.

Trusdale stared down at the approaching ship, pulled the horse into a sharp turn, and disappeared.

The dirigible's airbag soared above the cliff.

Was he going to face the cavalry alone? Why didn't he jump?

A rumble of hooves, and a black horse soared out from the cliff top and plummeted toward the deck ten feet below. Beelzebub landed like an angry two-ton cat and skidded across the boards on his metal shoes. The stallion's muscular chest slammed into the ship's side, sending Trusdale flying out of the saddle and over the edge.

Her heart caught in her throat.

She ran to the edge of the ship and peered over. Trusdale dangled by Beelzebub's leather reins, his face ashen. She grabbed the reins and coaxed the sweating stallion to back up as Welli and the servants hauled Trusdale aboard.

He flopped onto the teak boards, the reins still gripped tightly in his gloved hands.

Satisfied he was safely aboard, she shouted, "Head for the clouds, Mrs. Singh."

The airship shot skyward.

Welli helped Trusdale to a stand. "Are you all right, old boy?"

He nodded. "How's the horse?"

Constance checked over the stallion. "He's fine . . . are you . . . that is, why did you take him?"

"He looked like your fastest ride, and I had a few telegrams to send. There was a family matter I'd promised the Lord I'd clear up."

"Which Lord, exactly?"

Trusdale pointed up at the heavens. "The big one. Now, not to be nosy, but do you folks want to tell me how your great estate just disappeared?"

The servants and Welli stared at Constance. They all knew her family dabbled in science, but how much data should she share? She shifted her weight from foot to foot. "Would you believe me if I suggested moles were to blame?"

Trusdale chuckled. "Not in the slightest."

She sighed. "Fine. I used aether energy to create a fractal chasm that sent Haltwhistle Hall to a safe place. In another dimension."

Trusdale blinked. "I think I preferred the mole story. Oh Constance, your family home. You must be gutted."

She was, but this was an excellent opportunity to show her stiff upper lip in action. "As Maya said at my coming-out ball, it's only a house, after all." She ignored Welli and the servants dropped jaws. "Well, it is. It's the people who lived there that I care about, not stone and tile and mortar." It felt good to say it out loud.

Trusdale asked, "How exactly did you send your house—"

"Are you writing a report? If you absolutely *must* know, the transfer process was instigated using your Enigma Key, which I . . . liberated—"

"Stole."

"Do you want to hear this story, or not?"

He sighed and nodded.

"When your Key interacted with several others I had in my possession, a blast of aether energy ripped a tiny inter-dimensional vortex through which the estate slipped. In the process, the beings linked to the Keys were set free to travel to their own dimensions."

Welli raked his hair. "So, there are other worlds—"

"Inhabited by a plethora of non-human intelligent creatures and occasionally alternate versions of ourselves. The cosmos is a gorgeous mess. Isn't it wonderful?"

"Other versions of ourselves? So, if you've lost someone here—" said Trusdale.

"Then yes. They may exist in another dimension. Why, is there someone you'd like to visit?"

He gazed at her thoughtfully. "I have a family member I'd love to hug again one day. But for right now, I'm exactly where I want to be. Here, now, with you."

Her heart jumped.

Then he gestured to the servants and Welli. "And all of you too, of course. You're by far the best people I've met in this country."

"Well, that's not saying much," said Wellington. "To be fair, you haven't exactly seen the British at their best. Murderous princes aside, we're a lovely lot."

"We're also very discreet," said Constance. "Mr. Trusdale, will you promise not to discuss my family's inter-dimensional activities? The results could be—"

He crossed his heart. "You have my word."

She would need a little more leverage than that, but for now, his word would have to do. "Splendid. I trust you won't mention any of this to the scientists? The damage they could do if they continue investigating aether portals doesn't bear thinking about."

At the rear of the deck, the door that led down to the cabins and staterooms opened. Drs. Chauhan and Huang stepped out into the morning sunlight. A Yorkie puppy bounced happily at their heels. Trusdale muttered, "I swear, I won't breathe a word."

Constance exhaled. "Good man." She turned to greet the scientists who now strolled arm in arm. "Doctors, I trust our fluctuating altitude didn't disturb your slumber?"

Maya cocked her head. "Slumber?"

"Cawley said you two had availed yourselves of the cabins below. I assumed . . ."

Maya's cheeks reddened. Her dress was misbuttoned, and Huang's white tie hung loosely around his neck.

Huang cleared his throat. "We slept wonderfully, thank you for asking."

Boo ran to Constance and yapped. Constance knelt and cradled the puppy against her corset. Wet canine kisses covered her face, licking off the remnants of her makeup. *I must look an absolute fright!*

Even so, Trusdale was watching her with a broad grin on his face. She cleared her throat. "Hearn, please go and check that my livestock has survived this bumpy journey unharmed."

The burly man nodded and headed for belowdecks. The cargo hold had been transformed into a makeshift stable. While the bulk of the estate's livestock had either traveled with Auntie Madge or been gifted to the evacuated staff, the remaining ponies, sentry sheep, hedgehogs, foxes, and any other wild beasts the servants could cajole aboard were adjusting to their new quarters aboard the *Lady Penelope*.

Maya smiled at Trusdale. "Ah, J. F., you've returned."

Constance opened her mouth to inform the former Steamwerks matriarch that she was actually addressing J. F. Trusdale's lying younger brother, when her eyes met his. They were ridiculously blue.

If she wanted him to keep her secrets, she supposed she'd have to keep a few of his too. She closed her mouth.

Trusdale grinned at her, then said to Maya, "It was a close-run thing. There were 'Wanted' posters all over the village showing a sketch of me in my sunflower costume alongside Miss Haltwhistle riding her unicorn. If the locals weren't so protective of the Haltwhistles' and their guests, I'd have been turned in for the reward."

She was on a wanted poster? My, she would request a few copies to be sent over to Paris. What fun! That beat a boring old oil painting in a dusty hall any day.

"High society may barely know I exist, but the local staff, servants, and villagers are well acquainted with me. I've kept food on many of their kitchen tables for the past few years."

He held her gaze. "You're a good woman, Miss Haltwhistle."

"Who ever said I wasn't?" She smirked. "Anyway, in my new role as the debutante detective and captain of this vessel—"

Welli said, "Hold on a minute—"

"I think it's about time we put into action the final phase of my grand Plan." She called out, "Mrs. Singh, set a course for the royal parade route."

"Aye aye, Captain."

Welli shouted, "This is mutiny, Mrs. Singh."

The Indian woman laughed and brandished her cutlass.

Mr. Singh coughed. "My lord, perhaps discretion is the better part of valor. One warrior woman is a handful, but two united is a veritable army. Let us choose the path of wisdom and stay the hell out of their way."

Welli nodded. "You make an excellent point, Ajeet." He raised his voice, "Carry on, Mrs. Singh."

Trusdale raised a bushy eyebrow. "We're flying into the city? You know, traditionally, fugitives tend to flee the area where they're most likely to be hanged."

"And so we will, Mr. Trusdale, but as a British subject I feel duty-bound to warn the Queen of Lucien's Machiavellian machinations."

"Is that all?"

She scowled. "Well, I suppose the Prince won't have time to pursue me if he's facing her wrath."

"I thought your nobility might have its practical side."

"Besides, Maya would never forgive me if I let her former royal patron meet a grisly end. Right, Maya?"

The scientist shrugged. "No doubt she deserves it. Still, for a despot, she has grown a little softer in recent years. She's finally achieved the wisdom to see that imperial expansion is not always the best solution to every problem. If she wants a stable empire to hand down to Edward, she needs to consolidate her hold on those lands most loyal to the crown."

Trusdale asked, "So, Victoria's not marshaling her forces to invade the United States?"

Maya shook her head. "Heavens no—you're far more trouble than you're worth. The Canadians will hoist their flag over the White House long before the British Empire glances your way."

"But the upsurge in exo-suit production, the new weapons—" Trusdale pressed.

"You have the Brass Queen to thank for that." Maya gestured toward Constance. "Victoria is utterly smitten with her designs."

For the first time in her life, Constance thought she might actually faint. The deck went wobbly and she swayed. She balled her fists and focused her gaze on Maya. The sari-clad scientist glanced around the group. "I'm sorry, dear girl, I assumed that everyone here knew about your magnificent armaments."

Silence fell.

The cat was truly out of the bag, the house, and the county. Trusdale looked surprisingly unsurprised. "So, Miss Haltwhistle, you've been providing more than pork pies and cider to the masses?"

The Brass Queen, outed at last, cocked her head. "The masses? I'll have you know that only the most select clientele can afford my bespoke brass beauties. The personal armies of kings, sultans, and—"

"That bloke in Chicago," Cawley added.

She glowered. "Well, yes, Papa has made one or two unfortunate deals in his travels, but on the whole, our clients are—"

Maya said, "Buying weapons on an elite black market that circumvents local laws and taxes?"

Constance frowned. "You make it sound so sordid, yet you were chomping at the bit to place an off-the-books order."

Maya nodded. "We built an exo-suit for every flamethrower you could provide, with one goal in mind."

Trusdale asked, "Battlefield supremacy?"

"Celebration. The Queen was intrigued by Constance's desire to use F-451–equipped exo-suits as beverage dispensers. Her Royal Highness is going to install a dozen similarly equipped suits at every imperial palace. They'll be dispensing champagne, wine, and spirits at Jubilee parties from here to Zaire."

Constance groaned. "So much for my secret identity. Would you all mind keeping this information under your respective hats? I don't want people thinking that I'm an—"

"Arms dealer?" Trusdale said.

"Entrepreneur. It's so middle-class. Hardly befitting an ancient line of—"

"Rogues, dilettantes, and thieves?"

"Baronial blue bloods."

He laughed, and the worry lines that marred his forehead faded. He looked like the fresh-faced youth in the family portrait inside his fob watch: Captain Liberty Trusdale, unexpectedly dashing in his blue uniform, standing shoulder to shoulder with the brothers he loved.

She smiled, and he grinned back, setting her heart aflutter.

His new look suited him.

Chapter 44: A Sky Full of Heroes

CONSTANCE RESTED HER ELBOWS ON the handrail as the *Lady Penelope* floated over the city center. The pink dirigible joined a flotilla of civilian airships that drifted across the gray morning sky. They ranged from grand, gilded galleons to transparent tourist sightseers, repurposed cargo barges, and family cruisers. Every ship was packed with passengers eager to gain a bird's-eye view of the Queen's procession below.

Clearly, her decorative talents were the real star of the show. The silk flower garlands strung between the gas lamps cast a delicate rainbow web over the petal-strewn cobbled streets. Rose-covered effigies of mechanical shire horses, troop transport towers, and exo-suits provided color at every turn. Floral arches spanned the procession route, each celebrating a foreign colony or protectorate with an exotic display of its native blooms.

Thousands of flag-waving Sheffielders lined the procession route. Their jubilant cheers almost drowned out the trumpets and drums of numerous Steamwerks brass bands as the brown-and-white-uniformed musicians marched proudly between legions of redcoats and colonial troops from across the empire. Forty cavalry units, representing the world's finest dragoons, hussars, and lancers, trotted between twenty royal carriages, each more splendid than the last. The Queen's sons, daughters, numerous in-laws, and thirty-odd grandchildren traveled within them.

Victoria's nickname "the Grandmother of Europe" was no exaggeration. The crowned heads of almost every European country shared her bloodline. With few exceptions, the foreign royals had graciously accepted Her Majesty's invitation to attend today's parade. Accepting the invitation minimized the possibility of invasion by the Queen and provided an opportunity to visit the industrial powerhouse of Sheffield. The only event of comparable grandeur would be a Jubilee parade in the empire's capital city. But London wouldn't have Constance's floral genius to push the pomp and circumstance to beyond spectacular.

Trusdale clomped up to stand beside her. They watched the Queen ride her mechanical war elephant, Hiccup, through a Tasmania-inspired arch. The brass mastodon towered twenty feet above a crowd enraptured by the sight of their regent on her golden howdah throne. The plump seventy-seven-year-old wore a black leather battle corset over her gown, diamond-studded goggles, and a miniature crown, just as she did on commemorative teapots across the globe.

Trusdale said, "Looks like your foliage is a hit with the diamond-hat crowd."

"You think?"

"I'm sure. Victoria would be screaming for heads to roll if it wasn't to her taste. You've got a hit on your hands. Check it out, here comes the Royal Air Corps."

Bright against the gray sky, twenty scarlet-ballooned war dirigibles flew toward the city in a tight diamond formation. At full speed, they could cover the four miles from their base at RAC Norton in only ten minutes. Today, precision was more important than haste. Their flyby over Endcliffe Park was scheduled to take place exactly one minute after the Queen took her seat on the royal stand.

The fleet was shadowed by the dreadnought flagship HMS *Subjugator*. Built from Steamwerks supra-bronze, the two-hundred-foot-long behemoth boasted thirty cannons and two brass turret guns with the firepower to destroy an enemy ship or a city block with ease.

Eight captured pirate airships trailed the dreadnought. The ships included two dowdy Russian schooners, a sky-blue frigate, and five purple sloops seized from brigands foolish enough to try to raid the empire's spice routes. The air battle between the *Subjugator* and her faux pirate foes had been designed to entertain the crowd and delight a Queen notoriously difficult to amuse.

Trusdale rapped his fingers on the handrail. "Are you absolutely sure about this plan?"

She was always sure of all her plans. "Are you not?"

He rubbed the back of his neck. "I think it's as crazy as you chatting with interdimensional kraken in your head."

"Don't worry. They've gone now." A tinge of melancholy touched her. She hoped her tentacled friends enjoyed their newfound freedom.

"Good. I think you've got enough crazy stuff going on in that head of yours without adding inter-dimensional visitors."

"But they did promise to keep in touch."

He studied her. "Is that a joke?"

"Absolutely. Maybe. No."

He groaned. "Life never seems to settle into normal around you. All right, about this Plan of yours. What if we—"

"Get started? Excellent idea." She called up to the ship's helm, "Take us in behind the pirates, Mrs. Singh."

The pilot steered the ship to the aft of the aerial procession. Constance called out, "Excellent work, Mrs. Singh. Please keep your distance from the other ships. Let's stay inconspicuous as long as we can."

Trusdale muttered, "Because nothing screams 'inconspicuous' like a pink airship."

Constance sniffed. "It was my mother's favorite color. Welli hasn't had the heart to change it."

He lowered his head. "I didn't know. I'm sorry."

"Besides, the fleet is unlikely to feel threatened by the approach of a pink and gold luxury galleon. Looking harmless is our best defense. Do you have a telescope handy?"

He fished within his coat and drew out his battered brass telescope.

"Good. Your job is to watch the dreadnought. There should only be a skeleton crew left on board. The bulk of the redcoat aeronauts are pretending to be pirates on the captured ships."

"Why am I—?"

"The pirate ships will be shooting blanks from their cannons. So will the dreadnought, but it's carrying regular ammunition too. If the dreadnought crew starts to pay attention to us, we leave. One shot from the turret guns—"

"And we'll be walking home. Gotcha." He trained his telescope on the flagship. "Looks like you're right. I see about thirty redcoats milling about on the *Subjugator*'s deck."

"Of course I'm right. I took the time to study all the plans for the Queen's visit, including the logistics for the aerial display, while designing my floral tributes."

"Why am I not surprised?"

"Well, if they leave them lying around, someone is bound to—"

"Snoop?"

She huffed and turned her back on him to review the main deck. Beelzebub's slide across the teak boards had left long scrapes on the varnished wood. Sadly, none of her clothing trunks had survived the rescue of Trusdale from the redcoats. A solitary box of corsets and three lonely hatboxes were all that remained of her once-impressive wardrobe.

Welli sat on a barrel of blackberry cider reading through a stack of yellow notepaper. The armored water lily sipped purple cider from a silver toddy cup as he reviewed her handwritten message to the Queen. He'd started reading the pages in his cabin, but had graciously turned over his abode to Boo, who insisted on sleeping on the comfiest bed the galleon had to offer.

At Welli's elbow, Mr. Singh was in the process of unrolling four aerial semaphore flags. The wind had diminished to a gentle breeze that barely fluttered the square red-and-yellow flags.

Drs. Chauhan and Huang were involved in a far-too-passionate embrace beside the kneeling exo-suits. Constance averted her eyes from their unseemly display and glanced to the fore of the ship. Powerful brass telescopes were mounted to the handrail on each side of the bow. Hearn and Cawley manned the telescopes, their eyes trained on the royal parade below.

Constance called out to them, "Can you see Prince Lucien?"

Hearn nodded. "He's sitting in a carriage fifty yards behind Victoria's elephant. He's wearing the ponciest ostrich-feather hat you've ever seen in your life."

"Good. Don't let him out of your sight. Cawley, watch the Queen. It's imperative that she observes with her own eyes that we rescued Maya and Huang. Seeing is believing."

Cawley said, "Yes, miss. Her Majesty's brass elephant is approaching the park entrance. I reckon she'll reach the royal stand soon. Oooh, Miss Constance, she's started to read the VIP program!"

"Hah—I knew it. Pinder owes me one for correcting all his printing errors. The Queen would have had him arrested for grammatical heresy."

"Speaking of arrested," said Welli from atop the cider barrel, "you might want to rethink this message of yours to Her Royal Highness."

"Why? What's wrong with it? Don't tell me I dangled a participle?"

"Nothing so heinous. I'd assumed you were going to warn Victoria about Lucien's treachery—the kidnapping, invisible assassins, designs on the throne, and so on."

"Which I did."

"Indeed. It's this additional diatribe on your personal experience with the female inheritance law that is—"

"Succinct, timely, and entirely necessary. After all, when else will I gain an audience with the Queen? This is my chance to make a point. Besides, Maya agrees with me that the law needs changing, don't you, Maya?"

Dr. Chauhan removed her lips from her former colleague. "In principle, yes, but I don't relish my role as messenger."

Constance folded her arms. "Maya, why ever didn't you say? You don't have to do this, of course. I don't want you to feel that you owe me anything for rescuing both you and Huang from the Prince's evil clutches. Neither of you should consider yourselves beholden to me. Why, I'm sure you'd both have found your own way back from Sweden eventually. Probably not in each other's arms—you have me to thank for shining the light on your hidden passions—but somehow . . ."

Maya rolled her eyes. "All right, enough, I beg you. Victoria's head might explode, but I'll deliver your message in full." The scientist gazed up at Huang. "What do you say, Zhi, should we bite the hand that fed us?"

Her bespectacled paramour grinned. "Let the feast begin."

Welli sprang off his barrel and handed the stack of notes to the scientists. "Never let it be said that my cousin skimps on the details. You each hold a copy of her address to our glorious monarch. Loop the message as we fly so we can be sure the Queen has seen every line."

Constance asked, "Is everyone clear on the Plan?"

Mrs. Singh called down from the helm, "When you give the order, I will steer our ship directly through the air battle."

"Precisely. We will sail once through the fray, drawing the eye of Her Majesty toward us. Even if Lucien has infiltrated her court with a dozen of his lackeys, they can't stop Victoria from seeing the truth when it stands before her waving a semaphore flag."

"I'll watch for any response from Her Majesty's signalman," said Welli.

Mr. Singh handed him a diamond-encrusted telescope. "I'll plot our escape route to France belowdecks while keeping an eye on our animal passengers."

Constance clapped her hands. "Excellent. Hearn, Cawley, and Trusdale will watch the Prince, the Queen, and the dreadnought respectively. I think that about covers it."

"And what are you going to do?" asked Trusdale.

She stared at him. "I'm supervising, of course. Battle stations, everyone!"

The two scientists clambered into their exo-suits and slammed the transparent doors shut. Mr. Singh slid a red-and-yellow flag into each giant's fist. He stepped back from the suits as Constance commanded, "Doctors, start your steam engines."

The exo-suits rumbled into life, rose, and clomped to the ship's port side. In unison, they spread their metal arms wide. Using the flags, they began to transmit her message.

Constance turned to lean once more on the handrail. Trusdale murmured, "Have you considered that you might infuriate the

Queen? With thousands of people looking on, you're openly accusing her favorite grandson of attempted regicide. She could order the dreadnought to fire on us for our sass alone."

She patted the rail of the *Lady Penelope*. "Don't worry, looks can be deceiving. Beneath the refined exterior of this fancy airship beats the bold heart of a pirate queen. She's exceptionally well-armed, and ready to fight all comers. Trust me, she won't let you down."

"Are we talking about the ship, or you?"

She cocked her head. "A little of both, I suppose. Do you find that to be . . . alarming?"

He chuckled. "Not at all. In fact, I'm officially intrigued by the combination."

"Are you indeed?"

"I am. But I'm not too sure what you think of me."

She studied his almost-handsome face—his crooked nose, desert-sky eyes, and strong, square jaw with an adorable dimple. *How did I miss that before?* "I think you're a liar, a scoundrel, and probably much worse."

"And that is . . . ?"

She smiled. "Entertaining. Possibly even charming, with a wardrobe upgrade. My opinion will no doubt improve once you grant me exclusive rights to market the Trusdale Perambulating Kinetic Storm Battle Mitten."

He frowned. "That's not really mine to—"

"Your brother's legacy can live on. His greatest work, shared with the world."

"But I—"

"Would own five percent of the profits. I believe there's a substantial market for nonlethal weaponry. Between you and me, Mr. Trusdale, I'm tired of playing roles to please other people. I'm more than the Brass Queen, more than Miss Haltwhistle, more than

Cousin Connie, or any of the other labels they pin upon me. I'm one hundred percent my own woman. As such, I'll carve out my destiny, not by following in my family's footsteps, but by blazing my own trail."

"That's laudable, especially the non-lethal part, but, I don't know if I can . . . I mean, I'll have to think about it."

"Take all the time you need, or ten minutes, whichever comes first."

He groaned. "You are such a—"

Cawley shouted, "The Queen's family is seated on the royal stand. Her Highness is watching the military flyby."

Constance held up one finger. "Hold that thought, Mr. Trusdale. Our moment of glory approaches."

"Or our doom."

Either way, it was going to be spectacular.

Ahead, a diamond formation of scarlet airships soared over the park to the cheers of a packed crowd. Every man, woman, and child whooped with joy as the shadow of HMS *Subjugator* passed over their heads. The bronze flagship hung like an armored island over a sea of upturned faces.

The pirate ships swarmed down upon the bronze behemoth with cannons blazing. Smoke grenades aboard the dreadnought were activated to create the illusion of severe damage. The crowd gasped as black smoke billowed from every one of the dreadnought's cannon ports. The spectators cheered when the defiant redcoat aeronauts formed into a firing line and shot rifle blanks at their attackers.

The brigands brandished cutlasses at their redcoat foes. Although she could have dressed them better, Constance appreciated the pirates' costumes: jaunty tricorne hats, eye patches, frilly shirts, and a smattering of stuffed parrots. The pirates' cannons roared as the redcoats pulled eight antique cannons onto the *Subjugator*'s deck.

The redcoats lit the fuses, and the old cannons thundered. Naturally, the redcoats couldn't miss. With every cannon volley, a handful of pirates threw themselves to the deck to writhe in pretend death throes for the benefit of airship spectators.

Constance said, "This fight is remarkably one-sided." She called up to Mrs. Singh, "Take us in."

"His Royal Highness Prince Lucien just left the royal stand. He slipped out the back, and now he's heading for the park gates," called Hearn.

"The Queen's staring directly at our exo-suits. I reckon she sees your message. She's flushed bright red. She doesn't look happy," Cawley added.

"The Prince has reached the gates," yelled Hearn. "There's a blue carriage driven by a scar-faced servant pulling up. The Prince is heading for the carriage and—blimey! You won't believe this! An old bloke wearing a brown shepherd's cloak just launched himself at the Prince. They're on the ground, grappling. It's Dr. McKinley! He punched His Royal Highness right in the nose."

Constance laughed. "Good. Serves him right. What's happening now, Hearn?"

"The Prince is clutching his bloody nose. He's trying to stand up—McKinley's not letting go—five redcoats are approaching. That scar-faced fellow on the carriage is looking at the Prince; he's looking at the redcoats—and he's off! He's whipped the horses into a gallop—and he's gone. The redcoats have grabbed McKinley—the Prince is looking for his missing carriage—by heck, His Royal Highness is making a run for it, right down the middle of the street. Three redcoats are chasing him."

"I doubt he'll get too far."

Trusdale muttered, "You know, those crew members playing dead on the dreadnought are doing one hell of a job."

Constance frowned. "Only the pirate crews are supposed to play dead."

"Then we've got a problem."

He handed her the telescope. She peered through the device at the flagship's deck. Across the boards, redcoats clutched at their throats, their eyes bulging as they collapsed into squirming death throes. She tut-tutted. "Looks like none of our heroic boys would make it on the London stage. Talk about overacting! Why—"

"They're not acting."

She gasped. "You mean—they're fighting invisibles? Good Lord, why on earth—"

"I guess the Prince found a use for McKinley's batch of serum. He must have sent the Swedes over to the local airfield to board the *Subjugator* before it took off. Now, let's think. We've got a dreadnought armed with real ammunition, and just about every European monarch and their family sitting down there in one tidy box. One good shot and—"

"Every royal line in Europe will be simultaneously assassinated. Well, that's just awful!"

The color drained from Trusdale's face. "That's one way of putting it. This would create an instant power vacuum, which means anarchy, revolution, and war. The world as we know it will be torn apart."

A vision of Europe in flames danced through Constance's mind. She tilted up her chin. "Then we'd better get cracking." She shouted to the helm, "Mrs. Singh—take us in as close as you can to the *Subjugator*."

Trusdale gaped at her. "We're going to board?"

"Certainly not. We're hardly equipped to fight invisible assassins *en masse*."

"So, we're gonna ram the ship?"

She blinked at him. "Good heavens, how dramatic. I applaud your gusto, Mr. Trusdale, but the *Lady Penelope* would barely make a dent upon that metal monster. We need to be a little more creative."

Across the deck stood one empty exo-suit. She hurried toward it, lifted her ball gown clear above her ankles, and clambered into the kneeling titan. She settled her bustle on the velvet seat, pulled a lever to slam the transparent door closed, and hit the red ignition button. The suit's steam engine stuttered into life. Ignoring the engine's rumbling din, she ran her fingers across the mahogany instrument panel. She flicked a switch to disconnect the flamethrower's supply tube from its paraffin-filled fuel tank. There was a loud clunk as the hose detached.

Constance pushed a brass joystick into the stand position. As the suit rose, she engaged the right arm to draw the flamethrower out of its back-mounted holster. The dangling fuel hose clanked against the suit's sturdy bronze ankles as she took one step forward.

Trusdale appeared in front of the exo-suit and gawked at her through the transparent door.

Not wanting to waste time searching for the speaker button, she bellowed at him through the glass, "Bring me cider. Now!"

To his credit, he didn't ask if this was the best time to start drinking. She clomped to the ship's starboard as he tipped a wooden cider keg onto its side and rolled it toward her. He heaved the barrel to rest upright by her bronze hip as the *Lady Penelope* swung within fifty feet of the *Subjugator*'s hull. She punched one metal fist through the barrel's lid and sent a wave of hard blackberry cider slopping onto the deck. As Trusdale plunged her weapon's fuel pipe deep into the barrel, she pointed the Phoenix at two dozen besieged redcoats on the flagship's deck and pulled the trigger.

A jet of purple alcohol shot out of the gilded flamethrower and arced onto the *Subjugator*'s deck. The blackberry deluge rained down upon the redcoats as they struggled against their invisible foes. The liquid cast a violet hue over their naked Swedish attackers, making them partially discernible as they wrestled with the uniformed troops.

The odds were not yet even. The semi-visible assailants outnumbered the remaining soldiers by two to one.

She kept her finger on the trigger, pumping cider onto the deck. The great brass turret guns revolved into their firing positions, each with a naked, purple man sitting upon the gunner's seat. One barrel pointed down at the royal stand, the other at the *Lady Penelope*.

She gulped. Poor Welli, the servants, the scientists, the animals in the hold, and—

"Trusdale!" she screamed as the American jumped up onto the rail before her. He swayed, his black coat flapping like wings in the breeze. He raised his right arm, ensconced in his brother's battle mitten. A vast net of white lightning flashed from the gauntlet toward the dreadnought. The net fell upon the struggling soldiers and their invisible attackers and struck the purple spill of cider. A shock of electricity ran through the men. As one, they collapsed to the deck, stunned.

The recoil from the mitten knocked Trusdale back off the rail, straight into the exo-suit's arms. The Stetson-wearing cowboy grinned at her through the glass. "Shock tactics. That should hold 'em until the redcoats' brigand buddies board."

The pirate ships swooped in toward the dreadnought, packed with buccaneers ready to assist their beleaguered comrades against their purple-stained foes.

Constance dropped the suit's arms, and Trusdale fell with a thump onto the deck. He jumped up as she lowered the exo-suit to its knees and shut down the engine. As she stepped out of the suit, he offered her his hand. She took it, and a shock of electricity jolted through her.

Trusdale slapped the gauntlet. "Oops, sorry. The battle mitten needs recalibrating. Are you all right?"

She was so much better than all right. "I've never felt more alive! The invisibles are thwarted." She glanced around the deck, expecting a standing ovation, or at least a rousing cheer. Alas, Maya and Huang were still encased in their exo-suits, using the semaphore flags to send her message, while Cawley, Hearn, and Welli peered through their telescopes over the side of the ship.

She clucked her tongue in irritation. "Didn't any of them see us? That was a casebook example of using the resources at hand—"

"To obtain victory. Grandpa Haltwhistle would be proud."

Her chest swelled. "You helped, somewhat."

He beamed with such warmth, she laughed.

"Onward to France!" she said.

Welli called over his shoulder, "Hold up, old girl. It looks like the Queen's signalman is sending you a semaphore message."

"Oh no. Is it, 'You're under arrest?' or 'How dare you ruin my battle?'"

Welli adjusted the focus on his telescope. "No, it's—a thank-you. She's most grateful for your rescue of the scientists and your warning about Lucien. She says if your testimony against him proves true, you'll be amply rewarded. She will allow you to inherit your father's property—heavens, Constance, you'll be the sole female exception to the inheritance law!"

"Really? Goodness, I—quick, give me the flags."

Trusdale strode to Maya's exo-suit and tapped on the glass. She stopped waving her flags. The American pulled the flags from her metal grasp and handed them to Constance. Using the box of corsets as a step, she clambered up to stand precariously on the wooden handrail. Trusdale hovered behind her, ready to catch her if she fell.

Constance balanced upon the rail with the city spread before her. Three hundred thousand spectators stood in confused silence. They gazed up, watching spellbound as pirates boarded a British dreadnought for the first time in aeronautical history.

On the royal stand, the Queen stood in her crown and battle corset with a gold telescope pressed to her eye. She was remarkably tiny for a woman with the power to change the world with a single word.

Constance took a deep breath and swung her flags through her semaphore message:

T-H-A-N-K

Y-O-U

Y-O-U-R

M-A-J-E-S-T-Y

The crowd below broke into cheers and waved their flags. Gray clouds parted, and a golden ray of sunshine bathed her in light. The warmth flooded over her, from her emerald tiara down to her white ankle boots. A breeze blew her silver and blue skirts around her like a wild ocean wave. For a moment, she thought she saw purple kraken gamboling through the clouds. They disappeared as she glanced their way.

She contemplated her audience below. Housemaids, seamstresses, shopgirls, and duchesses. Every single woman from every social class bound by the same archaic laws.

She heaved a sigh and waved on:

B-U-T

A-L-L

W-O-M-E-N

D-E-S-E-R-V-E

T-H-I-S

R-I-G-H-T

Welli spluttered, "What on earth are you doing? She just granted you ownership of Haltwhistle Hall, your own personal property—"

"Which primarily consists of a ruined castle and a hole in the ground."

"And thousands of acres of land, and a baroness title, and—hold on, the Queen's shouting at her semaphore man."

She stared down at the monarch—an elderly woman in black surrounded by her daughters and granddaughters, none of whom truly owned the silk dresses on their backs. Victoria kept her telescope trained upon her as Welli reported, "The signalman says, 'Her Gracious Majesty will consider your petition most carefully.' Good heavens, there's a real possibility that British women might one day be able to inherit property in their own right."

The female half of the crowd below cheered ecstatically. Constance's head swam. She attempted a curtsey, almost fell headfirst off the rail, and felt Trusdale's strong hands tug her gown backward. She dropped to the deck, reveling in the applause from below.

He smiled. "That was quite the performance."

"It was the right thing to do."

"And?"

She sighed. "I suppose there's less chance of Victoria reneging on her offer to me now that she's considering changing the law for all women."

"Nice try. I think, deep down, you care about those folks down there."

"Tell no one. I have a reputation to maintain."

He murmured, "Your secret is safe with me."

"That's three secrets down and about five hundred to go."

"Hah, is that right? Now, about your offer. Do you really want to sell the Trusdale Perambulating Kinetic Storm Battle Mitten?"

Welli interjected, "Ugh, business. How ghastly. Mrs. Singh, kindly engage the autopilot for Paris. Everyone, I shall be opening six bottles of champagne belowdecks in exactly one minute. You are all welcome to join me in a series of toasts to our somewhat surprising survival."

He headed for the staterooms with the scientists and servants on his heels.

Constance gazed up at Trusdale. "It's quite the crew we've put together. And, yes, I'm interested in developing your battle mitten to its full potential. I must warn you though, I foresee some challenging times ahead. It could take us months to develop a more refined prototype that is worthy of being presented to my elite clients. We'll have to collaborate closely on the design, the distribution, the marketing. We'll need to travel the globe to source materials, components, craftsmen. I'm sure we'll become quite sick of the sight of each other."

"Sounds awful."

"Doesn't it?"

A slow smile lit his rugged face. "As it happens, I do have some free time available. All right, I'm in."

She clapped her hands. "Excellent."

A cheer rang out from Welli's cabin, accompanied by joyful yapping from Boo. Music from Welli's new-fangled gramophone swelled into a waltz. Constance cupped her ear. "Sounds like the party is well underway."

He grinned, and her heart beat a merry tattoo. "I'm looking forward to getting to know you a little better once we reach France."

Warmth spread from her chest to every toe and finger. "And I you. You're undoubtedly the most fascinating man I've ever met."

"Glad to hear it." He licked his lips. "So, um . . . I guess you're not looking to get married right now, are you? Because if you are . . ." He glanced down at the deck, perhaps contemplating dropping to one knee.

She reached out and touched his arm. "Not yet. I must blaze my own trail in life. But one day, I'll need an equal partner in more than business. A good man, with a good heart, who's willing to work on his wardrobe."

"I hear you. You, er, got anyone special in mind?" He straightened his appalling hat.

She smiled and stepped in close to the cowboy. Close enough, she fancied, to hear his heart beat time with hers. "I might. Time will tell. Perhaps we should take a moment to enjoy what we have right here, right now."

He bent down toward her, his eyes large and wondering. "What exactly did you have in mind?"

"Would you care to dance, Mr. Trusdale?"

He chuckled. "I thought you'd never ask."

"Oh, I know a decent partner when I see one. Eventually."

As violins sang, he wrapped his arm around her waist and held her tight. "Me, too."

Perfectly in tune, they swept into a glorious waltz as the airship soared into the heavens.

And everything was exactly as it should be.

THE END

Acknowledgments

There are so many wonderful people who helped me to launch *The Brass Queen*.

I wrote the first chapter as a worldbuilding exercise in one of David Farland's superb writing classes. His kind words of encouragement inspired me write the novel you now hold in your hands. This is the power of a great teacher. I count my blessings that I took my first steps toward becoming a writer with Dave's guidance.

Thank you to Sue Arroyo, Laura Wooffitt, Helga Schier and the CamCat Publishing team for their hard work and dedication. Special thanks to my brilliant editor, Cassandra Farrin. Cassandra transformed my manuscript with her innate understanding of story. She has the heart of a novelist and a poet's soul. Miss Constance Haltwhistle herself would be suitably impressed by Cassandra's elegant edits and perfect punctuation!

I'm eternally grateful to Natalie Grazian for her epic vision for this novel. Her passion for my writing opened the door that led to publication. Without Natalie, this book would not exist.

Special thanks to the awe-inspiring authors who were kind enough to read and review my debut. I truly appreciate your time and consideration, Cherie Priest, Cat Rambo, Rebecca Moesta, Genevieve Cogman, A.L. Davroe, and Leanna Renee Hieber. I love to visit the fantastic worlds you create!

Thank you, James A. Owen, for your artistic genius, your patience, and your kindness. James created the stunning illustrations that grace the cover and internal pages of this novel. The map of my alternate dimension Sheffield is simply enchanting!

This gorgeous book was designed by Olivia Hammerman and Lena Yang. Thank you for giving my humble words such a lovely home!

Kseniya Thomas and Erik Kraft, thank you for creating the logo for Pinder's Print Emporium, the letterpress invitation to Constance's coming-out ball, and so much more!

I'm so thankful to Dayna Anderson for championing my book through the publication process. It was a pleasure to work with you.

Many thanks to Kourtney Sokmen, Andrea Kiliany Thatcher, and Smith Publicity for their terrific support.

Thank you to my fabulous friends, Gabi Coatsworth and Steve Newton for beta-reading my manuscript. I couldn't have wished for a better first audience! Gabi is the official godmother of this novel. I was so fortunate that the first writing group I ever joined was led by her. Through Gabi, I learned so much and met many fine Connecticut writers including Alison McBain and the Fairfield Scribes, Roman Godzich, and Dave D'Alessio. Thank you all for your support and friendship throughout the years.

Hugs to my friends from the Superstars Writing Conference. It was a pleasure to meet you all in person at last! Heartfelt thanks to Wulf Moon, Mary Natwick, Kary English, Amanda McCarter, Chris Mandeville, and Joshua Essoe for their sage advice on my final draft.

Many thanks to my marvelous Pitch Wars mentors, Marty Mayberry and Léonie Kelsall. I raise a toast to the delightful Robin Winzenread, Anne Raven, Syed Masood, and LL Montez. I've had so much fun traveling with you on this journey. Here's to our future works!

Many thanks to Bill Harmer and the staff at the Westport Library for all your encouragement, and for hosting my book launch party!

Creating an audiobook is a team effort. Creating two audiobooks in the middle of a pandemic is a miracle! I have so much gratitude for the stellar work of actors George Ledoux and Aeric Azana, audio proofer Adriel Wiggins, and production engineer Matt Berky of Massive Productions.

Thank you to the multi-talented Hafsah Faizel for my whimsical branding and to artist Brian Kesinger for his charming illustration of Constance, Trusdale, and Boo. Many thanks to the exceptional editors Aja Pollack, Lisa Wilson-Hall, Barbara Rogan, and Heather Cashman.

Hanna Palm, thank you so much for your help with my Swedish assassins. I appreciate your guidance in making sure their dialogue is authentic. You're the best!

Thank you to the Calafell and Newton families for their friendship over the years. And thanks to Debra Southmayd for patiently listening as I chatted on endlessly about this novel. As promised, here is your signed copy!

I'll be forever grateful to my family, who encouraged me to read at an early age. I wish my grandmother, Ethel, and my Great Aunt Edna were still here to hold this book in their hands. For my Mum, Dad, Ann, and my step-siblings, I miss you all even more than the glorious hills and dales of Yorkshire. And thank you to my American in-laws for welcoming an eccentric British woman into the fold!

To my darling husband, *amor de mi vida*, I'll love you to the edge of forever and back again. Thank you for encouraging me to start writing.

And finally, my deepest gratitude goes to you, dear reader. Thank you for picking up this book and traveling into the Brassiverse with me. In another dimension, Constance and Trusdale tip their hats to you for joining them on their adventure. They hope to see you again soon!

Author Q & A

Q. What inspired *The Brass Queen*?

A. A minor character in H. G. Wells's *The Invisible Man* inspired my plot. In Wells's 1897 novel, a mysterious American tourist in an English pub whips out a revolver and shoots the invisible man in the knee. Upon reading this, I wondered—who is this curious interloper with the less-than-deadly aim? Thus began the adventures of J. F. Trusdale, an inept spy in a world where nothing is as it seems, including Trusdale himself. Such a man requires an exceptionally talented partner—enter Miss Constance Haltwhistle—weapons designer and amateur scientist.

Q. What is the central message you hope readers take away from the novel?

A. Constance demonstrates that you don't have to be perfect to be a hero. One person, however flawed, can change the world for the better. My heroine starts the novel hosting her own coming-out ball to find a noble husband. This is as close to playing by societal rules as Constance can manage! By the end of the novel, she's let go of her family estate and marital ambitions. She risks her own neck when she speaks up for women's legal rights to a despotic queen. From this point on, Constance will become a champion for the oppressed and forgotten. I hope this is a path we can all follow in our daily lives.

Q. You have said that you love to write about the passion of rogues, rebels, and renegades. What is it about these types of characters that attracts you?

A. I've always admired people who, through choice or circumstance, change society for the better. Even if they start from a place of selfishness, once people begin to care for something greater than themselves, they can transform into imperfect heroes. Flaws can become strengths, egoism can blossom into love, and the world—or even the universe—can take one step closer toward true harmony.

Q. What was an early experience where you learned that language had power?

A. I remember the terror I experienced as a toddler watching the Daleks on the *Doctor Who* TV show. The way they said the word "exterminate" literally gave me nightmares! And yet, I couldn't stop watching. Even today, the show is one of my favorites.

Q. What was one of the most surprising things you learned about yourself while creating this book?

A. I was surprised to learn that I had the ability and determination to create a novel from thin air! I hadn't penned a tale since I was a wee child in grade school. The moral of the story is that it's never too late to start writing!

Q. What does literary success look like to you?

A. If I can create fantastical worlds populated with characters you want to spend time with, then I'll have achieved what I define as literary success. With luck, I'll be able to spend the rest of my life creating such tales!

Q. For personal reading, do you prefer a specific genre?

A. I adore speculative fiction, as anything can happen! Dragons? Aliens? Androids who dream of electric sheep? I'm down for all of this and more! In terms of specifics, I love offbeat heroes on a perilous quest who face their problems with humor and hope. If there is also a romantic subplot, villains who almost redeem themselves (but don't quite make it), plus thrilling action scenes peppered with slapstick moments, sign me up!

Q. Are you working on any other projects at this time?

A. I'm currently developing the sequel to *The Brass Queen*, in which our intrepid heroes attempt to save the world from an interdimensional invasion!

About the Author

Elizabeth Chatsworth was born in the city of Sheffield in Yorkshire, England. After gaining a degree in English Literature, she traveled the globe until she finally settled in Connecticut, USA. Her home is shared with her husband and their rambunctious Yorkshire terrier, Boudicca.

Elizabeth loves to write of rogues, rebels, and renegades across time and space. A winner of the Writers Of The Future contest in 2020, she is also a Golden Heart® finalist, a Pitch Wars alumna, and a member of the SFWA (Science Fiction and Fantasy Writers of America).

When she's not writing, Elizabeth works as a voice-over actor. There's a rumor she possesses the world's best scone recipe. Contact her at www.elizabethchatsworth.com to see if it's true!

More from CamCat Books

An excerpt from

Shadows Over London
by Christian Klaver

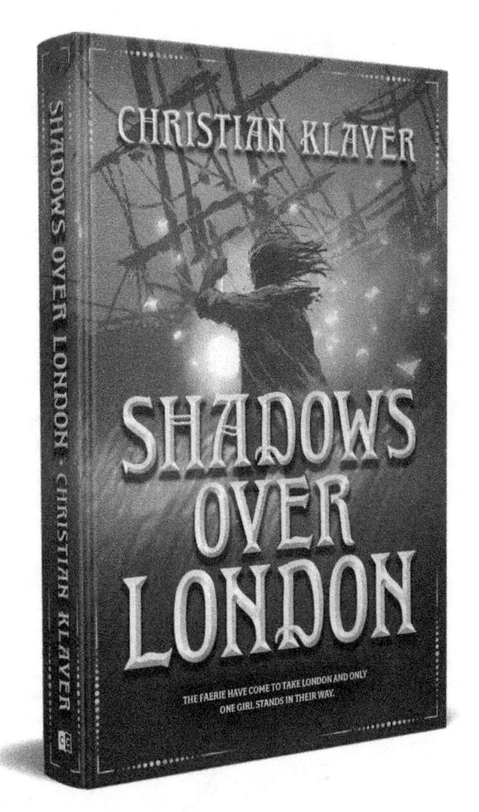

Prologue: The Faerie King

SOME DREAMS ARE SO TRUE that it doesn't matter if they actually happened that way or not. They're so true that they've happened more than once. My dreams about the Faerie were like that. Most of the rest of England got their first glimpse of the Faerie on the night London fell. But not me. I saw my first Faerie ten years before that, on my sixth birthday.

My name is Justice Kasric and my family was all tangled up with the Faerie even before the invasion.

Because I'd been born on Boxing Day, the day after Christmas, Father always made a grand affair of my birthday so that it wasn't all swallowed up by the other holidays.

That's why, long after Christmas supper had come and gone, I stood at the frosted window of my room looking out into the darkness trying to guess what kind of surprise Father had in store for my sixth birthday. I was sure that something wonderful was coming. Maybe a pony . . . or even ponies.

I crept quietly out of my room. I didn't want to wake Faith, my older sister. I didn't see or hear anyone on the top floors, but then I heard movement from down in the front hall. Father. He clicked his pocket watch closed, tucked it back into his dark waistcoat and pulled the heavy black naval coat off the hook by the door.

I was sure he'd turn around and see me crouched on the stairs, but he only stood a moment in the shrouded half-moonlight before opening the front door. A cool mist rolled noiselessly past his ankles as he went out.

I was in luck! Where else would Father be going except to feed the ponies? I drew on my rubber boots and threw my heavy blue woolen coat on over my nightgown, determined to follow.

When I opened the door and looked out into the front garden, the mist hung everywhere in soft carpets of moonlit fleece. Father was nowhere in sight, but I could hear him crunching ahead of me.

I paused, sensing even then that some steps took you further than others. The enormity of my actions lay heavily on me. The comforting, warm interior of the house called for me to come back inside. It was not too late to go back. I could return to the rest of my family, content with a life filled with tea settings, mantelpiece clocks, antimacassars and other normal, sensible notions. The proper thing would have been to go back inside, to bed. I remember shaking my head, sending my braids dancing.

I followed Father outside into the still and misty night.

We went across the front garden, past shrubs and frozen pools, and descended the hill into the snow-laden pines. His crunching footsteps carried back to me in the still air. I followed by stepping in the holes he'd left in the snow to make less noise, jumping to match his long stride. The stables lay behind the house, but clearly, we weren't heading there. We lived in the country then, amidst a great deal of farmland with clumps of forest around.

The silence grew heavier, deeper, as we descended into the trees, and a curious lassitude swept over me as I followed Father through the tangled woods. The air was sharp and filled with the clean smell of ice and pine. On the other side of a dip in the land, we should have emerged into a large and open field. Only we didn't. The field wasn't there. Instead, we kept going down through more and more snow-laden trees.

The treetops formed a nearly solid canopy sixty or seventy feet above us, but with a vast and open space underneath. The thick shafts of moonlight slanted down through silvered air into emerald shadows, each tree a stately pillar in that wide-open space.

I worried about Father catching me following him, but he never even turned around. Always, he went down. Down, down into the forest into what felt like another world entirely. Even I knew we couldn't still be in the English countryside. You could just feel it. I also knew that following him wasn't about ponies anymore and I might have given up and gone home, only I had no idea how to find my way back.

After a short time, we came to an open green hollow where I crouched at the edge of a ring of trees and blinked my eyes at the sudden brightness. The canopy opened up to the nighttime sky and moonlight filled the empty hollow like cream poured into a cup. This place had a planned feel, the circle of trees shaped just so, the long black trunk lying neatly in the exact center of a field of green grass like a long table, and all of it inexplicably free of snow. Two pale boulders sat on either side like chairs. The silence felt deeper here, older, expectant. The place was waiting.

Father lit a cigarette and stood smoking. The thin wisp of smoke curled up and into the night sky.

Then, the Faerie King arrived.

First, there was emptiness, and then, without any sign of motion, a hulking, towering figure stood on the other side of the log, standing as if he'd always been there waiting. I'd read enough of the right kinds of books to recognize him as a Faerie King right off and I shivered.

The Faerie King looked like a shambling beast on its back legs, with huge tined antlers that rose from his massive skull. He wore a wooden crown nearly buried by a black mane thick as lamb's fleece that flowed into a forked beard. His long face was a gaunt wooden mask, with blackened slits for eyes and a harsh, narrow opening for a mouth.

Except it wasn't a mask, because it moved. The mouth twitched and the jaw muscles clenched as he regarded the man in front of him. Finally, he inclined his head in a graceless welcome. He wore a cloak like a swath of forest laid across his back, made entirely of thick wild grass, weeds, and brambles, with a rich black undercoat of loam where a silk lining would show. Underneath the cloak, he wore armor that might once have been bright copper, now with rampant verdigris. He leaned on the pommel of a wide-bladed, granite sword.

The Faerie King and Father regarded each other for a long time before they each sat down. A chessboard with pieces of carved wood and bone sat suddenly between them. Again, there was no sense of movement, only a sudden understanding that the board must have always been there, waiting.

They began to play.

The Faerie King hesitated, reached to advance his white king's pawn, then stopped. His leathery right hand was massive, nearly the size of the board, far too large for this task. He shifted awkwardly and used his more normal-sized left hand. Father advanced a pawn immediately in response. The Faerie King sat and viewed the board with greater deliberation. He finally reached out with his left hand to make his move, and then stopped. He shifted in his seat, uncertain, then finally advanced his knight.

I could feel others watching with me. Invisible ghosts hidden in the trees. The weight of their interest hung palpably in the air. Whatever the outcome of this game, it was important in a way you couldn't help but feel. However long it took, this timeless shuffling of pieces, the watchers would wait and I waited with them. With only a nightgown on under my coat, crouching in the snow, I should have been freezing. But I didn't feel the cold. I only felt the waiting, and the waiting consumed me.

Father and the Faerie King had each moved their forces into the center of the board, aligning and realigning in constant readiness for the inevitable clash. Now Father sliced into the black pawns with surgical precision, starting an escalating series of exchanges. Around us, it began to snow.

As the game went on, Father and the Faerie King lined their captures neatly on the side of the board. Father looked to be considerably better off. The Faerie King grew more and more angry, and he squeezed and kneaded the log with his massive right hand so that the wood cracked and popped. Occasional bursts of wood fragments flew to either side.

Father's only reaction to this violent display was a long, slow smile. He took another Turkish cigarette calmly from a cigarette case and lit it. I was suddenly very chilled. That kind of calm wasn't natural.

The smoke from Father's cigarette drifted placidly upwards. His moves were immediate, decisive, while the Faerie King's became more and more hesitant as the game went on. The smile on Father's face grew. I watched, and the forest watched with me.

Then the Faerie King snarled, jumped up, and brought his massive fist down on the board like a mallet. Bits of the board, chess pieces, and wood splinters flew out into the snow. Twice more he mauled the log, gouging out huge hunks of wood in his fury. Then he spun with a swiftness shocking in so large a person and yanked his huge sword out of the snow. He brought it down in a deadly arc that splintered the log like a lightning strike. Debris and splinters had flown around Father like a ship's deck hit by a full broadside of cannonballs, but Father didn't even flinch. Two broken halves of smoldering log lay in the clearing.

"Perhaps next time," Father said, standing up, the first words either of them had spoken. He brushed a few splinters from his coat.

The Faerie King stared, quivering, his wooden face twisted suddenly with grief. Then his legs gave out and he collapsed in the snow, all his impotent rage spent. He sat, slumped with his mismatched hands on his knees, the perfect picture of abject defeat. He didn't so much as stir when Father turned his back and left.

I couldn't tear my gaze away from the rough and powerful shape slouched heavily and immobile in the snow. White clumps were already starting to gather on his arms, shoulders, head and antlers, as if he might never move again.

Father climbed directly to my hiding place and stood, looking down at me with amusement in his glacial-blue eyes. I'd forgotten all about hiding.

He warned me to keep silent with a gloved finger to his lips, then put a hand on my shoulder and steered me away from the hollow. Father fished his watch out of the waistcoat pocket and checked the time as we climbed back up the slope. We walked for a bit, surrounded only by the sound of crunching snow and the spiced scent of Father's smoke.

"Well," he said finally. "I've always encouraged you to be curious, little Justice, but this is a surprise. Did you follow me all the way from home?" He didn't sound cross at all, only curious. So it was a family trait.

CamCat Books

VISIT US ONLINE FOR
MORE BOOKS TO LIVE IN:
CAMCATBOOKS.COM

FOLLOW US

CamCatBooks

@CamCatBooks

@CamCat_Books